WHEN POWER FAILS

For Sarah,
Warm Wishes!
Gary M
10·26·23

GARY D. MCGUGAN

When Power Fails

ISBN 978-1-7779049-8-2 (Paperback)
ISBN 978-1-7779049-9-9 (eBook)
1. FICTION, THRILLERS

Also by Gary D. McGugan

Fiction

Three Weeks Less a Day
The Multima Scheme
Unrelenting Peril
Pernicious Pursuit
A Web of Deceit
A Slippery Shadow
CONTENTION

Non-Fiction

NEEDS Selling Solutions
(Co-authored with Jeff F. Allen)

What Readers Say About Gary D. McGugan's Books

"What an incredible story. Exciting, suspenseful, and thought-provoking, *A Slippery Shadow* by Gary D. McGugan is one of the best stories I have read."
~ Natalie Soine for Readers' Favorite

"As is the case with McGugan's two previous novels, *Three Weeks Less a Day* and *The Multima Scheme,* the plot of *Unrelenting Peril* is tight and complex. McGugan has a gift for well-paced, well-blocked flurries of nail-biting action that all lead up to a surprising finale."
~ Norm Goldman, Bookpleasures.com

"The chapters in this fast-paced plot jump from character to character, all interlinked by the hand of fate - some scheming, some grieving, and some learning valuable lessons about how stuff really works in the world beyond the headlines."
~ Barbara Bamberger Scott, Feathered Quill

"Gary D McGugan writes in a way that is easily understood and believable in this exciting book. He introduces characters to the story that allows you, the reader, to form a mental picture of what is going on in each scene while we are flown off in private jets to different parts of the world where crimes are plotted and put into operation."
~ Christopher Anderson for Readers' Favorite

"There is no point throughout this read where McGugan's audience has the remote chance of getting lost or confused. Rather, he spends just as much time tying loose ends together immediately after each crescendo in the plot before moving on with yet another whammy of a situation."
~ Diane Lunsford for Feathered Quill

"I highly recommend all of Gary D. McGugan's books. Though all the stories stand nicely on their own, please do yourself a favor and start at the beginning. The road from the first novel, *Three Weeks Less a Day* to his latest release is an incredible journey."
~ Sheri Hoyte for Reader Views

One

Montreal, Quebec, Friday April 21, 2023

It all started two days earlier. Suzanne Simpson had signed a contract committing her Multima Corporation to write a cheque for $6.38 billion to buy all the assets and liabilities of an archrival of her Supermarkets division. Though forced to make the call under entirely unreasonable time pressures, she'd made the fateful decision while thinking clearly and analytically.

After all, Jeffersons Stores was a major player in the US Southwest where Multima had no presence at all. It should have been far easier.

She'd fought fiercely with the Japanese corporation that owned Jeffersons. After almost a full day of strained negotiations, they finally agreed on a price that reflected a little more than half of Jeffersons' reported book value. Financially, it looked like a steal.

Her team had been ecstatic when they concluded the deal, boarded the company jet in Hawaii, and headed for home. So ecstatic they partied for several hours—until they'd emptied all the champagne bottles brought on board for the occasion.

But Suzanne hadn't participated. She'd sipped from a glass for a while, thanking each of her companions personally for the role they'd played in the demanding preparation for the negotiating sessions and their support with research, calculations, and ideas. She'd escaped to her private compartment in the rear of the aircraft, sealed off from noise in the main cabin. There, she slept soundly for almost six hours, waking as they touched down on a runway near the private jet section of Montreal's Mirabel Airport.

When she glanced outside her window that early morning, the sun had peeked above the horizon with joyful shades of orange. However, in the main cabin, her team hadn't appeared at all chipper about dawn. Still, she'd chatted with folks gathering up their belongings while the jet taxied to a parking spot, then assembled the group for a quick chat before they depaned.

"Take a few hours. Go home. Change your clothes and freshen up. Let's all meet in the headquarters boardroom at noon. Start thinking about the meeting as you travel, and plan to spend several hours there. I want to discuss our next steps in the acquisition process," she'd instructed.

Serge had caught her eye the instant she stepped into the open aircraft doorway. He'd arrived in Montreal minutes earlier, traveling on another Multima private jet with his entire security team. After she descended the plane's stairway, he greeted her with a long, passionate kiss—so long that Suzanne had to playfully push him away as others began to gawk.

Serge Boisvert was her chief of security and her guy. They'd announced their intimate relationship to the world a few months earlier, but there was no need to flaunt it on the tarmac.

Before the ragged team eventually arrived at Multima's headquarters at the agreed noon hour, her executive assistant Eileen had arranged a long table in one corner, laden with food and refreshments, and everyone loaded up a plate before taking a place at the table. At first, Suzanne spoke while her colleagues nibbled. Her comments were brief but demanded immediate attention and focus.

"We did the easy stuff in Hawaii. You may think we worked our buns off out there, but the past few days will pale in comparison to what lies ahead for our next two weeks. Get ready. It'll be hell until we close the deal, then maybe even worse for a while after that." She'd matched her grim facial expression and grave tone with the dire warning to set correct expectations and made eye contact as she looked around the room. Once there were a few shared nods of understanding, she'd breathed a bit easier and carried on.

"How intense our pain will be and for how many months it'll last will depend on how effectively we identify the coming challenges today and whether we take the actions necessary to address every potential pitfall." Suzanne had paused again, giving everyone time to absorb her words fully. When folks had started to shift uncomfortably in their chairs, she smiled and began the PowerPoint presentation she'd prepared.

Their session that Thursday afternoon and evening ended just before midnight. They'd discussed dozens of issues that required immediate action, ranging from when they should convert Jeffersons Stores' signage over to Multima Supermarkets to the composition of a transition team. Most critical of all: how they'd pull together the billions of dollars needed to close the deal in the coming nine days. Nine days.

That was the first thought that popped into her mind this morning, and it felt like a rough smack in the face. Suzanne jolted upright in bed, threw back the sheets and scurried toward the bathroom, retching. The sudden urge to throw up vanished during that rush toward the toilet, but she stood above it for a moment just to be sure.

Her watch showed 4:00 a.m., one hour before her usual wake-up alarm. Her heart pounded faster than usual, so she glanced at her watch again. 135 BPM, about the same number she reached running on a treadmill.

Suzanne took a deep breath, then a long look at herself in the mirror. For the past few weeks, it had seemed like she was living on a narrow ledge only a step away from disaster. Had she made a mistake of monumental importance? Or had it been right to catapult Multima Corporation to the top of the global business world with the massive acquisition? Either was possible, but there could be no safe space somewhere in between.

While she stood there, her right arm trembled and her legs felt weak. She gripped the counter, steadying herself. As she stabilized, Suzanne drew another long breath and exhaled slowly. She slowly bent each knee, stretching her legs for a moment, and repeated that modest self-therapy a few more times until her heart rate decreased and strength returned to her legs.

Her thoughts again darted back to the decision haunting her.

The time to pull it all together was so precariously short, and the list of tasks to complete so extensive; no wonder she found herself gazing into a bathroom mirror after less than four hours of sleep.

But there was little point in returning to bed. Further sleep that morning would be impossible.

On the other hand, Serge slept through anything. A thunderstorm outside? Frigid temperatures inside? A vital media interview the following day? She'd witnessed his uncanny ability to sleep through all those circumstances at one time or another in their short relationship.

Still, she tiptoed down the sweeping wooden stairway from their bedroom suite on the third floor to an empty kitchen at ground level. Florence Carpentier wouldn't arrive for another hour or two, but Suzanne could still perk a carafe of strong coffee on her own.

The instant she flipped on the kitchen lights, a commotion started outdoors. Muffled voices. Pounding footsteps, followed by a sudden flash of light in the yard. She scampered across the kitchen and leaned over the sink to peek out the window above it. A vehicle engine roared to life, and she saw it race out of their driveway.

She pressed the panic button on her watch, triggering an alarm on Serge's, then swept aside one section of the window curtain for a better view. It was a large vehicle, probably an SUV, and the driver swerved from side to side, driving in reverse, suggesting someone unfamiliar with navigating both the curves and the extended distance from the house to the road.

Serge dashed down the wooden steps two at a time, floorboards vibrating in protest as each absorbed his full weight for a fraction of a second. Breathless, he rushed toward the outside door and flung it open, a weapon in his right hand. He crouched quickly onto one knee and aimed in the direction of the speeding vehicle.

It was too late. Just as he prepared to fire, speeding lights disappeared over the crest of a small hill on the road, several feet beyond their driveway. Serge shook his head in disgust, gingerly set his weapon down on a table, then rushed to gather Suzanne in his arms.

He held her tightly for a moment or two before he asked, "Are you okay?"

Suzanne nodded, still shocked that a vehicle had rushed away from their countryside mansion at such an early hour. It was unlikely a stranger had stumbled upon their home by accident, and their visitor's sudden departure suggested some form of menace was probable. She took a deep breath.

"Yeah. I'm okay. Just startled. But you win. Have your security team implement that twenty-four-seven monitoring plan you recommended last week. It looks like we need it."

"Consider it done." His eyes widened. "But we need more than round-the-clock surveillance. I built a network of contacts while I was with the RCMP. I want your okay to draw on their expertise as well. Security works much like the business world; success is driven as much by who you know as how much you know."

She'd resisted that path since he joined the company. Of course, he might talk to someone he knew in Canada's national police force from time to time, but the "network of contacts" he referred to that morning was much bigger. He was talking about interactions with people he knew in the FBI, the Canadian Security Intelligence Service, and even the CIA. She abhorred the idea of association with spies or government operatives of any description.

She shook her head slowly. "I can't authorize that, Serge. It's not a path I'm prepared to follow. I'm okay with you talking occasionally to some of your old buddies within the RCMP or the FBI, but it's a slippery slope from sharing information to active participation. I want Multima Corporation to focus exclusively on winning in the competitive marketplaces where we operate. I've seen what happens to companies that become little more than subversive servants for government interests. Stay away from CSIS and the CIA."

He curtly nodded his acceptance, but there was little doubt the conversation would resume another day.

Two

Guantanamo Bay, Cuba, Friday April 21, 2023

Fidelia Morales pursed her lips tightly and groaned silently as she woke from a fitful sleep. It was important not to draw any unwanted attention despite the agonizing pain. At the same time, she coped with brain fog, disorientation, and throbbing twinges that started from the soles of her feet and shot up both legs with sharp, wince-inducing pangs that sometimes extended beyond her knees with even her tiniest movement.

She shivered but tried to camouflage her shift. They surely had cameras monitoring her every movement, and the sadistic FBI agent at the root of her problems made it clear last night that he'd start questioning her first thing this morning. The longer she could delay that ordeal, the longer she could postpone more physical agony.

Random snippets of the events leading to her current morass flashed in short bursts. Two FBI agents hidden on her private jet, hijacking her the moment she stepped inside the aircraft. Holding her for hours on the plane without food and only a bottle or two of water. Stomping on her feet twice, crunching multiple bones, because she refused to answer their questions. A clear threat to fly her out over the Pacific and drop her there from a helicopter. An almost entire collapse of her will to live, ending finally with a promise to divulge the location of her hundreds of millions of dollars stashed in bank accounts around the world—once she reached Guantanamo safely.

Opening her eyelids enough to let the room take on a hazy form, she spotted a camera, mounted near the ceiling, pointed toward her. Slowly, she shifted to her left so the camera captured her outstretched form only from the back, then opened her eyes fully.

More shivers followed, and Fidelia breathed deeply to muffle yet another groan forming deep in her throat and to fight back tears. She drew in a long breath once again, forcing focus on where she was and what could happen next.

The young doctor had bought her some time. He'd found her lying on the ground after the surly FBI agents had demanded she get down from her aircraft on her own. At least, she assumed the guy was a doctor. He wore army fatigues but had a stethoscope dangling around his neck. The fellow became enraged when he learned they'd forced her to crawl from her seat on the aircraft, down a metal stairway, and along the tarmac for a few yards toward a building before she passed out after screaming in pain.

Revived, she heard him yelling at the FBI agents, using words like torture, heartless, and coldhearted before he threatened to report their actions and have their asses thrown out of the FBI. It was the doctor who demanded the FBI agents—immediately and gently—pick her up, carry her to the assigned quarters and stay away from her until he completed a full examination and started treatment. Only then could they question her, he'd bellowed.

A sharp knock on a door broke Fidelia's reverie.

Without waiting for a response, someone entered the room, and a voice greeted her formally. "Are you awake, ma'am?"

A light above her bed suddenly brightened, and she recognized the voice of that doctor from last night. Still, she feigned sleep.

"I know you're awake, ma'am. The guards observed you on the cameras. Don't be afraid. I'm only here to help. Don't worry. Higher-ups ordered those FBI ruffians to leave you alone until I declare you fit for questioning. Please, lie on your back and let me examine your feet."

After a long moment, Fidelia shifted her body again to lie prone as the doctor lifted the sheet covering her body. She groaned when he gripped one foot, raised it a few inches from the bed, and then leaned forward to inspect the damage. Every touch and probe felt excruciating. Tears flowed down her cheeks unchecked, and she gasped for air several times as the doctor assessed first her left foot and then the right. When she focused through her tears, both feet were disgusting shades of navy blue and red rather than their usual light brown skin tone.

The doctor didn't telegraph any new information. Instead,

he tilted his head from side to side, observing Fidelia's reactions each time he touched somewhere on her feet. While he worked, a woman dressed in an army uniform appeared above Fidelia's head and gently dabbed a small towel against her face to wipe away flowing tears.

The room remained entirely silent. There was only the hum of an air conditioner in another building somewhere nearby. After several minutes, the doctor spoke with a gentle voice and a resigned tone. "You have several fractures in both feet. A couple soldiers will carry you to radiology for some pictures. Once I see the extent of the damage, we'll try to fix you up. I'm not an orthopedic surgeon, but I should be able to adjust some of the most damaged bones."

"Will I be able to walk?"

"Hopefully. I'll know better after I see the X-rays. But you won't be walking anywhere for a while. It'll be at least six weeks before you can put any weight on your feet and probably several months before you can walk unassisted. Your running days are over."

What about the FBI guys? As though reading Fidelia's mind, the doctor looked at her sternly, his brow furrowed and lips tight as he spoke.

"I can buy you one or two days before the FBI thugs have another go at you. It'll be much better for you to cooperate with them. My authority ends when I've treated you and you're stable. After that, they'll get permission to interview you again. Remember, if you don't cooperate, I have no influence over the methods they use. Should they decide to pack you up and ship you somewhere else, I also have no influence. If you value your life, I urge you to answer their questions fully and honestly."

Three

Montreal, Quebec, Friday April 21, 2023

Gordon Goodfellow adjusted a comfortable middle seat on Suzanne's corporate jet all the way back to the horizontal position. Just before midnight, their meeting had ended, and she'd given him the choice of staying in Montreal and flying back to Atlanta later in the morning or giving him a ride out to Mirabel International Airport in the wee morning hours. There, he'd find her plane and fly home immediately. Given the magnitude of the tasks ahead, he chose the earlier return.

Multima Supermarkets—the business he ran—had its own aircraft, but they'd used it to transport his team back to Atlanta while he stayed behind to attend the meeting at headquarters upon arrival from Hawaii. By then, his pilots had exceeded their legal working hours and were grounded to sleep a few hours. This worked out better anyway. Suzanne's jet was newer and more deluxe. He took a few minutes to try out all the bells and whistles before they took off, then resolved to get some sleep.

Predictably, as soon as he rested his head on a pillow, his brain started to race. Despite almost no sleep on that flight from Hawaii and his best efforts to resist, his mind insisted on replaying Thursday's demanding hours of the crucial meeting again.

~~~~~

Gordon had approached that noon meeting with Suzanne with some trepidation. He'd partied with his team most of the flight from Hawaii and was exhausted. As a Christian, he didn't drink alcohol, but he'd felt an obligation to celebrate their massive win with colleagues and subordinates. It was important to be a team player, after all.

She'd asked him to stay in Montreal for the headquarters get-together but specifically excluded his subordinates due to the number of people already expected to fill her large meeting room. That, too, was a concern.

Before they landed that Thursday morning, they'd chatted for a few minutes, and she'd shared sketchy details about her upcoming meeting agenda and things he might want to consider before the discussion started. Naturally, he would have preferred more time to prepare, but he trusted Suzanne and realized their timeline to close the most important deal of his career was almost impossibly short.

Even with her heads-up, it'd been surprising to see the number of people in Suzanne's expansive Montreal office that morning as they assembled around the table of food and refreshments Eileen had waiting when they arrived.

Seeing James Fitzgerald wasn't a surprise. Suzanne trusted the old codger more than anyone else in the corporation. Despite his advancing years, the guy's counsel was usually right. James had recently passed on the torch to a new leader at Multima Financial, so he'd have spare time on his hands. Suzanne would probably want to profit from that free time in the coming few hectic weeks.

Of course, Serge Boisvert was there. Since he and Suzanne had made their "secret" affair public, he seemed to pop up at every major company meeting. It was a surprise that she hadn't named him chief operating officer, considering his involvement in seemingly every aspect of the business.

Gordon had expected to see Pierre Cabot, CFO of the entire Multima Corporation, and watched him rush to a chair right next to Suzanne's spot at the head of the long table. He carried a ton of files under his arm, with a gigantic calculator balanced on top, appearing every bit the financial nerd. Gordon liked the guy, though. He seemed so smart you'd think he'd memorized every number in the pile of data he carried. Rushing to a chair by Suzanne probably signaled that he planned to play an active role in today's meeting.

Scurrying to a chair opposite Cabot, also next to Suzanne, Alberto Ferer carried another pile of documents. Two assistants followed the chief legal officer, each bringing yet more files. Alberto motioned for them to take chairs behind him against the wall. Neither assistant would be an active participant in the meeting. Still, Alberto could count on them to take notes for his role as secretary of the board of directors and to research any details on their laptops if necessary.

It was surprising to see Nicole Gagnon sit near Suzanne. The newly hired vice president for human resources for Multima Corporation had only served in the role for a few weeks. Maybe Suzanne intended to give the woman expanded responsibilities during the transition period, after they closed the deal for Jeffersons Stores.

But it was even more shocking to see Abduhl Mahinder, chief executive officer of the Bank of The Americas, from San Francisco there. The guy served on Multima's board of directors, but seeing a board member other than James Fitzgerald at a staff meeting was extremely rare. A tall Black man stood at Mahinder's side in full executive power garb, smiling warmly as the bank executive introduced him to each attendee individually.

Once the meeting was underway, it turned out the Black guy was there to coordinate between Multima Corporation and the consortium of lenders Abduhl Mahinder had put together. Joshua Monette was his name, and he was a high-powered consultant the banks trusted to fill in all the little details before they signed a loan agreement.

The first part of the meeting had little to do with Gordon directly. Naturally, he listened intently as Monette sparred first with Alberto Ferer over clauses in the acquisition agreement Suzanne had signed, then with Pierre Cabot over a few basis points in the consortium's proposed borrowing rate. Tensions rose on each issue until Abduhl Mahinder skillfully brokered a deal everyone could live with.

As they broke up the meeting for a coffee break, Monette said farewell to everyone, joking that he now had to get started on the "easy task" of getting eight different banks on three continents onside with all those conditions they'd just agreed upon.

When the group convened around the table again, Pierre Cabot briefed them on the financial audits. "Before our planes touched down in Montreal, our public accounting firm, OCD, already had teams en route to fifty Jeffersons Stores locations, six warehouses, and the company headquarters in San Francisco. Jeffersons was expecting them, so communication from the current Japanese owners went well despite some troubling rumors about violence and power struggles." Pierre peered over his glasses and showed a hint of a smirk as he assessed the room's mood.

Satisfied, he carried on. "OCD advises that each team has reported in successfully and that discussions are underway in all locations about the logistics and timing necessary to complete the physical audits before April 26. That will allow our people only four days to determine if there are any major discrepancies with their books before we wire the funds on Monday, May 1."

Then it had been time for Gordon to play.

"I'd like to get a few of my people on those teams for a few days," he remembered saying. "Candidly, although we all trust OCD, my folks understand some of the intricacies of our business the accounting people might miss. They can best assess the value of fresh meat and fish in the distribution network. The same is true for fruits and vegetables. How fresh the perishable food is will determine its value far more than simply accounting for quantities in stock."

Pierre Cabot saw the merits of that argument and agreed to get support for a dozen of Gordon's people to join different teams for a day or two. As Suzanne continued the meeting, Pierre and Gordon each sent email instructions from their phones.

Suzanne shifted to human resources and passed the leadership of the discussion to Nicole Gagnon. "We should anticipate some significant challenges integrating the management team and workforce of Jeffersons Stores into the culture of Multima Supermarkets. Let's talk about how the management team at Supermarkets plans to lead the integration."

With that simple suggestion, Nicole unleashed discussion and debate that had Gordon sitting in a hot seat for the following two hours. His team had carefully considered the issues and discussed various strategies before deciding on the one Gordon had carefully articulated. That plan had the current president of Jeffersons Stores reporting directly to Gordon. Despite his patient and detailed explanation, it was all to no avail.

As a shock to everyone, including Suzanne, Abduhl Mahinder instead suggested a new leader from outside Multima, someone the consortium of banks could agree upon. He pointed out the deal would only happen with the cooperation of the consortium. Since they were the folks taking on about $6 billion in risk, it was only reasonable for them to have someone they knew and trusted oversee the integration.

All eyes turned to Suzanne.

Her eyes focused on Mahinder and turned cold as stone, though her voice remained polite and amicable, even showing a hint of a smile. "That's not going to happen, Abduhl. I invited you to join us today because we value your counsel, and we need you to manage the expectations of the consortium. But our management team will decide who best meets the needs of the corporation and the consortium. You're welcome to share ideas and comments, but the Multima management team will decide. Serge, do you have any thoughts from a security perspective?"

"I do. We all know Jeffersons Stores is currently owned and controlled by Suji Corporation, which belongs to an organized crime outfit, the Yakuza. What we don't know is how deeply embedded the Yakuza is in the culture of Jeffersons. I'd like a Japanese speaker to lead or stay close to the leader so we can ferret out any undesirable people or practices early on."

Nodding heads around the table demonstrated agreement Serge was on to something, and it was an issue Gordon's team hadn't considered. He let others make suggestions before commenting.

James Fitzgerald wondered if they should consider a role for Yuki, the young woman from Financial Services who had served as a translator for the team in Japan. She didn't have the experience to lead a transition, but might she assist another leader and have the latitude to poke around?

Abduhl Mahinder didn't give up easily. With his preference to have the loan syndicate choose a transition leader thwarted, he tried another approach. "Why don't you consider an experienced hand like Mr. Fitzgerald here?" He smiled broadly and bowed in deference to James. "The old scoundrel can't be ready for full retirement yet!"

There was no laughter. Instead, all heads turned instinctively toward James. Gordon held his breath, waiting for a response. The last thing he needed was Suzanne's most loyal confidant involved in the reporting channels of a new acquisition. He didn't wait long.

Theatrically, James raised both arms in front of his body, his hands creating an unmistakable "hold it right there" sign. His crooked smile reflected a combination of appreciation and amusement, but his quiet words left no doubt. "No. Don't give Abduhl's generous suggestion a moment's consideration. This 'scoundrel' is most definitely headed to retirement. I'll stay on the board, but I've already ridden off into the sunset as far as any operating opportunity is concerned."

Gordon slowly exhaled, smiling broadly enough to blend in with the reactions of others around the table but not enough to draw attention to his sense of relief. A few other names were bandied about before Suzanne asked Nicole Gagnon if she had any recommendations from human resources.

"I don't know her personally, although we've chatted on Zoom a couple times, but I'm wondering if Amber Chan in China might be a suitable candidate. Her resume shows she studied in Japan and speaks the language fluently. She surely must understand Supermarkets' business since you've entrusted her with the China market. If we have a capable replacement groomed to fill her role, might we consider her to lead the transition?"

Gordon glanced around the quiet room while he gathered his thoughts, knowing the question demanded his feedback before that of the other attendees. It wasn't a bad idea. Amber Chan was already a direct report he respected. She'd carefully groomed at least three candidates they could choose from to become her replacement. Her knowledge of the Japanese language and customs would be invaluable. Suzanne had already hinted that she'd like to see him appoint a president for the American market, freeing up more of his time for more international acquisitions.

"What an excellent suggestion, Nicole." Gordon had raised his enthusiasm as high as he dared without appearing to be gushing. "I was just about to throw her name in. Amber has all the skills, experience and comportment to handle the role. I suggest we appoint her as executive vice-president for our Supermarkets of America division, with specific responsibility for overseeing the Jeffersons' integration into Multima Supermarkets."

~~~~~

The replay of that meeting winding down in his mind should have prompted relaxation, perhaps even sleep. Instead, his heart rate remained elevated, his skin felt damp from unexpected perspiration, and a sense of unease enveloped him, causing an unexpected chill to surge up his spine.

No sleep would follow that morning.

Four

Montreal, Quebec, Sunday April 30, 2023

A widely held impression that bankers work short, convenient hours clearly didn't apply to the high-stakes players who'd been working for less than two weeks to create a consortium to lend Multima Corporation a little more than six billion dollars.

Suzanne had slept little since sunrise on Friday morning, but her chief financial officer had warned her. She could either handle issues instantly by phone as they developed, coming and going wherever she pleased, or she could bring a couple changes of clothes and work from her office while they negotiated the final details of a complex transaction around the clock. Either way, he expected to close the deal within an almost impossibly compressed timeline.

Suzanne brought changes of clothes. She didn't have a shower in her office, but the fitness center on a lower level of their tower was well-equipped and open around the clock. Preparing for her next battle with the financial wizards, she looked into the mirror of the facility's change room, checked her makeup, and adjusted the collar of her business suit one final time.

The reflected image satisfied Suzanne. Her hair color switch to blonde a few months earlier had been a good choice. As she approached a milestone birthday in another couple years, those few wrinkles around her eyes from smiling and across her forehead from too many worries seemed acceptable. Regardless, her physical attributes shouldn't concern anyone at this stage in her career.

Her CFO, Pierre Cabot, knew all the banks' negotiators personally, so most of his conversations over the past week were by phone. After those calls, if Pierre thought Suzanne needed to either be in the loop or make a decision, he'd buzz her direct line in the office or pop by for a quick conference. There had been dozens of such interruptions over the week.

To close the massive transaction today, he recommended

she prepare for Zoom conferences instead. "The people I'm working with all appear to be onside now. But the amount we're asking for is massive, and none of those guys have ever put together a deal of this magnitude in such a short time frame."

"Maybe if we had a few women in the process, it wouldn't be so onerous." Suzanne smiled as she made the comment, but only enough to keep him wondering. For some time, she'd lamented how men dominated the lending arena, and she'd previously urged Pierre to bring more women into their borrowing relationships.

"Touché," Pierre said. "You're right. We need to get more women involved. But we have to close this deal first. The guys I work with are all in the upper echelon, but most of our lenders will still need to involve their CEO, and maybe even their board of directors, with such a large amount and the quick approval required. Those folks often want to look directly into a borrower's eyes. Some know you, and they won't need that reassurance. But others may need to assess you eye-to-eye before signing on the dotted line."

She was ready to meet their scrutiny.

That day, Abduhl Mahinder also worked from her office with Pierre, and it was he who had established a final deadline. Before 5:00 p.m. on Sunday evening, every participant in the loan syndication had to sign the agreement. By then, it would already be six o'clock Monday morning in Tokyo, and Multima's agreement with Suji Corporation required $6.38 billion in the company bank account by noon on that first day of May.

That day was pivotal. It was one of the few days that Japanese banks opened for business during the esteemed Golden Week. During that seven-day window, most companies closed their operations for five days, and Suji Corporation had another critical deadline to meet before the only other day banks would open for business.

They were waiting for freshly showered Suzanne as she returned wearing her best business suit. She liked bright colors and the sky-blue outfit picked up nicely a glint from her eyes and contrasted well with her golden hair. She displayed confidence. When she entered her office, six male faces were projected onto the large screen opposite her desk. She looked into the camera, smiled and waved, then headed toward the large oval table where Pierre and Abduhl argued politely with at least one of the participants.

Pierre nodded to her as he spoke to the camera. "Suzanne Simpson is joining us now. We haven't had time to brief her on your latest ask, but why don't you go ahead and explain your request directly to her? We'll probably need some time to discuss it and get back to you."

Pierre's face appeared drawn and pale. Beside him, Abduhl looked equally dejected. Her CFO avoided direct eye contact, swallowing an entire glass of water instead. She sat next to Abduhl, facing the camera.

"Hello, everyone," Suzanne said. "I'm delighted to meet you all. Who would like to explain the concern to me?"

Six individual faces on the screen looked around at each other as though they were all in the same room. One raised a finger. "Hi, Suzanne. I'm Roderick Vexation with Bank of the Middle East. These other gentlemen are all serving on a special committee our Prince Mustafa created to advise him about the wisdom of participating in the loan syndication with the Bank of The Americas."

The fellow paused momentarily, cleared his throat twice, and then continued looking at something just above the camera recording his message.

"We have great respect for you and Multima Corporation and, of course, great respect for Abduhl. But before we can recommend that our Prince put one billion dollars of his money at risk, we think it's necessary to ask you to provide one additional piece of security."

"What do you have in mind, Roderick?" She kept her tone neutral despite the unwanted last-minute complication.

"Since you are Multima Corporation's largest shareholder and the investor with the most voting rights, we think you should pledge your equity position to the consortium in the unlikely event Multima Corporation defaults on this more than six point three billion dollar loan."

No one spoke for several seconds. Suzanne masked her shock and anger as effectively as possible, pursing her lips and staring directly into the camera without saying a word.

Finally, Abduhl ventured a question.

"We've been discussing this deal for over a week, Roderick." His tone was muted and polite, but he paused long enough to show discomfort before continuing. "Why are you raising such a major change to the security package at this late stage? We're scheduled to transfer the funds in just a few hours."

"I apologize for not letting you know earlier, but the added requirement only came to my attention a few minutes ago. Prince Mustafa seeks the added assurance." His eyes dropped, and his brown face took on a reddish hue.

The silence on the Zoom call was profound. In Suzanne's office, a fan hummed from the ceiling in one corner of the long, narrow room. Abduhl's strong cologne had soured, now smelling foul, more like a boiled egg. Her CFO stared downward as though studying a just-discovered error on a page before him. On the wall-mounted widescreen, faces in every square appeared frozen, eyes downcast, no one daring to speak. Suzanne sat erect, her face impassive, waiting for someone to take a position on the Prince's last-minute demand.

When it was clear no one was prepared to lead, she stood up from her chair, looked directly into the camera and forced her tone to remain calm yet forceful. "Multima Corporation is an excellent, triple-A-rated company that stands entirely on its own. If every member of this assembled consortium cannot move forward with the loan in its current form—a loan that will generate hundreds of millions of dollars in interest income for each of its participants—I will walk away from this acquisition."

She stepped away from the table and continued out her office door without looking back.

Five

Guantanamo Bay, Cuba, Sunday April 30, 2023

Fidelia Morales had no tears left to shed. They'd questioned her, screamed at her, slapped her around, and made a dozen or more vile threats to intimidate her and weaken her resolve. She'd expected it, of course. Once Fidelia told that FBI agent in Hawaii that she'd reveal where the money was after she landed safely in Cuba, she knew she'd only bought a limited amount of time before the serious interrogations began.

Now, the rogue FBI guy in the rumpled dark blue suit had just lost his patience for the third time that morning in Guantanamo Bay. When she told him once again that she couldn't remember where she'd stashed her millions of dollars, he grabbed the food tray beside her hospital bed and threw it in her direction, missing her head by only inches, before he stormed out the door.

Leftover food and water from the tray splattered the wall, her pillow, and her face. Ceramic dishes crashed to the floor, breaking and scattering in all directions with an echo reverberating around the almost empty room. The metal tray bounced off the wall, hitting steel bedposts before clattering down to somewhere on the cement floor below her bed.

Both Fidelia's feet were still elevated in stirrups hanging from the ceiling. The staff had installed them to help reduce her swelling and discomfort after the surgery an army doctor had performed a few days earlier. Intense pain shot along her legs, almost to her hips, with even the slightest movements of her lower body, so she left the splattered sauces and ketchup from the partially eaten omelet where they fell and tried to lie still and regain her composure.

Each time became harder. Was today the third day of interrogation or the fourth? Would the next visit be a nurse or army doctor to offer comfort? Or would it be the bully FBI agent determined to steal the hundreds of millions of dollars she had squirreled away in a variety of secure offshore bank accounts?

She touched one finger to the side of her face and traced an outline along her jaw. Before the FBI guy threw the tray at her, he had slapped both sides of her face repeatedly. She'd lost count of the number of times he struck her once the initial vicious sting evolved into throbbing pain and before she felt her entire body shudder repeatedly from the force of his brutal bare hands. First, her skin burned; then sharp pain surfaced around her jaw. Touching that area now caused her eyes to blur with agony, but tears refused to flow and perhaps ease her torment. Eventually, exhaustion took hold, and she dozed.

Hours passed before she woke, and the door to her room opened again. Her hospital gown was damp from sweat, but a bit of fresh air filtered in as someone held the door open momentarily before entering. The breeze was still hot, but the incoming air offered some relief.

She tried to swallow again, but her throat was too dry, and instead, it sounded as if she had gagged. The noise caught the attention of the army doctor, the one who'd performed the surgery, and he stepped quickly across the room to her bed.

"Here, drink some water, but slowly." He pulled a plastic bottle from his jacket pocket, twisted the cap, and held it to her mouth. He continued to help her cradle the bottle in her trembling, cupped hands as he ran his eyes up and down her prone body.

"How do you feel?" His brown eyes probed deeply, but his facial expression was neutral and unreadable.

"Bad." Fidelia's voice sounded hoarse. The doctor waited for more but moved on when it became clear she had nothing to add.

"You should cooperate with them. It may seem unjust to lose the money you earned, even if you earned it illegally. I get that. But I fear for your health. Your body is already fragile from the trauma and surgery. I can see their questioning techniques are rough. If you don't give them the information they want, you might not survive, and there is nothing more I can do to stop it."

She closed her eyes without responding. He helped her drink more water from the bottle, then moved to her feet, where he poked and prodded for a few moments. He stepped back to her chest, reached into the gown, placed a stethoscope on the skin above her left breast, and listened. His face conveyed nothing.

When he finished, his facial muscles relaxed slightly. He looked down at her with deep worry lines creased into his forehead and around his eyes before he made one terse comment: "Think about what I said."

Then he left the room. It was easy for him to say, but quite another circumstance if one actually had more than a billion dollars and control of a massive operation at stake. Thousands of people depended on The Organization for their livelihood, even if it all came from crime. She could live on less, but her life would surely end if she gave away the money. Should the rogue FBI agents let her go free, as soon as someone in The Organization discovered the money was gone, her remaining lifespan could be measured in hours.

So, Fidelia became resigned to death, needing only to decide whether to let the FBI kill her with brutal roughness or give them access to the funds and wait for a former colleague to track her down and torture her to death, perhaps even more cruelly.

Unless. A faint outline of a smile formed on her battered face. Unless she could find a way to give them just enough money to satisfy their greed. If she offered them something, what might convince them they had everything and that letting her go was the best possible outcome?

Six

Atlanta, Georgia, Sunday April 30, 2023

The moment he heard the click of Suzanne Simpson ending their call, Gordon Goodfellow flung his phone at the far wall of his office with all the force he could muster. It clattered to the tile floor and skittered to a crooked stop somewhere under the sizeable oval table he used for meetings.

His head dropped in defeat as he wrapped both hands around the back of his neck and squeezed tightly, seeking relief. His eyes closed before he pointed his face upward, almost accusing God of abandoning him at such a crucial time. Suzanne said she'd literally walked away from the deal when an Arab sheik made a last-minute demand in exchange for his one billion dollar share of the loan in the fleeting minutes before the Jeffersons deal was supposed to close.

Months of research, planning, strategizing, and conniving were now moments away from total evaporation. The deal that could have made him one of the most powerful executives in the global supermarket business was disintegrating. Suzanne had ended their call with one ray of hope. Abduhl planned to explore one more avenue before he called it quits, but he didn't make any promises. They'd know one way or the other within hours.

Gordon slipped on his business jacket and left his office, closing its top button while he walked. The temporary office they had assigned Amber Chan for her new role as executive vice-president of Multima Supermarkets of America was only a few steps down the corridor. Her door was closed, but he knocked loudly and let himself in.

"We've got a problem. Suzanne has walked away from the deal. One of the lenders wanted more security, and she refused." He left out the particulars. Suzanne hadn't granted permission to share any of those. "It looks like the damned deal is off."

Just days before, Amber Chan had agreed to uproot her life entirely. She'd given up her home in China and her role as president of Multima's Asia Supermarkets' businesses to move to the US to lead newly acquired Jeffersons Stores. They had all been so sure the deal would close they'd already announced her replacement and listed her house in China for sale.

She gaped in shock for over a minute. "Wow. I can't think of a better way to ruin an otherwise perfect Sunday in April," she said. "What do we do now?"

"Hope and pray," Gordon replied. "There are still a few hours before the banks close in Tokyo. If Abduhl can find another partner, I suppose there's a slim chance we can pull it off. Suzanne didn't sound hopeful, though, and asked me to relay her apologies for what we're putting you through. Said she'd call you personally when they knew for sure. Let's keep it between us until a decision is final."

~~~~~

Amber Chan reached for her phone the moment Gordon left. After giving him enough time to return to his office, she opened her door and peeked down the corridor. Confident he was behind closed doors again, she dialed a long sequence of numbers as she scampered toward the elevator.

She wasn't afraid someone in the building would overhear her next conversation; only a handful of Multima Supermarkets executives were in the office that late Sunday afternoon. But Amber wasn't sure how thoroughly internal Multima security monitored calls and conversations. It would be safer outside.

As the elevator door opened in the ground floor lobby, she pressed 'send' on her phone and strode purposefully toward the outside doors. On the third ring, a male voice answered, and they greeted each other in Japanese. She recognized his voice when he said, "*Kon'nichiwa*," hello in Japanese.

It was Tak Takahashi, a former classmate at the University of Tokyo. They had slept together a few times during the school years but now were just friends. Amber liked the idea of maintaining contact with someone high up in the Yakuza. One never knew when it might be necessary to share or obtain information. Times like now. They continued in Japanese.

"I just heard the deal may be off. A lender wanted more security for the loan, and she walked away. It looks like there's no deal," said Amber.

"Yeah. Our guy from Dubai wanted her to pledge her shares as added security. We thought she might fold, but the deal's still alive anyway. Our guy from Argentina is negotiating with the Bank of The Americas as we speak. They should do a deal within the next few minutes. Sit tight. Your new job's safe."

"Did you find your boss yet?" Even when speaking outdoors, using Fidelia Morales's name on a phone network was too risky.

"Yeah. A rogue unit of the FBI has her. I'm working to spring her before she gives away any of the bank info. Hopefully, we'll get her out before they force her to spill anything. Don't call me at this number again. I'll give you a new number once the deal's done."

Amber paused a moment to think about his abrupt manner and somewhat brusque tone. She was turning her life upside down on one simple premise: before the end of the year, she could become one of the most powerful women in the world. If everything went right. But she couldn't appear either weak or impatient.

Adapting the tone and manner Tak had used a moment before, Amber said, "Sure. Just make it your first call when you see the money has arrived."

Seven

Montreal, Quebec, Friday May 12, 2023

"We should all celebrate this magnificent win and congratulate each other for an extraordinary job. Well done!" Suzanne fist-pumped for emphasis. It was the first meeting of Multima's board of directors after the acquisition of Jeffersons Stores closed on the first day of May.

"Gordon Goodfellow's team at Supermarkets contributed outstanding research and preparation. Pierre Cabot and his people did a marvelous job coordinating the audits and securing the financing. Alberto Ferer and his legal assistants answered the call and worked tirelessly to draft the documents, complete the searches, and close the deal. Everyone around this table made themselves available at all hours of the day, for weeks, while we tackled obstacles that arose from unexpected places and without warning."

The meeting participants leaned back in their chairs to bask in their moment of glory, smiles beaming, eyes sparkling, and bodies relaxed. They deserved some self-appreciation, and she was determined to let them all enjoy it.

When a reasonable few seconds had elapsed, she continued. "But our greatest thanks and heartfelt expression of gratitude certainly must be for Abduhl Mahinder. Using his clout as CEO of the Bank of The Americas, he saved our deal when a rogue investor tried to kibosh the deal in the final hours. With one phone call, Abduhl rescued the transaction, bringing a Latin American participant into the loan syndication only minutes before we had to transfer a few billion dollars to Suji's bank account. Bravo Abduhl!"

Suzanne sprang from her chair at the head of the long oval table. She clapped her hands vigorously as directors around the table also rose and joined in boisterous applause with shouts of appreciation. The uncharacteristic enthusiasm continued for a couple minutes before Abduhl grinned sheepishly, muttered his thanks, and waved at the faces around the table. With his gesture, the room grew silent again.

"There are only a handful of companies in the world strong enough to evoke a positive response to such a massive loan request in an unbelievably compressed timeline," Abduhl said. "Suzanne, you and your management team should take pride that our loan participant could make a billion-dollar decision in your favor so quickly."

With the platitudes and congratulations out of the way, Suzanne regained everyone's attention and moved on with the day's issues. For the next three hours, the board of directors listened to presentations, debated proposed modifications to the 2023 business plan, and voted on motions put forward by management and individual directors.

They took a break for lunch. For about a half-hour, everyone disappeared. Some found vacant offices. Others picked out a quiet corner of a corridor. A few rode down the elevator and outside the tall office tower to find private spots to check emails or return messages. But all returned to the meeting room by one o'clock, where Suzanne had promised lunch would be served.

Since the directors had held their first meeting in Montreal last year, all were aware the city was a special culinary spot. It was hard to explain precisely why, but every board member found Montreal's food, service, and atmosphere unique. That day in May, it was clear each director planned to savor the catered food as much as they might in a restaurant.

After the lunch break, Suzanne asked Natalia Tenaz to update the board of directors on progress at Multima Financial Services. The newly appointed division president was well prepared. She explained Financial Services' recent bond issue to finance the Latin American expansion.

"It was thirty percent oversubscribed," she said with satisfaction. "We were able to lower the offered rate by almost twenty-five basis points with surplus demand."

Then, she described deals that would close imminently. She named well-known lenders in Mexico, Chile, Argentina and Uruguay and described where her people thought they were at. With a smile and a nod toward her mentor, James Fitzgerald, Natalia told the group they would blow past the 2023 operating forecast.

"It's only May, and we have more than seven months when things might change, but I'm guessing we'll exceed our budgeted profits by fifty percent or more."

James Fitzgerald nodded and winked at Suzanne as Natalia wound up her presentation. Suzanne waited for the directors to question the new business leader's bountiful optimism. None took up the challenge.

Serge was up next. He looked gorgeous that morning. A new navy blue suit tailored to highlight his trim frame and taller-than-average height projected the desired power and polish. His recently styled hair had enough gray to project maturity while his smile showed charm, and those bright shining blue eyes drew her in every time he looked in her direction. He'd adapted well to the role of a business executive.

However, as much as she loved the guy, it hurt her that he insisted on presenting information to the board without discussing it with her first. She had a feeling his revelations that day might not be positive. His opening comments fueled that concern.

"When the Multima team left Honolulu a few weeks ago, I was terrified. Suzanne had concluded very tense discussions with Suji Corporation, and agreed to acquire all the outstanding shares of Jeffersons Stores. We also knew another rogue outfit ultimately controls Suji itself, and I had no idea how that criminal element known as The Organization might react. Did Suji have their permission to sell? Would The Organization become enraged by the meagre price Multima paid compared to Jeffersons Stores' book value? Was there a chance we might become innocent pawns in an international war among criminal factions?"

Serge paused and looked around the room, likely gauging the reaction of his audience. His brow remained furrowed and lips tight as he resumed. "I sensed something extraordinary was going on out there in Hawaii. Texts and cryptic messages from old allies in the FBI warned me to be careful but didn't divulge any details. This week, I tracked down a couple sources who must remain anonymous but whom I trust implicitly. Both confirmed a gang war unfolded in Honolulu in the hotel we were staying in—and while we were there."

There were gasps around the table. Directors appeared both surprised and shaken. Most leaned forward in their chairs, anxious for Serge to continue.

"The former head of the Yakuza, a guy named Sugimori, was overthrown and killed. They found his mutilated body at the bottom of a cliff outside the city. The young guy who finished those negotiations with Suzanne is, indeed, the new head of the outfit in Japan. His name is Tak Takahashi, and he's as corrupt and incorrigible as Sugimori, but smarter and more tech-savvy. I expect we haven't heard the last of him." Serge took another pause.

Everyone held on, assuming her guy was cleverly building suspense for the point of all of this. They didn't have to wait long.

After a deep breath and a glance around the room, he carried on. "A woman named Fidelia Morales was also in Hawaii, staying in a hotel next door. This powerful woman is the head of The Organization globally. She ordered Sugimori's death and okayed the sale of Jeffersons Stores with Takahashi. She also listened in on all the meetings and discussions between the two sides. Here's the most important thing I learned. One of my sources at the FBI divulged that they captured Fidelia Morales when she returned to her private jet at Honolulu's airport. It was parked close to our planes, possibly close enough to intercept our conversations." He paused again for dramatic effect, glancing toward Suzanne, no doubt to underscore his repeated warnings about even negotiating with these scoundrels.

She took care to bury any emotions and waited with the others to see if he'd drop another bombshell.

"What I'm about to tell you is so confidential within the FBI that only my source and three or four other folks are aware of it. There's a rogue unit within the FBI. Top leadership knows about it but asks no questions and never seeks reports or information about their activities. Maintaining plausible deniability, I'm told. You'll probably find this hard to believe. I certainly did. But my source says this rogue unit has captured Fidelia Morales, confiscated her private jet, transported her to an offshore location, and is secretly holding and questioning her there." Serge took another moment to let his audience absorb and ponder the significance of these allegations.

No one asked a question or commented.

Satisfied, he threw out his final gem. "My source tells me the FBI also has a plant in the Yakuza. She claims Takahashi already knows where that rogue unit is holding the crime boss and is formulating a plan to rescue Fidelia Morales from the FBI. They treat this information so seriously that the rogue unit plans to relocate the woman again within days if they can't immediately get the information they want."

Serge glanced at Suzanne once more before he unloaded another bombshell. "But that's really only gossip as far as we're concerned. Here's what's more important: Takahashi has a special technology team working around the clock to infiltrate Multima's computer systems. According to my FBI source, he plans to launch the world's largest known cybersecurity attack and demand a ransom that could bring Multima Corporation to its knees."

Serge surely hadn't wasted any time since she'd reluctantly granted approval for limited information sharing with the FBI. Had they already started down the slippery slope she feared?

Eight

Guantanamo Bay, Cuba, Friday May 12, 2023

Fidelia Morales's body tensed reflexively as she heard the door to her cabin squeak open. The doctor, nurses, and cleaning staff all knocked gently as a courtesy to their prisoner before entering her confined space. The FBI brute in the rumpled blue suit didn't bother.

"The medical guy tells me you're ready for more questions." He spat out the words. His tone of voice was restrained, but the smirk on his face and the flashing intensity in his dark eyes betrayed his clumsy attempt to project a calm demeanor. Clearly, he was anxious to resume his work.

Fidelia said nothing in response.

"We gave you a couple weeks like the doctor ordered. So that you know, I went back to Quantico for instructions. They approved the sale of your Bombardier 7500 business jet. I thought you might like to know we got fifty million dollars for it." The FBI lout taunted her with both his light-hearted scoff and mischievous grin. "Of course, we had to offer a big discount when we couldn't produce ownership papers. But that happens when you choose not to cooperate fully and immediately." He pounded his huge forefinger into the palm of his hand twice, emphasizing the possible consequences of not cooperating more fully this time.

Fidelia continued to stare at him without speaking. To say and do nothing appeared to be the safest course of action.

He slipped off his wrinkled dark blue jacket and threw it casually over the back of a chair. Ceremoniously, he unbuttoned his sleeves, then slowly and carefully rolled each up to a spot just below his elbow. He took a half-dozen steps toward her bed before hovering above her face menacingly, his lips drawn tightly, his face redder and more animated.

"Here are the ground rules. I'm going to turn on my recorder." He pulled a tiny device from his left front pants pocket. "I'm going to ask you some straightforward questions. You're going to answer those questions honestly and fully. If I like your answer, I'll ask another one. If I don't like your answer, I'll ask you again. There will be no third time. If I don't like what you tell me, I'll shut off the recorder and leave. An interrogation specialist will be your next visitor. He'll use enhanced interrogation methods to get the information I want."

To underscore how seriously he was taking the matter, he strolled around the room they used for her cell and closed each of the four open windows. Then he pulled the curtains on each window tightly together, blocking all outside light into the room. Finally, he moved to a switch mounted on a wall and shut off the light. The room fell into total darkness. Only tiny lines of sunshine peeked below the door and through a crack in the curtains of one window.

The questions started. At first, the FBI bully seemed almost civil as he asked her to state her name, citizenship, and addresses where she owned properties. She told him about the apartment in New York and the home in Uruguay. When he pressed for more, she divulged a recent purchase in Curaçao. He waited in silence for more, but she refused to tell him about her compound in Muynak, Uzbekistan. After waiting more than a minute, he seemed satisfied and went on.

His following questions were about stuff he probably already knew, and he likely asked them only to test her honesty and accuracy. Where was she born? When did she move to the US? What was her first job after she graduated from Columbia University? When did she get mixed up with Giancarlo Mareno and his prostitution businesses? At least an hour had passed before he asked the first tough question.

"What is your total net worth?" He asked the question casually, almost lightheartedly.

"I don't know." The answer was partially true. Anyone with so much wealth could only know *approximately* how much money she had. Equity shares changed in value every minute of every day. Interest on cash balances, certificates of deposit, and bonds accumulated daily.

"I'll ask the question again. What is your approximate net worth?" It was as though he had read her mind and rephrased the question to make it easier for her to answer.

She considered her response before responding. "Less

than a hundred million." She could cover that amount from one bank account and hoped that might satisfy the rotten dude and his FBI masters.

She heard an audible click and then footsteps as the burly agent wandered away. He didn't look back as he opened the door to her cell, went out, and slammed it shut.

Fidelia didn't move from her bed for several hours.

The promised interrogation specialist didn't appear.

She remained in darkness with her thoughts and fears until she heard a light knock at the door. It opened, and she could see the outline of the Cuban woman who occasionally brought her meals and cleaned her room.

The woman carried a tray and walked gingerly toward Fidelia's bed without turning on the lights. In Spanish, she told Fidelia she brought her food and water before questioning would resume during the night. Once the young woman set the tray on a lower table near the bed, she pulled a nearby chair closer to that table and invited Fidelia to sit on it and enjoy her food.

"My name is Agueda Diaz. You can trust me." The woman introduced herself in a whisper and met Fidelia's eyes as she spoke. *Agueda* meant good-hearted in Spanish, so that should count for something.

It was her first meal of the day, and Fidelia's stomach had been growling for hours already. Slowly, she worked her way out of the bed and took two tentative steps to reach the offered chair and table. The pain was excruciating, and she gasped. As Fidelia reached out for the chair back and tried to ease her way into the chair, the young woman firmly gripped her left wrist to add support.

Fidelia felt a tiny piece of paper press against her palm as the Cuban worker squeezed her hand tightly.

Their eyes met for only an instant. Fidelia might have detected a curt nod before Agueda stepped away, turned her back on Fidelia and hurried from the room. She hesitated only long enough to flip a switch, turning on an overhead light before she clicked the door latches securely from the outside.

Fidelia nibbled a warmed bun nonchalantly, occasionally glancing upward at the cameras mounted in each corner of the wall she faced. Neither showed any indication they were operating. There were no tiny red or blue lights, but there could be little doubt both were recording. She tried to remember where and how the doctor stood when he gave his subtle warnings that she should cooperate with them.

Each time, he took a step or two away from her bed, shifted his body slightly away from her, and spoke with his eyes cast downward, seemingly looking at something on the floor at his feet. Perhaps he was resigned to someone hearing every word he shared with an injured patient, but his nervous manner had suggested maybe he had discovered a way to keep his face from being detected by the cameras.

Fidelia first guessed, then estimated, the angles and range of the cameras, looking for a spot where she might discreetly read whatever was written on the paper without detection. Nothing was obvious.

When she finished the bread, with her right hand, she poured milk from a tiny carton onto a bowl of cereal that occupied one corner of the tray. She reached to her left and set down the milk carton near the bowl, close enough to block the piece of paper from the left camera. With one smooth operation, Fidelia leaned toward her left, blocked the camera's view behind her, and slid the tiny sliver of paper into a space on the tray between the milk carton and the bowl.

She looked down and saw nothing. The paper was blank. *Was it folded?*

Fidelia took a few mouthfuls of the cereal to avoid the suspicion of anyone monitoring her in real time. Without looking down, she gingerly felt for the morsel of paper and moved it to the edge of the table. Before she set down the spoon and reached for another piece of bread, she slid the paper behind the bowl out of view of the cameras with her left hand. She then squeezed the paper where she felt a fold and opened it with her right hand, still blocking the view from the cameras behind her with her body. The cereal bowl blocked the front cameras.

She broke off and ate a couple pieces from the bread, then glanced down as she leaned forward to pick up the spoon again. The font was small but clear.

We know where you are. Have plan to rescue. Give nothing.

Nine

Atlanta, Georgia, Thursday May 18, 2023

Gordon Goodfellow stretched his arms high above his head, held them there, and wrung his hands together several times. On his way back down, he stopped to rub his eyes and shake his head. Everyone else in the room appeared equally exhausted.

A glance at his watch confirmed that afternoon was morphing into evening, but the interminable meeting showed no signs of ending. This pattern had repeated every day since they'd first convened the technology wizards on Monday. That meant five full days of discussions, arguments, and computer jargon he barely understood at the best of times.

More significantly, Gordon could only roughly estimate the thousands of dollars this exercise cost Multima Supermarkets every minute they continued. The consultant from Japan alone charged a thousand dollars an hour, and his team of six crack technicians each billed more than five hundred dollars an hour for their services.

In San Francisco, the three security specialists, who looked to be just out of their teens, charged twelve thousand dollars daily, but they also seemed to work about 20 hours a day. And he had counted more than forty Multima technicians appearing on the Zoom screen at one point or another to explain concerns about their narrowly specialized ownership of some aspect of the computer system software or the hardware itself.

Just moments before, the guy in the center of the Zoom screen had boldly proclaimed he'd found another way to infiltrate the Jeffersons Stores computer systems with his hacking expertise. Amber Chan and Multima Supermarkets' chief technology officer tilted their heads toward the speaker, nodding occasionally, frequently posing questions Gordon understood only superficially, tapping information into their laptops almost continuously.

What a godsend that woman has become! Gordon looked

toward Amber at the other end of the long boardroom table and admired her composure as they waded through all the problems those teams of technicians had discovered. Vulnerabilities, as the techies liked to call them, now numbered in the dozens, maybe even more than a hundred. He'd lost count and would check with Amber later to get the actual tally.

Until he saw her in action—when Gordon returned from Montreal and started this marathon session to save the Multima Supermarkets operating system from a cyberattack Serge Boisvert thought imminent—he was entirely unaware his new chief of the Jeffersons Stores integration team was herself a computer genius.

It was her MBA from the University of Tokyo and her astute management of Multima's massive operations in China that first caught his eye. That she also was an expert computer programmer and formidable hacker in her own right came as a brilliant revelation and welcome news.

Like today, Gordon dropped into the meetings every few hours between his other obligations. But Amber had attended every session for more than twelve hours a day since Monday. Gordon examined her closely, trying to detect signs of fatigue, but he found none.

"We'll need to involve Serge's team in this one." Amber suddenly called out to Gordon from the end of the table, pointing at a schematic diagram someone was holding up to the Zoom camera. "Do you see how that information flow diverts to a second channel?"

Gordon nodded.

"Someone is siphoning information off the Jeffersons mainframe. Someone is capturing everything deemed confidential in that server. That's the first problem. Worse, though, is the susceptibility it creates. The hacker can also inject new information into the server, corrupting the data or bringing down its operation entirely. That's the third one we found just today!"

Gordon froze. If the Jeffersons Stores' systems were so easily vulnerable, what would it cost to fix? How long would it take? Would they have time to plug all the gaps in security before someone decided to cripple, if not kill, Jeffersons

Stores?

He looked around the table and glanced upward at the screens.

Everyone waited for his comment or guidance.

"Is it a futile process to fix the vulnerabilities?" His expression was grim, and his voice barely above a whisper.

"No," one of the techies replied after an uncomfortably long silence. "We can catch and correct every vulnerability. We're using an app that uses artificial intelligence. It will be extremely slow for the first few weeks because we'll have to recheck every line of code and teach the app how to correct its errors and omissions. But it will get easier over time."

"Your best guess?" It was Amber, eyebrows raised and head tilted, who asked.

"Nine months to a year," the nameless techie replied.

"We'll need to get Suzanne and Serge involved for sure." Gordon shook his head slowly, still shocked by the enormity of the task.

"Yeah, we'll need corporate support," Amber said. "But I wonder if it might be better for us to consider an entirely different path. Has anyone estimated how long it would take to migrate Jeffersons Stores onto Multima's system, throwing out Jeffersons' technology entirely?"

Eyes shifted nervously around the table and on the large wall-mounted screen where the remote technicians appeared equally unprepared.

"Let's get a team together now. We need to whip up a time and cost estimate over the weekend. Who's in?" Amber's warm, infectious smile and enthusiastic tone prompted a few hands to raise hesitantly on the screens.

Ten

Montreal, Quebec, Friday May 19, 2023

Suzanne Simpson swept into the massive conference room at Multima's Montreal headquarters, expecting to see only Edward Hadley. Instead, at least a dozen people greeted her. The senior executives—her chief legal counsel Alberto Ferer and Hadley—remained seated, but more junior team members rose from their chairs, almost as though coached, to say hellos and gain visibility with their CEO. On the side wall, the massive screen was populated with another dozen faces.

Suzanne smiled and waved dismissively for everyone to take a seat, looking over her eyeglasses at her director of public and corporate relations for an explanation.

"Alberto and I thought we needed to bring the full team this morning. This one has the potential to shake the food industry to the core. We'll need all hands on deck to avoid a tsunami of bad publicity and maybe even new government legislation."

She nodded and tried to assess the level of concern on the participants' faces while she looked around the room. "Fire away."

Edward Hadley carried on. "You know the feds have been making noises for a few months now about summoning CEOs from major Canadian supermarket chains to Ottawa to appear before a parliamentary committee dealing with high rates of inflation."

He waited for Suzanne to nod again before he broke the news. "Today, the chief-of-staff for the minister responsible called and told us they want you to attend and gave three possible dates. They want all six CEOs to testify simultaneously, so we'll need to coordinate with the other guys and agree on a date."

"Fair enough. But why are they asking me to appear? Shouldn't Gordon Goodfellow handle that?" Suzanne glanced at his image on the screen as she posed her question.

Goodfellow answered. "When Edward, Alberto, and I

spoke earlier, I asked the same question. The minister's office was quite insistent that only the CEO was welcome and demanded you attend by name."

Edward added more. "Even if they hadn't insisted, we'd want you there anyway. There's a huge media uproar building around the price of food. It might look less than respectful if we send Gordon. As important as he is at Multima Supermarkets, he's not the CEO. Politicians and the media are looking for accountability, and it's doubtful anyone other than a CEO would satisfy their blood lust. Besides, Gordon's Georgian drawl would probably irritate the nationalists in all the political parties."

Everyone around the table and on the Zoom screen laughed, including Gordon.

Alberto Ferer raised a finger, indicating he'd like to add something. "This inflation issue has become highly political, especially around food prices. The leader of the left-wing NDP thinks CEOs are outright criminals. The new leader of the right-wing Conservatives operates a rage farm, cultivating anger and anxiety as a defined strategy to defeat the governing Liberals. The Green Party screams for attention wherever it can, and the Bloc Québécois sees inflation as a tool of the nasty Anglais to eliminate the French language, forcing his Québec population to learn to swear in English to get the attention of disinterested governments."

There was a murmur of restrained laughter again while Alberto paused to sip his coffee before continuing. "If we're not careful, this fragile minority government might lose control. We might see radical action. Things like government-mandated price freezes. There might be attempts to break up the current dominant companies. One member of parliament is even talking about inviting foreign competitors to start up business in Canada—no doubt with some generous federal subsidy to force us to compete with lower prices."

"I've never appeared before a parliamentary committee," Suzanne said. "What's involved?"

Hadley motioned for the chief legal counsel to reply.

Alberto nodded and started. "Representatives from all political parties form the committee. In a majority government, the party in power ensures it has more members than all the opposition combined. In a minority government like we have now, the committee composition more accurately reflects the actual percentage of seats each party holds. So, you can expect more difficult questions as each party tries to score points in the court of public opinion. Committees are no longer devoted gatherers of facts to make informed recommendations to their parties. Rather, the committee members are more like performers, scheming to trip up the testifying witnesses for political gain."

When Alberto paused, Edward pounced before Suzanne could follow up. "There's another dynamic at work, too. Social media drives the agenda. Each committee member will have a parliamentary assistant in the room during the process. Often, individual members perform for the cameras, creating drama and posing questions only to generate embarrassment or discomfort for those being questioned. The goal is to have a one-minute video to post on social media, making the questioner look heroic and the respondent look bad. It gets vicious sometimes."

Suzanne took a deep breath. She furrowed her brow and tightened her lips, showing her concern. "What happens if we refuse to participate?"

"Legally, you can only delay. If you refuse to show up, a committee can oblige you to attend, or you can be found in contempt of parliament. The legal consequences of that are substantial." Alberto looked Suzanne directly in the eye as he spoke. It was clear he was warning her to avoid that path.

After a few seconds of silence, Edward added more. "Even delaying an appearance before the committee would be risky. The public mood about inflation is so grim right now we might see immediate dips in sales. Lots of people already think CEOs are arrogant billionaires, insensitive to the average person's concerns. To delay an appearance would stoke that sentiment."

Suzanne shrugged and looked at Edward. "I'd like you to see if there's another way we might meet with government officials, privately, if possible. If you can't get that, coordinate an appearance with our competitors through the association. Work with Eileen to find a date for the hearing and have her block some time on my calendar for preparatory sessions too.

46

Have your team put together some sample questions I might expect. That sort of thing."

She glanced toward Alberto but continued to address Hadley. "Find time on Alberto's calendar as well. I want another session with both of you to review all the legal pitfalls."

She waited as the men made quick notes and nodded their agreement. Then she addressed Gordon via the Zoom camera. "Can you have your team prepare a couple comprehensive summaries? All the measures we've currently taken with suppliers to moderate price increases. Any ideas you're working on to reduce prices or margins without negatively impacting the bottom line. And we better start working on measures we might need to propose that would impact profitability and quantify the impact on our shareholders. Be sure to get Pierre Cabot's financial people involved early in those conversations."

There was a flurry of activity around the table and on the Zoom screens as associates scribbled notes on paper or tapped the keyboards of their electronic devices.

Suzanne paused to let them finish before introducing a new complication. "I see Eileen was able to reach Serge out in California. You may have noticed he's joined our conference." She smiled affectionately into the camera and gave him a slight hand wave. "I asked him to join the meeting on short notice because we've got good representation here from Supermarkets, legal, and public relations. He made me aware of an issue that might affect all those operations. Before I turn the microphone over to him, I want to emphasize that what you're about to hear is highly confidential and should not, I repeat, not be discussed with any of your colleagues. Go ahead, Serge."

Suzanne sat erect and erased any hint of a smile as she surveyed those seated around the table, then gazed at the widescreen on the wall. Serge appeared equally concerned, his forehead creased with worry lines and the bags under his eyes suggesting insufficient sleep.

"We've discovered some activity on the dark web that's concerning. It's too early to make any announcements, and there's still a chance our information is wrong. But we've seen enough messages to raise the alarm and now ask each of you to be extra vigilant in the coming days. Someone is trying to buy information about behind-the-scenes activities at Supermarkets. Be extra alert to any requests for information about our business. Don't explain why to your teams. Just remind all your direct reports that all inquiries must first come to you, and you must forward them to me. Whoever's seeking this information is willing to pay up to fifty million dollars. If our information is accurate, these people are serious."

Eleven

Guantanamo Bay, Cuba, Saturday May 20, 2023

Fidelia Morales no longer knew what day it was. She wasn't even sure if she was alive or having a terrible nightmare. She pinched herself gently to confirm she was conscious. Even that tame touch caused her to shudder.

Pain was a constant, but she no longer had tears to cry. Days ago, her eyes had dried up entirely, even if she made sobbing noises or screamed out when they touched live electric wires to her feet or forcibly held her head under water or ran gushing water over her face for what seemed like hours.

She realized the words coming from her mouth now sounded like gibberish. They made no sense to her or her tormentors. The burly FBI bully cursed and swore at her continuously, threatening even more violent measures if she didn't cooperate. But she could no longer recall details to give. No matter how hard she tried, she couldn't remember the names of the banks where she hid the money, let alone individual account numbers.

Their torture created a result completely opposite from what they expected. Even when she was prepared to give them bits of information some days ago, her mind couldn't recall specifics. What she sputtered under duress proved inaccurate, and the next day, they subjected her to more torture, for even longer. Since then, she'd been disfunctional, unable to remember simple details about her life before capture.

A gentle knock on the door disturbed her latest efforts at thinking. When the door opened, the expected Cuban worker, Agueda Diaz, appeared. She wasn't alone. Two large men wearing dark suits stood behind her.

New FBI guys?

One waved for the young woman to move away, and then both men stepped inside Fidelia's room and walked toward her. Every muscle in her body tensed, and pain from past torture resurfaced. She tried to speak, but nothing came out.

One of the men asked, "Can you walk?"

Fidelia shook her head slowly, still unable to form words.

"Get a stretcher," the voice ordered. The other man in a suit hurried out of the room and past Agueda, whom he addressed next. "Bring me a bottle of water for her. Now."

There was silence as the big man looked her body up and down. Roughly, he yanked back the sheet covering her body, and his eyes grew wide as he silently surveyed the scars, bruises, and burn marks all over Fidelia's lower body. His facial expression remained stoic for what seemed like a few minutes before he finally spoke.

"We're taking you someplace else."

Fidelia's body recoiled at the thought of moving. Her mind raced with fear and trepidation about what was to come. She wrapped her arms around her chest protectively, waiting for the pain to start again. She felt a single prick to her upper thigh; then the world turned dark again.

Twelve

Atlanta, Georgia, Tuesday May 30, 2023

He scheduled the town hall meeting for noon on their first day back from the long Memorial Day weekend. Gordon used that weekend—when Multima Supermarkets' headquarters was virtually empty—to put the final touches on a speech he'd make to the technology teams today.

More than five hundred people would join the town hall remotely from Jeffersons Stores' headquarters in San Francisco. About one thousand team members would cram into the usually spacious lobby of the high-rise office complex that towered over other buildings on the outer edges of Atlanta.

After the brilliant work of Amber Chan's task force had scoped the magnitude of converting the entire information systems at newly acquired Jeffersons Stores to Multima Supermarkets' more robust and secure technology, they decided to move forward. Serge Boisvert and his security team in Montreal supported the decision, and Suzanne had signed off on the $100 million projected expense.

That day, his job was to convince the assembled town hall participants they should celebrate a bitter dictate he would announce. Effective immediately, all vacation time would be canceled until the project was completed in October. Of course, that ruined summer for everyone. All managers and employees were to work ten-hour days, five days a week, until further notice. Any absences required advance managerial approval, except in the case of illness. He shuddered as he thought about the potentially disastrous consequences if his audience didn't accept the carrot he'd offer.

Moments ago, he'd shuddered again as he remembered the probable, and almost unimaginable, consequences if they didn't get the job done.

At eleven o'clock, he switched off alerts on his phone, told his executive assistant to hold any calls or visitors, and stood before Edward Hadley and his communication specialists who'd come to his office for one final rehearsal of the speech he was about to deliver. He'd practiced it five times already. Each time, after whispered conferences among Edward and his team, they'd made at least one minor suggestion. It might have been a voice inflection, a few words changed, or something subtle he'd unknowingly conveyed in his body language, but they pointed them out in search of perfection.

Of course, he'd deliver the speech without notes or a teleprompter. Edward had emphasized that employees would react more positively if they believed his important comments came from his heart rather than a prepared script. So, every pause had been calculated, every gesture orchestrated, and every smile or frown timed for optimum impact.

While his audience of five watched his every movement and hung on each word, Gordon pretended he was in a crowded lobby with hundreds of people and an unforgiving camera transmitting his message to hundreds more. He delivered his message like an actor on stage might impart his lines to win the adoration of a theater audience. When he gave his last, heartfelt rehearsed plea, Edward Hadley and his team jumped to their feet as one and applauded as if they'd just been thrilled by a live performance on Broadway.

Gordon could only hope the real deal, minutes later, might generate a similar result.

They strode into the lobby in single file, Gordon leading. Edward and his team gradually dropped out of the procession, spreading themselves throughout the crowd. Only Gordon stepped onto the makeshift platform, elevated about three feet so everyone in attendance could see him clearly. When he reached the center of his stage, he made a sweeping circle, smiling and waving to the crowd surrounding him, plus the four cameras pointed downward from the high lobby ceiling. Then he paused.

The crowd stood shoulder to shoulder, not jammed together tightly, but close enough for some to feel a degree of social discomfort. Most faces looked patient and interested, some smiled, a few showed early signs of boredom. The hall was bright, with all the overhead lights beaming down and spotlights attached to the cameras glaring at him. The room became silent except for the low drone of the air conditioner fan blowing cooler air from above. Two security guards had positioned themselves outside the front entrance, hands behind their backs, blocking the path of anyone trying to enter the building.

Gordon stood before the crowd, hands relaxed at his side, wearing a beige casual sports coat and dark brown pants, colors Hadley's communications specialists long maintained projected the friendliest image. A stylist had carefully trimmed his brown hair, so none fell over his ears, then blow-dried the manicured cut to ensure every hair remained in place for the duration of the speech. He looked and felt like a successful leader.

Flashing a broad smile showing lots of teeth, he clicked on the microphone attached to his left lapel.

"Hello, everyone! Thank you for taking time away from your many responsibilities to join me here for a few minutes. I'll keep it brief, but I need to share with you personally the most important message I've delivered in the twenty-three years I've been with Multima Supermarkets." Gordon paused to let that settle in and shifted ninety degrees to face another section of the lobby.

Eyes followed his movement.

"It appears our company is a prime target for a cyberattack. Many of you know we've been assessing our systems at Multima headquarters and in the San Francisco offices of Jeffersons Stores, which we recently acquired. Unfortunately, our experts concluded that we are vulnerable. No one in either company is to blame. Both organizations have spent huge amounts of money continuously upgrading our systems to keep the bad guys out. But the bad guys have gotten better, using new artificial intelligence tools and unprecedented financial backing from bad actors around the globe. Some are criminal elements. Some are government-backed. Any of them might cause serious harm to Multima if we don't act quickly." Gordon paused again, turned another ninety degrees as rehearsed, then explained the circumstances in more detail.

He glimpsed furrowed brows and grimaces of concern on individual faces in the crowd as his message took hold. He described the urgency. Then, he shifted to his left again before he outlined the plan to upgrade the entire Multima Supermarkets computer information systems, building in more intelligent protection technologies and converting servers and technology at Jeffersons Stores to the same new, more resilient system.

He saw widened eyes and a few gaping mouths when he described the timeline for completion. Some glanced worriedly at colleagues. A small minority rolled their eyes in disbelief.

Gordon shifted ninety degrees to the left again to break the bad news. "If you have doubts about that timeline and our ability to complete it by October, your doubts are well-founded. Our expert team reached the same conclusion. We won't complete it that quickly if we continue to use our current processes and work habits. From today until we complete the project in October, I'm asking each of you to rise to the unusual challenge of modifying our processes, work hours, and human resources policies."

Gordon watched bodies become more erect and tense as he outlined the new working hours. Then saw an expected restless shifting of feet among some in the crowd before he explained the cancellation of vacations and disallowance of any absences except for illness.

"I'm as sorry to make these requests as you are to hear them. I never imagined that I'd have to take steps like this when I became the leader of this great company. Let me assure you. If you have already made vacation plans—flights, hotels, car rentals, anything like that—the company will reimburse you for any expenses you incur canceling those reservations."

He observed shoulders slumping forward among the crowd, a few faces relaxing in relief that they at least wouldn't lose money, and an occasional thumbs-up. He promised the company would be reasonable, carving out exceptions dealing with extraordinary circumstances like childcare or eldercare. He would be flexible with starting and finishing times as long as everyone put in ten hours a day. There were no smiles, but little anger surfaced either. Success would ride on Gordon's closing comments.

"As you would expect, Suzanne Simpson and the

corporate team fully support this crucial project. They'll absorb the huge costs we'll incur, so everyone's annual bonuses—based on achieving our established performance objectives—are safe."

Gordon saw more tension evaporate after he paused, raised his voice an octave, as he'd rehearsed, and shared the surprise news.

"There's an added special bonus for everyone. It's payable one day after we complete this vital project. Last Friday, the closing price for Multima shares trading on the New York Stock Exchange was twenty-two dollars and forty-seven cents. Suzanne Simpson has agreed to grant each of you publicly traded shares in Multima Corporation equal to ten percent of your annual salary, calculated at a guaranteed value of twenty-two dollars per share!"

Applause started the instant Gordon paused for breath. It grew so loud and quickly that he had to shout into the microphone over the whistles, high-fives, cheers, and hand-clapping.

"Let's all get back to work now and finish this job so every one of us can share in the success of this great company!"

Thirteen

Singapore, Saturday July 1, 2023

The moment Suzanne heard how well Multima Supermarkets' workforce had accepted Gordon Goodfellow's challenge, she imposed the same temporary long working hours and vacation ban on her headquarters team for symbolic support. It would require sacrifices from the entire company team to convert Jeffersons Stores' computer systems and upgrade Supermarkets' systems to better thwart outside cyberattacks.

She clarified to everyone that they'd observe statutory holidays, regardless. Following her own rules, she canceled her personal summer vacation plans and modified her business travel schedule slightly. That's what brought her to Singapore on Canada's national holiday. She also rationalized that since Saturday was a day off for the company's office employees, everyone should also have a day off on the US's Fourth of July.

But first she scheduled two working days with Serge in Shanghai before the weekend. She wanted to meet in person with the new Supermarkets president for the Asia region. Serge had also brought along two technology experts to assess whether there was any substance to the dramatically increased talk about hacking from Japan and North Korea. When the technology experts drew no conclusions after two days of testing, they flew home on a Friday morning flight, while Suzanne and Serge left after dinner for the five-and-a-half-hour flight south to Singapore.

It was their first romantic interlude since Memorial Day. That is to say, as romantic as it could be with two of Serge's bodyguards in tow, Jasmine Smith-Field and Willy Landon. Both were tall, fit and heavy-set specimens of good health and brute strength. Suzanne loved them both, and Serge often assigned them to watch over her when she traveled in the US. Neither had relocated to Canada when Multima moved its headquarters to Montreal, so she'd missed their good humor and now welcomed their companionship during sightseeing and walks around the Asian city-state.

Suzanne had reluctantly agreed to full-time surveillance after that early morning incident at their home in the Laurentian Mountains near Montreal. Law enforcement still hadn't gotten to the bottom of it, but she knew Serge considered that unknown visitor a genuine threat, and she respected his judgment. He'd agreed they could be more relaxed in Singapore, and the security pair more resembled travel companions or friends while they checked out Singapore's sights, history, and eclectic mix of international foods.

She wanted their first night there to be special and remembered seeing an email from months earlier promoting an exclusive restaurant named Siri House on Dempsey Hill. As they wandered through the spectacular and unique National Orchid Garden, she noted a sign for Dempsey Hill and wondered out loud if it was nearby. Willy instantly researched their location, determined the restaurant was comfortably within walking distance, and offered to jog over and see if they could get a table.

Thirty minutes later, he returned with a confirmation of a private room in an area usually reserved for corporate events. He'd checked, and it was luxurious, comfortable and secure. They resumed admiring the thousands of varieties of orchids in the garden for an hour or two, then returned to their hotel to refresh and dress for their special dinner. A limousine Serge had booked for the evening dropped them off at the upscale restaurant.

Its manager met them at the front door and welcomed everyone with enthusiasm and charm. He led their procession in single file through the main seating area to a beautiful, secluded garden in the back. Tall, dense hedges towered behind a single large table set for four. Suzanne marveled at the quiet of the area, only feet away from a noisy street.

Silver ornaments, like those on a Christmas tree, sparkled overhead. Lush, green grass, just steps from their table, threw off the scent of a recent cutting. Brightly colored orchids decorated the table and filled pots carefully positioned throughout the private seating area for maximum beauty and elegance. A beautiful young Asian woman bowed and introduced herself.

"My name is Ashley, and I'm pleased to serve you this evening." Her radiant smile attracted attention first. She bowed slightly, her hands clasped before her breasts in a motion most foreigners equate with prayer.

"*Selamat,*" she welcomed.

Dressed in a colorful, full-length traditional gown, Ashley gracefully slid chairs out from the table for Suzanne and Jasmine. Serge and Willy seated themselves.

Their dinner was exquisite. Each chose different dishes from a menu that featured various types of Asian cuisine and enthusiastically graded each of their four courses offered as "outstanding." The bottles of dry red wine Serge ordered were equally enjoyable, and Suzanne probably drank more than she should have because the bodyguards had covered their glasses with napkins after their first few sips.

Eventually, she grew anxious for some quiet time alone with her lover. Suzanne suggested they leave as soon as the food service finished. Her smile was intended to telegraph to Serge that she longed for his warm embrace and a delightful night together under the sheets of their hotel suite's gigantic bed.

Their reserved limousine waited outside the front entrance after the group paid the bill and stepped out of the restaurant. Jasmine stood by her side and chatted as they walked. Serge and Willy followed behind them.

Halfway to the limousine, Jasmine suddenly grabbed Suzanne's shoulders and roughly thrust her downward into a flower bed beside the walk, falling on top of her with a heavy thud.

When Suzanne cried out and lifted her head from the dirt, she saw Willy lying flat on the sidewalk behind her, his left shoulder red with spreading blood, and Serge sprinting furiously toward the street.

Fourteen

Dubrovnik, Croatia, Saturday July 1, 2023

Fidelia checked the date on her phone and did a quick calculation. It was almost six weeks since they'd brought her here. The bones in her feet had begun to feel more normal. On her own today, she'd climbed the stairs from the upper deck, where her suite was located, to a rooftop sitting area. Most of the scars and burns on her arms, legs and feet had now healed.

She could once again look into a mirror without bursting into tears. Damage from their vicious punches and slaps had permanently scarred her skin, but a cosmetic surgeon that Tak Takahashi and Klaudia Schäffer flew over from Milan had worked wonders.

Tak had saved her life. She still marveled at how effectively he had used a hidden resource in the FBI, once Fidelia's longtime friend finally consented to help. Klaudia knew about that FBI resource, how to contact her, and how to manipulate her.

In earlier days, Fidelia and Klaudia had even been sometime lovers, but their relationship had soured miserably in the days before the fiasco in Hawaii. Fortunately, in the chaos and confusion of that disaster in Honolulu, Tak had smartly seized Fidelia's former friend and took her back to Japan with him. For Fidelia, the magic started when Klaudia realized Tak would simply kill her if she didn't cooperate fully.

That secret FBI resource pulled back the FBI bully detective in the rumpled suit for "consultations". Klaudia had then enlisted the support of their secret plant in the Cuban Dirección de Inteligencia, their secret service, who managed the worker, Agueda, at Guantanamo. Eventually, it was she who passed Tak's messages to Fidelia.

When that secret FBI source arranged credentials and an FBI aircraft for two goons from The Organization in Florida, they swept Fidelia out of the grasp of the rogue FBI agents, abruptly ending her illegal custody in Guantanamo Bay.

Most recently, Klaudia again proved helpful. She convinced The Organization's country head for Italy to loan her this palatial vacation home in Dubrovnik. Now, they were all nestled in the three-level home built into the mountainside of the picturesque Croatian city, overlooking the Adriatic Sea.

The Cuban worker, Agueda Diaz, had demanded they also pull her out of Cuba in return for her help, and the fake FBI officers had stashed the woman in a compartment of the FBI jet. She took care of Fidelia on the nine-hour flight as they crossed the Atlantic, then served as housekeeper and nursemaid while Fidelia recovered from her ordeal in captivity.

The fake FBI officers stayed in Europe for a while as well. Fidelia's Miami crime boss assigned them to protect her until further notice, so they took turns surveying the walkways and streets leading to her temporary home. So far, they had nothing to do but watch.

During the previous night, Tak and Klaudia had arrived from Tokyo on his newly purchased Bombardier 7500 jet, an aircraft he'd bought weeks earlier on the dark web for a fraction of its value. The pair had flown the twelve-hour flight from Tokyo on a route south of Russia and over the "Stans," avoiding the war zone in Ukraine, before dipping down over the Balkans and arriving in Dubrovnik just after midnight this morning. Although they'd slept during the flight, both had said they wanted to begin adjusting to Croatia's time zone after a few more hours of sleep. She expected to see them soon.

Fidelia's mind and emotions still weren't up to snuff. She often cried uncontrollably for extended periods for no reason at all. Her dreams were usually nightmares, waking her with screams that sounded horrible even to her and with her entire body sometimes trembling for hours afterward. She still couldn't recall many details about The Organization, the criminal outfit she supposedly still ran. But each day seemed a bit better.

Tak was a brilliant protégé in the Japanese Yakuza, The Organization's affiliate in crime in the Asian country. During those last hours of havoc in Hawaii, she'd eliminated his predecessor and handed Tak the crown to run their operations in Japan.

He was probably grateful for that. Still, she found it difficult to understand why he was visiting her when he should surely be solidifying his position at home. It seemed downright risky for him to leave his country at such a delicate stage. Maybe he chose to come now to assess her health personally and perhaps plot his next steps.

Klaudia was always a wild card. She'd worked for Fidelia in the escort business, and they'd become close enough to share nights of passion from time to time. But her former close friend rebelled foolishly when Fidelia snatched her off a Caribbean island and forced her to help in the botched Hawaii deal. Which version of the woman would show up to chat with her in the coming hours?

She didn't have long to wait. Echoes of shoes clanking on a metal staircase leading to the roof deck carried clearly to Fidelia's ears. Thick layers of dark clouds covered the Adriatic as far as she could see. Birds chirped in the orange trees growing beside the house. Faintly, from off in the distance, she heard a piece of heavy equipment drilling into the mountain rock for some new construction project.

Fidelia took in one deep breath of salty sea air before she saw Tak's head surface above the patio floor. Klaudia followed. The two Miami bodyguards took no chances with the visiting pair. They came into view and staked out positions on each corner of the roof deck, facing her. Their ever-present jackets were unbuttoned, and their weapons of choice were in clear view from where she reclined on the canvas sun lounge.

After taking a long moment to inspect and assess Fidelia, Tak spoke first.

"How is your recovery progressing?" When she didn't immediately respond, he tried again. "Really, how are you feeling after your ordeal?"

His voice sounded genuinely interested, but she remained silent.

Klaudia tried next, her tone more pressing. "Are you able to speak, Fidelia? Are you alright?"

Fidelia pushed herself more upright on the lounge chair to better read their eyes. She cleared her throat to ensure the most resounding voice she could muster. "Send the Miami guys downstairs. Then strip down. Take off all your clothes—both of you—and pull up chairs."

Fifteen

Atlanta, Georgia, Saturday July 1, 2023

Gordon knew Suzanne had exempted Saturdays, Sundays and public holidays from the increased work-hours mandate for all technology-related staff and the managers who supervised them. But Amber Chan had persuaded—or cajoled—her teams to work anyway. The systems conversion and updates ran about a week behind her established schedule, and she seemed determined to regain lost time.

It also provided a good excuse to escape the tensions at home. For months, the relationship with his wife had been strained with frequent arguments about the maturing kids, her demands to augment financial donations to the church, and the ever-increasing frequency of her "headaches" when they turned in for the night.

That morning, he cheerfully gave his wife Priscilla a peck on the cheek, thanking her for understanding his need to go to the office, and dropped off his teenage son at a baseball practice on the way. His wife would collect their eldest child when the practice finished about noon.

Upon arrival at the office, his mood brightened at the sight of dozens of cars in the parking lot. Amber sure had her team galvanized. It was hard to imagine how she maintained such highly motivated staff when she demanded so much from them. He made a mental note to chat with a few that day to see what he might learn from her methods.

Intentionally, he followed a longer route to his executive suite on the top floor of the building. He took the elevator to the fourth floor and stepped into a vast area covered by individual work cubicles. A hum of activity greeted him. Conversations in muted tones. The click of keyboards as workers processed data. According to a schedule posted over on the far wall, Amber already held court in the meeting room, with a dozen or more experts.

He waved through the meeting room's glass windows, and his greeting was eventually returned as participants noticed him passing. But he didn't interrupt their discussions. His objective was only to show them he too was sacrificing his Saturday for the Multima cause. Return waves were friendly, with lots of smiles, reassuring him that Amber must be handling her subordinates well.

The president of a nationwide supermarket chain never lacks work. Printed reports and correspondence left over from preceding days lay piled high on his desk. Unlike most executives today, Gordon hadn't adapted entirely to the digital world. Instead, he preferred to study data already screened and analyzed by others. Since he could add little to the technicians' work, he'd leave them alone for a while. Instead, he set out to shrink the pile of reports and absorb as many details as possible about Supermarkets' performance globally.

He started with Jeffersons Stores. For the entire morning, he read the numbers and the notes either Amber or her team had added for background or clarification. Comments said sales were more robust than budgeted, primarily due to inflation. Gross margins were also better than budgeted for the same reason. As he worked his way through the data, Gordon was continually reminded about his recent conversations with Suzanne and the pressure the Canadian government and consumers there exerted on Multima.

He also became concerned about budgeted expenses at Jeffersons Stores.

Surprisingly, during June, labor expenses had skyrocketed in the stores. Actual costs were far higher than planned. Why?

June was usually a stable month in retail. No holidays or special events caused disruptions or required fluctuations in staff. There had been no changes to the union agreement. After considerable thought, Gordon concluded that Amber's focus on the computer upgrade project might have detracted from her day-to-day management oversight. Today might not be the time to address it, but he made a mental note to approach her with his concerns when appropriate.

A glance at his watch showed it was already noon. Amber's team had ordered a spread of food and snacks, so he took the elevator from his office down to join them. His timing was perfect.

Staff clustered around two large tables of food and

refreshments, loading up their plates, and then pulling up chairs wherever they found space to chat with a colleague. Gordon grabbed two slices of pizza and circulated.

He'd learned much about employee relations under the tutelage of Suzanne Simpson when she was president of Multima Supermarkets, before acceding to the CEO role. Gordon knew the first names of most employees who worked in the headquarters building, and they appreciated his personal hellos and brief chats. He introduced himself to every new face and listened intently to anything anyone chose to share with him.

It became clear that Amber had them motivated. Enthusiasm for the project was high. Several commented about the pleasure of working with a leader who actually understood technology. With no offense to him, they usually added with an apologetic grin. He detected no ill will about their need to work that day and sensed optimism they'd achieve the October deadline.

As he finished making the rounds, he stopped at the makeshift desk in an uncluttered corner that Amber used when she spent time on this floor. Her regular office was next to his upstairs, but he'd seldom seen her there since they'd launched the project to integrate Jeffersons Stores' information systems with Multima's.

"How's it going?" he asked.

Amber looked up from her keyboard and stood to greet him. "Oh, hi! I saw you wandering about. I'm really pleased with the progress this morning. The team has accomplished a lot, with a complete focus on the project and no interruptions from the day-to-day stuff. Did you get enough to eat?"

Gordon smiled and tossed his empty paper plate in a nearby wastebasket. "Plenty, thanks. Morale seems high. The team seems to be having fun despite it all. Anything you need help with?"

Amber took a long moment and looked him in the eye before she replied.

Is she looking for a hint of concern? Gordon maintained a passive demeanor and returned her eye contact.

"I think we have the project under control," she replied, "but I'm not entirely satisfied with performance in the stores this month. I think we have a problem controlling expenses. Can we chat about that when you have some time?"

"Any time will work for me. When would you like to get together?" Gordon kept his tone light, avoiding any sense of concern.

"We'll finish today at about five. Would you have a few minutes then to meet and chat?" Her light tone conflicted with her sense of urgency. Nothing he'd said or shown suggested it was vital for them to meet right away. Something must be worrying her.

He didn't need to pile on and create pressure, but he surprised himself with his next question. "Five o'clock today would be fine. Would you like to chat over dinner?"

As a result, Gordon found himself sitting across from Amber in a darkened restaurant after telling his wife an emergency would delay his return home that evening. It was a problem in China, where the day was just starting. It might take a while to resolve.

He wanted to avoid any tension or putting pressure on his colleague, so after they each ordered a glass of red wine, he started their conversation with the light stuff. How was she settling into life in America? How did she find her apartment?

For a few minutes, he listened. She liked where she lived, but she found the pace of life very slow in the US. The weather was almost like Shanghai, and traffic in Atlanta was a breeze compared to home.

They ordered dinner, and both had finished their glasses of wine, so Gordon ordered a bottle of the brand Amber had first chosen to accompany their meal. Before the food arrived, she made her confession.

"I've really messed up on the day-to-day management at Jeffersons Stores. I've become single-mindedly focused on the systems project, and store management has taken advantage of my lax oversight. I assumed my direct reports monitored labor hours and expenses, but they let me down. I may have to make some changes."

Gordon nodded while she told her story but stopped agreeing when she implied some changes in staff might evolve. It didn't work that way at Multima.

"What kind of changes do you have in mind?" He

maintained a tone of interest or curiosity and tilted his head to welcome a reply.

Between mouthfuls of their meal, Amber outlined her concerns and ideas to correct the over-expenditures in the future. As he listened, Gordon's mood improved considerably. His leader of the Jeffersons Store integration articulated excellent ideas and never recommended discipline or terminations. Instead, she sought his support to establish new communication channels among her direct reports, new performance metrics, and urgent training in expense management.

When Amber finished her overview, he asked a few questions to clarify her proposals, testing how well she'd thought them through.

Impressed by her ideas and poise, he responded without hesitation. "You have my full support for all those changes. Just one suggestion. You might want to ask Pierre Cabot to have someone on his team lead your training exercise." He allowed a smirk to form. "Getting him involved now might head off a future problem."

She got the unspoken message that it would go easier for her if the company's CFO saw her quick recognition of a problem and the wisdom of involving him in the solution. She laughed, nodding in agreement. Then she surprised him.

"I'll send him an email tomorrow. Thank you so much for your support." She leaned in toward him, looked him directly in the eyes, then unexpectedly planted her right hand on his on the table and squeezed gently. The sparkle in her eyes suggested more than gratitude, and Gordon felt an unusual stirring in his groin. He didn't withdraw his hand, and Amber held on delicately.

"Can I offer you a coffee at my apartment before you go home?" Her hand squeezed again, more sensuously this time. And her eyes continued to sparkle mischievously.

Without much consideration, Gordon smiled and answered more quickly than he expected. "Why not? It would be great to get to know you better."

He followed her to her apartment less than ten minutes from Multima Supermarkets' headquarters, where she pointed from her car to the visitors' parking section before driving a few yards further along to her assigned spot. When they met up again on the walkway to her apartment, her manner was friendly, and she chatted about the building and its superintendent as they entered and rode the elevator to her tenth-floor suite.

The apartment was exquisitely furnished. Colorful but tasteful modern art adorned each of the walls. The beige carpet was plush and warm. Shades of brown colored the walls, and the lighting was subdued. Gordon imagined she had contracted with a designer to furnish the place, and she confirmed his guess.

"Yes. Nicole Gagnon from the Montreal headquarters recommended the designer. She once lived and worked here in Atlanta and knew the company from personal experience. I think they did a wonderful job. Now, would you still have a coffee or maybe another glass of that wine we were drinking? It's my favorite brand, so I always keep some here."

Gordon guessed the added bit was to clarify her preference, so he agreed to the wine.

"Make yourself comfortable. I'll get the wine and be right back." Amber switched on some music and disappeared into the kitchen.

Gordon took a seat on the enormous beige sofa. It had a unique shape. More than ten feet long, there were four individual components. At each end, sections with backs and arms stretched out from the wall. In the middle was a large chunk with a back but no arms. And at the end Gordon selected, there was a section jutting out beyond the section with an arm. It occurred to him that it wouldn't take much effort to slide that last piece of the puzzle against the others to form a more-than-king-sized bed.

As he finished that thought, Amber returned with two glasses of wine.

She'd shed only the red jacket of her business suit for that day but now displayed a sheer, almost transparent, white blouse with the same short black skirt. As she stood before Gordon and handed him his glass of wine, she looked a bit like a server, but it was also impossible not to notice that she wore nothing under that blouse.

She paused, letting him have a good look as her smile

grew. When Amber sat on the sofa, she picked a spot just inches from him despite the length of the sofa. There, she clinked her glass with his and drew a long sip before slowly placing her wine on a short decorative table. The lighting showed the outline of her beautifully formed breasts enticingly, and Gordon felt a yearning grow in his groin. It occurred to him that things were moving too quickly, and in the wrong direction, but he dismissed that concern almost immediately.

She slowly shifted away from the small table, turned to face Gordon directly, and subtly ran the tip of her tongue across her lips before reaching out for Gordon's glass. "May I?"

When Amber had taken it and set it on the table next to her, she turned, facing him more directly, and moved closer to touch her lips with his.

He lost all restraint.

He pulled her tightly to him and pressed his tongue deep into her mouth. She responded with a fury of passion, inviting his tongue inside, teasing and exploring. They squirmed to get closer, touching erratically and probing every orifice accessible. There was no boundary, and before Gordon realized it, she was naked, and his hands had moved well beyond her inviting breasts and probed between her legs, seeking her most sensitive nerves.

Amber finished undressing him in a manner approaching desperation, forcefully pulling buttons apart as she tore his clothes away before reaching for his penis, then she squeezed it possessively, drawing him into her already damp vagina. The next few moments became a blur of activity as Gordon thrust, and Amber encouraged him to penetrate even deeper.

Suddenly, it was over. *Shit! Much too early!*

Amber didn't miss a beat and whispered the right words at the right time. "Don't worry, Gordon. It was a little soon, but I'll have you again."

As he started to answer, she put her forefinger over his lips, kissed him and slid off his body, cuddling closely. Settled, she began kissing and stroking him in ways he'd never experienced, stirring his groin into desire once more. He felt himself harden and enlarge until Amber once again mounted him and kissed his mouth hungrily, her firm thighs urging him to respond.

The second time he came, she squealed with pleasure and pulled him tightly to her body. They stayed there for several minutes without speaking. Each listening to the other's pounding heart and taking in the satisfaction of the other's fulfillment.

Then Gordon's guilt emerged. He had sinned. As an evangelical Christian, he promised lifelong fidelity to his wife, and he had just broken that promise for the first time since they'd married. He continued to hold Amber in his arms but felt awkward, unsure of what to say and what to do next.

Worse, the woman reported directly to him. A company policy violated, one that could ruin his career. As he lamented his moment of weakness, he heard what sounded like a sniffle. He loosened his hold on her slightly.

"Is everything all right?"

The sniffle became a sob, then several sobs. He tried again.

"I'm sorry, Amber. I'm sorry I've made you cry."

She struggled to regain control and sat more upright, still crying with dramatic heaves. "No. It's not you. You were fine. That's not the problem."

Gordon waited momentarily, looking at her despite his shame and discomfort. "Why are you crying then?"

"I got a disturbing phone call from China this morning. One of my closest friends, someone I used to work with, accidentally overheard a horrible conversation."

"A conversation?" Gordon tilted his head to one side, and his brow furrowed deeply with both confusion and curiosity.

"Yes. A few days ago, when Suzanne Simpson visited my old office in Shanghai, this friend accidentally overheard a conversation a terrible woman from another part of China was having with Suzanne's bodyguard. They were sitting in a quiet corner near some file cabinets, and my friend overheard them speaking in English when she went to retrieve a file. She heard the awful woman tell the bodyguard that I had a boyfriend in the Japanese Yakuza and that I'd been a member of that gang since living in Japan."

Gordon bristled. He sensed danger for a fleeting instant

before focusing his full attention on her story. "Why would she tell such a lie?"

"The woman is an ethnic Uyghur from Western China. They always complain of mistreatment by the Chinese government and ethnic Chinese people. This woman often complained to co-workers that I was too close to the government and equally to blame for their plight. I had one meeting with her to diffuse the issue, and she promised never to defame me again, so I took no further action. Now, she's spread that malicious rumor again. If that bodyguard relays this terrible lie to Suzanne, my future with Multima may be finished!"

Gordon held his head in his hands in disbelief. Could there be any simple way out of this mess?

Sixteen

Singapore, Sunday July 2, 2023

She insisted on staying in the emergency waiting area at the Singapore General Hospital until they knew bodyguard Willy was out of danger. Attending police officers assured Suzanne, Serge, and Jasmine the hospital was one of the best in the world and they had no doubt Willy would get the best medical treatment available.

While an ambulance had raced the wounded bodyguard to medical care, Serge and Jasmine tried to convince Suzanne to return to their suite at the Four Seasons Hotel, a five-minute drive away. But she had genuine concerns about the condition of her assigned protector. She reasoned that she felt safer in a crowded hospital area, guarded by armed police officers than in a hotel with unarmed security with who knew what level of training.

One of the older Singaporean police officers persuaded Serge, who convinced Suzanne that they should at least sit in a more private area while waiting. He guided them to an empty, quiet lounge reserved for politicians and dignitaries off to the side of the main waiting area and stationed two officers outside the door.

Once they were alone and settled into the more private surroundings, Serge wanted to know what they'd seen. He asked Jasmine to report first because she had pushed Suzanne safely to the ground.

"I was scanning the horizon as we always do. A short Asian male made a sudden movement at the side of the roadway ahead of us. He shifted from a slow walk to a few running steps, then suddenly whirled toward us. I could see him raising something from his side. I assumed the worst and shoved Suzanne downward into the flower bed with all my strength, then fell on her to protect her. I figured if I was wrong, I'd just apologize."

"Great thinking," Suzanne said. "I value your dedication." She reached out and touched Jasmine's hand and squeezed tightly for a moment.

Serge nodded in agreement. "You made absolutely the right call, and I commend your quick thinking, too. Did you notice any distinguishing characteristics about the guy that we can share with the police?"

"Not much. It all happened too quickly. He was young and Asian, probably about five-foot-six, and in excellent physical shape. His movements were quick and slick. Dressed casually. Blue jeans and a green T-shirt, I think. I didn't notice glasses or a hat."

"Well, that's something for the police here to start with. They'll probably want you to check their photo library of known offenders. The guy had disappeared by the time I reached the street. I didn't see anyone at all. Anything else come to mind?" Serge asked the question casually but focused intently on Jasmine as though he expected more.

"Well, since all this happened, I've been thinking about a weird conversation I had on Friday with one of the staff members at Supermarkets' Asian headquarters in Shanghai." Jasmine paused, shook her head slowly, and took a deep breath. She seemed uncertain or uncomfortable or both.

"A Chinese woman approached me in the cafeteria and tapped me on the shoulder. She spoke English quite well, said she had something very important to tell me, and motioned for me to follow her. She led me to a quiet nook a few yards down from the cafeteria, where they stored a ton of files in taller cabinets than I'd seen before, probably about six feet high." Jasmine took another moment to collect her thoughts.

"The woman's manner seemed odd to me. She seemed unusually angry. Her nostrils flared when she began to speak, and her face reddened. I'm not used to seeing people react like that. But instead of shouting, she spoke very quietly, like she was afraid of being overheard, and leaned in so close to me that I recoiled a bit. She first confirmed I worked directly with Suzanne. I just nodded in reply. Then she said she had something significant to tell me, and that I must pass it along to Suzanne. She waited for me to nod again, confirming that I would."

Jasmine took another deep breath and again shook her head from side to side a couple times as though building courage or seeking insight. She paused.

The only sound in the lounge was gurgling water from an aquarium on the opposite side of the room. Half a dozen small, brightly colored fish swam there, darting in continuous circles. The entire lounge was covered by royal blue, plush carpet, but a golden line extended a few feet below a window where lights outside the room squeezed through a gap in the window curtain. The room was comfortable, but it still couldn't escape the ever-present stench of powerful hospital antiseptics.

Jasmine started again, her tone implying doubt or disbelief. "She wanted me to tell you that Amber Chan is mixed up with Japanese criminals. According to her, the woman hates Chinese people and got involved in the Yakuza when she was a college student studying in Tokyo. The woman claimed that Amber was a lover of one of the kingpins in the gang. I didn't pass along this information before because the woman seemed so odd and unstable. Her story seemed ridiculous at the time."

Serge nodded as she spoke, then waited a moment. Perhaps he hoped for more; maybe he wanted to gather his thoughts. "I understand your dilemma. I know neither Suzanne nor I fault your judgment. But it's probably better to let us know everything in the future, even if it seems far-fetched. Why do you think it's significant now?"

Jasmine's hand, resting on the leather armrest, trembled. "Willy was walking right behind me as we came down the sidewalk. I'm wondering if Willy was shot accidentally when I lunged to protect Suzanne. Did I avoid a bullet meant for me?"

Seventeen

Dubrovnik, Croatia, Sunday July 2, 2023

Fidelia felt more confident climbing the steps to her rooftop patio that morning. Almost two months had passed since her torture in Cuba and her feet and legs had responded well to physiotherapy and gentle exercises.

When she stepped onto the marble surface, she turned and looked down at the beautiful sights below. It wasn't the same as Puerto Rico, where she grew up, but it was the seaside and stunning in its own special way. She breathed in deeply soothing, salty sea air.

In the distance, the rich, blue Adriatic Sea stretched beyond the mountains as far as she could see, an early morning sun glittering brightly on its gentle waves. Below her, a massive, colorfully painted cruise liner docked on the opposite side of the port, its passengers appearing like energetic ants scurrying off the ship for a day of sightseeing.

Closer, the lazy port of Dubrovnik was showing signs of life as a dozen or so smaller fishing, sightseeing, and pleasure boats untied from the piers and slowly chugged out of the harbor toward the open sea.

The small city built on the side of a mountain surrounding the harbor was quiet that morning. A flock of birds squawked as they glided over the water, hoping to spot breakfast. She saw only a single car on the narrow two-lane road that connected Dubrovnik with the rest of the Balkans and wound its way gradually from the top where Fidelia was staying and down into the city's central business area.

It was a perfect time and place to think. Tak Takahashi and Klaudia would climb up here to join her soon, and the Italian crime boss who loaned her this place was expected sometime later as well. In her few precious moments alone, she needed to make decisions—lots of them.

Yesterday, Tak and Klaudia hadn't appreciated her sudden demand that they both fully disrobe in front of her immediately. Of course, she'd seen both nude before, so there was no sexual intention behind her demand. Instead, she had two other motives. First, each had sworn loyalty to her—total and complete loyalty. If they couldn't accept a simple order to get naked, how could she rely upon them if she gave a more complicated command like eliminating someone?

Her other motive was fear. Although she still hated to admit it, the torture and physical punishment she underwent in Guantanamo Bay at the hands of the abusive FBI thug left her fearing almost everything and everybody. Were Tak and Klaudia secretly carrying weapons? Were they wired to record everything she said?

She could no longer take chances with even her closest associates and wanted to deliver that message to them loudly and clearly.

After a couple quiet and grumpy, mumbled expressions in Japanese and German respectively, both had followed her order and sat naked before her for the rest of their one-hour meeting.

Tak did most of the talking. He brought her up to date on the state of the Yakuza in Japan. Although they came within a hair of losing the Japanese government's exceptional tolerance of the lucrative pachinko parlors, Tak described how he engineered the last-minute connection between The Organization's guy, an Argentinian venture capital fund, and the Bank of The Americas.

That shrewd move had allowed the deal with Multima to move forward and meet the Japanese government's deadline for payment of years of unpaid taxes. Accordingly, the authorities continued to look the other way when it came to the Yakuza's illegal activities in the pachinko joints.

Fidelia smiled at the irony. The Organization still earned income from Multima Corporation via the Argentinian fund even though they had lost billions with Suzanne Simpson's plunder of Jeffersons Stores when they were forced to sell at such a low price. However, they'd recover their loss another way.

His control over the Japanese wing of The Organization seemed solid, and Tak outlined planned proactive measures to weaken the influence of a couple rivals who might try to undermine his authority. Fidelia had voiced no objection.

Klaudia was in a different situation. She remained

repugnant. During their dialogue, she spent more time examining her fingernails than participating in the conversation. While she appeared to listen, she never voiced an opinion or asked a question unless Fidelia confronted her directly. At the end of every question Fidelia posed, her former close friend ended her sentence demanding release from The Organization. She never expressed an interest in Fidelia's health or recovery. She didn't display one iota of friendship or affection.

Fidelia had weighed her options with both subordinates for hours after that little talk.

The scent of strong coffee interrupted her thoughts before she caught the distinctive echo of shoes climbing the metal stairs to her perch on the roof patio. It was Tak.

"I thought you might like something strong to start your day." His cheerful greeting seemed a touch overdone, but she shared the basic sentiment: coffee would be good.

"I plan to leave for Tokyo today if you have no objection." He watched her carefully as usual, always sensitive to her moods or preferences—good qualities for a subordinate. "I want to discuss Multima Corporation. I'd like your candid opinions, and I thought it better for us to have that conversation alone. Is now a good time?"

Fidelia took a long sip of her coffee before she answered, using that time to read the expression on his face. His eyes were penetrating, more aggressive than subservient. His facial expression was taut, and his lips pursed. He wanted something and wanted it badly.

"Before we talk strategy, tell me what you've managed so far," she said.

"Financially, the Argentinian venture capital fund is under our control. The guy that runs it has a weakness for both women and drugs. We've got photos and videos that will ensure he does whatever we want until he runs out of money. But he's got enough."

"So you think Multima might miss an interest payment or something that would let the guy yank out his part of the loan and cause some instability?" Fidelia's tone dripped with sarcasm. The idea that Multima couldn't make interest payments on a billion-dollar loan was absurd.

"It's a long shot. I agree. More important, though, is his relationship with the Bank of The Americas. He's close to the CEO there, Abduhl Mahinder. Married to the guy's only daughter. Mahinder serves on the board of directors at Multima. I think we can gradually use that relationship to disrupt the management and direction of Multima using the bank's powerful board position and leverage over the company."

Fidelia considered that for a moment, reserving any criticism with the logic for later. "Perhaps. But what about the woman? Where does she fit?"

"Amber Chan?" He waited for Fidelia to nod. "I first met her at university. We keep in touch. Money and visions of grandeur drive her. But she's also brilliant. It was her idea to plant information the chief of security at Multima would discover about our intention to launch a cyberattack. She was right. Suzanne Simpson's lover persuaded her and the board to fully rework their information systems to defend against us. Then, she wormed her way into leadership of the team making all the changes. When she's done, we'll know the secret computer codes to infiltrate and control the entire system."

He tried but failed to control his excitement. His grin stretched from ear to ear, and his wide eyes sparkled. Until Fidelia dropped a bombshell.

"But you have a problem. Amber Chan's prickly personality and odd relationships with some of her Chinese colleagues might bring all that to an end."

"What ... what are you talking about?" Tak seldom sputtered, so Fidelia forced herself to suppress a budding grin. His shock was genuine, so she filled him in.

"You recall Marie Dependente? Do you remember I put her in charge of the American operations before the fiasco in Hawaii? Although some evidence suggests she might have fed the FBI information that led to my capture, I've left her in power. She's doing a commendable job so far, with money flowing to my accounts every month." Fidelia paused. It was good to remind Tak about the importance of those monthly remissions.

"When I put her in charge, I instructed her to pass on any information she received about Multima Corporation. A plant we have in the Atlanta offices of Multima Supermarkets business discovered that your Amber Chan is about to be uncovered. We have a recording from her apartment following a torrid night under the sheets. It reveals her confession to the president of Multima Supermarkets that an enemy in China has alerted the Multima security people to Amber's relationship with you."

Tak stood there with an open mouth. His brow furrowed more deeply than Fidelia could recall seeing before. His head dropped. He was speechless.

Fidelia was relieved the guy was too shocked to pose questions. It would have been hard to avoid revealing how her communication and control persevered so effectively despite the FBI illegally incarcerating her in Guantanamo.

"I suggest you find out who the gossipy Chinese woman is. Amber Chan knows. You'll have to deal with that woman quickly. Suzanne Simpson and her security chief are still in Asia—in Singapore, actually. We can expect Serge Boisvert to return to China once the bodyguard who received the tip from Amber Chan's vindictive enemy shares that information with him. My informant in Singapore thinks that may be soon since someone took a shot at the Simpson party yesterday evening and wounded one of the bodyguards."

Tak still stood openmouthed, but he eventually nodded. However, Fidelia wasn't finished with him yet.

"When you fly out today for Tokyo, make a stop in Uzbekistan. I want you to drop Klaudia there. I'll arrange for my people to meet you at the airport, so you'll only be delayed by a few minutes."

Tak nodded his agreement; then she asked the question that had been nagging her for weeks. "That Bombardier 7500 jet you bought at such a bargain basement price on the dark web. It's mine. You flew on that jet with me, and you know it's mine, right? When you get back to Japan, tell the pilots to return it to me here. You'll eat the fifty million dollars you paid. Got it?"

Tak nodded, then bowed deeply before returning to the stairs to prepare for departure.

Eighteen

Atlanta, Georgia, Sunday July 2, 2023

Gordon Goodfellow left Amber Chan's apartment an emotional wreck. After he showered and gargled a capful of mouthwash, he intended to return home. Halfway there, he lost his nerve. There was a good chance Priscilla was still awake, or he might wake her entering the house. She was a light sleeper; awake, she'd read him like a book.

It was bad enough dealing with the emotional turmoil of such a flagrant sin. He'd need time to pray for forgiveness before he could entertain the reality that he'd need to sin once more with some deceptive story Priscilla might not believe. And where would that land them?

He decided to take a room at a Hilton Garden Inn just off the Perimeter Highway 285. Gordon paid cash at check-in. He was tempted to use a false name, but the clerk requested some ID before asking his name. At least, with cash, Priscilla wouldn't come across some credit card charge she didn't recognize. She paid all their bills because he always used the Multima Corporate American Express card when he traveled for business.

When he got to the room, Gordon dropped to his knees beside the bed and prayed to God for forgiveness. As an Evangelical, it was absolutely mandatory. There was no need to confess to a priest as the Catholics did, but for several minutes, Gordon told the Lord how sorry he was for being so foolish. The tears he shed were genuine, and as he closed his prayer session, he begged not only for forgiveness but the wisdom to avoid further damage to his marriage and career.

He knew the Lord might find the last two requests a little self-serving, but the stark reality was that this mess he had become involved in with Amber could cost him both his marriage and the job he'd worked so hard at for over twenty years.

God's forgiveness assured, Gordon walked over to the hotel's honor bar and found a coffee maker and three envelopes of coffee, one decaffeinated. He set it aside and brewed a full-strength pot to better control his thinking and nerves. Some people avoided caffeine in pressure situations, but Gordon always felt it stimulated his thought processes. With a fresh cup in hand, he glanced at his watch. It read 2:00 a.m.

What were his options to control the damage from this fling with Amber? Would she use their one-night stand as leverage in their business relationship? Was there a chance she surreptitiously recorded their romp? How would Suzanne respond if she learned of his indiscretion? Was Amber really connected to the Japanese Yakuza? Could she be working with them to destroy Multima?

Gordon paced slowly around the room in circles as he sipped his cup of coffee and pondered a growing list of problems and alternatives.

After almost an hour of identifying all the possible challenges, Gordon went to the tiny desk provided by the hotel, reached in its drawer for a pen and pad of paper, then started listing potential courses of action.

Should he pull Amber off the computer conversion project? Should he reach Suzanne in Singapore and tell her about the nasty rumor Amber had shared about the clandestine conversation in China? Was it better to use Serge Boisvert, Multima's chief of security, as his information conduit to his CEO? Gordon weighed all the alternatives he could identify.

Of course, there was always the option of doing nothing, hoping there was no substance to the rumor out of China and keeping it all under wraps as long as possible. However, such an approach was foreign to a guy trained to get out in front of potential problems.

With coffee, some time to reflect, and fundamental optimism that he always found the right solution, Gordon called Amber and woke her while it was still dark outside.

"We need to talk, see how each of us feels, make sure we're on the same page after last night," he said.

"Okay. I'm just waking up here. Is tomorrow at the office alright?" Her tone was low, and she formed her words slowly, probably still half asleep.

"I'd rather do it sooner and not near the office. I got a hotel room last night. Can you drive over here?"

"I'd rather you come back. I'm still not familiar with Atlanta and don't like driving when it's dark. Would you like to come here? I'll make some coffee."

Knowing their conversation would be sensitive, Gordon acceded to her request. After fetching a throwaway toothbrush and sample-size toothpaste from the front desk, he cleaned up again and set out for her apartment. When she opened the door, he smelled a strong scent of coffee and noticed Amber dressed casually in a tank top and shorts—very short shorts and still no bra under the skimpy top. He resolved to stay focused. But where to start?

Amber pointed toward the sofa where it all happened. She sat close enough to touch him if she reached out, but not so close she might tempt him again.

"I'm sorry for what happened last night. It was completely out of character for me, and I apologize unequivocally." He looked into her eyes as he spoke, and they flickered twice. She seemed to feel his discomfort.

"There's no need to apologize." She smiled warmly, with her eyebrows arched and pearl-white teeth showing. "We're all human. We have desires. We have lapses. If you want it to be a one-time thing, I'm fine with that. Don't worry, I have no intention of lording it over you for personal gain."

Damn. Did she have to use a form of the word Lord?

"I trust you, Amber. You know I'm a married Christian, and as much as I may be attracted to you, it won't happen again." He watched her nod, understanding, but not necessarily with enough enthusiasm to accept that reality. "You know we could both be in a lot of trouble at work for our indiscretion, right?"

She smiled coyly. "I suspect that trouble might be greater for you than me, but don't worry. Our night together will stay entirely between us. I won't say a word to anyone."

"I appreciate that. If it's okay with you, I'd like to move on to the information you got from China. How do you think we best deal with that?" He cocked his head to the side attentively, welcoming her thoughts.

"I've been thinking about that since you left. I know you're in an awkward position and probably feel you have to do something, tell someone. I'll make it easier for you. I'll step aside from my direct involvement in the computer systems conversion and the integration. We already chatted about my failure to keep expenses and operations in focus. If you like, I'll voluntarily move aside, let headquarters technology management take over, and spend my time controlling our expenses to optimize profits."

Gordon drew a deep breath. He couldn't have made a more elegant proposal himself. Plus, making that kind of sacrifice voluntarily bolstered his belief that she must be telling the truth.

"That sounds perfect. We also have to share the information you received with Suzanne and Serge. If they discover it later, we might be unable to manage their response." He used a tone as casual as possible but leaned in, underscoring the importance he attached to the pathway.

"I agree. I'll even encourage her to talk with the woman and investigate the allegation if necessary." Amber's tone reflected her complete confidence that any investigation would clear her of any suspicion.

Both relaxed visibly. Amber drew her legs up beneath her and slouched forward slightly. Gordon stretched his legs out and clutched his hands together in an arc, flexing them to relieve tension.

"Shall we call her now? It's already evening over there."

Amber nodded, unfolded her legs from beneath her, and shifted toward Gordon's phone on the sofa between them. He pressed Suzanne's name on the phone's directory. Withdrawing his hand, he couldn't help but notice Amber's beautiful bare breasts peeking out again from behind her flimsy top.

Suzanne answered on the second ring.

Gordon kept the opening pleasantries brief, like she preferred, and got right to the heart of the matter. "Amber Chan is on the line with me. She shared some concerning information with me, and we agreed we should pass it on to you and Serge immediately. Are you somewhere you can use the speaker for confidential information?"

"That depends on how discreet you need the conversation

to be. I'm in the ER of Singapore's General Hospital, but there are just three of us in a private lounge. Serge, our bodyguard Jasmine, and me. Willy's been shot. He'll be okay, and it will be another hour before we can visit him in his room. So go ahead."

Gordon froze. Amber tensed, her sitting posture erect and rigid. The pause was long enough for Suzanne to ask if they were still on the line.

"Yes, sorry about that, Suzanne. We were both just shocked to learn about Willy. Is everyone else okay?"

"Yeah. We're all a bit shaken by it all, but everyone's fine. Go ahead before anyone else comes into the room. I have you on speaker." Her tone was businesslike, no-nonsense, no time to chat, so Gordon jumped in as instructed.

"Amber just shared with me a call she received from a close acquaintance at Supermarkets' headquarters in Shanghai. It's serious, so I'll let Amber relay the message she received directly."

Amber read Suzanne's message and tone. Briefly and succinctly, she shared the name of the person who called her, the information the contact shared, and the name of the person who allegedly made the comments to Jasmine. Then she moved directly to what they'd agreed upon.

"I am not involved with the Yakuza or any other criminal organization, and I'm confident any investigation will establish that. However, I realize how sensitive this allegation is. Gordon and I have discussed it, and if you agree, I'll refocus my attention immediately. We propose that Marcel Dubois assume hands-on leadership of the systems conversion and updates. I'll move away from the project entirely and focus on improvements in expense controls and general operations within Jeffersons stores."

Serge spoke next. "Thanks for making us aware of those allegations from your former colleague in Shanghai. Jasmine shared them with us a few hours ago. Suzanne will speak to your proposed shift in responsibilities, but I want you to know that I deem a full investigation of her allegations essential. Suzanne will drop me off in Shanghai on her way back to Canada tomorrow—provided Willy's well enough to travel. I hope you understand we have no other choice."

There was a pause. Suzanne normally would speak next, but she took her time, apparently still processing her decision or formulating a response. Gordon looked over at Amber, projecting confidence he didn't yet feel. Her hands were tightly wound into fists, and she appeared to be holding her breath, her face pale.

When Suzanne spoke, her tone was uncharacteristically subdued, lacking her usual warmth and enthusiasm, although she chose the right words.

"I have confidence in you, Amber, and in your judgment, Gordon. Your proposal makes good sense and I'm confident Marcel will step into the day-to-day leadership on the technology projects. Pierre Cabot already sent me an email of concern about the cost overruns on Jeffersons' operating expenses, so adjusting your focus there is also beneficial. However, as Serge said, we have to investigate those allegations out of Shanghai and that may cause you some discomfort. You'll both have to live with it until Serge is satisfied that employee was merely a malcontent with malicious intent."

Their conversation continued for a few minutes as Suzanne provided more background on the shooting, Willy's current condition, and her meetings with the new management in Shanghai. As the conversation continued, Amber relaxed, drew her legs up under her again, and leaned toward the phone. Of course, it was hard for Gordon to avoid looking into the skimpy top with the perfectly formed breasts inviting his attention.

Again, his groin stirred.

When he pressed the "end" button on the phone, Amber raised her hand for a high-five and a hoot of relief or satisfaction. Then she suddenly leaned forward and wrapped her arms around Gordon in a desperate embrace.

"Thank you so much," she whispered seductively.

Within seconds, it led to another impassioned kiss as they gripped each other tightly. Before long, he sinned again.

Nineteen

Singapore, very early morning, Monday July 3, 2023

After their call with Gordon and Amber in the VIP area beside the Emergency Room at the hospital, Serge took Suzanne's hand and guided her off to a quiet corner far away from Jasmine for a whispered conversation.

"The Mounties and FBI can't help us here. We're communicating as effectively as we can with law enforcement in Singapore, but I have no established, secure or dependable sources here. I need your okay to get CSIS involved. They'll have contacts."

She peered into his eyes, hoping for a glimpse of his intentions. Those eyes pleaded more strongly for her support than his words. Someone had taken a shot at them, and no one knew who or why. Worse, unless they dug deeper and solved the mystery, there might be another attempt.

Suzanne processed the alternatives and then gave her approval with a single nod and a warning. "I'll authorize you to draw on your contacts at CSIS and get whatever information you can about this incident. However, I want your understanding and agreement that we share no other information with them."

He nodded acceptance of her terms and reached into his pocket. As she returned to sit again with Jasmine, waiting for information about Willy, Serge dialed a number from his phone and was soon in conversation.

They continued waiting and were still hard at work in those early morning hours, but not without some tension.

After his call with someone at CSIS, Serge first warned against Suzanne attending a planned speaking engagement in Hawaii. No conference was worth risking her life. They had no idea yet who shot Willy or who that shooter was aiming for.

"Cancel everything," he suggested.

Of course, that was easier to say than do, and Suzanne initially had set the matter aside, hoping Edward Hadley might eventually aid the process. They'd first dragged him out of bed the day of the shooting. Although the incident occurred on the evening of Canada Day, Singapore time, it was early morning for him.

Those first conversations were about managing the media. Even in Singapore, it's impossible to keep a shooting quiet when it involves the bodyguard of the CEO of one of the world's best-known companies. Edward appreciated the heads-up and immediately started working with trusted media contacts to prepare them for the news.

In the early hours of that Monday morning, Edward broached the subject of Suzanne's speaking engagement at the Moral Money Conference in Hawaii, scheduled for that coming Wednesday. It was a large international gathering of banks and other lenders to focus on environmental, social, and governance investing, and the Bank of The Americas sponsored it.

"If you intend to cancel, we need to let them know as early as possible. I'm confident they'll understand if you feel a need to pass after all you're going through in Singapore, but you're the keynote speaker. They'll have to scramble to get a replacement, and we don't want to burn any bridges with Abduhl Mahinder."

Serge still didn't want her to speak at the event. He couldn't be there to personally oversee her security because they'd already agreed he should fly to Shanghai with Jasmine to investigate the allegations from the Chinese worker about Amber Chan. That had been decided before their conversation with Gordon and Amber, and that conversation did nothing to allay Serge's concern about the woman's possible connection to the Japanese Yakuza. He was torn between competing priorities.

Edward had contacted the Bank of The Americas conference organizer discreetly and sought her advice. He reported back to Suzanne that the organizer was desperate. At such late notice, on the Fourth of July long weekend, finding a speaker of Suzanne's caliber would be impossible. The woman had begged for some time to come up with a strategy to keep Suzanne safe and secure, hoping Edward could somehow keep his boss onside with the engagement.

Over a matter of several hours, while Edward, Serge, and

Suzanne argued on their respective cell phones, they worked toward a consensus.

Midway through their impromptu meeting, she felt her eyes drooping and energy evaporating until a nurse dropped into the lounge to deliver some good news: the doctors had patched up Willy and he was stable enough to travel. He'd need another month to recover fully, but the surgeon thought he could leave the hospital soon. Minutes later, the doctor himself visited them and confirmed it.

"I think it's fine for him to travel to Florida on the corporate jet with a stop in Hawaii. I'd recommend you have a nurse accompany him in case of any sudden changes from the altitude or with his breathing, and I can give you the name of a good respite care facility in Honolulu to watch over him should you decide to spend a short time on the ground there."

Serge summarized his understanding for everyone from his detailed notes on a scrap of paper.

"Suzanne, Jasmine, Willy, a private nurse, and I will leave Singapore today, at 7:00 p.m., for Shanghai. In Shanghai, Jasmine and I will debark. I'll arrange for the jet to be refueled and ready to leave for Honolulu by 1:00 a.m. With almost nine hours of flying time, the corporate jet will arrive in Hawaii on Tuesday at about 3:30 p.m. local time. Suzanne will stay at the Prince Waikiki Hotel." As he mentioned the hotel's name, Serge paused to shake his head and looked directly at her. It was the hotel where the final Jeffersons Stores negotiations had taken place only three months earlier, and he hated the location.

Suzanne offered only a half-hearted smile as Serge finished his summary.

"At nine thirty on Wednesday morning, Suzanne will deliver her speech, and by eleven thirty should be back at the jet. An ambulance has been arranged to deliver Willy to the respite center on arrival and pick him up again at 10:00 a.m. to have him back to the jet before Suzanne arrives. The plane will fly directly to Ft. Myers, where an ambulance will meet Willy and deliver him to Lee Memorial Hospital for medical reassessment."

With everyone as satisfied as possible under trying circumstances, she agreed they could all leave for the hotel and Serge summoned a car within minutes. But her day wasn't finished yet.

Instead, back at the hotel, she guessed there'd be another hour or more with Edward Hadley dissecting and rebuilding the speech he had prepared for her delivery before the Singapore shooting. With that disturbing incident, she was now determined to focus less on climate change and environmental sustainability and focus instead on the governance part of environmental, social, and governance investing.

She knew Edward would resist. However, by the end of their conversation, she was determined he would craft a speech that drew much more attention to the perils of organized crime. It was time for those cursed government officials everywhere to quit harassing companies for inflation they couldn't control, and start enforcing laws to rid the business community of the criminals genuinely responsible.

She didn't intend to live her life in fear of the criminal sons of bitches.

Twenty

Dubrovnik, Croatia, Monday July 3, 2023

With Tak and Klaudia on their way to Japan and Uzbekistan, respectively, Fidelia turned her full attention to Antonio Verlusconi. A few years earlier, she'd given The Organization's Italian business to him after it became necessary to eliminate his predecessor to make a point and solidify her control of the outfit.

He was a large man, more than six feet tall, with broad, muscular shoulders that met his large round head with almost no neck showing between the two body parts. The skin on his face always had a tinge of red in it and his black eyes seemed never to stop darting about. Although he had enormous power in Italy, he never took his privilege for granted. She couldn't describe his manner as humble—that would overstate his humility—but he displayed fundamental respect toward everyone until they crossed him. Then, he had all the ruthless qualities she admired and that he needed for his job.

"Thanks for lending me this magnificent home while I get my feet on the ground again."

Fidelia emphasized her genuine appreciation with a solid hug of his big shoulders, careful to avoid any gesture of affection beyond a smile. They'd slept together in earlier days when he was an enforcer, and she ran The Organization's escort business. In those days, she'd rewarded his punishment of more than one scoundrel who mistreated her women with sex in lieu of money. She'd learned long before that such rewards instilled a special loyalty money couldn't buy. Today, there was no room for mixed signals.

"Glad I could help," he said. "Use the place for as long as you need it."

"I'd like to buy it." Fidelia delivered the words softly, with a crooked smile, but looked him directly in the eye.

Verlusconi squirmed in his chair. His eyes widened a bit in surprise, but his expression remained impassive. "I bought it for my mistress. She's living in another apartment in town while you're using this place, but she really likes it here. It was she who oversaw the design, construction, and decor. She wouldn't be happy if I sold it."

"What did it cost you to please your mistress?"

"More than a million euros," he replied without hesitation. "She's kinda special to me."

Fidelia read his wry grin and uncomfortable demeanor. "I'll give you two million. You can build her a nicer home. I need a place to live. The FBI forced me to disclose my properties in New York, Uruguay, and Curaçao. They'll be watching them forever, so I'll have to get rid of them. I want you to sell me this place."

Verlusconi was smart. He nodded, smiled, and shrugged his shoulders in resignation. "Of course, Fidelia. I swore loyalty to you, and your wish is my command. My mistress will probably be miserable for a few weeks, but your generous offering price will eventually bring her around. But I must ask a favor of you in return."

Fidelia didn't reply. Her semi-nod implied he could ask, with no assurance of success.

"Get Klaudia Schäffer working in the escort business again. Since you let her walk away from The Organization's recruiting in Eastern Europe, our business has dropped dramatically." His tone didn't condemn. It seemed more like a statement of fact.

Fidelia appreciated that and nodded that he should continue.

"Her replacement gets a few acceptably well-performing girls from Africa, but you know Italians don't like the dark-skinned ones as much as they like Romanians or even Russians."

Fidelia didn't care much about which skin color Italians preferred to pay for sex, but she did realize the escort business had plunged in Italy. That impacted her monthly proceeds from the country. She thought about Verlusconi's demand and wondered silently if there might be a way to lure Klaudia back into action.

While she pondered the possibility, he continued. His tone remained calm, but he leaned in as he spoke, his brow furrowed and his eyes animated.

"Besides the challenges in the escort business, we've got a problem with the Russians again. Last month, I lost two good men in Trieste, up near the border with Slovenia. They were making a drug delivery. Their driver stayed in the car outside and watched helplessly as their bodies were tossed from a balcony on the fourteenth floor. A trademark Russian Mafia murder. And a month before that, Juan Suarez in Spain lost two of his men the same way in Ayamonte. Klaudia grew up in the secret services that became the Russian Mafia. You should do whatever it takes to get her back in The Organization, helping us with both women and information."

When he finished, he leaned back in his chair and waited for her reaction. It was impossible to miss the undertone of a threat.

She took her time answering. "You may be right. Klaudia's got access to the Russian Mafia, and I share your concern they're getting more aggressive and infringing on our territories. But Klaudia's in a tough spot emotionally right now. Something happened. She's changed. I don't know if we can bring her back."

Fidelia shook her head as she spoke, conveying her bewilderment and temporary helplessness, but it was necessary to leave her conversation with the Italian crime boss positive and hopeful.

"You know Nadine Violette, Boivin's favorite in France?" She waited for Verlusconi's nod. "She's got good contacts in Romania. I'll ask her to find a few women there. Help you get those escort numbers back up again. With Klaudia, we'll have to give her a bit of time to work through her issues. But I'll try to find a way."

Twenty-One

Atlanta, Georgia, Friday September 1, 2023

Gordon Goodfellow stood beside his desk, stretched his arms upward, and shook his head slowly back and forth. This day couldn't get much worse.

It started with a visit from Marcel Dubois, Multima's chief technology officer. He was in town to meet personally with the leaders of the systems conversion and Jeffersons Stores' integration project. He reported that work had slowed dramatically since they moved Amber Chan away from the project to focus on other issues. They'd encountered some snags that were taking time to resolve. It looked like achieving their October deadline was in danger. He now guessed the end of November looked more likely.

An hour after Dubois left his office, Gordon's executive assistant announced that someone from the sheriff's office was waiting in the lobby to see him personally. They wouldn't reveal the purpose of their visit.

He told her to send the fellow up to his office and was surprised when a tall woman in uniform introduced herself and asked Gordon to confirm who he was. Once he stated his name, she reached into a pouch, pulled out a document, stepped forward and handed him the piece of paper.

"Your wife Priscilla is serving notice of her intention to file for divorce. This document instructs you to give me all keys you have for the home you share and formally requests you advise her of a date when you'll remove all your personal belongings from the home. It also provides the name and number of her attorney. You must channel all future communication through her."

Shocked, Gordon read the document several times. Priscilla had not reacted well when he shared the news about Amber and their affair a couple weeks earlier. She had screamed, shouted, and cried incessantly. Basically, she threw him out. She was not at all forgiving of his sinful dalliance and didn't behave in a Christian way, he'd thought at the time.

He'd been staying at Amber's since, expecting things would blow over in a few weeks and they could have a calm, rational conversation about where they'd go next. Now, it looked like a courtroom was their next stop.

Later, Edward Hadley called with the results of the most recent public opinion polls for August and a summary of recent focus group sessions related to food inflation. Multima Supermarkets' customers were an angry bunch. Overwhelmingly, the poll participants felt Multima was gouging its customers and hoarding wealth at their expense. The worst results were in Canada, but customers in England, France, and the US were almost as unhappy.

During the focus group sessions, Hadley reported some participants displayed open hostility, and in one session, a participant threatened violence. The language was frequently vulgar, and many participants claimed they were looking for shopping alternatives like dollar stores. A few said they were forced to use food banks for at least some of their weekly requirements. It didn't look good at all for Suzanne Simpson and other CEOs in the food industry who'd been summoned to appear before a Canadian parliamentary committee in about two weeks.

Now, he stood by his desk, waiting for Suzanne to come on the line. Her assistant, Eileen, had called a few minutes earlier and asked him to stand by for a conversation. She was finishing up another meeting and would join the call as soon as possible. He'd been waiting ten minutes already without further communication. That was unusual for both Eileen and Suzanne.

Finally, his CEO greeted him. "I have Serge, Alberto Ferer, and Nicole Gagnon from HR here in my office. We need to speak with you about Amber Chan. Are you alone and is our call private?"

The formality was surprising. Gordon had to clear his throat before responding.

"Yes, I'm alone. The office door is closed."

"For the past month, Serge has been working on that information Jasmine received during our China visit. I'll let him share his findings with everyone." Her tone remained crisp. He detected none of her usual warmth.

"Yes, I spent two weeks in Shanghai, Beijing, and Tokyo right after the shooting incident in Singapore. Jasmine was with me in Shanghai and arranged a private meeting with the woman from Multima's China office at our hotel. We talked with her for more than three hours and had a Mandarin speaker from my team sit in to translate. The woman is a credible witness. Clearly, as a member of China's Uyghur population, she's angry with her country's government. She also equates Amber Chan with the governing communist party, but she also provided facts we could follow up on and investigate independently."

Serge's tone was confident. His speaking pace was slower than usual, his emphasis on words like "credible witness" telegraphed where he was headed.

Gordon sat down in his executive chair to concentrate fully. He reached for a pen and scrap of paper in case he needed to make notes.

"She named Tak Takahashi as the person in the Japanese Yakuza Amber Chan was acquainted with. She claimed their relationship dated back to Amber's university days in Tokyo and provided specific dates when they had conversations on her private mobile number. She refused to divulge how she got information about the private mobile calls but invited me to verify it with SmarTone Mobile Communications. I checked. Her private telephone records show calls with burner phone numbers in Japan on the dates the woman provided. The most recent call was the day before Amber moved to Atlanta."

Gordon shifted uneasily in his chair. Amber had maintained the woman's allegations had no merit or foundation. Calls with a burner phone in Japan reasonably raised suspicions. He continued to listen to Serge's monologue.

"The woman claimed that Amber was an informant directly connected to the State Security Ministry. While I was in Beijing, through a contact provided to me by the Canadian government agency CSIS, I found she may have some sort of link. But I couldn't determine that conclusively."

Gordon sighed. Amber had insisted she had no connections to the Chinese government, but that denial could still be true. He made another note as Serge carried on.

"In Tokyo, there is no doubt the guy we negotiated the Jeffersons Stores deal with, Tak Takahashi, is now the top crime boss in the Japanese Yakuza. My contacts in the Tokyo police force confirmed he has seized total power and solidified his control over the criminal outfit. There's also little doubt he and Amber Chan know each other. They were classmates in at least three subjects in each of the four years she studied in Japan. They appear in photos together in the university yearbook. Their body language in some of those photos suggests close friendship, perhaps more."

Gordon sighed, looked down at his desk, and shook his head. He had most feared that bit of information. His problems had just grown exponentially. He waited for the bad news to stop, but Serge continued.

"In my role as chief security officer, I can't over-emphasize my concern about this woman. While I don't have conclusive proof, all the evidence strongly suggests that she has a continuing relationship with someone in a criminal outfit we understand intends to launch a major cyberattack against Multima. I recommend we remove her from her role at Multima, pay her decent severance, and terminate her employment without delay."

The silence that followed was profound. No one said a word. Gordon heard only a deep breath taken, probably by Suzanne, who was likely the nearest to the speakerphone. As Amber's direct superior, he should respond first, but what could he say? Was he supposed to agree that the woman he was currently living with was a possible criminal and a threat to the company?

Alberto Ferer saved him from responding. "Legally, I think we have to slow down. As Serge admits, proof of wrongdoing is inconclusive, although he presents a very plausible case. I'm sensitive to the potential harm to Multima from the Japanese Yakuza. I'm also fearful that if we terminate Amber Chan, and she lawyers up, we might find ourselves liable for a lot of compensation, maybe well into the millions."

Nicole Gagnon jumped in next. "I agree. From an HR perspective, I think I'd have a tough time justifying to a jury why we fired an employee we uprooted from her career and home in China, moved to the US, placed in a key operating role, and then terminated mere months into her new assignment. And let's not forget: her direct reports think she is a wonderful leader, doing a magnificent job for Multima."

As they spoke, Gordon prayed silently for divine intervention or inspiration. This conversation had all the hallmarks of a career disaster—for Amber and for him. As the silence extended, he realized they were waiting for his opinion. He was grateful the call wasn't on Zoom as he looked skyward and carefully chose his words and tone.

"I think we're all overlooking one important fact. Let's not forget Amber brought the initial conversation with Jasmine to our attention. She approached me with the issue, and we immediately brought everyone into the loop."

Of course, he didn't mention that conversation took place as she shed tears after two passionate sessions in bed. He paused to let them think about his point before he asked his question.

"If there was substance to the allegation, why would she volunteer the information? Wouldn't it have been better for her just to ignore it? If she really has this connection to the head of the Yakuza, rather than bringing it to our attention, why wouldn't she tell him instead and have the Chinese informant eliminated before she could do more damage?"

"Whoa there, Gordon," Serge cautioned. "You're starting to sound like you've watched too many gangster movies. There's a big difference between having a contact in the criminal world and killing people because they're inconvenient. I'm not implying Amber is part of the Yakuza's plan. She may or may not be aware that information she could inadvertently share with Takahashi might eventually be used against Multima. It's the connection that's dangerous."

There was another long pause, giving emotions time to cool.

Suzanne always mastered these interactions, knowing when to speak and when to listen. Until now, she'd listened carefully, and everyone on the call knew it was her turn.

"I wish we could deal more with the nuances of running a profitable business and less with the drama of the outside world. But as John George Mortimer liked to say, 'We have to play the cards we're dealt.'"

Suzanne often made references to Multima's founder and her deceased biological father when things got tense around the boardroom table. Everyone on her management team knew and respected the man, and mentioning his name and sayings was her way of refocusing everyone's attention on finding a practical and workable solution. But the one person pushing for dramatic action against Amber never knew John George, and Serge was also Suzanne's chosen lover. Gordon took a deep breath as she continued.

"There's surely something amiss here. Our colleague Willy was seriously injured when someone in Singapore took a shot at our group. No one knows who the intended target was, but we have an employee still recovering from his injuries and unable to work." Suzanne paused again. Gordon realized she was trying to reframe the discussion without offending any of the participants. She did this often and expertly.

"We can also be confident in Serge's investigation. Clearly, there is evidence that Amber knew and associated with Tak Takahashi as a student. Telephone records suggest they had recent contact, and even if the calls were to Takahashi, those records don't give us any insight into what was discussed. The calls were short. She may have shared information or received instructions, but the calls might also have been entirely social. We don't know."

Gordon's neck muscles started to relax as he listened. He continued to pray silently. There was still hope.

"We must consider the tip Serge received from sources on the dark web as a genuine threat. After all, we've already agreed to spend a hundred million dollars to defend ourselves against a cyberattack. And it would be foolish to ignore the possibility Amber is involved. But we need to proceed slowly, and with caution, before we terminate her employment. She also moved away from the project voluntarily. She's no longer receiving briefings on the system conversion or attending meetings. Is that correct, Gordon?"

He froze for an instant. Of course, she no longer received memos, attended meetings, or was part of the project design process. Still, they were living together temporarily and chatted often about the project's progress. But divulging that information would probably toss both their careers onto the garbage heap.

"That's correct. Amber is entirely out of the loop concerning the systems modifications." He mouthed another silent prayer, looking upward and asking the Lord for forgiveness once again.

Suzanne paused once more, preparing the group for a conclusion. "I'll defer any decision about removing Amber for a while longer. Serge, I'd like more concrete evidence before we pull the plug on her. We'll have an offline conversation about continuing your investigation."

Oh Shit! That probably means surveillance.

Twenty-Two

Montreal, Quebec, Friday September 1, 2023

"Okay, start your digital monitoring," Suzanne said the moment Alberto and Nicole closed the door on their way out of her office. "If you think you need to tap into Amber's personal phone as well as her office line, I'm okay with that."

"Okay. Thanks for your support on that ... at least." Serge glared across the table, clearly upset with her decision.

She'd expected disappointment but was taken aback by his almost hostile manner. This was the first time she'd noticed it in their relationship, and her stomach tightened with tension. She chose not to reply immediately. Instead, she locked into the pupils of his eyes until he blinked and looked downward, relaxing his shoulders somewhat.

She explained. "We've talked about this. I trust you. I value your opinions, and I respect everything about the way you work. But this is one of those times when I can't accept your recommendation. No matter how well-founded you believe it is. I must also listen to and respect the views and opinions of others. This is one of those times when we're going to have to differ."

She continued looking directly at him, and eventually, he raised his eyes and made contact. She saw less anger and more determination and waited for his response.

"I get it. I'm not happy about it, but I get it." His eyes softened, and his posture relaxed. They wouldn't have a major battle today, but he was telegraphing his next move. She waited for it.

"I'm also concerned about Goodfellow. Don't you find it odd that he and Amber called us to report the incident with that woman in China early on a Sunday morning, immediately after the shooting in Singapore? Is it normal for them to be together in the office at eight or nine o'clock on a Sunday morning? Or were they perhaps somewhere else?"

Suzanne listened intently, without comment, but she tilted her head inquisitively.

He took the hint. "I'd like to tap into his lines as well, private and office. If we don't find anything in a week, I'll drop it. But I have a gut feeling he's not telling us the full story."

She dropped her eyes and considered the extraordinary request. It was illegal to wiretap in Georgia. She'd already taken risks authorizing him to tap Amber's lines. Was he testing limits? Seeking some sort of retaliation? Was this a quid pro quo? Or did he have a point about Gordon? She'd already turned down one big ask today; dare she decline another?

"Okay, but just for a week. Gordon's worked for me for over ten years, and I know him well. I'll agree on that basis."

She stood from the meeting table, signaling the end of their session as Eileen knocked on the door. Alberto was back, this time with Edward Hadley and Multima's president for Canada, Bob McKenzie. They were ready for their scheduled eleven o'clock meeting about the Canadian parliamentary committee appearance.

They made small talk around the table as Eileen worked on the Zoom link to Gordon Goodfellow in his Atlanta office. Unsuccessful, she called his executive assistant and learned he had left the office. He wasn't feeling well, the woman said.

"We've only got eighteen days until your command performance with the Canadian parliamentary committee investigating food inflation," Edward said. "Shall we continue without Gordan and bring him up to speed later?"

Suzanne nodded, "Yeah. But before we get into the nitty-gritty, did you have any luck changing this inquiry to something more private than a committee hearing?"

Edward shook his head. "So far, no. I spoke with our contact in the prime minister's office. She agreed to ask him but wouldn't commit."

On that disappointing note, they launched into preparations for an event fraught with potential peril.

"The polls are worse," Edward started. "The NDP leader's continuous harping that billionaire supermarket CEOs are ripping off the average consumer is gaining traction. More than eighty percent of poll respondents agree with him. I've talked with my counterparts at the other companies. They all get the same survey results and claim their customer satisfaction has also plummeted. They'll pressure us to give up something in the committee meetings. If not, it looks as if the minority government will be forced to pass new legislation to create at least an appearance of doing something."

For hours, it was more of the same. Edward painted a picture of bitter consumer discontent while they worked through a list of more than a hundred hypothetical questions his team had devised.

Alberto played devil's advocate, ripping apart the answers Suzanne formulated based on her best knowledge of the current state of the supermarket industry. Not having Gordon there for instant responses wasn't ideal, but some of his subordinates in Atlanta had joined the conversation on Zoom, and they also threw out possible answers.

By the end of the session, Suzanne was exhausted, Alberto was annoyed and Edward Hadley was fearful. They took away only one benefit from their hours of dialogue: it was crystal clear they had mountains of work ahead to be adequately prepared for the coming public hearing in a roomful of calculating and cunning politicians.

With her office vacant again, Suzanne asked Eileen to arrange a quick lunch. Even though it was mid-afternoon, hours of work remained preparing for the upcoming meeting of the board of directors. And that meeting was scheduled right after Labor Day.

When Eileen returned with a sandwich and bottle of water from the Starbucks in a nearby building, she set them on Suzanne's desk before asking: "When should I schedule the helicopter to take you home?"

"Helicopter? Why a helicopter? I'll just ride home with Serge and the bodyguards in the car."

Eileen pulled back her shoulders, her voice timid. "Didn't he tell you? Serge left with the car before lunch. For Atlanta. He said he'd be there for a few days."

Twenty-Three
Dubrovnik, Croatia, Monday September 4, 2023

It was Labor Day in the US, a quiet day even in the world of organized crime. Her country boss there liked to enjoy one of the last long weekends of summer, and the rest of her crowd around the globe had adopted the habit, too. One mark of a good leader is knowing when it's best to just back away for a day or two and let people enjoy things in their own way.

Fidelia had learned that lesson while she ran The Organization's global escort business, and she continued to practice the principle while she climbed rock stairways in Dubrovnik that afternoon. She'd discovered those stairs carved into the mountainsides during her recovery from the surgery on her mangled feet after her ordeal at Guantanamo Bay.

Healing had been long and painful. Even today, she'd awakened with stiff ankles and sharp pangs of discomfort when she put weight on the bottoms of her feet and fumbled to put on socks and shoes. It eased somewhat with movement, so Fidelia had increased her levels of physical activity each day for more than three months.

She'd started out with a hundred-yard walk along the laneway leading up to the house. Then she walked twenty yards farther each day. Gradually, she increased the distance to more than a mile, and at that point, she discovered a well-maintained stairway built of rocks and cement. She learned the city of Dubrovnik had hundreds of those stairways built for pedestrians to navigate the mountainsides without using the narrow and dangerous roadways.

With a bit of research, Fidelia learned the city had 5,423 of those steps spread around the city, more than one thousand in the old town and more than four thousand spread around the rest of the picturesque location used for filming *Game of Thrones*. She created a pastime to ease her recovery and made it a goal to climb every one of those steps.

For weeks now, she'd mapped out different paths that

allowed her to climb up and down the city's stairways while enjoying the hot climate and spectacular views of the Adriatic. Her game was paying off.

She glanced back at her two bodyguards, and heard them huffing and puffing to keep up with her pace on the steps behind her. She smiled. These were her regular guys from Uruguay. The duo from Florida, who accompanied her for the first couple months after she escaped from Guantanamo, could never match the fitness of this team. The new guys joined her in August, after she bought the house she was living in from Antonio Verlusconi, then bought a smaller one next door for the bodyguards and Mia Vasquez.

Mia was a childhood friend who'd been with her throughout her career in The Organization and served as her administrative assistant. She set up the meetings, coordinated arrangements with the pilots, and made sure everything went smoothly for Fidelia as she oversaw the unruly mob that made up The Organization. Mia was back at the house, finalizing arrangements for a trip starting tomorrow.

That thought forced Fidelia back to the real world.

Over the past few weeks, she'd shored up her communication and support from her worried European country bosses. After the US and Japan, Italy, Spain, Portugal, and France generated more monthly income for The Organization than any other part of the world. She had to compete with the Italian Mafia, of course. But there was enough opportunity for both if her country leaders minded their manners and didn't become too greedy.

Or if someone else didn't squeeze into her territory.

Unfortunately, over the past few months, someone had indeed started to worm into each of those prime territories, and it had alarmed those country bosses.

Antonio Verlusconi had complained about a drug deal gone bad, and his delivery guy's fall from an apartment building balcony. In Portugal, Estavao Sereno had three of his enforcers ambushed on a roadway near Porto after visiting one of the vineyards they protected. Juan Suarez reported that a high-speed boat pursued and overtook two of his drug runners from Morocco just off the shore of Marbella, stealing more than two million dollars worth of high-grade heroin.

And Pierre Boivin reported that his supply of women from Tunisia for the lucrative French escort business had utterly dried up.

In each case, the culprit was the Russian Mafia. Her people were sure of it and showed her the evidence. Fidelia was mortified.

Giancarlo Mareno—her patron in The Organization until she eliminated him—had always warned against antagonizing the Russian Mafia. "It's like waking a sleeping bear," he'd often said. "Those animals are vicious and unpredictable. And they're at least tacitly supported—and maybe even more—by the autocratic president of Russia. Let them sleep."

But the Russian bear was no longer in hibernation. It had now decided to infringe on The Organization's territory. Another lesson Fidelia learned early in her career with organized crime is that territory is sacrosanct. Any infringement on it must be dealt with quickly and decisively. If not, her authority over the country's crime bosses would wilt and their business disappear. After all that Fidelia went through with the FBI only a few months ago, she didn't intend to cede one inch of her territory to the Russians or anyone else.

For that reason, she'd schemed with her country bosses, individually and collectively. They had a plan. When she returned from her Dubrovnik step-counting walk today, she'd shower, dress, and head to her private jet at the airport. From there, it was about five hours flying time to her compound near Muynak, Uzbekistan. Fidelia had already spoken with Zefar Karimov, her friend and the Deputy Finance Minister of Uzbekistan.

He'd greased the palms necessary to ensure there would be no immigration formalities when her plane touched down, nor any data recorded at the airport concerning her flight or the private jet that would park there while she did her business.

At dinner, she'd plant the seeds of The Organization's determination to rid Europe of the Russian bear; for that, she needed Klaudia. Again.

Twenty-Four

Eagle Beach, Aruba, Monday September 4, 2023

It was their last day in Aruba.

Gordon Goodfellow facetiously hoped he'd reacted the way any other company president would behave under the same duress. He'd grabbed his secret lover by the waist, guided her to the company jet parked at Hartsfield-Jackson International Airport, and flown off to a Caribbean Island where they could lie low for a few days and think more clearly.

He was dripping with sweat this morning, enjoying a combination jog and walk. It'd started with a good run along the shoreline from their condo at the Eagle Beach resort complex into the main town of Oranjestad. The sky was a brilliant blue, and the path he followed ran along a winding road next to the sandy beaches all the way to town.

As he arrived, the popular tourist destination was coming to life. He saw two cruise ships. One was already parked, and the other awkwardly chugged its way toward the dock with the help of two or three struggling tugboats. Across the street, vendors restocked their covered stalls and built enticing displays of their wares to attract the money of landing visitors. Farther along, a few people strolled, chatting and pointing to sights of interest as they took in the history and unique architecture of the former Dutch colony.

Outside the Renaissance Resort, taxis and tour buses loaded their charges for the day, but the street from there to the airport was lightly traveled as most flights arrived later in the morning or early afternoon. Just past the Renaissance, Gordon headed northeast on Route 6 toward the village of Paradera.

He knew the path well. Priscilla had often jogged or walked the same path with him during their short stays on the island. He felt a pang of regret at that memory. After all, he was still absorbing all the implications of her serving him with divorce papers before the weekend. Their marriage had included many great times in places like Aruba. They also had a condo in Banff up in Canada for the ski season and another in Avignon, France, when they wanted to visit Europe.

He'd probably have to sell them all to settle the divorce. They didn't have much cash or many investments other than real estate, and there was no doubt Priscilla would want at least half of everything they owned. He silently cursed at how things were turning out, then again quickly begged the Lord for forgiveness for his lapse. The last thing he needed at a time like this was to lose God's support. As he jogged, he promised the Lord he'd do better.

Just before arriving at Paradera, Gordon turned onto Route 4 and, about a hundred yards along, stopped at the tiny Subway outlet for water. He wore a pouch with a small bottle, but he'd used the entire few sips just before leaving Oranjestad, and it was essential to take on more.

With a large, ice-cold bottle in hand, he decided to walk the rest of the way back to Eagle Beach. He thought more clearly when he walked, and clarity of thought was a definite priority that morning. They had only a few hours left on the island, and there'd be one more delicate conversation with Amber before they flew out. Of course, they'd be the only passengers on the jet, but Gordon thought it would be better if they could reach an agreement before they left.

Amber remained adamant she had nothing to do with Tak Takahashi and the Japanese Yakuza. He'd brought the subject up twice during their weekend chats, and both times, she was not only insistent but became somewhat aggressive. Her face had clouded with anger, but her self-control was remarkable. Her voice remained calm, her manner reserved, and her eyes wary each time he pushed her to the brink.

Surprisingly, she hadn't rejected his hypothetical suggestion that perhaps she should consider resigning from Multima to make all their problems disappear. He'd pointed out that her immigration status let her work anywhere in the US for anyone she chose. With her skills and his network of contacts, he was confident she could find a new role—maybe even a better one—with another major corporation. And if she didn't find the job she wanted, they could comfortably live together on his earnings, even if Priscilla was about to take half his assets.

It had all happened suddenly, but Gordon became increasingly convinced that it was God's will for Amber and him to become a couple. But first, they had to find a way to do it without him losing his job at Multima Supermarkets.

Given the telephone conference with Suzanne and her team the day they left Atlanta, Gordon had no doubt Suzanne had issued orders to Serge to keep digging. He knew his boss and mentor well. She'd fired James Fitzgerald for a single indiscretion with a subordinate a few years earlier—before she brought him back later to help bail her out of another problem. He'd heard about the wiretaps Serge had planted at Multima Financial Services when they once suspected an employee there was feeding information to The Organization or some other illegal outfit.

Gordon stood under a tree for a moment of shade and processed all those thoughts, concerns, and fears again while sipping from the bottle of water. As he set out for the last mile or so before reaching the condo, he plotted a strategy, but he was unprepared when Amber greeted him at the door, wearing nothing but a charming smile.

Her head tilted to one side, she held her hands behind her back, revealing the front of her body entirely, and her grin grew more mischievous by the moment. Once Gordon recovered from her delightful surprise greeting, she twisted her hips seductively, drawing his eyes to the breasts he had loved from his first peek.

She waited for him to move forward, wrap his arms around her tenderly, and pull her in tightly for a long embrace. He planted gentle kisses around her neck and ears, and then she drew him closer, parting his lips and flashing her tongue inside his receptive mouth for a long, lustful kiss.

Playfully, she pushed him away much too soon. "You need a shower after that run. Let's start there."

She grabbed his hand and tugged sharply, leading him toward the bathroom shower. He stripped while they meandered along the hallway, leaving a trail of the shoes and clothes he'd worn for his run. By the time they reached the shower, he was as bare as she was and already showing signs of an erection. He wanted to wash himself quickly and hop into bed to avoid a repeat of that first early release he still had bad dreams about.

Amber wanted it differently. She teased and taunted him with a sponge and water, going through the motions of cleaning sweat from his body, massaging tired muscles, and stroking his penis and testicles in ways he'd experienced with her only once before. His breathing quickened, his exaggerated lunges for kisses and playtime with her tongue became more desperate, and his erection felt ready to explode. When she grabbed him firmly and kneeled, he came with uncontrollable force.

Amber took him in her mouth regardless, licking and sucking and spreading the gushing semen on her breasts and vagina in turn. Then she asked him to clean her up with a smile no man could resist.

Following her example, he wiped the cum from her body with the sponge, intermittently digressing to touch a nipple, run a finger down her neck or up her thigh, or delicately tease with his fingers in her most sensitive areas. She welcomed his exploration, even guiding him to her most arousing spots and squeezing his hand with her thighs, begging for more.

When it was clear she was ready, Gordon shut off the water, swept her off her feet, and carried her from the shower to the bed, dripping water across the tile floor. Leaving the bathroom, Amber had grabbed a towel from the rack, and she motioned for Gordon to dry her off.

Neither spoke as Gordon gently drew the soft, fluffy towel across her body, drying the beads of water from her skin and replacing the droplets with teasing kisses and gentle touches. She moaned with delight and arousal until he dried the area surrounding her vagina. Then she leaned forward and wrapped her hands around both shoulders, drawing him down and guiding him into her.

He lost track of time. They touched, kissed, rollicked, shifted, squeezed and finally released in mutual exhaustion, both satisfied and breathless. After a few minutes, Gordon shifted off her, then cuddled up close, stroking and massaging her gently and silently. Her breathing slowed shortly after, and her body relaxed more. After a final moan, she shifted to her side, facing him with her large brown eyes, only inches away from his.

"I'll resign tomorrow. As much as I love my job and love working for Multima, I know what we're doing is precarious for both our careers."

As Gordon started to answer, she gently but firmly placed one finger across his lips. "I want to. What we have together is special. I don't want to put anything at risk. I'll just hang out and make love with you for a while. We can decide together what should come next."

Twenty-Five

In the Laurentian Mountains, near Montreal, Monday
September 4, 2023

Florence Carpentier served as housekeeper, chef, and chief listener in the Simpson household. Suzanne considered the petite, almost entirely white-haired woman as a friend, almost a family member.

Suzanne's mother had died suddenly a few years earlier, and her father, John George Mortimer, had passed a year later. She was an only child, and close friends—the ones you could share everything with—were rare when one reached the executive suite. The connection between Suzanne and Florence was odd but remarkably comfortable.

From the day Florence first welcomed Suzanne to the house as a short-term rental client, they'd connected on an emotional level better described as intimate friends than employer-servant. They shared jokes quietly and privately. They told stories to each other when they were alone. Surprisingly, within weeks of first meeting each other, they often finished each other's sentences or blurted out punchlines to jokes at the same time.

Serge liked her, too. When their day was over, with the bodyguards away in their lookouts for overnight protection, Serge would often invite Florence to stay the night rather than drive twenty minutes along a dark road home. When she was exhausted, Florence would accept the invitation and join them to listen to music or chat, watch a TV program, or play a card game, all things Suzanne and Serge liked to do to relax.

Each time she stayed, within minutes, laughter filled the room, voices grew louder and sounded more joyful, and everyone present felt a tangible increase in energy and enthusiasm. Such was her personality, and such seemed Florence's outlook on life.

When Serge took off for Atlanta without a word to Suzanne that Friday before Labor Day, the first thing Suzanne did when she reached her home in the Laurentians was to look for Florence. She called out her name, scurried about the house searching for her, and upon discovering her yanking laundry from a dryer, embraced her as though they hadn't seen each other in years.

Before she knew it, she was sobbing uncontrollably as she held Florence suffocatingly close to her. The poor woman didn't know what to do or say for an instant and let her employer release whatever had built up inside. After a few moments, Suzanne realized she was acting like a fool, uncoiled her arms from around Florence, and watched her take a deep breath of relief.

Of course, Florence asked what was bothering her, discreetly glancing around Suzanne to see if Serge stood somewhere nearby. Her eyes bulged uncomfortably behind gold eyeglass frames, and new, deep furrows etched into her brow aged her dramatically.

"Serge went to Atlanta today. Out of the blue, without a word to me, he booked a flight with Air Canada and took off for Atlanta." Suzanne realized her shrugging shoulders, shaking head and louder-than-necessary tone sounded more desperate than intended. She slowed it down and mumbled, "He's never done anything like that before."

Before tears could gush again, she smiled half-heartedly at her friend. "Let me help you unload that machine. Pass me the laundry basket; I'll bring it upstairs."

Florence displayed mild surprise, but her sky-blue eyes had recovered their sparkle by the time Suzanne followed her up the plush carpeted flight of stairs from the luxuriously finished basement into the modern kitchen.

"I think this would be a good time for some *soupe aux pois* et *tortière,*" Florence announced as they reached the top. Québécoise mothers often prescribed the traditional soup and baked ground pork dish as cure-alls.

Suzanne nodded. "And maybe after dinner, we can bring the bodyguards to town with us to find some *crème brûlée.*" She giggled like a teenager dreaming of meeting a rock star.

They chatted as she helped Florence prepare the meal, and then they dined together for only the second time Suzanne could remember. It was therapeutic. She asked her housekeeper questions about her private life and family, and

Florence rewarded her with tales of escapades and events that left them both laughing as though they were enjoying an evening of comedy in a downtown bar.

The bodyguards loved her idea of dessert in town and chauffeured them all to a quaint restaurant with live entertainment and lots of activity on a Friday night before a long weekend. Montrealers flooded into villages in the Laurentian Mountains year-round, but the Labor Day holiday marked the unofficial end of summer and always drew the most visitors of the year.

Suzanne sipped a couple digestifs after the dessert and, as the restaurant filled, suggested they leave. Before their car left the village of Saint-Sauveur, Suzanne heard an alert from her phone and retrieved it from the bag in her lap.

> *My bad. Apologies. Should have let you know where I was going. In Atlanta. Nothing major but some curious stuff going on. Will be home by Monday. Don't worry. It won't happen again. Love, S.*

She held up the phone for Florence to read the message. There was nothing there she was afraid to show, and Suzanne wanted a moment to decide how best to respond. After observing Florence's arched eyebrows but wordless response, she prepared the words and keyed them in.

> *Apology accepted. Be careful. It better not happen again. See you Monday. Love, S.*

Suzanne revised the punctuation, inserting an exclamation mark instead of a period after the word again. With the faintest of smiles forming, she pressed "send."

Serge provided brief updates by text on Saturday and Sunday. She acknowledged each of them—sometimes after a considerable lapse of time—but provided neither encouragement nor feedback. Both could wait until she could assess his body language as well as his words.

She expected friends and colleagues had already made plans for the long weekend, so she was reluctant to interrupt them by suggesting a flight to Toronto or New York to take in a couple plays or some other weekend diversion. Instead, she had Florence book the helicopter each day and worked from the Montreal headquarters.

The bodyguards made coffee for everyone because Eileen enjoyed her weekend off, and they whiled away their time in the comfortable waiting area outside her office. Suzanne used the time to wade through stacks of reports on her desk, do some reading and research on food inflation issues around the globe, and study the briefing documents prepared by Edward Hadley's team of communications specialists.

Each day, one of the bodyguards slipped out of the office, found an open restaurant, and brought back a sandwich, slice of pizza, or container of soup for each of them. Then, she and the bodyguards used the gym in the building for a few hours each afternoon. With the long weekend, it was almost empty.

Evenings, Florence prepared typical Québécois dishes, to everyone's delight. Suzanne had invited her bodyguards to join her in the formal dining area rather than in the kitchen/dining section of the four-bedroom apartment in the furnished basement they usually used. She served wine and enjoyed conversations with her protectors and housekeeper that were seldom possible during her usual routine with Multima Corporation and private time with Serge.

She found it refreshing—even stimulating—listening to their stories, interests and even a few expressed concerns. When Serge opened the door on Monday evening, sheepishly poking his head into the hallway, he found them all huddled around the cleared dining room table, playing a board game and laughing uproariously at someone's wrong move.

When the group noticed him, there was an uncomfortable silence for a moment, her subordinates uncertain how to react. Suzanne stood from the table, told the group she'd be right back, and welcomed Serge at the hallway entrance with a friendly peck on the cheek, an obligatory hug, and an ice-breaking, "Welcome home. Do you want to join us?"

Serge got the message. "No, you all carry on. I'll take my things upstairs, then enjoy a glass of wine while I watch you play."

Suzanne encouraged the players to continue well past

midnight. Each of them had glanced at their watches several times in the hours after Serge arrived, but they played on at her urging until she decided to call it a night. Serge assumed the role of good sport, laughing when appropriate, encouraging the losers, and high-fiving brilliant moves. By the time they reached their bedroom, Suzanne was ready for real conversation.

Serge read her well.

"Life goes on without me. I get that. Don't worry. It won't happen again, and I apologize once more. We should have talked before I acted." He reached out to wrap his arms around her, and Suzanne accepted the embrace without returning it.

"If we're going to continue to be a couple, I expect communication in advance, not after the fact. If you accept that, I accept your apology. If you find that too restrictive, life will go on, maybe not as happily, but it will continue." She looked directly into his eyes without blinking as she delivered the ominous warning. She studied his eyes briefly, watching them soften as he returned her gaze. Their sparkle returned, reassuring her.

"I accept your apology." She leaned in, wrapping her hands gently around his neck, drawing him closer for a long kiss. When it ended, she finally asked the question. "So, what did you learn in Atlanta?"

"I'll admit the trip wasn't nearly as productive as I expected. Although I don't have the necessary evidence yet, I think there's something there. My team placed all the plants on the business phone system. It was a great time to do it with no one in the offices. But we couldn't get a tap on Gordon's phone. He's out of the country with the Supermarkets' jet. Atlanta airport showed the destination as Aruba with a return scheduled tonight."

He paused, probably looking for Suzanne's reaction and to give her time to think about that inappropriate use of the company's assets. When she frowned, he continued.

"Curious thing, though. Mrs. Goodfellow spent the weekend at their home in Atlanta with the two kids. According to my observers, they didn't leave their place for the entire weekend except to attend church on Sunday. Almost like a family in mourning, with no one outside, and no friends coming or going. I tried to meet Amber Chan. However, there was no answer on her phone. No responses to my three voice messages. No answer at her apartment when I knocked on the door. However, a car registered to her and using her assigned apartment parking spot didn't move all weekend."

Serge paused again, giving Suzanne time to assemble all the puzzle pieces. His lips curled with a tinge of disgust as he delivered his last thought on the matter. "While I don't have enough evidence yet, I'm convinced there's something there. I'm afraid it's soon going to become much more complicated."

Seconds after he delivered that pronouncement, Suzanne felt the vibration of an alert on her phone. She glanced down to see a text from Eileen.

> *Urgent. Gordon Goodfellow has requested a 30-minute phone slot tomorrow morning. Shall I confirm?*

Twenty-Six

In flight, Tuesday September 5, 2023

Fidelia boarded the Bombardier 7500 first, and headed directly to her preferred swivel chair at the round table in the middle of the first compartment, pointing for Mia to take the chair opposite.

She secured her few belongings in a cupboard behind the seat, then made herself comfortable as the six bodyguards filed into the jet and headed toward the middle compartment where they could watch the big screen and enjoy some entertainment in the air.

Hopefully, all six wouldn't have much to do on this flight, but Fidelia preferred not to take chances. Left behind at her new home in Dubrovnik was the Cuban worker, Agueda Diaz, from Guantanamo Bay, who continued to serve as housekeeper for the new place. The youngest Uruguayan bodyguard, Ricardo Schirillio, also stayed behind.

He'd be fine minding the house, and Fidelia hadn't missed the interest the young guy had shown in Agueda. His eyes followed her constantly, and Fidelia could almost smell the suppressed desire. Leaving the pair together was practical and likely would prove delightfully rewarding for both. She liked to build loyalties. Letting them explore each other while she traveled might bring Fidelia benefits down the road.

She looked around the aircraft as one pilot closed the doors. The other played at the bank of controls, preparing for departure. She stifled a grin as she thought about getting the jet back from Tak Takahashi. It was a pure power play to force him to return the private aircraft to her and take a fifty-million-dollar hit. But the scoundrel must have known the plane was hers when he agreed to buy it on the dark web. He knew the FBI had stolen it. So, she was entitled to feel a sense of satisfaction in teaching the young fellow a lesson. That thought reminded her she should call during the flight to see what he was up to in Japan.

She turned to Mia, now also settled in across the table.

"How are your parents doing?" Mia had been taking care of her ailing parents in Puerto Rico only a couple months earlier. Then Fidelia told her it was time to put her parents in a care home. She needed her full-time and nearby after that Hawaii fiasco and physical torture at Guantanamo Bay. The combination of the new demands had created an emotional time for her assistant. Her reply showed her struggle continued.

"I spoke with them last night. They're getting used to the place."

"You did the right thing. Your parents will get excellent care there, and I'll continue paying their expenses as long as they need the help." That meant she'd keep paying until they died, which wouldn't be long. Both had suffered from dementia for years. "I'm going to pay you a special bonus, too. I know it's been hard for you, so add a hundred thousand dollars to your December paycheck."

Mia sat straighter in her seat, a grateful smile crossing her face before she spoke.

"Thank you. I appreciate it."

"Klaudia knows we're coming today?"

"Yes, I confirmed with her and the staff members there yesterday. They're expecting us."

"Klaudia's mood any better?" Fidelia looked deep into Mia's eyes as she asked the question. Her assistant always showed excellent judgment and seldom held back essential details. However, with "problem child" Klaudia, it was helpful to have every perspective possible. Much was at stake.

"She's still demoralized and resentful. She really wants out and feels you owe it to her to let her move on from The Organization."

Fidelia nodded her understanding but studiously avoided any display of emotion. Instead, she shifted the subject and dictated a list of people she wanted Mia to line up on the phone as they traveled. Their flight would take about five hours, crossing Bulgaria to better avoid Russian airspace later in the flight, then over the Black Sea on a flight path across Azerbaijan before crossing the Caspian Sea up into Muynak in the northwest corner of Uzbekistan.

She planned to use most of those five hours talking with

country bosses as part of her monthly routine. It was important to remind them who put them where they were and listen carefully for any wavering loyalty or threatening ambition. Giancarlo Mareno taught her that lesson, and she practiced the routine almost religiously. The first name on the list she handed Mia was Tak Takahashi.

"Good evening, Tak. Mia probably told you I'm calling from the plane. Thanks again for returning it to me so promptly." The extra dig wasn't necessary, but she wanted him to remember who the boss was from the beginning of the call. "How's everything going in Japan?"

He chose to ignore her power play. "All under control here. I just reviewed the proceeds for the month. I think you'll be happy with your commission. You'll see that most of it came from the pachinko parlors, but drugs are gaining traction. Despite the government putting in place penalties for possession, young people are using cannabis more. We've had a couple guys arrested, but still lots of volunteers to sell the stuff."

Fidelia listened as he carried on with his brief overview of the Yakuza's activities and events in the preceding month but would take a keener interest when she saw the funds deposited in her accounts in Singapore. Then she'd compare the amount received with the detailed written report he'd provide.

"What's your Amber Chan doing with Multima? Still making headway on that new computer system you want to blow up?"

"Actually, we have a problem with that. Amber's planning to resign from her role in the company."

"Did you say resign?" Fidelia raised her voice more than a notch, incredulous at the news. Why did he wait so long to tell her this bit of important news?

"Yeah, she has to. It's a long story, but she told me she had to get out, and I gave her the okay." Tak's voice wavered and trailed off as he said it.

"Make your long story short. What happened?" Fidelia kept growing anger out of her voice, but a tone bordering on threatening left little doubt she expected answers.

"She chose to reward the president of Multima

Supermarkets with a few romps in bed, and the fool fell in love. He was married, and the wife found out and took divorce action. Multima has rules against that kind of employee interaction, and Amber expected Suzanne Simpson would throw them both out as soon as she became aware. Amber has a plan to keep the project on track using her influence over the Supermarkets president, a guy named Goodfellow."

"What's her plan?"

"We didn't have time to discuss it. She asked me to be patient and trust her, but Amber's confident she can still pull it off."

"Has she submitted her resignation yet?" Fidelia's tone became more urgent, more demanding.

"No. She plans to do it during a call with the president of Supermarkets and Suzanne Simpson first thing this morning, Montreal time."

"Get that fucking call canceled right now," Fidelia ordered. "Contact Amber immediately and tell her she's not to resign under any circumstances until I personally approve her alternate plan. Tell her to develop a migraine, cramps, or any fucking excuse she chooses to delay, but I need her in her current role. Don't share this with her, but I have a huge problem developing in Europe. That Multima cyberattack is an important piece of my plan."

She pressed "end" on her phone with an exasperated thrust of her forefinger, then breathed deeply and signaled to Mia that she was ready for the next call.

Over the ensuing hours, she talked with the guys running Italy, France, Spain, and Portugal. There were no surprises. The guys had made all the arrangements and were ready to execute as soon as Fidelia got Klaudia onside.

Next, Mia reached her woman in charge of Australia. She was getting ready for bed, so Fidelia kept the call brief. Aretta Musa was a woman she had pulled out of Africa to run the Australian escort business. She had performed so well that Fidelia eventually gave her responsibility for running all The Organization's business Down Under. Aretta even took care of eliminating her greedy predecessor the same day she received the order. Fidelia's kind of woman.

The Russian Mafia was active in Africa. Fidelia used their

brief conversation to check on a couple known operatives and leaders and get the woman's perspective on their strengths and weaknesses. As an afterthought, she ended the call by asking Aretta to check with her contacts in Algeria to see if getting a hundred or so women to France on short notice might be possible. She needed a backup plan.

Her last call before touching down was with Marie Dependente, her recently appointed boss for the crucial US businesses. She'd appointed the French woman to replace her longtime protector, Luigi Fortissimo. Marie had personally taken the sonofabitch out of the game when he attacked Fidelia on her jet. The woman's prowess as a fighter was undoubtedly impressive, but Fidelia gave her the role because she found her exceptionally smart. Of course, she also valued the woman's past support, including years of providing information about Multima's operations in Europe.

Fidelia found Marie well-informed and well-connected to influential people in important offices around the world. She swore an oath of loyalty without hesitation, and Fidelia gave her all the information she needed to run the American activities of The Organization. The woman's first few months in power proved mainly uneventful. She had to eliminate two guys loyal to Luigi when they were late with their first payments, but she did it quickly and decisively.

US operations seemed stable, and Fidelia received the woman's monthly commission payments in her Cayman accounts promptly. Still, there was a nagging concern.

A well-paid—and usually reliable—source of information in the upper echelons of the FBI had planted a seed during those conversations when she had conspired with Tak and Klaudia to spring Fidelia from Guantanamo. Although the woman had no evidence to support her hunch, she suspected that Marie Dependente might have provided information on Fidelia's whereabouts, which resulted in the devastating fiasco in Hawaii that led to her confinement in Cuba.

The source guessed that Marie may have tipped off the immigration authorities, who then tipped off the FBI.

In her three conversations with Marie over the summer months, Fidelia listened carefully for hints of disloyalty. So far there had been no indication Marie may have switched sides or was acting in any way harmful to either Fidelia or The Organization. However, as she signaled to Mia that she was ready to talk with her US crime boss, she'd decided to probe carefully again. She started with Multima Corporation.

"Have your people in Atlanta come up with anything I might want to know?" Fidelia asked.

"I just talked with the guys there yesterday. They've made a couple discoveries. Both are kinda gossipy issues I didn't think urgent and thought we could cover today," Marie replied.

Fidelia sat more erect. "Non-urgent" issues often had a way of assuming more importance than expected.

"We're monitoring her cell phone as you asked, and there's nothing of note there. She calls Japan once or twice a week, different numbers, so we're assuming those are to Tak on burner phones. Other than that, a few fast-food orders, a few calls to Gordon Goodfellow's line, and one call to a hairstylist." Marie paused, perhaps for a sip of water or coffee, before she continued.

"However, the cameras we installed in her apartment show she's indeed a busy woman. First, she's carrying on a sizzling affair with her boss. Goodfellow has slept there every night for the past two months, except for the Labor Day weekend. There was no activity in the apartment that weekend."

Fidelia interrupted to reconfirm one detail. "When you say 'sleeping there,' can I assume they're doing more than sleeping?"

"Oh, yeah. The boys said they have enough material for a full-length porno feature. Apparently, Ms. Chan and Goodfellow are mutually enthusiastic participants, and scarcely a night goes by without considerable action in the bedroom."

Fidelia told her to go on.

"As I said, this is all gossipy. Still, you might find it interesting. During the last two weeks, Amber Chan also entertained two other guys while Goodfellow was at work. Both are young guys, fresh out of university and about half her age, working at Multima Supermarkets. Both visited at separate times—once each week—during August. Each time, they discussed technology issues for about an hour. Ms. Chan took notes while they chatted. After she finished those conversations, she left the table and went into her bedroom, then returned to the living area where the guy waited. Each time, she came back stark naked and proceeded to reward the guys, first with a blowjob, then at least another half hour fucking in every position imaginable, according to our guys."

Fidelia listened intently. The sex was no big deal. She couldn't care less if the woman had an appetite for lots of partners. Still, she found it odd Amber Chan contemplated resigning from Multima to maintain her relationship with Gordon Goodfellow, yet apparently had no qualms about servicing others.

Unless these guys are part of the plan Chan is supposedly hatching?

"Have your guys continue monitoring. And if you get any other bits of information—gossipy or not—call me. Don't wait for our regular updates," Fidelia said.

The jet started its descent into Muynak as Fidelia finished her calls. She took a deep breath and focused on the view of the surrounding countryside. She spotted her compound in the middle of an almost barren field, the one place in the world she felt secure. It was a large home on a massive property, with several adjoining buildings set back more than a mile from the nearest road. One was devoted to her security detail. It could accommodate up to ten bodyguards, although she'd never felt a need for more than six.

Another small building housed her caretakers, a local married couple who managed and maintained the property and prepared meals for her when Fidelia stayed at the compound. Yet another smaller building accommodated any guests, and Klaudia would be there. But she changed her mind and now wouldn't visit tonight. Her petulant former friend could wait until morning.

As the plane touched down on the runway, Fidelia noticed three black Mercedes Benz limousines sitting on the edge of the tarmac a few hundred yards from the terminal. That's where her pilot would park the jet. Standing beside those limousines, she recognized the confident posture of her friend Zefar Karimov, the Deputy Finance Minister of Uzbekistan.

As she stepped off the jet's stairway, he turned on his engaging smile, opened his arms broadly, and wrapped her in a warm but formal embrace like he might greet a dignitary from a foreign country. He followed with the obligatory peck on each cheek. Then, for any curious eyes watching from the terminal, he stepped closer to block any view of her face as they circled around the jet toward the limousines.

Of course, they wouldn't enter the terminal. There would be no immigration formalities. The airport would pretend the empty jet at the end of the tarmac was an apparition that didn't truly exist.

In the limousine, his manner changed dramatically. Zefar had been a friend for a long time, and she owed him much. His embrace became predictably more sensual. His tongue ravaged her mouth as he pressed deeper and deeper. If she wanted it, she could easily become a third wife. But she had no interest in such an arrangement.

Instead, though she might be the most powerful woman in a potent outfit, she would spread her legs just like Amber Chan. She, too, had to reward the guy who made it possible for her to escape from the rest of the rabble on Earth, if only for a few days.

Twenty-Seven

Montreal, Quebec, Tuesday September 5, 2023

Suzanne asked Serge to join the unplanned conference call Gordon Goodfellow had requested. After the gossip her chief of security shared with her from his impulsive trip to Atlanta, she expected a revelation—maybe even a confession or two.

Surprisingly, the conversation took an entirely different path.

"Thanks for making some time for us this morning, Suzanne. I had hoped Amber Chan might join us to outline her excellent progress in getting expenses under control at Jeffersons Stores, but she called earlier to say she's unwell this morning. She tested negative for COVID but seems to have caught one of those other pesky viruses floating about."

Suzanne raised an eyebrow slightly but fought to avoid any expression of surprise. That was a challenge. He made no mention of the trip to Aruba without his family. No confession about using the company jet for personal entertainment. No acknowledgment of the other obvious missing bits of either information or gossip. She kept her good wishes for Amber's quick recovery to a bare minimum and asked him what else was on his mind that morning. As the camera in his Atlanta office expanded its view, it was clear why none of those issues surfaced.

"Besides Amber's great progress getting those Jeffersons Stores expenses under control, I wanted my team to share with you directly the information they collected for your appearance before the Canadian government's parliamentary committee." His tone seemed an octave higher than usual. Enthusiasm sounded manufactured. But she nodded and told him to go ahead.

Five of Gordon's direct reports sat with him and took over the Zoom conference for succinct six-minute segments. They were all well prepared. They had studiously researched their information, and a shared PowerPoint noted where they had gotten all their facts.

One presenter explained their five-week-long battle last year with the processed-food giant Snackco. She detailed how Multima strenuously resisted a fifteen percent increase demanded by the supplier, refusing to pay the new prices they demanded. In return, Snackco withheld all shipments to Supermarkets. Ultimately, Multima gave in because their customers started buying Snackco-branded chips and soft drinks elsewhere.

Another team member described how badly labor negotiations were dragging with Multima unions in the US, Canada, and Europe. In all those markets, organized labor had demanded wage increases approaching, or exceeding, ten percent—a more significant increase than any time in the past twenty-five years.

A third presenter summarized current negotiations with suppliers of meat, dairy products, and other perishable goods. He talked about continuing shortages as some belligerent growers simply reduced the number of animals they raised, the amount of milk they produced, or the products they harvested on their farms—all forcing prices higher.

A fourth focused on real estate. Multima Corporation owned many of the properties where their stores were located. Municipalities had increased property taxes into double digits in some cases, and the cost of maintenance and repairs had skyrocketed, with some service providers demanding unprecedented increases in their hourly rates. Multima managed to control those costs by delaying needed renovations, keeping expenses to the minimum required for safety and an acceptable appearance.

The last presenter was the most positive. She outlined the recent company successes with Multima's private label goods and their customer loyalty program. Sales of private label products had surged as customers switched from more expensive name brands to Multima's "Mom's Picks" label to save money. Produced and packaged to Multima's requirements by the same companies that sold well-known, popular name brands, Mom's Picks products sold at lower prices but also generated higher gross profits for the chain. They didn't need the same massive advertising budgets that brand-name products spent. So, Multima profits would continue rising, even if prices didn't increase.

But the Multima More program was even more powerful. Multima offered bonus points for specific products purchased. Those bonus points served as discounts, and vendors of those products often reimbursed those discounts to increase their market share. Customers redeemed bonus points whenever they chose, saving actual dollars on their weekly shopping bills.

The beautiful irony for Multima? The more challenging things became for customers, the more loyal they became, with a greater desire to accumulate more bonus points for saving money and purchasing more Multima house brands, which cost them less. Many customers thought of it as "double-dipping" their savings, which drove Multima sales and profits ever upward.

Gordon Goodfellow carried on from the last presenter. "I hope that gives you the background tools you'll need to prepare for the government inquiry, but I hope it also demonstrates how our Multima More program can be a powerful tool to offset any new measures governments might impose. Of course, if we can get Financial's credit card program more entwined with the Multima More loyalty program, customer benefits also expand exponentially."

His tone was confident, more natural and ebullient than when they'd started the call less than an hour earlier. He seemed to be back in his comfort zone. He became more relaxed, showing a genuine, unforced smile with the usual sparkle in his eyes.

Suzanne tested her read. "I think I hear a strong recommendation for us to grow the Multima More program. Your analysis suggests we can slow price increases on our Mom's Picks products. We'll increase sales more than enough to offset any cost increases we incur. So, we'll attract customers back to our stores because we are the only place they can buy Mom's Picks products. And we'll encourage even greater loyalty by expanding Financial's Multima More credit card benefits, again available only by buying from our stores."

"That's right," Gordon said. "But one further step—one that will create the most dramatic results the most quickly—is the full integration of those programs into Jeffersons Stores.

Signing up Jeffersons Stores' millions of customers to the Multima More loyalty program can make us not only resistant to any government measures, it should make us almost bulletproof."

Suzanne smiled. A strong statement, perhaps, but only modestly exaggerated if they did this right. She set the wheels in motion.

"Okay, Gordon. If I'd known you and your team had all this great info to share this morning, I would have invited more folks here at headquarters who should be in the loop." She smiled to soften a direct admonishment in front of his team. Then she resumed.

"Organize some time with Pierre Cabot. His people need to analyze your suggestions, assess the cost-benefit ratios, and look at the tax impact. Bring Edward Hadley into the discussion. He needs to incorporate all that information into a briefing document for my appearance before the government committee. He also needs to have his team develop a marketing integration strategy to get Jeffersons Stores' customers onboard if we decide to move more quickly on that strategy. Finally, share all this with Marcel Dubois. If our computer systems can't handle it, we can't do it. I'll have Eileen set up a meeting for everyone we need involved. Let's make it a week from today."

Suzanne looked into the camera and held her gaze there for a moment, looking for any sign of unease from any of the participants. They looked confident and relaxed. Then, with a tone breezy and casual, as though she might have had an afterthought, she ended the meeting.

"Oh, Gordon, please call me on my private line. Right after we finish here, if you can." She smiled only enough to put his team members at ease.

Twenty-Eight

Muynak, Uzbekistan, Wednesday September 6, 2023

Zefar's watch alarm woke Fidelia at 4:00 a.m. He had to return to the capital, Tashkent, for an important meeting that morning and started early. After a quick shower, he dressed and readied for a formal government meeting. His mind had already shifted to business as he planted a nondescript kiss on her lips, with no effort to part them. Last night's passion was already a page turned, she supposed.

The sex had been enjoyable for Fidelia. Zefar was a robust and fit man, well-endowed where it mattered, and his sexual appetite was almost without limit. During the five hours between their arrival at the compound and falling asleep, he managed to satisfy her three times. It was indeed a rare male specimen who could perform at that level.

Now, it would probably be weeks—maybe months—before they met again. He had two legal wives to satisfy, after all, and although Fidelia enjoyed his company and an occasional romp in bed, she had no expectations for the future.

Still, few people had helped her more. When the FBI had ordered Interpol to issue a code red for her arrest—that first time almost a decade earlier—Zefar arranged everything she needed to stay free. The guy got her an Uzbekistan passport. He found, bought, and renovated her secluded compound.

Enterprising resources that he knew searched for, bought, and installed the latest and most sophisticated communications equipment from a source in Israel. When the place was ready, he staffed her compound with relatives who needed a place to stay and a steady income but were folks who also understood the meaning of total discretion. And it all happened within a month.

She cheerfully bid farewell to Zefar and then headed outside for a leisurely walk as the sun rose. Fidelia loved the area around her compound even though it was now an arid desert.

It was still hard for her to imagine, but the nearby town of

Muynak was once a bustling fishing port on the Aral Sea, the fourth-largest lake in the world at that time. Then, it dried up entirely—in only forty years—from unsustainable cotton production in the area. Now, the town sat almost a hundred miles from the nearest water, and photos of the area often depicted abandoned fishing boats dotting the sandy terrain, miles into the now-barren desert.

There were no longer tourists, and visitors were rare. Fidelia relished that seclusion. Zefar told her thirteen thousand people remained in the area, but none lived within miles of her remote compound. The landscape was dirt and sand as far as she could see, with scarcely anything else in sight. Maybe an occasional clump of brownish grass or a scrawny shrub. Only an off-course bird or insect broke her comforting silence that morning.

It was the perfect place to think, calculate and prepare. She needed that space because her next task was to have the most important conversation of her life with her former friend Klaudia.

Before Fidelia had dispatched her now bothersome friend to Uzbekistan, she knew that as much as she loved the solace of the desert, Klaudia had always hated it. She identified herself as a German and carried a European Union passport issued by that country. But Klaudia's origins were in Russia, where she'd served as an operative in the Russian secret services. She'd fled because she hated the country intensely and the thugs in the secret service who'd mistreated her so brutally for so long.

In times when they were closer, Klaudia had tearfully recounted bitter tales of misogyny, rape, and cruelty. That horrid treatment left her with both physical and emotional scars that time had only partially healed. Fidelia suspected the lingering memories of that miserable period in her life could be the catalyst for getting Klaudia to participate in the grand scheme she had plotted during the past weeks in Dubrovnik.

She chose to discuss it over breakfast in the spacious dining area next to the kitchen. Fidelia asked her housekeeper not to return after she served them each an omelet with fresh eggs from chickens housed behind the compound and vegetables grown by the chef's husband in an irrigated greenhouse Zefar had built. Irrigation was possible because of the enormous tank behind the house where they stored imported water.

Klaudia looked terrible. She was approaching fifty, but even in recent months, she'd remained younger-looking and exceptionally beautiful until they'd snatched her from the streets in Curaçao. She'd been resentful and angry when they'd seized her and required attitude adjustment therapy.

As Fidelia assessed her appearance today, it looked like her face had never quite recovered from the severe sunburn she'd suffered that day they forced her to lie, bound and naked, outdoors. The scorching Caribbean sunshine beamed down on her for almost an entire day. Before Klaudia almost died of thirst and exposure, she acquiesced and began to cooperate. But her skin was as red as embers in a fire and blistered with ugly blotches.

Today, her skin looked pale and Klaudia's long, brown hair, streaked with naturally graying strands, hadn't been trimmed in months. Her nails were chewed to the skin on each finger, and several teeth—broken when Fidelia used her clenched fists to get her attention in Hawaii—still displayed ugly chips. Large dark circles below and around her eyes suggested prolonged poor sleep. Wrinkles on her forearms and neck indicated that exercise and workouts were now a thing of the past, and her left hand trembled slightly but continuously.

Klaudia wolfed down the breakfast as though she hadn't eaten for days, although that wasn't the case.

"What have you been doing with your time here?" Fidelia used a soft, friendly tone, followed by a smile, to show she cared about the response.

"The usual. Thanks, I guess, for arranging the new computer. It doesn't let me communicate with anyone outside the compound, but it doesn't limit my research."

"What kinds of research have you been doing?" Again, Fidelia feigned interest with a tone of curiosity.

"Mainly, I'm learning as much as I can about artificial intelligence. If you ever let me out, that's a field I'd like to explore more." Still the defiant monotone.

"I see you're still bitter."

"Bitter? Maybe. Disillusioned might be more like it. I'll never understand how—at this stage in your life, and with the power you wield—you can continue to treat other women as though they are simply pawns on a chessboard. Pawns you can move at will to play your sordid games. Mere names you expect to accept the physical and emotional abuse heaped on them by vile men or dispatch to a graveyard should they fail to cooperate."

Fidelia listened, but she'd heard it all before. Unlike Klaudia, she didn't view her experiences in the escort business with either shame or disgust. Sex was part of life. That some people were prepared to pay for it was neither good nor evil. It just was. If men were willing to pay enough to put a few dollars in the pockets of women who needed it, and the people who managed those women were prepared to share some with Fidelia, who was she to turn away a few million tax-free dollars a year?

"So, you still want to go your own way?" Fidelia asked, hinting at that possibility. Klaudia raised her head for the first time and looked into her eyes.

"I pray for it. I don't even believe in a deity, but I still pray every day that you'll let me go."

Fidelia waited, choosing just the right words and inquisitive tone. "Do you still know how to reach Yuri Federov? Or Boris Ivanov?"

Klaudia's face reddened almost instantly. She hated those two men more than any others on earth. They were the names she'd shared most often for humiliating her, sexually torturing her, and making her life in Russia so unbearable that she was forced to escape.

Klaudia didn't answer at first. For a long moment, she looked at Fidelia without blinking, her eyes hardening until they looked like stone. Finally, she nodded curtly, twice.

Fidelia chose not to speak further right away. This was one of those times when silence could be more persuasive than words. *Let her chew on that for a bit.* The thought prompted her to finish her cooling omelet, gulping down the remaining few bites without looking up.

Finished, Fidelia reached for the white linen napkin at her side, dabbed at the corner of her mouth, and asked her most important question. Most important for each of them.

"My guys in Europe complain about two growing problems. Since you left, they don't have enough quality women from Eastern Europe. Plus, there's Russian mob interference again. We're losing people. I plan to send a message and am prepared to use Federov and Ivanov to deliver it. I have a plan to eliminate them both in a manner that will tell the Russkis to stay at home—in a way they'll understand. Are you willing to help me achieve that goal?"

"What's in it for me?"

"I'll move you back to your place in Düsseldorf by the weekend as a gesture of good faith. As a retainer, I'll deposit a million dollars in your Cayman bank account. I'll deposit another five million in your account when the deed is done."

"And my freedom?"

"You'll just have to trust me on that one. Nothing I can say or do will guarantee freedom, as you call it. I know your preference. I'll try to honor it. But there are no guarantees."

Fidelia waited for a response. It took more than a moment.

Far in the background, the housekeeper cleaned up, and dishes clinked. A breeze gently fluffed the curtains on an open window and carried inside the scent of herbs growing outside the windowsill. A solitary black fly hummed near the top of the twelve-foot-high white ceiling. A faint tapping of sandals beneath the table telegraphed her former friend's inner turmoil.

Finally, she sat upright and looked directly into Fidelia's eyes. Klaudia's expression was pained, her mouth forming almost a grimace. She swallowed twice before she spoke.

"You're clever. You knew my passion for eliminating that pair from the face of the earth would offset my well-founded suspicion you'll never honor the freedom part. I'm torn. I'll probably regret it, but I'll take a chance with you again."

Twenty-Nine

Atlanta, Georgia, Wednesday September 6, 2023

After Suzanne's private dressing-down the day before, Gordon decided it was time for him to buck up and do more for his corporate survival than pray.

He closed the door to his office and asked his executive assistant to reschedule his calls for the next hour. He dimmed the monitor on his desk, leaned back in the comfortable swivel chair behind it, and swung his feet up. He realized it was an odd habit, but he found that he did his best thinking when he shut out the world like this and let his body relax while his brain churned.

What had happened to his self-control? Why did Amber have such a powerful influence on his judgment? How did he get himself headed for a divorce? And was he now in danger of losing his job?

It was quite the reprimand he'd received from Suzanne after that conference call. She'd told him she was alone in the room, but she'd used the speaker on her phone from the moment she answered her private line. His gut told him that Serge had probably listened in on the call.

When she asked about Amber's health, Gordon didn't lie, but he didn't tell the whole truth either. "She claims to have a bug that's left her feeling unwell and didn't want to spread it around the office."

He hoped his choice of words correctly left Suzanne with the impression he wasn't entirely convinced of an illness without creating too much doubt. In fact, Gordon had serious misgivings about any illness. True, he awoke in the middle of the night in Amber's bed while she was retching loudly in the bathroom. But she flushed the toilet quickly before he could check for any evidence, claiming she must have eaten something tainted before leaving Aruba.

His suspicions grew with the first thing she said when they returned together to the bedroom. "I feel awful. I can't go to work today. You'll have to cancel the call with Suzanne this morning. Besides, I'm rethinking my resignation. I'll think about it today and tell you what I decide when you return from work."

Gordon knew he couldn't cancel the call with Suzanne without raising concerns. One simply didn't ask the CEO for some time for a conversation, then arbitrarily cancel it. Instead, he'd texted the five direct reports, claiming he forgot to tell them, but he needed them to get something together to present to her by Zoom. They all met at his office at 7:30 that morning to hash through their respective recommendations, put them into a semblance of order, and rehearse their pitch once before the conference call started.

Recalling the panic he felt sending those early morning texts, he made a mental note to call each of the presenters later that morning to thank them again for bailing him out on such short notice. Those small gestures built loyalty, and he might need a lot of loyalty soon.

He thought longer about the call after the Zoom conference. Suzanne had been calm and polite throughout, but formal. No kibitzing at the outset. No humor anytime during the conversation. Both were unusual. She'd often coached subordinates that both gestures were essential to effective communication. Instead, that morning she jumped right to the real reason for her informal inquiry.

"The security team reported unusual flight activity on the Supermarkets corporate jet over the weekend. Anything I should be aware of?"

Gordon hadn't expected the question, so it took him a second or two to devise the best strategy. He was moderately satisfied with his performance, and he did it without any overt lies. "Yeah, that was me. I know I should have requested an exception to the policy, but I needed to get away for the weekend. If you want me to reimburse the company, I will."

Suzanne took a moment to reflect before she answered with another question. "If you don't mind me asking, is everything going okay at home?"

He couldn't lie. There were too many ways she could find out about the divorce, and lying at this stage could be fatal to his career. "I don't mind you asking at all. We are going through a rough patch. Nothing you should be concerned about, but I needed some time alone to think it through."

She didn't pursue the marriage question, merely offering her hopes that everything would work out okay, and if he needed any time away from the job to let her know. It would be inconvenient, but personal relationships were important, and the company made resources available should he need them.

Then she threw one more curve to close that matter. "That said, weekend jaunts on the company jet at the company's expense aren't considered therapeutic. This time, I'll note an indiscretion in your HR file. If there's a recurrence, the consequences will be severe."

He was relieved when she switched the topic to the computer systems upgrade and listened while he recapped their progress from his perspective, making a point to compliment the efforts of her chief technology officer, Marcel Dubois. Suzanne also clarified her understanding of a couple points related to the earlier presentations on Zoom, then suddenly switched back to Amber.

"I know we just moved Amber to Atlanta a few months ago, but I'm wondering if she wouldn't be more effective in San Francisco. Atlanta made sense when she worked with the technology team every day on the conversion. But now that you have her focusing on operations, might it be better for her to be physically closer to the team there?"

Sonofabitch! Talk about a new complication. In return, he mumbled a few thoughts about an interesting idea, something to think about, needing to talk with HR and other meaningless drivel.

Suzanne told him to consider it, especially if the board agreed to accelerate the integration of Jeffersons Stores branding to become full-fledged Multima Supermarkets immediately.

Now he had to find a way to navigate through this mess. Amber and he had been living together for two months, and more than living together. They'd been passionately making love almost every day during that time. How could he ask her to move across the country? What would he do without her nearby?

He stood up from his desk, shook his head a couple times, stretched his arms above his head to ease tension, and then started pacing around the perimeter of the spacious office.

At least Amber had opened the door a crack. In Aruba, they'd agreed it was best for her to resign from Multima. It was the best way to address their current violation of a significant company policy and salvage at least his job.

However, that had all changed when he'd returned to her apartment the previous evening. She told him she'd changed her mind. She loved her job, didn't want to leave it, and thought they should find a way to make it work without her quitting.

He couldn't miss the determined gleam in her eye, her passion as she almost spit out the words. She clenched her fists while she spoke, emphasizing her conviction and telegraphing her intention to fight for her job. All this struck Gordon like a punch to the stomach.

They had argued about her decision for hours. He tried logic, emotion, reasoning, and every tool he could think to draw on. It ended without a night of lovemaking and without a consensus about how they should move forward. The only point of agreement: Amber should take another day away from the office while they both mulled it over. People would easily understand her need for more recovery time.

When the pacing around the office ended, Gordon had made his decision. Amber would relocate to San Francisco. Now, he had to find a way to sell that move and keep her a willing bed partner—even if those sessions would become infrequent—and a loyal protector of their secret.

He had work to do. Skillfully managing those outcomes would take more thinking and a ton of finesse.

Thirty

Ottawa, Ontario, Monday September 18, 2023

Edward Hadley, lobbyists for the other supermarket companies, and the grocers' association team had all magically made the threatened parliamentary committee appearance go away. It took some shrewd backroom manipulation by members of parliament and the office of the prime minister, but today, Suzanne, Edward, and her CEO counterparts marched down a long corridor in the historic Canadian House of Commons toward a meeting with two senior government ministers.

No one spoke as they walked because a flock of reporters scurried along the same hallway, pressing closely to the striding grocery industry representatives, shouting out questions, flashing photographs, and holding phones high in the air to record anything anyone said.

Edward had warned her about a media scrum when he'd given his final briefing a few days earlier. He'd also reminded her again about the dangers during their forty-minute helicopter trip from her home in the Laurentian Mountains to Ottawa, the capital of Canada.

Suzanne processed and reprocessed the key points they expected to discuss. Although the atmosphere in the meeting should be considerably less tense than the committee format first proposed, the current minority government had a lot riding on the outcome of this meeting. Only a few days earlier, the prime minister had declared that his government was summoning the CEOs to Ottawa to "hold them to account" for the stubbornly high inflation rate in the supermarket business.

So, officialdom had already made up its mind about whom to blame. Today's goal was to minimize damage to the industry and the companies' bottom-line profits. It would be a challenge. The two cabinet members they were meeting were tough negotiators. One had already bedazzled a former US president who tried to change some rules in the game of trade between the two countries. The other cabinet minister oversaw a range of industry issues, including the agency responsible for anti-competitive behavior.

Both ministers would probably be polite but forceful.

When their guide for the journey to the meeting room announced they'd arrived, and the cabinet ministers would join them momentarily, she suggested the guests help themselves to coffee from an urn on a table in a corner of the dark, wood-paneled room.

The CEOs and their entourages took advantage of the short delay to shake hands, say hellos, pat a few backs, and reduce the tension. They all knew each other, of course. They met at least a few times a year at association get-togethers or supplier events. All knew better than to compare notes in an environment like this, but there were still a few winks and nudges as the executives bolstered each other's spirits for the battle about to begin.

They didn't wait long. The finance minister arrived one step ahead of the minister for innovation. She was a tall, confident woman wearing an expensive business suit in a soft pastel blue. She wore little make-up, but her long hair was groomed meticulously. She smiled broadly as she approached Suzanne first, a subtle recognition she should first greet the CEO of the largest corporation and the only woman among them. The handshake was firm but curt.

As the finance minister moved on to greet the next CEO, the minister of innovation filled the vacant space and introduced himself to Suzanne with a similar formal shake of the right hand. His dark eyes looked foreboding, like a boxer's might in those last seconds of waiting for a bell to ring to start the fight. His lips curled up slightly, but the smile never reached his eyes.

The minister of finance took one of two seats at the head of the long boardroom-style table. Her counterpart took the other as both waved for the CEOs to choose a vacant chair. Edward Hadley, assistants to the other CEOs, and the ministers' staff attending, all took chairs lined around the room's perimeter to make notes, record dialogue, or pass messages to their respective bosses.

The minister of finance started the meeting. "Thank you all for coming today. Our government is extremely concerned about the confluence of two significant events. Inflation has increased by more than fifteen percent in the three years since COVID first hit Canada. In the grocery segment, inflation has increased by more than twenty percent and is still rising every month. During those same three years, the profits earned by your companies have increased more than forty percent cumulatively."

When the woman paused for effect, Suzanne eyed the minister directly, trying to guess how aggressively the politician would frame her following remarks. She didn't have to wait long.

"I realize those results don't apply equally to everyone here today, and I can accept the premise that profits in the years before COVID might have been challenging for one or two of you. But to Canadian consumers, the people who elect us to protect their best interests, all arguments end with these indisputable facts. Supermarket profits have increased almost three times as much as the rate of inflation. Further, wages haven't kept pace with inflation, so many Canadians are struggling to maintain their standard of living, and some have difficulty putting food on their tables."

Cleverly, the minister of finance took a sip of water to again let her audience mull over the implications. When she resumed, her tone hardened, she spoke more slowly, and she emphasized action words.

"Our prime minister *told* the Canadian people that we brought you here to *hold* you to account and *demand* action. We want to know what you will *do to bring down* prices, how you will *do* it, and when grocery prices will *stabilize* and *reduce* from their current unacceptable levels." The finance minister then turned to her cohort and motioned for him to continue their prepared opening statements.

He looked around the table while speaking, making direct eye contact with each CEO. "As my esteemed colleague said, our government expects clearly defined action from each of you and your industry collectively. We're not here to threaten you with specific government action. We just want to remind you that a failure to reach an acceptable understanding before we all leave here today will result in my department and others exploring all options available to us. Within weeks, we'll be ready to recommend specific government initiatives to achieve our goal of reducing inflation in supermarket prices."

The minister tapped his forefinger in the palm of his hand to emphasize the seriousness of each point he made, then turned back to the minister of finance once he finished.

"From each of you, we want to know your company's planned actions to help our government achieve this goal," she said. "May I suggest we work around the table alphabetically? I know you all have type A personalities and would each like to go first." She pointed to the CEO across from Suzanne, whose company name started with a C.

He nodded and thanked the ministers for the opportunity to discuss the issues everyone faced with increasing costs. Then, he promptly rejected the premise that food retailers were the cause of inflation. He pointed out that supermarkets produced nothing but bread in their in-store bakeries, and even there, all the ingredients were purchased from a myriad of suppliers.

Articulately, he pointed out that retail prices were increasing because farmers were forced to pay higher prices for everything, from the seeds they planted in the ground to the fuel for their tractors, and they demanded more for their crops. Food processors experienced inflation not only due to farmers' demands but also increased prices for the equipment they used to process and package their products.

Retailers paid higher prices not only because of the increases from farmers and processors but also because of the dramatically increased cost of transporting those products from where they were grown or processed to stores across the country. He ended his allotted ten minutes by reminding the ministers that their government's policy of setting a price on carbon also directly impacted the cost of every product supermarkets sold.

Both cabinet ministers frowned, but they avoided comment until they'd heard from everyone.

Each of the speakers who followed carried a similar message using different examples. One CEO claimed bottom-line supermarket profits were higher only because companies improved efficiencies with technology that allowed them to turn over inventories faster at the same gross margins.

Another argued that putting pressure on supermarkets without addressing costs throughout the entire distribution chain was discriminatory and would change nothing for Canadian consumers.

The cabinet ministers' poker faces revealed little about what impact, if any, the CEO presentations were having. When the finance minister pointed to Suzanne, she leaned forward in her chair and turned to face the government officials.

"First, let me emphasize my agreement with the comments of those who spoke before me. You're targeting the wrong people. What do I mean by that? Let me use as an example the months-long war Multima waged with Snackco last year. May I remind you that we fought a major price increase demanded by Snackco, and they refused to sell us any products? Our shelves that should have displayed their snacks and soft drinks sat empty for weeks, costing us millions of dollars in lost sales. We had to eventually give up our battle and accept their higher prices because some customers abandoned our store to shop at competitors just to be able to buy Snackco products at higher prices!"

Suzanne let her tone of disbelief hang in the air for a moment.

"Supermarkets' prices are driven by our suppliers. We take the price they charge us and mark up those prices by long-established percentages, letting the marketplace decide whether customers choose to buy the higher-priced goods or not. If customers don't buy, we don't order more from the supplier. If we don't order, suppliers usually reduce their prices to incent us to buy more. During this inflation cycle, some suppliers are ignoring customer demand and keeping their prices higher no matter what."

Again, she paused to give the ministers time to process that unusual trend. When she resumed, she lowered her tone a notch, leaned further toward the officials and made penetrating eye contact with the minister of finance.

"I started by telling you that you're accusing the wrong parties. I'll finish by reminding you what I told attendees at last year's American Grocery Association meeting. The real culprit in the supply chain is organized crime. Sophisticated and powerful entities are buying out individual, private farmers in entire geographic areas and for many types of products. They've bought up meat-packing plants and fruit processors. Our security department at Multima thinks organized gangs have penetrated—and now also control—a significant chunk of the trucking industry."

She took another breath, then shifted her gaze to the minister of innovation. When their eyes met, Suzanne took one last plunge for the team.

"Respectfully, ministers, our supermarkets might be easy, high-profile targets, ripe for attack from your government and some of our customers. You may be able to browbeat us to help you in the polls with measures that provide temporary relief. But if you're serious about defending the integrity of the Canadian food industry, you should call the Royal Canadian Mounted Police and demand they investigate the flood of recent business acquisitions and find out who ultimately owns hundreds of numbered companies that are buying them up. We can only keep food prices realistic for Canadian customers if you address that real and fundamental crisis."

Neither minister offered the courtesy of a nod, a hint of understanding, or agreement with Suzanne's plea. Instead, the minister of finance pointed to a CEO on the other side of the table to go next.

With a shrug of her shoulders and a shake of her head, Suzanne wordlessly showed her disdain for the process and crossed her arms defiantly across her chest. The minister of finance caught the movement from the corner of her eye and frowned before she focused on the fifth CEO's comments.

The charade continued for another few minutes until all the CEOs had shared their views. The minister of finance tried to demonstrate that she had been listening by asking follow-up questions from notes she'd made. Her tone remained respectful, but it became clear that nothing the CEOs said had swayed her position. The minister of innovation didn't bother to ask any questions and even seemed bored with the process at times.

After almost two hours of unproductive dialogue, the minister of finance finally issued an ultimatum. "We're putting you on notice. By Thanksgiving—and that's Canadian Thanksgiving, by the way—we must see the increases in food prices in your stores stop. We understand that legally you can't collude about how you'll stop the inflation. That would be anti-competitive behavior. But we demand that each of you provide details on how your stores will accomplish that goal by Thanksgiving or we'll start drafting tax legislation to recover for the people of Canada those excessive profits earned by your corporations."

The minister of finance wagged her finger, as a teacher might scold a naughty child. She paused only long enough to emphasize the gravity of the situation.

"Please understand that this action is taken at the direction of the prime minister's office. It's non-negotiable. It's serious. Will we have your compliance?"

Suzanne and the other CEOs nodded without enthusiasm. The ministers stood up simultaneously and walked around the table, shaking hands in farewell with each CEO, with one perfunctory pump of the hand for each.

Government staff offered the CEOs two possible escapes. One was by the door they had entered to a hallway outside the room full of anxious media people. The other was a back door that led toward the parking lot and was not accessible to the probing reporters. Suzanne elected the rear door.

As she, Edward, and a half-dozen others followed the government escort toward the exit, they didn't speak. But outside, there was a torrent of foul language as each contingent shared its perspectives with nearby colleagues. None were happy.

Inside the limo Edward had reserved for the morning, they closed the window that blocked their conversation from the bodyguards up front as they motored back toward the airport.

Edward pulled out his phone and located the app formerly known as Twitter. He clicked a couple times on the phone's screen and brought up the volume on the speaker so they could listen to the minister of finance gloat to the media about their demands of the CEOs and the nasty consequences for any who failed to comply.

Suzanne shook her head, gritting her teeth. "The prime minister sang an entirely different tune back in 2020 when we agreed to move our global headquarters from the US to

Montreal, appeasing the French government when we bought Farefour Stores. Back then, he was like a puppy begging for a bone. Maybe it's time for another conversation."

Thirty-One

Muynak, Uzbekistan, Monday September 18, 2023

When Fidelia stopped running outside the back entrance of her compound, she leaned against the stone wall, huffing and puffing like an old man. It was her first run in almost six months. She felt some pain in her feet where bones had healed from the torture in Guantanamo, but cartilage and tendon damage couldn't be repaired. Still, she was satisfied with a slow, twenty-minute jog in the sandy desert surrounding her home.

The pain was tolerable as the sand provided enough cushion for the bottoms of her feet. The clear air and hot sun soothed her spirit as she ran, and now, as her heart rate slowed, she felt the familiar adrenaline rush athletes feel from physical accomplishment.

Her watch showed enough time to shower before an upcoming call with Klaudia, so she dashed inside the house and completed her mission. She slipped on a clean T-shirt just as the secure burner phone buzzed. Almost two weeks had elapsed since Fidelia sent away her German-Russian friend on her latest mission. There was no time for small talk.

"I have a nibble," Klaudia reported. "As we agreed, I tracked down Yuri Federov. He's as horny and clueless as ever. He bought the story. I think he also buys that I'm currently living in Spain. I used that burner phone Juan Suarez sent over with the Seville number from Telefónica. We've talked three times since, and he's warming up each time. He rambles on about never finding anyone as good as me. Talked about how lonely he is as a middle-aged bachelor. He's giving all the right signals."

"Good work. I never doubted the power of your charm." Fidelia drew heavily on her own reservoir of charisma to make the compliment sound genuine. "Have you made any progress on a personal meeting?"

"That might be a problem. Because of the war, even guys in Russia's secret service now have trouble traveling. Most

European countries have banned travel for known operatives like Federov. I planted a seed that we could meet up in Algeria or Morocco. Both are close to Spain. He hasn't agreed yet, but he might bite when he gets desperate enough."

"Is he still reporting to Boris Ivanov?"

"Yeah. Ivanov's still in Moscow. Fedorov's in St. Petersburg. But it seems they're still close, and Ivanov still has a direct line to the Kremlin."

It was only a nibble, as Klaudia correctly described it, but they had to start somewhere. There were other things they could do in the meantime.

"Let's relocate you. If you continue calling him from Germany, he'll eventually track you down and blow the Spanish cover. We need him to be convinced you're living in Spain to make the plan work. I'll get Suarez to find you an apartment there for the next few months."

Klaudia didn't object, so Fidelia gave a few more instructions. "If he agrees to meet, you'll probably only get one chance to lure him in. Get your teeth fixed as quickly as you can. Join a gym and get that body of yours in top shape. Spend a few dollars on a ravishing hairstyle, get a manicure and a facial, anything you think will increase your appeal, and play into his libido."

Again, Klaudia did not resist the orders. She probably already knew she needed some repairs.

"Last thing for today, find a way to get him talking to Ivanov about your ideas. Tell him you've got connections, not only for women but also some opportunities for cybercrime. See if he'll approach Ivanov about working outside the secret services, so they keep all the income. Maybe offer to do some work for them in Spain to get started. To make the grand scheme work, we need to ensnare them both."

"Yeah, I already planted the seed about cyber ransom. There was a long pause when I mentioned it, and he didn't show any enthusiasm for the idea. I'll keep working on it, though."

Good, she was coming around. Her show of initiative was encouraging. When Klaudia was totally committed to a project, no one was better. They'd need several weeks more plotting, enticing, and teasing before seasoned professionals like the two Russian agents might fall into her trap.

It was still too early to plan with certainty, but Fidelia remained convinced the two selfish bastards would eventually succumb to greed. She knew she held a winning hand. Both women were confident they'd take the bait when they saw a clear path to recover the five hundred million dollars snatched from Russian Mafia bank accounts on Monday, March 16, 2020.

It was a date the Russian mob remembered as clearly as Americans recalled 9-11. And if they saw a way to recover it without the knowledge of their superiors, their hunger might become even more intense.

Thirty-Two
San Francisco, California, Monday September 25, 2023

In just a few days, they would spend their last night together for a while. Gordon processed that thought with mixed emotions. While he would surely miss the nights of passion in bed, a part of him begged for less drama and upheaval in his life. Time apart might also give him a chance to think more—and more clearly. For the past few months, his brain seemed to have operated in a fog, something like the feeling COVID survivors described: thinking less clearly, having problems remembering things, and feeling sluggish at times.

Worse, he wasn't living the faith he'd pursued his entire life, and it left a void he could neither explain nor accept. Prayer had become rare, and Amber never let him speak about his religion or faith. She didn't grasp the concept of God.

Amber remained a puzzling juggernaut. She'd shed a few tears when he first tested Suzanne's suggestion that she move to the West Coast to be closer to Jeffersons Stores' primary operations. The net result seemed more like sniffles of uncertainty than an outpouring of grief or anger. Strangely, minutes after she went out for a walk to think it all through, she returned and said she accepted the suggestion. "When should I make the move?"

Something else seemed out of place. Within a couple hours of that brief awkward discussion, she'd opened a bottle of wine, poured a glass for each of them, and seduced him again as skillfully and fervidly as she had that first time months earlier. What had shifted her mood from disappointment to sexual hunger in such a short time?

The following few days were a whirlwind. They seemed to be constantly dodging potential bullets. Amber first suggested Gordon sublet her apartment so he'd have a place to live and free the company of her lease obligations. A reasonable idea until it occurred to Gordon that to make that switch, they'd have to get HR involved. Multima's human resources team at headquarters had negotiated the lease for Amber as an expat.

How could Amber now involve HR without divulging that Gordon needed a place to live because his wife threw him out and was seeking a divorce?

Gordon was forced to confess his marital situation to his executive assistant so she could help him find a place to live quickly. She promised she wouldn't divulge anything to anyone but also said she'd already suspected he was experiencing problems at home. Others in the office might share those suspicions.

Suzanne first seemed surprised when Gordon told her—only a few days after their initial conversation—that he accepted her suggestion and that Amber was prepared to make the move west.

"She offered no resistance?" Suzanne had asked.

What did you expect?

Cautiously, he said, "Amber seemed a bit annoyed about uprooting and relocating so soon after moving from Shanghai, but she's loyal. After she thought about it for a bit, she said if we wanted her to move, she'd do it."

"No bonuses or salary adjustment?" Suzanne had asked to be certain. He'd confirmed that was the case.

Gordon's executive assistant came through with a new place for him to live, although he hadn't seen it yet. He'd take possession on October 1, so working from California for a few days made sense. He'd help Amber settle in at the former Jeffersons Stores headquarters and get to know the management team there better.

Amber had commandeered a spare conference room, and they sat across from each other at one end of the table with laptops, phones and a pile of reports to wade through.

Once settled, Gordon began responding to the messages left on his voice mail. When he looked around after a while, he realized he was alone in the room, then pushed through the queue of calls needing his attention until he emptied his voice mailbox. The entire morning had evaporated, but that was okay. It was already mid-afternoon back in Atlanta, and colleagues across the country would soon start winding down their activities in the office for the day. For a company president, one advantage of working from the West Coast was the ability to cram more into the day with an early start.

He decided not to wait for Amber's return and set out to poke around the office area. Gordon didn't know most of the employees in the newly acquired location, so he wandered about saying hello, introducing himself to people sitting in cubicles or offices, and then asking them about their jobs. What did they do for Jeffersons? How did they enjoy working here? What did they like about the company? What might they like to change if they could?

With his contagious smile, casual demeanor, and genuine interest in listening to what people said, Gordon quickly engaged with several employees of different ages, experience levels and expertise. Before he realized it, three hours had passed, and he was hungry.

He asked the last person he spoke with where he could find the company cafeteria, and she offered to show him the way. She was on the way there herself.

They chatted as they waited for an elevator and again during the climb to the top floor of the building, where Gordon discovered a well-appointed dining area with a magnificent view of San Francisco Bay. He thanked the woman for her help, wandered over to large floor-to-ceiling windows, and admired the view. From a corner near that window, Amber caught his eye and waved for him to come over.

She introduced Harold Lemington, vice president of store operations in the Jeffersons hierarchy. He had some information to share. Despite a growling stomach, Gordon pulled up a cafeteria chair and joined their conversation.

"Harold thinks we need to communicate our strategies and intentions better." Amber laughed as she started the conversation and playfully tapped Harold's forearm to put him at ease. "He thinks you should do a town hall while you're out here and explain what's happening."

The Jeffersons' executive grinned tentatively, unsure how warmly his new senior managers might welcome constructive input. "There are a lot of rumors out in the stores. People are talking about layoffs and headcount reductions. Some even worry that Multima might close unproductive stores."

"What's causing those rumors and concerns, do you think?" Gordon asked.

For the next hour, Harold inundated them with unpopular policies, management actions, and cases when Multima had failed to act. He explained that the new owner needed to articulate better the company's business philosophy, values, and guiding principles. To him that was a more useful strategy than just ordering cuts in spending, store operating hours, and employee hours. Gordon and Amber listened without interrupting him, keenly interested in his perspective.

When the man ran out of things to say, Gordon was the first to speak. "Thanks, Harold. Amber and I value your input—the criticisms and the suggestions. Leave it with us."

Back in the conference room, carrying two of the scarce sandwiches still on display in the cafeteria and a bottle of water each, Gordon asked for Amber's impressions of their impromptu meeting. She addressed each of Harold's points from memory, agreeing with some, questioning others, and adding context to a few. Gordon detected a hint of defensiveness or uncertainty from Amber for the first time.

He chose to treat the exercise as a learning moment. They dissected the issues, discussed how they might address weaknesses, and how problems should be prioritized. Amber demonstrated her leadership skills by absorbing, analyzing, and seeking solutions for each issue. Gordon smiled in satisfaction as she summed up her understanding.

"I've got lots to work on in the coming months. Clearly, interacting with Americans is different from Asians. I see that I need to seek more input and listen better before we implement new procedures rather than expecting people to follow directives from the top down. And I'll do that. But I also think it would be helpful if you could do a town hall for all the store employees as you did in the spring for the technology and finance teams."

For the remainder of that week, Gordon and Amber met with each of the Jeffersons Stores executives in San Francisco, listening as they had with Harold Lemington. At the end of each day, they chose a different San Francisco restaurant for quiet meals, in darkened corners. There, they compared notes and discussed various options while enjoying excellent cuisine and fine California wines.

Each night, they returned to Gordon's suite at the Hotel

Via. For the sake of appearances, they had booked and paid for a separate room for Amber. Neither expected her to use it any time before he departed for Atlanta on Saturday. Instead, each night, they enjoyed wild romps on the sofa in his suite's living area or in the king-size bed, depending on their urgency. Gordon sensed their mutual sexual desperation forewarned how challenging their geographic separation might become.

On his last day in California, after hours of consultation with the management team in San Francisco and Edward Hadley's team in Montreal, Amber and Gordon performed for the Zoom camera. She started the dialogue with a *mea culpa* about her communication shortcomings in the prior months and a resolution to do better in the future. She asked for everyone's support to help her build a robust, vibrant and profitable part of Multima Supermarkets. Then she passed it to him.

Prepared well by Hadley's communication specialists, Gordon felt comfortable carrying a positive message for the future. He revealed that Jeffersons stores would soon carry new signage and become full-fledged members of the Multima family of supermarkets. He talked about a new advertising campaign that would start even before the signs began appearing. Finally, he reassured employees no store closures were planned. Indeed, before Thanksgiving, he expected to announce several new locations that would be opening in 2024.

Where employees gathered in groups to view the town hall, he saw applause as he built toward a climax; individuals also smiled broadly. To cap it off, he announced that every store employee would receive a one-time bonus equivalent to one week's earnings to welcome them to Multima. Arms raised in cheers, high-fives were shared, and a few celebrated with happy dances.

After the event, Gordon, Amber, and her direct reports in San Francisco all enjoyed a sumptuous dinner at Saison, one of the city's most expensive restaurants, to celebrate the town hall and a new beginning. All agreed they should have done this months before, but they'd make the most of the excitement now, and try to turn Jeffersons Stores into Multima Supermarkets' best-performing region.

Back at their hotel, Amber wanted him immediately. She started in the elevator with deep, passionate kisses, pulling him close with one arm and unbuttoning his shirt with the other. Once they reached the suite, they undressed each other as though it was their first time. When both had climaxed and lay holding each other in their arms for several minutes, Gordon thought he detected a sniffle.

He pushed away from Amber and saw tears dribbling slowly down her cheeks. When they made eye contact, she used a finger to wipe away the tears and looked downward again before she started sobbing. Tomorrow morning, they would separate for at least a few weeks, maybe longer.

He supposed she'd miss all this, but he asked the question anyway. "Why are you crying, Amber?"

The room was silent, with only her faint sobs. After their rush of passion, the bedsheets felt warm and slightly damp in spots. A grandfather clock in the living area ticked at an even pace, while light from a bedside lamp at its lowest setting cast a long shadow across her gorgeous face, shimmering across her rumpled jet-black hair, with a few stray locks sensuously blocking the corner of her left eye.

Her lips parted to speak, but nothing came out the first time. She audibly sucked in another breath, deeper this time, then swept the stray hair out of her eyes to probe deeply into Gordon's.

"I think I'm pregnant." She searched his eyes and face for a reaction. "I took a Clearblue test yesterday. It was positive."

Thirty-Three

Montreal, Quebec, Wednesday October 4, 2023

They had two days left to comply with the Canadian government's deadline. Suzanne had given it her best shot at the meeting with the cabinet ministers. She'd tried again with the prime minister, but couldn't speak with him directly. Instead, she pled their position on rising prices with his chief of staff, who listened politely and then committed to nothing.

Edward Hadley reported all the other summoned CEOs intended to satisfy the cabinet ministers' orders. Two had already submitted their confidential undertakings to help stabilize food prices. Not surprisingly, neither would divulge any aspect of their official responses for competitive reasons.

All the key players sat around the huge, polished mahogany table in Multima headquarters' conference room. She'd asked Gordon to fly in from Atlanta that morning, and he brought a half dozen of his direct reports. Curiously, Amber Chan wasn't among them. Perhaps it wasn't crucial for the person in charge of converting Jeffersons Stores to Multima Stores to be there. That new division operated only in the Southwest US, but she made a mental note to check Gordon's reasoning during a break.

Suzanne asked Multima Supermarkets' Canadian president, Bob McKenzie, to outline his recommendations. He turned on a projector with a handheld device and looked toward a PowerPoint image forming on the screen at the end of the table opposite her armchair.

"We've developed a three-point strategy to satisfy the government demands." He pressed a button, and a new slide popped up to emphasize his message. "First, for all Multima Mom's Picks branded products, we'll freeze the current prices until the end of January. We already have inventory for almost ninety days in the stores or regional warehouses. If we run short and need to order, we'll tell the supplier we need to have the same prices, or there's no additional order. In a worst case, we'll forego some revenue in January, but our buyers think most suppliers will be sensitive to the spot we're in with the government and maintain current pricing for us."

He paused to look around the room for any questions. There were none, so he popped up another slide.

"Our second strategy is to gain market share from our competitors. Our buyers have negotiated special purchase prices for one-week promotions with major brands, meat suppliers, and produce importers. We'll feature those in all our usual flyers and promotions. These promos will lower our gross margins, but we expect to offset fewer margin dollars with greater sales revenues. Our analysts project that bottom-line profits will stay constant. Still, there is always a risk that we over-estimate demand and are stuck with some inventory to sell later or discount for quick sale in the case of perishables."

McKenzie checked the room with his eyes to see if everyone was with him so far. There were no questions, so he continued his presentation.

"Our third strategy will cost us some money. We'll sacrifice some profit in the short term, but we treat this profit erosion as an investment. We're going to use Multima More as a strategic weapon. First, we'll make the government happy by increasing the number of Multima Points we award buyers' purchases. Those points effectively reduce the prices for buyers who shop strategically and redeem their accumulated points. The win for us will be using those incentive points to sell slower-moving and higher-margin products. Plus, we can use the cash those purchases generate until customers redeem their points and we take a hit on our revenue and margins."

He appeared less confident about the strength of that argument. His tone waffled slightly, and his pause implied a brief reality check. About to challenge the premise, Suzanne shifted in her chair but stopped at the last moment, deciding to wait until he finished.

"I know there are risks with our third strategy, and I was reluctant to pursue it until we got our colleagues at Financial Services involved. They saw our idea as a big win for their business. Why? If customers pay for their groceries with Multima More credit cards, they earn even more Multima More points, further reducing their purchase costs. So,

Financial Services will run in-store promotions, encouraging the sixty percent of our customers who don't already use our branded credit card to apply for one. Financial Services have great data on customer payment habits and the profits they earn on unpaid balances. We're confident their increased profits, resulting from our food promotions, will more than offset any profit erosion from Supermarkets' pricing on groceries."

Suzanne shifted her attention toward Natalia Tenaz, president of Multima Financial Services. That explained why Gordon Goodfellow had invited her to fly in from Chicago.

She was ready to play her role. "Yeah. We support this initiative one hundred percent. First, if we get only twenty percent of Jeffersons Stores customers to sign up, our finance volume increases by a third next year. If we also increase our share of Multima Supermarkets customers by only five percent, and their payment habits are like our current base, we'll add another hundred million to our bottom line annually without significant increases in overhead. Plus, we're rolling out a premium version, and I think the timing is perfect for converting lots of existing card customers to the premium card, where cardholders pay a fee that covers all our overhead costs. We think it's a win for customers, Supermarkets, and Financial Services."

Natalia's answer was persuasive, accented by a broad smile and high-energy tone. Suzanne shifted her attention to Pierre Cabot. "I'm onside, too," he said. "My team ran the numbers. Our estimates took a more conservative outlook on both revenue and expenses, and we'll maintain current bottom lines in a worst-case scenario. There's potential for about ten percent upside over two years."

Suzanne turned in the other direction toward Alberto Ferer, her chief legal counsel.

He nodded. "From a legal perspective, we're satisfying the Canadian government's demand if we share these strategies with them by Friday. If you approve the plans today, I'd like to have a few hours to review the draft of the letter Edward will prepare for your signature. Otherwise, I see no problems."

"Okay, let's run with it," Suzanne said. "Edward, can you have something ready for Alberto to review tomorrow morning and for me to sign by noon? I'd like to have it there one day before the deadline."

She waited for Hadley and Ferer to nod their understanding, then took a deep breath.

"It's good we handled that part of the meeting quickly. Thanks, everyone, for your excellent preparation. Now, let's deal with that other deadline. Where are we on the computer systems upgrade and overhaul to integrate the Jeffersons Stores business? That deadline is about three weeks away, right?"

She turned toward Marcel Dubois, her chief technology officer.

He wasn't smiling. "We can't make the deadline. Period. Problems developed this week that will require at least thirty days to repair. We have to fix those problems first, then we'll need another thirty days to complete everything. Completion is looking closer to Christmas than Halloween."

Suzanne took in his grim expression, then asked for more.

Dubois obliged. "Our routine scan of completed code discovered almost a dozen errors. Each error allowed penetration of the system in multiple ways. The coding was so poor that it would have been like leaving doors open and unlocked in twelve different spaces. Unsophisticated intruders could have easily penetrated our entire system. We have no choice. We have to rebuild those walls from scratch."

Suzanne shifted to Gordon Goodfellow.

He squirmed in his chair before he spoke. "I just learned about this yesterday. Marcel told me about the issue and said he'd update us this morning after they had time to complete their analysis. I understand we had some communication problems and found it necessary to terminate a couple employees." He looked at Marcel as he finished his sentence.

"Yeah. Two software engineers brought on board while Amber Chan led the project. They're Chinese university graduates and everyone thought they were brilliant at writing code. Unbelievably fast with elevated analysis skills. When we confronted each of them, they claimed a misunderstanding in translation from English to Chinese. They misunderstood the instructions. I knew that kind of misinterpretation was impossible, so I contacted Nicole Gagnon in HR immediately.

We terminated their contracts yesterday."

"Was this sabotage?" Suzanne was incredulous, and her tone reflected impatience and suppressed anger. She focused her eyes on her technology chief.

"Nicole and I discussed that at length," Marcel said. "She wondered if we should bring in Serge's people to investigate, but I didn't think we'd gain much by doing that. All our security people could conclude—with absolute certainty—was that potential threats existed. If the engineers' position is that they made those mistakes through a language misunderstanding, I don't know how we could prove otherwise."

"First of all, I want Serge notified and involved in any such instances in the future." Suzanne continued to look directly at Dubois. "Your assessment and conclusions may be entirely correct, but I also want to hear Serge say it. Please get with him as soon as we finish this meeting."

They discussed the computer systems issues for several minutes longer. Suzanne and Gordon both questioned the chief technology officer to learn if more resources could help or if greater employee incentives might speed up the process. When Marcel Dubois had convinced her that he'd explored all those avenues and determined his latest estimate was the best possible, she dismissed him from the meeting to focus on that critical project.

Her attention turned to Gordon Goodfellow. "How are you going to manage the timing of the planned Jeffersons Stores integration, the advertising and marketing campaigns planned for Thanksgiving, and our employees' expectations for full integration with Multima as you promised them last month?"

"You're right. We'll have to go back to square one on all those issues. I don't have immediate answers for you, but the team and I will start addressing them as we fly back to Atlanta today. I expect some of the advertising can be modified or delayed. I doubt we can do much about the signage installations, but we'll check what might be possible. Can I get back to you next week?"

Suzanne let him save face in front of his direct reports.

"A week Friday, I have a meeting with the Board. I'll need your revised strategy to review and approve before I meet with them." There was no need to explain the gravity of reporting this setback to the board of directors. She stood up to signal the end of the meeting and threw out one last comment. "Gordon, can you come to my office with me for a moment before you leave? I have something I'd like to discuss with you privately."

Thirty-Four

Seville, Spain, Friday October 13, 2023

Fidelia and her personal assistant, Mia Vasquez, had just arrived in Spain. While Mia attended to her ever-growing list of tasks, Fidelia wandered around the apartment her country boss, Juan Suarez, had loaned to Klaudia Schäffer. She admired the luxurious suite and wouldn't mind staying there a while herself.

It was located on the third floor of a recently renovated building in the heart of the old town of Seville. Although Suarez kept the exterior appearance conservative to fit comfortably with the *Mudéjar* architecture typical in the historic city, he spared no expense with the luxury inside.

The living area contained two large navy-blue sofas, wrapping the room in opposite directions, with four end tables, modern lamps and subdued lighting. A formal dining room, with eight chairs and a polished oak finish, filled the space between the living area and kitchen. That kitchen could easily be featured in *Mi Casa* magazine as an example of all the latest home appliances, with the trendiest colors and most modern technology. Suarez probably spent more on the apartment's kitchen than many people pay for a modest home.

Off to one side, she spotted two bedrooms, but Fidelia didn't bother checking them out. Given the attention paid to the rest of the apartment, she had no doubt the guest room she'd use for the next few nights would be more than adequate for a good sleep.

She first thought it curious that Suarez chose Seville as the location to house Klaudia for their project with the Russian Mafia. Neither of the two Russians targeted would be welcome in any European country, so they'd already established that any meeting would occur in Morocco or Algeria. Both countries were still friendly with Russia and regularly welcomed highly placed officials from the country's Federal Secret Service, better known as the FSB.

Fidelia first thought a spot close to Gibraltar would be

best. After all, it's less than ten miles across the Strait of Gibraltar, probably less than an hour in a yacht. Even Malaga or Marbella seemed more logical.

Juan Suarez patiently explained why he chose the town of his birth. "With all the illegal immigrants trying to enter Europe right now, the southern coast of Spain is swarming with government authorities. Every branch of government, policing, and defense is represented, including hundreds working undercover. Even though Klaudia looks European, and carries an EU passport, curious minds might be drawn to a single, white northern European woman who's hanging around for an extended period. People with that profile are often sympathetic to illegal immigrants and come here to assist in moving those people farther north."

It made sense. Seville was only a two-hour drive or a half-hour helicopter trip from the coast. Besides, it was where he also housed his most elite protectors and enforcers. More than a dozen shared four separate apartments below Klaudia's palatial temporary residence on the third floor.

Fidelia asked Suarez to send one of his people to make coffee and asked everyone to sit around the large dining room table. In addition to Suarez, Estavao Sereno from Portugal and Antonio Verlusconi from Italy had flown in that morning. Pierre Boivin from France joined on a secure burner phone, but his favorite woman, Nadine Violette, had joined them around the table. She, too, had a role to play in the charade.

Before coffee arrived, Fidelia asked Klaudia to bring them up to date.

"Yuri Federov will come alone with five women. He says that, but I know he never travels without protection. Through an old friend, I learned he now usually travels with two former FSB companions. They'll all be heavily armed, and they've all been trained in the martial arts. He'll fly on an FSB jet from St. Petersburg to Chisinau Airport in Moldova. That's where he'll pick up the women. They're eastern Romanians, all involuntary. From Moldova, they'll fly to Rabat, Morocco, arriving shortly after midnight. We'll need to exchange the money for the women on the tarmac at the airport." Klaudia noticed the coffee had arrived and paused while a female bodyguard distributed cups from a tray.

Fidelia used the break to ask a question. "How many hours is he planning to stay in Rabat?"

"He told me he was staying only one night. That's why we have to meet on October 20. But that's a Friday. If the horny bastard hasn't changed his ways, my guess is he'll stretch it out over the weekend, finding different local women each night," Klaudia said.

"So, when you arrive in Rabat, you go to the FSB apartment to meet Federov once he arrives. At the airport, we give him a hundred thousand US dollars, and then we transfer the women from the FSB jet to mine. Nadine takes charge of the women with the five guys provided by Suarez to ensure they all get to Spain okay." Fidelia checked her notes as she spoke. "Then Federov meets you at the apartment, and Pierre Boivin's guys take over from there."

The voice of her French country boss boomed from the phone. "We've got a half-dozen good people on the ground in Rabat. They should be able to plant microphones and cameras where Klaudia and Federov will stay. Did he give you the apartment number yet?"

"Yes, and a code to enter when I arrive. He made it clear he wanted me completely undressed to welcome him when he stepped through the door." Klaudia groaned.

"Give me all the address details, including the code. My people won't use that code to plant their tools. The lock is probably monitored. They have other means to get in." From his tone on the burner phone, Fidelia could picture him confidently crossing his arms with a satisfied grin.

"Carry on, Klaudia. Tell everyone what you plan to accomplish," Fidelia said.

"He'll probably arrive with an erection and expect me to play with him and let him fuck me until he's satisfied. He plays rough, very rough. There's nothing I fear more about this mission than those first few minutes after he arrives."

"So you think he's more interested in sex than talking about the hundred women you're offering to buy?" It was Boivin from France again.

"No doubt about it," Klaudia replied. "The money is far more important to Ivanov. Federov is mentally unsound. Stupid. And motivated only by cruel, dominant sex. It's Ivanov who's motivated by money and power. That's why we need to be sure Ivanov learns about our planned meeting after Federov leaves Russia and before he arrives in Morocco."

"Timing is everything here." Fidelia looked around the table to underscore her point. "We can't allow anything to happen to either Klaudia or Nadine, understand?"

Both Suarez and Sereno nodded wordlessly. Both got the message. Now, the details.

"Pierre, tell me all about your guys in Morocco. Why should we trust them? How will they get inside to plant the devices? How will they overtake the FSB protection? And how will we get Klaudia back out of there?"

Thirty-Five

Atlanta, Georgia, Friday October 13, 2023

It had been three months of hell. Of course, Gordon had experienced moments of absolute delight. Those times with Amber had introduced him to an entirely different world. Despite marriage to a beautiful—some would say gorgeous—wife for twenty-five years, he'd never experienced the same passion for sex with Priscilla that he found with Amber.

But apart from the sensational rollicks in bed, Gordon's life invited disaster after disaster. So far, none had proved fatal, but he was walking a fine line. Once he crossed that line, who knew where he might end up?

He was a believer. His faith in God was absolute, and his evangelical upbringing taught him that his behavior over the past months had been sinful. Gordon had begged forgiveness from the Lord several times, but recently, even that proved less than satisfying. He no longer attended services at his house of worship; his soon-to-be ex-wife would be there with their two kids, and he had no idea how to behave.

Priscilla refused to talk with him, ignored his calls and texts, and had poisoned the children's outlook toward him. Although she allowed the kids to speak with him when he called, most of their conversations consisted of monosyllabic responses to his questions. He no longer slept well, wasn't eating properly, and worry lines on his face etched deeper.

He hadn't seen Amber since she dropped the bomb about her pregnancy almost three weeks earlier. They'd talked about it every night on FaceTime, and he'd taken pains to assure her of his support and enthusiastic welcome of their coming child. So, it came as an unsettling shock when she casually told him yesterday that she wouldn't fly in for the weekend like they'd planned. Her doctor had recommended no air travel for a week or two after the abortion.

Abortion! That contradicted everything he'd been taught about the sanctity of life and God's will. That Amber could take such action without his agreement—without consultation, even—grated far more than he expected. It caused his thoughts to wander in a way he never foresaw. How well did he know this woman? How much more should he know? Was there a chance she really was working for other interests, as Serge Boisvert believed? How could all of this affect his life and career?

Hesitantly, he reached for his phone and pressed the number for Reverend Wally Aposeur, minister of the Evangelical Church of God. While he waited for someone to answer, he thought about the pastor, probably preparing his sermon for Sunday's services. He might be busy or unwilling to meet. Then his thoughts drifted to the thousands of dollars Gordon contributed to the church with his weekly tithes, automatic deductions from his bank account for the past twenty years that continued to this day.

The reverend picked up the call on the seventh ring, breathing heavily. "Sorry for the delay in responding. I'm out for my daily jog. It took me a few seconds to get the phone out of my pouch."

Gordon used the time he guessed the minister might need to get his breathing under control for a greeting and small talk.

When he was ready, the reverend signaled it with a question. "I'd been hoping you'd call, Gordon. Priscilla shared your marital challenges with me, and I've been coaching her through the trauma. How can I help you?" His tone was non-committal, neither sympathetic nor hostile.

"I need to talk, Reverend. I've tried prayer, and it hasn't helped. I'd like to ask for an hour of your time. Could tomorrow work?" He hoped he'd struck a balance in his tone—not desperate, but anxious. He was relieved when the minister replied.

"Saturday's a busy day for me. You know I have my sermon to prepare for the flock on Sunday. But I hear your concern. If you can join me in the pastor's study at eight tomorrow morning, I'll be happy to meet with you."

Gordon slept even less that Friday night and arrived at the church well before the agreed-upon time. He thought again about Amber, her aborting his child, and the mess he was in with Multima Corporation should Suzanne learn about his stupidity and sinfulness over the past months. By the time he left his car and knocked on the outside door to the pastor's study, he felt tears welling in his eyes.

"Come in," the pastor called out. The reverend extended his right hand to shake and wrapped his other arm around Gordon's back with a pat of assurance. "Let's sit over there on the sofa, and you tell me all about it."

Gordon breathed deeply to choke off tears continuing to well and spilled the entire story. Without all the racy details, he confessed to his marital infidelity with Amber, careful not to use her name. He explained how this lapse in judgment violated Multima's policy. He explained Serge's suspicion that Amber might somehow be wrapped up in organized crime targeting his company's computer systems. Nothing was out of bounds except her name.

The pastor listened intently, his head tilted first to the left, then the right, nodding where appropriate. His eyes conveyed sympathy, not blame. The only signal of judgment Gordon could detect was the pastor's tendency to blink every time a new sin, variance from company policy, or lapse in judgment was revealed. He maintained his calm demeanor until Gordon dropped the bombshell.

"Things hit rock bottom a few days ago as I prepared to leave her in San Francisco and return home. Out of the blue, this woman"—his new term for Amber instead of her name—"without any warning, announced she was pregnant. I offered her all my support, financially and morally. We talked about it every day for a week until she finally confessed that she had an abortion and wanted to move on."

The pastor reached across and patted Gordon's knee twice, clasped his hand tightly, and said they should pray together for God's wisdom and forgiveness. They both closed their eyes and respectfully lowered their heads.

"Oh, mighty Lord, together we beseech you to have mercy on Gordon's soul, to forgive his repeated transgressions of your will and his failures to resist earthly temptations. We beg you to give us the wisdom and strength to move on from this horrible disobedience of your laws and to make right the grievous harm he has caused his wonderful wife and loving family. In thy name, we thank you for your love, patience, understanding and guidance, and in the name of thy only holy son, Jesus. Amen."

The pastor continued to grasp Gordon's hand for a moment before raising his head and gazing into Gordon's eyes for a long, penetrating moment. Then he slowly drew his hand away, sat more upright and asked, "How much does your CEO know?"

Gordon told him about Serge and his investigations. He shared bits of the conversation they'd had when they decided to move Amber away from the computer systems project. He pointed out that Suzanne suggested they move the woman to San Francisco to be closer to Jeffersons Stores' operations. He reminded the pastor that Suzanne was the woman he had reported to directly for more than a decade, first when she ran Multima Supermarkets and then when she promoted him to his current role after she became CEO.

"I expect Suzanne already knows more than you might think. If she's as perceptive as you say and has navigated the treacherous cliffs and precipices of corporate life to reach the summit, at the very least, she must have strong suspicions. You'll have to make the risk calculation for yourself. But, to clear your conscience, you must do what's right. That means coming to terms with your poor judgment, recent behavior and violation of company policies."

Gordon listened impassively, then took a moment to weigh the minister's message.

The office was virtually silent. A bird chirped outside an open window, letting in enough air for the metal slats of partially drawn venetian blinds to tinkle in harmony. Stacks of paper, held down by a paperweight on a desk across from the leather sofa, rustled slightly from the incoming breeze. And the bright green eyes of a black kitten peeked out at Gordon from below the desk as though intrigued by his dilemma.

The pastor shuffled his position on the sofa, waiting for a response.

Gordon stood up, prompting the minister to rise as well. "I'll think about it, Reverend. I'll think about it."

He took the longest route home he could imagine, driving down I-75 to I-20, then back up I-285 to his new apartment in Riverside. There, he sat in the parking lot, still thinking, until the interior of his car became too hot and stuffy. Finally, he walked into his apartment, grabbed a bottle of water from the fridge, and plunked down on a chair at the kitchen table. He glanced at his watch and decided mid-morning on a Saturday would be an alright time to call her. With a decisive press on the phone screen where her private number was displayed, Gordon waited for Suzanne to answer.

The greetings and pleasantries lasted only a moment. He wanted to give her just enough time to absorb the surprise of an unplanned call. Then he plunged into his purpose before losing his nerve.

"Suzanne, I'm afraid I have some confessions to make."

Thirty-Six

Montreal, Quebec, Saturday October 14, 2023

The surprise phone call caught them enjoying a second cup of coffee after finishing a delicious breakfast of crepes with authentic Quebec maple syrup, the first they had tasted since the previous spring harvest.

As soon as she heard the word "confessions," Suzanne caught Serge's eye with an upraised finger and then quickly activated the speaker. "Serge is with me. I put the phone on speaker."

She set the phone in the middle of the table so they could both hear clearly. They leaned in, heads down and shoulders hunched forward, intent on absorbing every word and nuance.

Serge's posture stiffened the moment Gordon confessed to a relationship with Amber. Her lover's fingers tapped on the tabletop when her president of Supermarkets acknowledged that Priscilla had initiated divorce proceedings, and their case would soon be before the courts. A signal his impatience was growing, Serge's frown deepened further when Gordon revealed the news that Amber had become pregnant and then had an abortion.

Neither commented as Gordon walked them through the alarming confirmation of Serge's suspicions about their relationship, but nothing about her chief of security's demeanor suggested a coming "I told you so." Still, Suzanne felt the weight of her inaction after Serge first alerted her to the likely scenario.

When Gordon apparently thought he had shared enough, Suzanne looked across the table at Serge. He continued to gaze downward. She took a deep breath, cleared her throat, and gripped her hands tightly in her lap. She forced her tone to remain calm though grave.

"That's quite a bundle of information you've unloaded on us this morning. What prompted you to make this confession. And why now?"

"I've felt awful for weeks, even months. You know I'm a

Christian. It's been like hell for me knowing that I've sinned, letting you down, letting my family down, betraying everything I believe in." His voice broke, and he took a moment to regain his composure.

"This morning, I met with my pastor. I confessed everything to him. We talked it over and prayed about it. He persuaded me that I should also confess to you. I know I've violated company policies. I realize I've breached the trust and confidence you've shown me for more than a decade. I am truly sorry for what I've done, and I apologize unequivocally." His voice broke again.

She waited a moment to see if there was more. Satisfied that Gordon had revealed all he was prepared to share that day, she took another moment to let him squirm in discomfort while she collected her thoughts and chose her words.

"To say I'm disappointed with these revelations is an understatement. You'll face repercussions for your behavior and serious lapses in judgment. I'm going to take some time to decide how serious those consequences will be. I suggest you take Monday and Tuesday off as personal days. Stay home. Don't travel, delegate any scheduled meetings to a subordinate ... and don't talk about any of this with anyone anymore, including your pastor."

Gordon acknowledged her directive, apologized again and meekly left the line.

Suzanne looked at Serge again. This time, she waited until his head lifted and met her eyes. He shrugged, shook his head and grimaced. She continued to wait.

Finally, he spoke. "I realize you're in the worst position imaginable. He's a protégé. You groomed him. He runs your most important business division. Setting aside these past few months, he's done an astounding job, making billions for the company and for you. But any one of his stupid actions, lapses in judgment, and violations of company policies is easily reason for immediate termination from the company."

Serge paused, took another sip of his coffee, and peered over the cup for a moment before continuing.

"I'm not going to try to influence your decision except to say this. You know he's been duped. You know Amber Chan was never pregnant and didn't have an abortion. We picked that up in a recording of a call she conducted in Japanese from her hotel room in San Francisco. She told the person she talked with that it was all a ruse. We couldn't hear the other side of that conversation, so we can't be sure who she spoke with and we don't know why she created the story, but we can guess."

Suzanne waited to see if he would add more, hoping for more insight. None came.

"Let's keep this between us for a few days ... until I decide," she said. He nodded in return. "But let's also watch both of them as closely as possible. Use extra staff if you need to."

Suzanne picked up her phone and wandered outside for a solitary walk. At the end of the long laneway, after she had turned onto the winding road and no one from her home could see her, she pulled out her phone again and pressed a number.

Thirty-Seven

Rabat, Morocco, Friday October 20, 2023

Fidelia's jet carried Klaudia Schäffer to Morocco to execute the first stage of their complex plan to teach the Russian Mafia a lesson and give her the satisfaction of evening old scores with at least one of the FSB thugs who had so cruelly abused her years earlier. Fidelia chose not to join the fun. Instead, she had twisted the arm of her French country boss, Pierre Boivin, urging him to "volunteer" his favorite companion. Putting his sex life at risk—even though that risk was minimal—had taken more effort than expected.

Nadine Violette sat in the comfortable reclining chair across from Klaudia as they chatted. They knew each other, of course. Nadine had reported to Klaudia when she ran the escort business for Europe. The gorgeous French woman had been one of the most sought-after women in all of France in her early twenties, earning hundreds of euros for only a few minutes in bed, into the thousands if she spent the night.

French men loved her sensuous smile, teasing giggle, and incomparable body. Nadine enjoyed her work until Boivin became so enamored with her that he persuaded Fidelia to release her to him. He still shared her with friends or business acquaintances occasionally but made it clear to everyone that she belonged to him.

Klaudia was happy to have her along. First, she spoke French like most Moroccans. Although she had learned a bit of the language in her European role with The Organization, Klaudia didn't consider herself at all fluent. If things went awry tonight, Nadine might become very useful.

The flight from Seville to Rabat was less than an hour, and the plane touched down in almost total darkness before midnight. As far as she could see there was no other activity on the runway or around the terminal. When the plane parked in the section reserved for private jets, Klaudia spotted her ride immediately to the left of the terminal at the end of the tarmac. As Pierre Boivin had promised, four men stood beside a white Mercedes SUV, and they all appeared extremely fit.

The leader stepped forward with a curt smile and a few words in French. Nadine replied immediately, then translated for Klaudia. "He told me they're ready to take you to the house."

Klaudia nodded, then gave Nadine a heartfelt hug. "Good luck with the women. And thanks in advance for coming back after you drop them off in Malaga. I should be okay, but it will be great to know you're around the airport here if I need some help."

The two women hugged again before Klaudia straightened her outfit and stepped out of the doorway and down the stairs of the private jet. She wore a traditional Moroccan long flowing robe with her body entirely covered. The fabric was lightweight, but it was black and stretched from her shoulders to just above the ground. She also wore a long scarf that covered her head and was designed to wrap around her face in the company of men. On her feet, she wore comfortable open-toed sandals.

After she worked her way into the SUV, the driver explained in French that the ride to the home on Rue Madani Ben Houssain would take about twenty-five minutes. Klaudia used the burner phone to check in with Fidelia, as agreed. Their conversation lasted only a few seconds, as she assured her boss that all was according to plan so far.

For the rest of the short drive to the drop-off spot, Klaudia gazed out into the darkness. Rabat is a capital city, so it was surprising to see so little light, but she had read that authorities dimmed or turned off many streetlights and those in office buildings after midnight to conserve precious resources.

Regardless, the ride was uneventful until they reached Rue Hackmi Meddoun in the Souissi quarter, where the SUV stopped. The driver parked there because Federov had insisted she walk the remaining few hundred yards to the FSB property.

The driver picked an alcove around the corner on a side street where the vehicle would be partly hidden by shrubs. From her review of a map of the area, Klaudia realized they were about three miles from the Atlantic Ocean and less than a mile from the US embassy compound; but only a few hundred yards from the FSB apartment.

They'd be watching her. The four men in the SUV would follow at a distance and two others were already concealed on the property only moments away from the apartment where she would meet Federov.

She took pains not to show either fear or concern, as she strode along the street toward the address he gave her, then up a long brick sidewalk in the center of the property, leading to the entrance of the gray cement-block building. It looked like they'd built it in Soviet times with no architectural appeal and straight lines in every direction. The dull design and color immediately brought back a flood of unpleasant memories of her homeland. She shuddered unexpectedly.

No guards were visible, but Pierre Boivin's people had warned her a handful of FSB operatives would be both inside and outside the building monitoring her movements. Klaudia keyed in a code at the doorway of a section leading to the right. The door swung open and automatically closed moments after she stepped through.

She walked along a short hallway with doors to three apartments on either side. The one she needed was the last on the right side. A light illuminated a digital box the second Klaudia touched the keyboard. She entered the six-digit code Federov had provided and waited for the click. Nothing happened.

She tried again. Still no reaction after she pressed the keyboard. Then, she spotted the problem, a box in the bottom right corner of the keyboard with a lock icon. This time, after keying in the six digits, she hit that icon and the door lock immediately released.

Klaudia looked around the room after stepping inside and shook her scarf free from her head as she took in a living room that was as unappealing and poorly designed as the exterior. An old, gray fabric sofa stretched across one wall. Two wooden chairs sat opposite the couch, with a small coffee table in between. On the other wall, there was a kitchen equipped with appliances from the last century, a hum from the small refrigerator loud enough to become a distraction.

Drapes on the window shared the ugly gray hues of the

sofa and hung unevenly. The kitchen table had chairs for two. The floor was cement, and it looked like the faded red paint had been applied years before, with gray blotches worn through. Musty air suggested the suite was used infrequently.

Klaudia sent a message from her burner phone that all was okay so far. Then she plunked herself on the ugly sofa to wait.

Thirty-Eight

Montreal, Quebec, Friday October 20, 2023

He felt like a schoolboy summoned to the principal's office for a chat about his bad behavior. Initially, she had given Gordon a two-day time-out, then tacked on another two days before instructing him to report to her office at headquarters that morning.

He checked the mirror in the men's room before entering Suzanne Simpson's office suite where the 'interview' would take place. His face looked a little sullen, so he practiced different smiles until he found one that seemed a good mixture of contrite but not defeated.

When he'd shaved earlier, he took care to ensure his grooming was flawless, even trimming his nose hairs and eyebrows. But he couldn't fix the gray pallor of his skin. He slapped his face a couple times to add a little color and wished it was okay for guys to add makeup to brighten themselves up when needed.

He wore a tie that day. Around Multima, business casual was usual, but he'd guessed that he might offset any upcoming humiliation by dressing formally and showing Suzanne optimum respect. He adjusted the knot slightly, checked the tie was straight, took a final deep breath, and then headed toward a discussion he dreaded.

Suzanne's assistant, Eileen, stood to greet him as he approached the executive's suite. She smiled politely before she said hello, but there was no early morning humor, offer of coffee, or casual kibitzing in her manner. Today, it was all business. She opened the office door for Gordon, then stood aside while he entered, before closing the door again on her way out.

He moved toward Suzanne. She'd stepped from behind her desk and was approaching him to shake hands and welcome him. From the corner of his eye, he noticed movement in an alcove to his left, where a large boardroom-style table sat. Lifting himself slowly from a chair was none other than James Fitzgerald!

Gordon forced himself to focus on Suzanne. Her face was drawn. Her usually energetic blue eyes appeared cold and unfeeling. She made no attempt to flash her trademark smile that usually disarmed everyone, and when she took his hand, it was brief, formal, and without her usual enthusiastic grip.

Without so much as a good morning or hello, Suzanne said, "I've asked James Fitzgerald to join us."

She took his elbow and turned him toward James, then walked him toward the executive table before she dropped her grip on his elbow. James also looked grim. His lips were tight, his jaw fixed, and his handshake perfunctory. But his dark eyes looked softer, almost sympathetic, until he looked away toward Suzanne, who motioned for everyone to take a seat.

"You're in an awkward spot, Gordon, and you've put me and the company in an equally uncomfortable position." Suzanne paused to underscore her point, and he felt her eyes almost burrowing inside his own to maximize his discomfort. "The business textbooks would tell me to fire you immediately, without severance, strip you of all your company benefits, and wait for you to mount a legal challenge no jury would ever support."

Gordon squirmed as she spoke. He'd never experienced an interaction like this with Suzanne. She was renowned for her people skills and remarkable ability to put people at ease.

"But you know I don't always follow textbook wisdom. You've been a tremendous resource. You've made significant contributions to our company's success. And you've built a loyal following among your direct reports and employees throughout the organization. I admire all those qualities and would hate to lose them. But I'm fully prepared to play by the textbook rules if you choose not to accept a remedial path I'll explain. Are you following me so far?"

Gordon nodded. It probably wasn't a good time to say anything.

"James is here today in his capacity as a director on our board. I asked for his help despite his plea a few months ago not to get involved in any business operations after leaving the helm of Financial Services." She glanced toward James with a curt nod and the tiniest of smiles.

"I've asked him to team up with you for the next few months, probably until March. If you accept this arrangement, he'll share your office with you, travel with you, and provide guidance and advice. As a director, he'll provide regular updates to me and, as he deems appropriate, to the board. He'll share your mission. Simply stated, the smooth integration of Jeffersons Stores into Multima, including the systems upgrades and integration, switching the marketing banners to Multima Supermarkets, and achieving all the performance metrics already in place. You'll continue to act as the president of Multima Supermarkets worldwide, but you'll have a coach in that role until I decide he's no longer required."

Again, Suzanne paused and drilled into his eyes with enough intensity he involuntarily blinked a few times. James sat silently, observing Gordon intently, causing him to squirm in his seat again despite trying not to. The atmosphere suggested strongly that it was better to wait for her to give him permission to speak. She was clearly on a carefully defined mission.

"So, what will it be? Are you prepared to accept James Fitzgerald as your personal coach for the next few months, or shall I hand you the termination letter sitting on my desk?"

He'd feared the meeting would be unpleasant. Had fully expected a formal warning letter, perhaps termination. Mentally preparing for this meeting, he never once considered this outcome. James Fitzgerald was a reasonably good old guy. He understood the financial world intimately, and he had served as the chief financial officer for John George Mortimer back when Supermarkets was the only business Multima had. So he knew a bit about the food industry.

But a "coach" watching everything he said and did for the next five or six months? That was demeaning. It was unfair after all he had accomplished. But the alternative was to throw away everything he'd worked for over the past almost twenty-five years.

"I'm prepared to work with James as a coach and welcome the opportunity to benefit from his experience and knowledge." He looked at Suzanne as he spoke, letting her study his eyes for sincerity, but he made sure he didn't project any signs of defeat.

He turned to make eye contact with James. "I'm sure we'll have some details to sort out working together, but I trust your judgment and have long admired your business smarts. While I regret that Suzanne decided this entire exercise is necessary, I'll do all I can to make the arrangement work smoothly."

She nodded twice and kept her eyes focused on him. James remained silent.

"Let's get started. Eileen has reserved a quiet meeting room for you. She'll take you there and get you set up for the day. It's relatively private. Talk over how you'll work together, develop some parameters, get a good understanding of each other, and discuss Amber Chan and where she fits into the new working relationship. I'd like to meet with you both again at about four and hear what you've decided on processes, boundaries, et cetera. When we're done, I want you both to fly out to San Francisco. This issue is so critical that I need both of you focused. And it needs to start this weekend."

No doubt this twist had already been discussed and agreed with James, so Gordon nodded his acquiescence.

"One last thing. While the two of you are working together, the Supermarkets' jet will be assigned to James. Living in Virginia, he'll need to travel farther, more often. When you're working together, it shouldn't make any difference."

Left unsaid, but impossible to miss, was a further clear admonishment. For the next while, there would be no temptation for Gordon to use Multima's resources for personal travel.

Thirty-Nine

Montreal, Quebec, Friday October 20, 2023

Serge called in at the end of her day. Moments after her helicopter had touched down, Suzanne answered, at the same time waving to the bodyguards as she walked toward the house. He had little to report, and the frustration of that reality reflected in his tone.

"There's something amiss with this woman. She's just too damn perfect on the job," he sputtered.

Unsure how someone could be "too perfect," Suzanne elected to say nothing and see where the conversation went from there.

"Everyone who reports to her loves her," he said. "They can't stop talking about her good humor, her charm, and her intelligence. They say she seems to remember every word she hears and number she reads

"That fits. She's been an outperformer since the day she joined the company. That's why she won the job in Asia, and it's that star quality that caught Nicole Gagnon's attention, the reason Nicole put her name forward for the Jeffersons Stores job. But I suspect Amber's business acumen is not the source of your current irritation."

Serge laughed easily and took a breath before he continued. "Right. What's got me baffled is how cleverly she covers her tracks. The burner phone we tapped hasn't been used in weeks, so she must have a new one. However, my people can't find a trace of a device. They've checked her bags electronically. They've done multiple scans of her room at the hotel. Technicians searched her rental car. The gals I have following her have never seen her stop at anything other than takeout food outlets since they started tracking her movements."

"Has she traveled during the time you've monitored her?"

"Three flights. Single-day trips to LA, Houston and Phoenix. First class each time. Staff in each city picked her up, drove her to four or five stores, then back to the airport."

"Is there a chance she knows you're following her? Maybe recognizes your team's faces or something like that?"

"Maybe. My folks are careful though. When she travels like that, I have three people fly as well, two women and a guy. Only one sits in first class each time, and they use disguises when they follow her into a store. Anything's possible, but it's not likely she's spotted us." Serge paused, maybe to choose his next words carefully. "I think it's more likely she expects to be followed and uses other strategies instead. My people noticed the drivers who picked her up and chauffeured her around each city were Asian."

"So you're wondering if she used those drivers to communicate with Takahashi?"

"Yeah, him or whoever she's taking orders from. I've asked my people in all three cities to check out the drivers." Serge's tone signaled more than annoyance or frustration. She detected a hint of curiosity or perhaps ambiguity.

"I'm hearing some uncertainty in your tone. Are you no longer confident it's the Yakuza trying to attack us?" Suzanne asked.

"Oh, I still think it's probably the Japanese, but there has been a subtle change on the dark web. There's still talk about a cyberattack on Multima, but the tone has changed. My people recently noticed different vocabulary. We still see words like 'ransom' and 'CA' which we interpret as cyberattacks. But, over the past few days, they've also noticed words like 'snatch,' 'hit,' and 'remove.' These words lean more toward a theft or maybe even a kidnapping or an assassination. I've alerted my entire team globally, but I think we need to warn our staff to be alert."

"Okay. Send a text to Gordon and James asking them to get a message out to everyone. Let's be sure they're alert to anything that seems unusual at our locations, any odd emails or social media, even changes in shipments from suppliers. Maybe you can draft something and ask them to pass it on."

"Consider it done. But I need more help. You gave me the okay to work with CSIS in Singapore, but I also need help with Japan, China, and maybe Europe. The CIA and Interpol have far more extensive networks than the Canadians. I have one hand tied behind my back because of your reluctance to cooperate with the more sophisticated agencies."

She'd expected a request for more. With a morbid fear of a cyberattack that could come from anywhere on Earth, it was difficult to resist the temptation to seek help—wherever it might come from.

"Okay, Serge. But the same condition as before. We ask for help and share information about current incidents only. Take care of yourself and come home soon."

"Thanks. I will. But you need to be careful, too. I don't want to dampen your weekend plans while I'm away, but this might not be the best time to hit those after-hours clubs in Saint-Sauveur or elsewhere in the Laurentians."

Suzanne heard a giggle escape before he had all the words out and laughed along with him. She couldn't remember the last time she'd been to any after-hours club, anywhere. They chatted a few minutes longer, then said their goodbyes with professions of love.

As they hung up, an alert sounded on Suzanne's phone. The message caused her to freeze.

> *A bomb exploded in Jeffersons Store 929 in Houston at 5:47 local time. Reported deaths and injuries. More than 50 ambulances dispatched. Gordon & I are OK. Left store 15 minutes before attack. Gordon launching emergency plans now with Serge. Will update as info received, James.*

It had been a couple years since a Multima supermarket had been bombed. The last time was in Florida when The Organization had tried to weasel its way into the company with threats and violence, and the last thing she wanted to learn was that her company was once again under attack.

With her outdoor call completed, Suzanne continued walking toward the rear of her home, when its back door suddenly burst open just before she arrived.

From inside her mansion in the Laurentian Mountains near Montreal, two bodyguards stormed out the rear door and dashed toward Suzanne, shouting at her and waving frantically for her to run inside. She dashed the remaining few steps, then fell heavily to the floor inside, a bodyguard landing on top of her a second later.

After that she wasn't entirely clear what happened. When Suzanne tried to lift herself up, she heard a distant hum as the bodyguard pressed down her head and screamed, "Don't move. There's a drone above!"

She heard other bodyguards shouting among themselves. "It's over the house."

"No, it's past the house, in the backyard ... close to the chopper."

"It dropped something. Everyone, stay down."

Their shouts all sounded desperate.

Suddenly, everything fell quiet. At first, no one dared move, but after a few seconds, Suzanne felt the bodyguard push up his bulky frame from her body, allowing her to breathe more easily. He twisted and turned toward the helicopter.

"Nothin' happened," he muttered to himself. "What the fuck did the drone drop if nothin' happened?"

Slowly, he slid off Suzanne entirely onto his knees, then bounced to his feet with the help of his arms. Upright, he extended a hand to Suzanne and pulled her to standing with one tug. His face was both apologetic and sheepish.

"Sorry, madame, but we saw the drone and feared the worst. It did drop something, and I'm recommending we get the police out here to see what it was. I'll have two of the other bodyguards take you and Florence to town with the car. Have dinner there, and we'll check it out."

Suzanne made repeated attempts to reach Serge. The situation in Houston frightened her, and she felt horrible for those injured and the families of those killed. After bouncing repeatedly to his voice mail, she tried James Fitzgerald instead. A good, calming conversation would be nice.

"We're at the site now," James explained. "As soon as we heard the news, we reversed direction and got back here. Gordon's been working the phone with Serge and Edward Hadley to get advice on the best way to handle police and media relations here. He's doing a good job."

"Are the police giving any info at all?"

"Very little. They told us they found five bodies so far and about thirty-five people were transported in ambulances to three different hospitals in the area. Injuries appear to range from minor to life-threatening. To my inexperienced eye, the damage at the store looks severe. I'm guessing we'll be out of business here for several months."

"Has someone contacted the insurance company yet?"

"Yeah. That was one of the first things Gordon instructed Amber to take on. Someone should be here momentarily."

"She's there with you today?"

"Yes, again. Gordon asked her to come along while we did the store visits and employee meetings. She seems to enjoy a very good rapport with the employees, has been moving around a lot here at the site, comforting them and getting help where people need it."

Suzanne asked James to keep her informed of developments. Once more, she tried Serge, again without success, and decided to follow her lead bodyguard's advice. She invited Florence to join her and headed to a restaurant in town with two guys from the bodyguard team. Neither woman had an appetite. They both picked at their meals after calming their frayed nerves with a couple glasses of red wine.

Two further attempts to reach Serge failed. She'd left a voice message, but there was little doubt he was swamped with the bombing in Houston. When it came time to pay their bill, Suzanne called the lead bodyguard while the server processed her credit card.

The fellow was very direct. "It's better for you not to come home this evening. The police confirmed that a bomb dropped from the drone. Lucky for us, it was a dud and didn't detonate. I reached Serge by text, and he wants you to stay in town tonight, at the Hotel Bonaventure. He asked Eileen to book you a suite. Said he'll meet you there in the morning. I've already told your driver."

Suzanne felt the blood drain from her face, and she felt faint and numb. Was she involved in an all-out war? All she could manage to reply was a weak, "Thank you. I'll do that."

Forty

Rabat, Morocco, Saturday October 21, 2023

It was almost two in the morning when one of the guys from the airport called Klaudia. She was drowsy. It had been a long and stressful day, with the past few hours inactive and alone in the FSB apartment. She forced herself to become alert the moment she heard the ring, a technique learned while she served in the scurrilous FSB outfit.

"Federov is on the way. Just left here with two other guys and a local driver. So, four of them. Plus three we saw in the neighborhood."

Klaudia swallowed hard but said nothing as the French speaker spoke in broken English. "He brought five women. All are high-quality, young, and attractive. All drugged. My men carried them to Fidelia's plane. On the runway for takeoff now. Be back in two hours to get you out. Hopefully before light."

Klaudia took another mouthful of the bottled water she carried in her bag, then unwrapped her headscarf before a mirror and arranged it to cover as much of her head and face as possible. Federov could take his order for her to undress before he arrived and shove it. But he wouldn't need any temptation. If she guessed correctly, he'd demand sex the moment he burst through the door whatever her garb. She paced for the few minutes she expected the trip from the airport to take.

After an hour, she was still pacing, and wondering why the delay? Did he drop off the hundred thousand US dollars somewhere? Was there a mechanical problem with his car? Was he dallying along the way just to annoy and upset her? Regardless, she had no control over his timing, so she returned to the grungy sofa and waited.

Another hour later, there was still no sign of Federov and she started to worry. Sometime after four in the morning, despite her most valiant efforts to stay awake, Klaudia dozed off.

The click of the door lock woke her, and she turned toward it, lifting herself off the sofa to a full upright position. It wasn't Federov. Another man, appearing more local than Russian, stepped through the door first, and two others followed, all walking toward Klaudia wordlessly, expressions grim.

"Slap the handcuffs on her," Federov ordered in Russian from the hallway behind them. He carried the same brown leather bag on his shoulder, in the same casual way, as the first time they'd met on the job.

It was pointless to argue, so she held out her hands in front to make it easier for the guy who produced the cuffs from a pocket.

"Hands behind her," Federov commanded. He now stood just inside the closed door, a few feet away from her, and waited until he heard the click of the locking cuffs before he approached her. "Don't you look cute in your foreign costume?"

His tone seemed friendly enough that Klaudia started to form a smile. Before her lips made it all the way there, he reached out, viciously grabbed the top of her kaftan and hijab, and ripped both from her body in one violent motion that almost pulled her off her feet.

"I told you to wear nothing," he seethed.

The other men's eyes all focused immediately on her bra and panties, the only things left covering her front, though the garb stuck in the back at her waist because of the cuffs on her hands. One guy stepped forward, laughing, and yanked the garment from below her hands. He gave her a friendly pat on the ass as he pulled her clothing away.

"Okay, we've established you're not wired or carrying a weapon. Sit down on the sofa again." Federov's tone became curt but not hostile. He slid one of the wooden chairs closer and set it directly opposite her. He slipped off the bag and set it beside his feet. Then, he stared for another moment before asking her a question with little enthusiasm. "Your guys at the airport liked the women I delivered, and they paid my fee. So, what else do you want?"

"Your people in Europe appear to be more active recently. The person I work for is concerned about some recent deaths that have all the hallmarks of FSB punishment. My boss wants to avoid a gang war and wants to make a deal instead."

Federov listened. His face showed no emotion, maybe no interest in what she was saying. But his eyes shifted downward to her breasts and back a few times. Some things never changed.

"Don't try to hide your boss's identity. Can you be so naïve as to think we don't know Fidelia Morales sent you here? What's the stupid bitch proposing?" He almost spat out the last phrase with open disdain.

"She wants to buy women, lots of women. She knows how to operate in Europe, has the network, and has the political and police connections. She wants to buy the women from you instead of running her own network in Eastern Europe. She'll let you guys control the human trafficking business in the old Soviet Union and buy a hundred women a month at the same twenty grand each she paid today. Two million a month and you guys agree to leave her people alone."

"Boris will never agree to that," Federov said. "I can't imagine he'd be interested in double or triple that amount. You know, some of those girls we snatch bring in twenty grand a month. Why would we want to give that up?"

"Fidelia's guys are pushing her to take out two of yours for every operative of The Organization you kill. Do the math. It wouldn't take long before there's a full-scale gang war. All those highly skilled resources you spend all that time and money training could disappear faster than you can recruit them. Remember, Fidelia has no inhibitions about knocking people off. She's even happy to do it herself if needed."

Klaudia planted the less-than-subtle reminder that Fidelia had shot her mentor Giancarlo Mareno while he begged for mercy from his knees. The story was legendary in the underworld everywhere.

"I'll take it back to Boris and see what he says." Federov's tone suggested that he was wasting his time but would carry the message without enthusiasm.

It was the reaction Klaudia had predicted, so she used the carrot Fidelia had suggested. "Did you ever hear about a half-billion US dollars that inexplicably disappeared from bank accounts controlled by your Russian masters on Monday,

March 16, 2020?"

Federov leaped from the chair. "Outside," he motioned to the three flunkies. He waited until the door clicked closed behind them. "What do you know about that?"

Klaudia waited, hoping to build suspense. Instead, she evoked anger. Before she could react, Federov stepped forward, slapped her face hard with his right hand, then grabbed her bra violently and jerked it from her body.

"Now, if you don't want me to start playing with my cigarette lighter and those nipples, tell me what you know about that heist. Everything."

With the shock of his treatment, Klaudia's first inclination was to sob from the humiliating tactics the Russian had resorted to. But she remembered. She'd prepared for this, knowing his treatment of women wouldn't have changed over time. She had to get this next part right to get the ultimate revenge.

"I'll only tell you this. We know where the five hundred million went, and we know how to get it back. If you touch me again or harm me in any way, you will never see the money. Not one dollar of it. Release me from the handcuffs now, and I'll tell you what the next steps will be."

Federov paused, took a long look at her breasts again, then spun on his heel and went to the door. In the doorway, he summoned the guy with the key, and within seconds, came back with it, ordering her to stand up. She complied. Although it was awkward rising from the sofa with her hands bound behind her back, Klaudia managed it while he stood a step or two behind her, still gawking over her shoulder at her nipples.

When he released the cuffs, she reached first for her garment on the floor and threw it around her, torn or not. When her breasts were covered, she continued to stand and laid down the terms of their cooperation.

"Going forward, we talk only to Boris Ivanov. You'll give him my number in Spain and tell him to call me within a week to agree upon a meeting date and location. Only he and Fidelia will meet. No bodyguards. No assistants. No weapons. Got that?"

Klaudia pressed hard because that was the only style of language this jerk understood. She knew a half-billion dollars for Federov's boss would eliminate any further mistreatment today. Should anything happen to her, and the FSB lose an opportunity to regain that money, even an idiot like Federov knew it would be his last bad decision.

"Fidelia's willing to share the recovery in any way Ivanov proposes. But she's only willing to meet and discuss conditions if Ivanov comes prepared to back away from Europe. If she doesn't hear from him by next Saturday, your people in Europe will start disappearing. And you can be sure their departures from this world will be far more exotic than tumbling from a high-rise balcony. Do we understand each other?"

He didn't answer, and she didn't press further. Instead, she gathered her headscarf from the end of the sofa, swung it around her neck, and started toward the door. Before she completed her first step, her flowing robe appeared to drag against Federov's leather bag, causing Klaudia to lose her balance, and she tumbled awkwardly to the floor.

He laughed.

As Klaudia freed her torn robe with her right hand, using a move she'd practiced a hundred times, her left hand slid into his bag and affixed a hand-painted, dark brown, and trackable Apple AirTag on its inside flap.

Fedorov laughed only for a moment, then watched her recovery with little apparent interest as she got back to her feet and scrambled sheepishly toward the doorway. When she reached out her hand for the doorknob, Federov shouted for the men to let her pass.

Forty-One

Houston, Texas, Saturday October 21, 2023

The police finally insisted Gordon Goodfellow had done all he could at the scene for that night and should take his two friends with him and go to a hotel. They were polite but insistent, and James Fitzgerald had nodded his agreement with the police officer's request.

By the time they checked into The Post Oak Hotel, it was already past one in the morning. In the elevator to their rooms, James said goodnight, but both Gordon and Amber said they needed to find something to eat. Once James left the elevator, Gordon suggested they have room service send something for both of them to his room. Amber nodded with a smile. She looked exhausted.

Her assigned room was a few doors further along on the same floor, and she wanted to head there to clean up before the food arrived. Gordon arranged for a bucket of chicken wings and a bottle of red wine from the all-night kitchen and took a shower while waiting. The stench of the burning store and residue from the explosion seemed to be everywhere. His skin, his clothes, and even his briefcase carried the smell, so he stayed in the hot shower much longer than usual, rubbing scented gel into his hair and all over his body multiple times.

He heard a faint knock on the door just as he finished dressing. Assuming it was either Amber or the wings, he wandered to the door, still buttoning his shirt. It was neither.

Instead, the bell captain who had greeted them at the front door handed him an unmarked envelope, holding out his empty hand for a tip. Gordon found him a couple bucks, thanked him and examined the envelope. It was highly unlikely either James or Amber would send him a message as a note. If they had something to share, surely a call or text would be more efficient.

He was wary, and opened the hotel envelope with his plastic room key, sliding it into a tiny opening, then touching the paper surface as little as possible. He'd heard about people receiving envelopes containing deadly poisons. Was the unsettled situation here giving him pantophobia, a fear of everything?

There was no killer powder, only a folded message, hand-written on a piece of matching hotel stationery. He opened it and felt his heart rate surge.

"This is only the first pitch of the game. Get out while you can."

Another knock on the door. This time louder than before. Setting the envelope and message aside, Gordon strode to the doorway to greet the room service delivery. After signing the chit, and adding a ten-dollar tip to the total bill, Gordon called Amber's room to let her know their food had arrived.

Surprisingly, there was no answer. Could she still be in the shower?

By three in the morning, Amber still had not arrived at his room and had not answered his calls. Gordon called the front desk and asked them to try. They, too, were unsuccessful. Worried, he asked if hotel security might check her room, but they were reluctant to invade her privacy. He texted Serge Boisvert to see if Multima's security chief might help.

Although Serge was traveling on a red-eye commercial flight, he received the text and seemed to find the situation curious. He sent a return message asking if there were any other details Gordon could share. He hesitated before replying but concluded the odd written message delivered earlier might be significant. Seconds after adding that bit of information to the text stream, he received another message from Multima's chief of security.

Don't touch the message any more than you have already. Call Houston police immediately and ask them to check Amber's room. Give them the piece of paper and envelope. I'll call you when I arrive in Montreal in about two hours.

Houston police responded to his request about an hour later with a knock on his door. Two police officers and a hotel security agent stood in the hallway when Gordon greeted them. He retold the story: Amber's plan to return for food that was now cold in his room, his telephone calls and knocks on her door that produced no responses, the mysterious letter delivery, and Serge Boisvert's instruction that he call.

Within a couple minutes, the more senior police officer asked Gordon to stay in his room while they checked the one assigned to Amber.

Since her room was only three doorways further along, he stood instead outside his room in the hallway and watched the next steps unfold. The older officer knocked loudly on the door, identifying himself and asking her to open up.

After the knocks on the door, the hallway became silent. Light fixtures on the walls cast a bright glow in large circles on the dark brown carpet below. The police and security guard stood erect in a semi-circle around the door to Amber's room and didn't move for several moments. Then, the officer knocked and called out twice more, each time in a louder tone of voice.

After a suitable wait, with no response to his third request, the senior officer nodded to the hotel agent who stepped forward, entered a plastic card into the lock mechanism and opened the doorway. Light from the room filtered into the corridor, but there was no sound. With weapons drawn, the police officers entered with the hotel agent trailing, but they all came out of the room less than a minute later.

The senior officer waved for Gordon to join them, and he rushed over to Amber's doorway.

"As you can see, there is no one here. This suite hasn't been used. Everything is exactly the way the hotel cleaners left it."

The senior police officer suggested they all go down to the front desk and see if someone had made a mistake, or perhaps she had changed rooms. On the way, he stopped again at Gordon's room to pick up the envelope. Pulling on plastic gloves from his pants pocket, he inserted both the envelope and note into a plastic bag and tucked it into a large pocket in his vest.

The woman managing the front desk looked familiar. Gordon recognized her from their earlier check-in when he had whispered to James that while she might not be the brightest bulb in the room, she appeared competent. She was a Christian, too. As they headed toward their rooms, she wished them all a blessed stay in Houston.

The senior police officer interviewed her and the hotel security agent, while the younger fellow stood to one side with Gordon, close enough for him to feel part of the process but far enough away that he couldn't eavesdrop on the conversation. The process lasted for several minutes before the senior officer stepped away with a tip of his hat and a smile for the desk clerk.

"I don't think there was any mistake. Ms. Chan was registered to the room we checked, and there is no record of any request for a change of room. There's not much more we can do at this stage. Amber Chan is a mature adult. She has the right to do as she pleases. Absent any signs of violence, struggle, or suspicious behavior, we need to allow twenty-four hours before you can file a missing persons report. Maybe she was just a little spooked by that Multima store explosion and needed a little time alone to absorb it all."

"Why do you think that might be the case, officer?" Gordon hadn't shared any info about the previous day's trauma with the man.

"The front desk clerk overheard you all chatting about it during check-in. She said you were all pale and oddly quite dirty for businesspeople. Of course, she also noticed you all work for Multima Corporation from your registration documents, so she assumed you'd all be aware of the disaster."

Gordon retreated to his suite on the top floor again. It was too late to try sleeping. He was scheduled to meet James Fitzgerald and Amber for breakfast in about two hours, so he decided to make some coffee with the packets the hotel provided in the room, wait an hour, then give James a call.

While the coffee brewed, Serge Boisvert called. His plane had just parked at the terminal, and he wanted to know what was happening in Houston. Gordon brought him up to date on the police visit and its failure to produce any new information.

The security chief cursed silently, almost under his breath. Gordon asked him what they should do next.

"I don't think there's much you can do. I'll contact

Houston police later this morning. I have the contact details for a senior detective there. I'll see what I can find out," Serge said.

"You don't have anyone from your team stationed here? I thought I talked to one of your people last night." The guy had given Gordon a card, and he reached inside his jacket to find out the fellow's name.

Serge didn't immediately reply. Then he took a deep breath. "Yeah, Joey Wansom. He told me he met you at the scene." Another long pause. "Unfortunately, he's now missing as well."

Forty-Two

Montreal, Quebec, Saturday October 21, 2023

She was already awake when Serge called from Pierre Elliott Trudeau Airport in Montreal, where he'd just cleared customs and immigration. Suzanne heard the loud background noise as he strode toward whatever car he had waiting for him there.

Once they'd reassured each other that they were alright and coping adequately with the stress from both the dud bomb in the backyard of their home in the Laurentian Mountains and the tragic bombing in Houston, Serge got right down to business.

"It feels like we're at war on multiple fronts. There's something strange going on, and I feel somewhat helpless at the moment." His tone sounded more bewildered than angry, and less confident than usual.

She chose to listen, and he eventually continued. "As if the two bombing incidents weren't enough for us to deal with, there are three more bits of news I have to share with you. Amber Chan is now missing. She hasn't been seen since Gordon left her outside his room at a hotel in Houston, and the hotel claims her room was never used."

Suzanne drew a deep breath, audible enough that Serge paused, probably to let her process the information.

"But it gets more complicated. Someone delivered a mysterious handwritten note to Gordon in his room last night, implying the bombing in Houston was just the beginning of our problems. The forensic specialists are examining the note this morning to try to get a lead on who may have sent it. The hotel employee who delivered it claims no knowledge of who asked him to deliver the note and can't help with a description other than it was a short Asian male."

"How is Gordon reacting to all this?"

"Surprisingly well. He's calm, under control, and seeking advice on any further steps he should take." Serge's tone suggested his confidence in Gordon might be growing.

"How about James?" Suzanne asked.

There was a short pause before Serge replied. "Damn it! I don't know. In my conversations with Gordon, I never thought to ask, and he made no mention of James. Would you like me to call him?"

"No, you have your hands full. I'll give him a call when we finish here. It's still about five in the morning out there. When will you get here?"

"I'll be there in about a half-hour. The car is leaving the airport now. Before we say goodbye, there's one more piece of information that might be important. Not only is Amber Chan missing, but the guy I had tailing her in Houston isn't reachable either. Worse, before I called you, I received word they located his rental car. It's parked in the private aircraft section of Bush Intercontinental Airport. I've got people checking private flight records for departures overnight to see if we can get any information. But this jumbled mess just gets worse by the hour."

James was up when Suzanne called. He was preparing to leave his room to meet Gordon for breakfast. The pair had already spoken about all the overnight developments in Houston, but James was unaware of the incident at her home when Suzanne mentioned it.

"It's all troubling, like someone is in the background pulling multiple levers to create havoc for Multima. Who would want to do that?" he asked.

Suzanne assumed he was asking a rhetorical question and didn't answer. Instead, she poured a cup of coffee from the pot she'd brewed while talking with Serge. She savored a good sip before James decided to continue.

"This doesn't feel like Japanese Yakuza work to me. The bombing in Houston, perhaps. Maybe even Amber Chan and the disappearance of Serge's guy. But dropping a dud bomb from a drone at your place in Montreal suggests somebody less professional. Have you heard anything from that character called the Shadow lately?"

The Shadow was an anonymous American who'd caused havoc with Multima in the past. No one could be one hundred percent sure about his real identity, but all signs pointed toward someone very close to a former president of the United States. No proof existed, but rumors had circulated for years about the Shadow's supposed yearning to take over Multima Corporation by any means possible, legal or otherwise.

"Nothing recently. But you raise a good point. I have an attorney friend in Washington who's well-connected to some of the unsavory elements that contaminate the capital. I'll give her a call. In the meantime, is it safe for you and Gordon to stay in Houston, or are you planning to move on?"

"I expect we'll discuss that at breakfast. I don't think we're in danger here, but I'm not sure what else we can do either. Gordon's done a great job with the media and cooperated well with the police investigation. He already spent time consoling the staff at the store. We might want to consider quick visits to other Houston store locations today to reassure employees and management there, but I'm guessing we'll be back in San Francisco by tonight. He'll have to plug the big hole left by Amber until we get a handle on her whereabouts."

Suzanne squeezed in a call to Edward Hadley before Serge arrived. She rousted him from bed that Saturday morning. Still, his report was relatively positive.

"I was on the phone with Gordon Goodfellow almost continuously until past two our time. I helped him with a string of reporters, and he handled it well. We'll have to monitor the media this week to be sure our messages of condolence and assurances worked effectively, but early indications are good," Edward said.

She told him about the dud bomb in the Laurentians and the missing duo in Texas. Then, she suggested he scout around and see if more was going on that she should know about.

"Two incidents on the same day in Canada and the US seem odd, but I'm wondering if there were any anomalies in Europe or Asia we haven't heard about yet. Let's not create any alarm, but ask your people to work discreetly with their global contacts to see if anything unusual occurred over the past few days," she said.

When Serge knocked on the door of her suite at the Hotel Bonaventure, she opened the door to his widespread arms for a long, almost desperate embrace. They held each other tightly for a moment or two before they kissed. Neither spoke. Instead, they explored each other with their eyes and then their tongues, longing to reconnect completely after days apart and the ugly incidents both had dealt with alone for the past hours.

It wasn't sexual, although she longed to be close to him and hold him tightly. A few moments passed before time caught up with them, and she realized the door to her suite was wide open. People in the corridor were gawking at them. She broke away from his arms and playfully tugged him into the room, where they reengaged precisely where they'd left off. It felt wonderful to have him close to her again, and it was astonishing how invigorated his presence made her feel.

Eventually, the weight of the issues at hand prevailed. They both realized, simultaneously, that duty must once again take priority.

Serge started. "After we spoke on the phone, I received another call from Texas. The body of my guy watching Amber was found in a ditch near the airport. Strangled, it appears. Dead for several hours. Sixteen private aircraft took off from Bush Intercontinental last night. Ten of them belonged to US corporations. Latin American interests—probably drug dealers—owned two jets and three aircraft belonged to American billionaires or entertainers. One was registered to a numbered Japanese company. It filed a flight plan with Seville, Spain, listed as its destination."

Suzanne drew a deep breath as she absorbed the implications, but she didn't interrupt. There was more.

"In the terminal, they checked security cameras and discovered three people boarded the jet. One was an Asian woman matching the description of Amber Chan. She was escorted by two extraordinarily large men who appeared to be of European descent, and one of those guys carried a piece of luggage. That plane left the terminal at 2:03 a.m.—about an hour after Gordon Goodfellow reported seeing her for the last time in Houston."

Suzanne's shoulders slumped and her head dropped. This could only mean there was more to come. *How much more?*

Forty-Three

Seville, Spain, Sunday October 22, 2023

For Fidelia, it had been a no-brainer. The jet was in Mexico City that day anyway, picking up another half-dozen women that Aretta Musa had rounded up. Surprisingly, she'd been shut out of North Africa. Governments there were collectively becoming more diligent. They'd started searching private aircraft randomly with multiple agents, making it harder to bribe folks to look the other way.

However, Aretta's people in Mexico had found six excellent new recruits. Her people found them in a time-tested way: invitations to young, beautiful women to apply for roles in upcoming porno films. The invitations to a swank downtown Mexico City location drew in a couple dozen. The most promising were moved to a separate room where they were told to undress to see if they were suitable for the role. The guys sedated the nude women, hid their clothes in another room in case they awakened too early, and destroyed the SIM cards from their phones.

Fidelia had received word of an explosion at the Multima Supermarket in Houston and a call from her US country boss, Louise Dependente, minutes after it occurred. She immediately contacted Tak Takahashi to find out what he knew about it and learned he was entirely in the dark. Later, when Tak reported back that he couldn't reach Amber Chan on either of the two secure burner phones he'd given her, Fidelia made her decision.

Minutes before the scheduled transfer of the captive women to her private jet parked at *Aeropuerto Internacional Ciudad de Mexico*, Fidelia issued three orders. The first was to the pilot of the jet, instructing him to fly to Houston right after leaving Mexico City. In Houston, he would take on three more passengers, two men and a woman.

Her second call was to Louise Dependente, ordering her to have her tail on Amber Chan intercept the woman and have her at Houston Intercontinental Airport by 2:00 a.m.

Saturday morning.

Then she issued a final order to Louise. Get the two big lugs from Miami who had protected Fidelia on her escape from Guantanamo and fly them to Houston to meet her guy there, then take control of Amber for a flight to Spain.

It was a tight schedule, but the only casualty was the Multima security officer. He tried to intercept Louise Dependente's people as they seized Amber and escaped from the basement garage of The Post Oak Hotel. They threw his body in his rental car and assigned one guy from the kidnapping group to dump the body somewhere en route to the airport. Unfortunately, both the car and body were discovered earlier than Fidelia would have liked, but so far, there was no other collateral damage.

Her country guys in Spain, France and Portugal had already divided up the six beautiful, kidnapped Mexican women. Probably they had already started earning money.

The Chinese woman was another story. Fidelia studied her as Amber started to revive. She didn't trust Asians, especially Chinese. From her days overseeing the escort business, she knew Chinese women were always more difficult to manage than Japanese, Thai, or Indonesian women. There just might be some truth to the allegations of the woman's disgruntled former colleague at Multima's Shanghai office. If it turned out Amber Chan had two-timed Tak Takahashi by working with the Chinese Triads, it would be even worse.

As much as Fidelia feared the Russian Mafia, she was even more terrified of the Chinese thugs. While the Russians were ruthless and brutal, she found the Chinese more cunning. They found ways to infiltrate and control that the Russians hadn't discovered yet, and it was time to find out exactly where Miss Amber Chan's loyalties lay.

She motioned for the big guy from Florida who was guarding the door to go in and wake her up. He shook the woman a bit. Slapped her face once. Then, yanked her into a seated position facing Fidelia, who was standing at the foot of her bed. With her eyes now open wide, Amber Chan looked pale and terrified.

"Where am I? ... Who are you?" Her tone was measured despite the fear in her eyes. She seemed ready to cry, with a pout on her face, shoulders slumped forward, and her arms protectively wrapped around her bare chest.

"It doesn't matter who I am or where you are. Your job for the next few minutes will be to answer my questions. How well you answer those questions will determine your future career path. You look like a smart woman, someone who wants to advance in life, so I suggest you answer honestly and truthfully the first time. Failure to do so may result in undesirable alterations to your beautiful face and body as well as harm to your career trajectory."

Fidelia spoke calmly, almost softly, moving her body as little as possible and enunciating her words slowly and clearly. There could be no misunderstanding.

"Tell me who you are and what you do for a living."

Amber looked at her strangely, as though she might recognize the face of the woman confronting her. It was unlikely she could place Fidelia's face with her name. She'd permitted only a handful of photos over her entire career and none in the past decade. Besides, she'd done extensive repair work in the meantime. She repeated her question.

At first, it looked as if the woman might ask a question, but instead answered, simply and honestly.

"Whom do you report to at Multima Supermarkets?"

Again, she answered honestly.

"Are you Japanese or Chinese?"

She confirmed her correct nationality.

"Have you ever lived in Japan?"

"No. Only China and the US." Lying. Either she'd decided that she was not being interrogated by Fidelia Morales or chose to lie to see where the next questions led. *Cunning Chinese.*

For more than a half hour, Fidelia posed unthreatening, easy questions that required neither truth nor lies; any answer was suitable to her. Then she started to probe.

"Do you know about the explosion at the Multima Supermarket in Houston on Friday?"

She nodded, so Fidelia asked, "What happened?"

The answer simply affirmed the basic details anyone could have seen on TV news.

Fidelia pressed for more. "Everyone knows those details. I

want to know who ordered the explosion. Who did it?"

Amber's eyes widened perceptibly, and she appeared shocked by the question. "Nobody knows! The police are investigating, but they still don't know who is responsible or why they bombed the store."

A convincing performance, but she'd need more work. "That's an incorrect answer. I'll give you another chance to tell me who ordered the bombing."

Amber shriveled in size, squirmed, and started to cry. "I honestly don't know. I'm telling you the truth. If I knew, I would have already told the police."

"You're lying. You're a great actor, but you're lying. Think about it overnight. I'll come back in the morning, and we'll chat again. If you don't give me the right answer, tomorrow we'll ship you to one of our field offices. There, you'll spend the rest of your useful life making men happy. You'll do whatever they demand. You'll do it cheerfully and even masterfully, and you'll do it for as long as we consider you useful. Think carefully about your answer."

Fidelia turned on her heel and stepped outside the room, pulling the door closed behind her. She paused to speak to the guard outside Amber's room and spoke just loudly enough for the woman to hear her tell the guard, "Let your partner know it's okay for you guys to play with her a bit. No rough stuff and no marks at this stage, but you can play with her."

Fidelia heard desperate sobbing as she walked away from the room.

Forty-Four

San Francisco, California, Sunday October 22, 2023

Friday's bombing of a Jeffersons Stores outlet in Houston was now old news. As Gordon Goodfellow scrolled through the TV channels in his hotel room that morning, three mass shootings over the weekend, in different parts of the country, and the war in Ukraine now dominated the newscasts. None of it was good news, but it surely took some attention away from Jeffersons Stores and Multima.

Sales at the newly acquired division had plummeted Friday and Saturday throughout the Southwest. Customers got nervous about their own safety when a supermarket was attacked like that. Might it happen while they're shopping in their local store? In Texas, people stayed away in droves, but even in nearby Oklahoma and Arizona, store traffic was down as much as thirty percent. It would have real repercussions on the bottom line for the month.

Sure, most of those people might be back in the stores during the coming weeks, but only a percentage of those lost sales would be recovered. The reputational damage also made the rebranding of Jeffersons Stores to Multima Supermarkets more urgent. With his business leader for that conversion now missing, responsibility for getting it back on track would fall directly on Gordon's shoulders.

For most of the day she went missing, Gordon felt angst about Amber's disappearance. He loved the woman, after all. When he had a moment or two free from the stresses of the bombing and its aftermath, he prayed. He prayed before he ate breakfast with James Fitzgerald, after his second interview with the police in Houston, twice on the flight to San Francisco, and finally before turning in for sleep again at the hotel. Every time he prayed, he felt more unease. Rather than relieving his angst, each prayer session seemed to increase it.

Was it possible she knew something about the bombing before it occurred?

He thought back to their tour of the store and their

interactions with the staff. At the time, everything seemed normal. Nothing stood out to alert him to danger or make him suspect anything out of the ordinary might occur in the store. Amber had excused herself to take a couple calls, but that wasn't unusual for a busy executive in charge of operations. She stepped outside, but seeking out privacy or a quiet setting wasn't abnormal either.

As he reviewed the tour over and over in his mind, only a couple tiny bits of conversation now made him wonder if she had some sort of advance knowledge or warning.

At each of the other store visits that day, she'd pressed the local team to be sure they had all the store arrangements for new Multima signage completed before the planned installation dates. They needed to clear space in the warehouse to store the new signs for a week or two. They needed to be sure the areas around the existing signs were cleaned, with tape and barricades ready for the workers to safely block off the area. As much as he tried, he couldn't recall her discussing those arrangements with the team in the store where the bomb detonated.

The other piece that continued to haunt his memory was Amber's insistence they all needed to leave the store to stay on schedule. It troubled him because their schedule wasn't that crucial at that time of the day. It was their last store visit, and the only flight they had to catch was the Multima Supermarkets' jet, now entrusted to James Fitzgerald and parked at the airport. Yet he could recall three separate times when she'd leaned in toward him while someone else spoke, whispering that they needed to move on as soon as possible.

At the time, Gordon didn't notice those little prods because they were part of the store visit routine. When executives chatted with team members, to avoid appearing unconcerned when one went on a little too long about their pet peeve, subordinates always made it easier for the executive by appearing to be the person guilty of cutting short the conversation to keep the boss on schedule for all their other equally important discussions.

Now, when Gordon looked back on those interactions, it felt odd that Amber was filling that role. Usually, it would have been one of her subordinates doing the nudging. Neither of those curious issues alone merited a call to Serge Boisvert, but to protect his ass, he probably should make him aware of them. The guy had sent an email to everyone asking anyone who might have noticed anything at all out of the ordinary prior to the explosion to share it with him, no matter how insignificant it might seem.

He dialed Serge's phone. As he hit the number, he noticed it was almost noon on the East Coast. Multima's chief of security answered on the second ring, as usual.

"I hope I'm not interrupting anything. Is now a good time?" Gordon always liked to ask that question after the pleasantries were out of the way. It usually assured the person he was calling wasn't distracted by some other more pressing issue.

"It's fine, Gordon." Serge paused for a second and added, "May I put you on speaker? It looks like our CEO might like to listen in as well."

Gordon laughed at Serge's lighthearted reference to Suzanne and assured him that would be fine. Then he sought information.

"I'm planning to meet James in a few minutes and wondered if there were any new developments in the search for Amber. Heard anything?"

"I don't think we can call it a search yet. The official position of the Houston police department is that Amber isn't a missing person until a report is filed and we're only able to do that today. I have someone out there in Houston now to get that process underway. But I intended to call you this morning to give you a heads-up about another unfortunate development. The police are already actively searching for her because she is a person of interest in a murder investigation."

Gordon's heart skipped a beat, and he swallowed hard. He could feel the blood rushing from his brain to his face and felt it grow warmer by the second.

"Did I hear you correctly? Did you say a murder investigation?"

"Yes, you heard correctly. I assigned a security team member named Joey Wansom from the San Francisco office to keep an eye on Amber after the information we received about her and Tak Takahashi. Remember you said you met him at the bombing site? Early this morning, his body was discovered in a ditch near the airport."

Gordon was enraged, but not about the murder. "Jesus Christ! You had a company tail watching Amber? Does that mean there's someone tracking everything I do, too?"

"Don't need one for you. James Fitzgerald's handling that." *Cold. Insulting.*

Gordon decided to tack in a different direction—Suzanne was listening in, after all. "I'm bewildered here. You'll have to help me. I get why you had someone following Amber, but why would anyone think she was involved in his murder?"

"Two security video clips have emerged. One, from the parking lot of The Post Oak Hotel, showed two large men striking Joey repeatedly, then stuffing his body in his own car and driving it away. Another video clip from the private jet terminal at Bush Intercontinental shows the same two large men escorting Amber to a waiting plane. There are no indications of any resistance by Amber in that video. The police also found Joey's car parked outside the airport terminal. I think the police have good reason to consider her a person of interest."

Again, Serge's tone was cold, unfeeling, maybe even bitter.

What has Amber gotten herself into? Gordon calculated quickly. First, he had to save himself.

"I'm really sorry to hear about your guy Joey. My thoughts and prayers are surely with his family, and I know he's a tragic loss to you as well. I appreciate you sharing these awful details with me, but the reason for my call was to let you know I thought long and hard about your email yesterday. A couple small anomalies came to mind, and I thought I should share them with you."

He succinctly and calmly outlined them for Serge, emphasizing that they only came to him that morning after considerable thought. The chief of security's reply didn't give him much reason for optimism.

"Every bit helps. Thanks for that. I'll keep it in mind as the investigation unfolds. Let me know if you think of anything else. One other thing. Going forward, it's probably best for me to handle all communications with the Houston police. If they ask you any more questions, you should consider consulting with an attorney before you answer them."

Suzanne quickly jumped in. "We have every confidence in you, personally. But things are not looking good for Amber. Your recent relationship with her might kindle police interest. We just want you to be careful."

Gordon sagged into the easy chair of his suite. That she had no questions for him about Supermarkets' business that morning told him his days with Multima were probably numbered.

Forty-Five

Montreal, Quebec, Sunday October 22, 2023

When she was sure Serge had hung up the phone, Suzanne looked over at him, tilting her head in curiosity.

"You didn't tell him everything." She said it softly but conveyed with her eyes that she wanted a response.

"You're right. I'm not sure I share your confidence in the guy. He may just have poor judgment. Maybe he's thinking with his dick instead of his brain. I don't know. Candidly, I'd expect the president of a multi-billion-dollar global business to ask many more questions and assess far more objectively the people he deals with. Despite his 'thoughts and prayers' and Christian lifestyle, I don't trust him at all."

Suzanne took a sip from her coffee mug.

"What purpose did the bombing of our Houston store serve for anyone?" Her tone seemed more plaintive than intended, so she added a clarification. "Really, even if we are in a war, as you say, what purpose did that bomb serve?"

"I have two theories. The most likely purpose was to throw us off. Maybe they want to distract us from the computer systems modification project, get us refocused on security at the stores, and push us toward spending money on store safety instead of focusing on a potential cyberattack. Less likely, but still possible, perhaps there's someone other than the Japanese Yakuza or The Organization trying to worm their way in. Candidly, both the unsuccessful drone attack on our home and the bombing of a supermarket sound more like the unhinged bungling of someone like the Shadow than organized crime."

Suzanne mulled that over for a minute, especially after James had raised the same concern. Her conversation with the attorney in Washington didn't support Serge's theory about the Shadow though. According to Beverly Vonderhausen, his gang was already deeply immersed in the 2024 US election cycle and far too busy to bother with Multima or other potentially juicy targets.

"Are your contacts in Europe sure it's Amber they have in their sights?"

"No doubt. Fidelia Morales must have been careless. She probably decided to snatch Amber on short notice and forgot to check for any new airport protocols in Houston. Thanks to those in Texas who abhor immigration, the airports now have far more sophisticated cameras. They not only caught Amber and her two escorts on camera, new technology also captured the plane's identification details, then locked digitally into the jet's navigation system."

"So, they followed the flight all the way to Europe?"

"Yep. And, with a ten-hour flight, once we learned about the tracking details, I reached a contact at Interpol. He had people waiting at the airport in Seville. They followed the thugs who picked her up to an address owned by a known organized crime leader in Spain."

"Why didn't they arrest her?"

"They're watching the place twenty-four hours a day. Interpol wants to catch the big fish. Amber's a minnow in their eyes. Based on the information I shared with them about her— and our challenges with Tak Takahashi and the Yakuza—they want to try to snare him or Fidelia Morales, or the Spanish country head at the very least. By the way, that jet was registered to a numbered company in Japan, so it probably belongs to Takahashi. I agree with their strategy."

Suzanne sipped more of her coffee. It tasted better.

"What about our place in the Laurentians? Is it safe for us to return?" She used a confident tone and smiled hopefully.

"It's your call, of course, but I don't think it's safe yet. You have that board meeting later this week in Florida. If you don't have a lot on your calendar before the annual post-Thanksgiving tour, after Florida I'd recommend another trip to Asia. Spend a few weeks over there while your team back here finishes up the computer programming and conversion of the Jeffersons Stores to the Multima brand. Then do your post-Thanksgiving tour as you always do. Follow that with a vacation for a few days in Europe. By then, I'm guessing we'll have more answers, and life at home should be safer."

"So you think I'll be better off gallivanting around the globe, staying in hotels, than I would be at home?" Although not her first choice, the idea had some appeal, which she conveyed with a mischievous smile.

"Absolutely safer. I'll stay on the West Coast with James and Gordon, getting to the bottom of the Houston bombing, and letting the police here solve the dud bomb incident."

She called her executive assistant, Eileen, and asked her to meet at the office that afternoon. By dinner hour, they'd plotted a travel route and itinerary, identified all the events and commitments they'd need to change, and confirmed with Eileen's spouse that she'd be away for a month.

When Suzanne caught up with Serge after their dinner in the hotel dining room, she slipped into clothes that made her intentions more than obvious. It was the only negligee she had thrown into her carry-on before leaving their home, and it was completely transparent. When Serge stepped out of the shower and came into the bedroom of the suite, he dropped his towel, took her in his arms, and made love to her like it was their first time.

Forty-Six

Seville, Spain, Thursday October 26, 2023

Instead of revisiting the Chinese woman the next morning, as she had threatened during their Sunday conversation, Fidelia left her to stew for a few more days. They fed their captive enough to keep her alive and gave her water to drink twice a day. Fidelia reminded the big American guys guarding the woman that it was okay to play with her from time to time. Both had confirmed multiple "play sessions" and reassured her they'd done no permanent damage, inside or out.

Fidelia was tempted to let the woman vegetate longer, but she hadn't yet heard from Boris Ivanov with a response to Klaudia's demand for cooperation during the meeting in Morocco. Saturday was the deadline. Should they fail to respond, or if the response was not positive, her people had already targeted three unlucky Russians for elimination, and none of those murders would be pretty to watch. Of course, she'd also have to prepare for probable retaliation, so she might have a lot on her agenda in the coming weeks.

Hopefully, greed would overcome Boris Ivanov's anticipated trepidation. Of course, he would be fearful. If he intended to work with Fidelia to retrieve five hundred million dollars stolen earlier from the FSB, she relied on him wanting his share of the heist deposited into a personal account he controlled somewhere offshore. That money couldn't go back to the FSB easily. If that happened, he'd have to explain how his negligence lost the money in the first place, and there were special cells in Siberian jails to accommodate people that stupid.

The guy still had a couple days to respond before the shit hit the fan, but The Organization was ready either way. So, today was the day to break the Chinese woman.

Fidelia dressed entirely in black, wore no makeup, and checked in a mirror that her facial expression conveyed enough anger that Amber would eventually succumb.

The big lout from Florida, whose perpetual grin always

threatened to become a genuine smile, guarded the door and opened it for her to enter. She waved to close it before she approached Amber Chan's bed.

The Chinese woman didn't stir. She was completely covered by white sheets drawn close to her curled-up body, lying on her side, facing away. As she approached, Fidelia heard a faint whimper, no louder than a whisper, but the covered body didn't heave like she was sobbing.

Fidelia said nothing for a moment or two. She simply observed.

A faint whimper continued, but the woman's rate of breathing seemed calm. Perhaps she was asleep.

Fidelia took a step closer and called out loudly, "Wake up."

Without shifting her body, the young Chinese woman simply said, "I'm awake." She paused. "You're Fidelia Morales, aren't you?"

"It doesn't matter who I am. You have a question to answer. Have you thought about it long enough to give me an honest answer?"

"About thirty minutes before the explosion, Tak called ..."

"Who is Tak?" Fidelia interrupted.

"You know, Tak Takahashi. Your guy in Japan. He called and told me he had just learned there would be an explosion at a Jeffersons Store in Houston. He didn't know which store and didn't know who planted the bomb. He said he heard it was a crazy American, and if I was still in Houston, I should get outside as soon as possible."

"How did he know you were in Houston?

"I'd called him a few hours earlier to report in."

"How do you know Takahashi?" She finally asked a question that gave the Chinese woman a reason to shift her position.

She turned to face Fidelia, still pulling the bedsheet tightly around her so only her body above the neck was exposed. She tilted her head and lifted her eyebrows in bewilderment.

Fidelia continued to stare at her prisoner, arms crossed, demonstrating impatience but no other emotion. Finally, Amber relaxed her grip on the sheet enough for it to fall downward and stop at her breasts.

"You must be Fidelia Morales. You know Tak Takahashi. And you must also know why I was calling him to report in. Why are you torturing me this way?"

"As I said, my job here today is to ask the questions. Your role is to answer them fully and truthfully. Start talking, or your next career move will involve 'playing' with a lot more men than the two you've had for the past few days."

Amber started talking. She confirmed her role in the cyberattack plot and spilled her guts for several minutes, telling the whole story. She talked about knowing Takahashi from her university days, her affair with Gordon Goodfellow, her banishment from the project to San Francisco, and ended with the gory details of the explosion she narrowly missed witnessing. She shuddered, then shaking, she burst into tears.

Fidelia was unmoved. She waited until the tears subsided.

"Crazy Americans don't call up Takahashi to tell him they've planted a bomb. How did he find out about it in advance?" Fidelia stiffened her posture but remained silent.

Amber continued to sniffle for another couple moments, looking down, probably considering her options.

Finally, she spoke. "Tak has a contact in North Korea, another friend from university. He's high up in the security apparatus of the government and oversees a chunk of their cyber spying in the US. He came across a message sent by someone there giving instructions for the bombing to someone in Houston, routing that message from Miami through Germany, Russia, China, and Hawaii before it landed in Texas. Both Americans had encrypted email, but the Koreans could still decipher the message. The guy in Korea knew about Tak's connection to Jeffersons Stores and gave him a heads-up."

Fidelia processed that information for a moment or two. Amber didn't speak.

"You had a good job with Multima in China, making lots of money, with lots of power and responsibility. Why did you get involved with Tak's plan to attack the company?" Fidelia asked.

Amber relaxed her shoulders, letting the sheet slip further down her breasts until she noticed and quickly tucked it back under one arm to keep it in place. Then her face brightened, and a smile formed.

"I saw an opportunity to become as powerful as you." She made direct eye contact for the first time. "I realized Suzanne Simpson's days at Multima would be numbered if we could launch a successful cyberattack. Tak shared enough details about the data interceptors the Yakuza had planted and the damage they would do when he launched the attack. His 'secret' announcement on the dark web was designed to give Multima a sense of urgency about trying to fortify their systems."

She paused and looked around, seeming to ask if everything was clear so far, so Fidelia nodded and let her continue.

"He has a plant inside Multima who put forward my name. I became confident that I could guide the technology process and execute the attack exactly as Tak planned. After we pulled a few billion dollars out of the company with our hack and ransom, I expected to see Suzanne Simpson thrown out by her board of directors. My name would be put forward to replace her by one of the influential men who serve on that board. If it worked, I could become as rich and powerful as you. That's why I switched sides."

"And then it all seemed to fall apart," Fidelia said. "They became suspicious of your role, cut you out of the technology process, and banished you to operations in the western US, far away from their computer technology. Is that right?"

Amber looked downward, and her shoulders slumped slightly. She shook her head sideways a couple times, either in disgust or disappointment.

Fidelia waited for her answer, crossing her arms again to signal time was running out.

"I asked you a question. I expect an answer." Fidelia used the same firm tone as earlier, when she'd threatened banishment to her European escort service.

"If Tak or you still want to do it, I have all the information we need. Sending me to San Francisco changed nothing for Multima. Even today, I've received all the data I need to thwart all the changes Multima is spending a hundred million dollars to fix."

Forty-Seven

Ft. Myers, Florida, Friday October 27, 2023

As the car driving James Fitzgerald and him from nearby Page Field pulled up to the side entrance of the building, Gordon Goodfellow thought Suzanne should probably sell the old, pale yellow brick headquarters tower in downtown Ft. Myers.

But Suzanne probably found the building hard to part with. There were likely too many fond memories. John George Mortimer chose that location to manage a small team overseeing all of Multima's operations around the globe. Rumor had it that he not only picked that spot for its great Florida weather but also to vacate his long-time office in Atlanta. He'd said he wanted to give Suzanne space and distance to run the Supermarkets business after he'd promoted her from the Canadian supermarket chain he'd acquired.

Most of the facility was rented out now, and only a handful of Multima people remained there to support the staff working out of the company's new global headquarters in Montreal. But the beautiful, large conference room John George had furnished with the finest furniture, and beautifully decorated to feel like a meeting room of a Fortune 50 company, remained intact. It was still lovingly cared for by the few employees remaining.

Suzanne liked to schedule at least one of the quarterly board meetings there. Most of her current directors had been appointed years earlier by John George himself, and they always appreciated her gesture of remembrance. They also tended to relax their diligent oversight of her and the Multima team on those occasions.

With everything they'd been dealing with lately, Gordon was happy that she chose this location before she summoned him to report to the board. Today, he'd need all the help that fond memories and goodwill might provide.

Entering the meeting room moments later, he saw most of the directors standing around in small groups shaking hands, patting each other on the back, smiling and occasionally enjoying a short laugh. He headed to his assigned chair to the left of Suzanne and noticed a name card for James Fitzgerald on the table next to his. Unusual.

What message is Suzanne sending to the directors now?

Gordon dropped off a USB drive with Eileen, who was organizing the resident techie and would ensure the PowerPoint presentations appeared on the screen at the right time for the correct speaker. Then he sought out Suzanne, who held court with her seemingly ever-present chief of security, a director from the mid-west, and James Fitzgerald.

He interrupted their conversation only long enough for a quick good morning, a brief shake of each of their hands, and enough time for her to flash her most dazzling smile. That it sparkled brighter than usual gave him some comfort as he made the rounds and greeted all the participants.

No one needed to call the meeting to order. As soon as Suzanne moved toward her chair at the head of the table, everyone else in the room took their assigned place and conversations stopped.

When Alberto Ferer, serving as secretary of the board, cleared his throat twice and started to speak, the meeting was underway.

"This will be our last quarterly meeting of this fiscal year. The management team has created an aggressive agenda for us to review, and you'll note that four directors have requested time to discuss specific subjects. I expect this meeting will take most of the day, so Eileen has arranged for breaks and lunch here in the boardroom. For those directors who can stay, Eileen has also planned for everyone to dine at The Veranda this evening. I know that's a favorite among this group, and I hope you'll be able to stay and join us."

Judging by the enthusiastic nods and broad grins around the table, most planned to be there. That was a good sign. Gordon nodded with equal enthusiasm and turned on his most charming smile. Directors might go a little easier on him, knowing they might sit beside him for dinner. He'd need every little edge possible today.

As Alberto droned on with his other opening comments, Gordon tuned out the background noise and focused on those sitting around the table, looking for signs of discontent. Most sat erect, some with arms crossed, others sagging comfortably into the dark brown leather chairs. Only Abduhl Mahinder signaled mild impatience. He tapped his fingers on the tabletop slowly and methodically as he listened, his brow already furrowed.

When Alberto finally finished, he ceded control of the meeting to Suzanne, who wasted no time. She spoke briskly and minimized words, a stark contrast to her chief legal officer.

"Let's get right down to the financial results and outlook for the quarter with a preliminary forecast for fiscal 2024. Pierre Cabot, will you please lead us through the numbers?"

According to Pierre, Multima was headed for a colossal quarter. Sales revenues were up everywhere except with Jeffersons Stores' recent "softness" due to the Houston bombing incident. Gross margins were stronger in the Financial Services and Supermarkets divisions and across the globe. Expenses were well under control, although technology costs were up a hundred million for the systems conversions and enhancements. Shareholders would be delighted with the profits he'd announce in February, but the board might brace itself for some more negative media coverage of those spectacular results.

Several board members applauded spontaneously when Pierre sat down from his formal presentation, gradually drawing in all the others, with a few even standing while they clapped to show their delight with the news. Directors of Multima Corporation were legally required to own at least one thousand shares in the company, so this bit of news surely added significantly to their personal wealth. Gordon tried to show as much enthusiasm as those around him.

Suzanne glanced toward him while she joined the applause, probably only to remind him he was up next. Her broad smile disappeared when she passed the meeting to him.

"Gordon Goodfellow will give us a picture of how things are going at Supermarkets. You all know that last quarter we closed the biggest acquisition in our history. We knew that takeover came with some challenges. That's why we paid only about sixty percent of its book value. However, the integration of Jeffersons Stores has proven more challenging on a couple fronts than we anticipated. I've asked Gordon to give us an accurate picture of where we stand with this new operating division and its integration into the Multima corporate family."

His knees weren't shaking as he strode to the lectern beside the large screen, but he felt some limpness. A large head-and-shoulders photo of him superimposed over a picture of a large Multima Supermarket appeared on the screen. His underarms already felt damp, despite applying twice as much deodorant as usual. Before he approached the lectern, he sent a silent prayer to God to help him get through today.

He started with the bombing in Houston to get the worst news out of the way first. Once again, Edward Hadley and his team had coached him on the appropriate facial expressions to use and the preferred tone of voice to tell the story. His audience listened respectfully—without interruption—as Gordon described being near the site when the explosion occurred and some of his interactions with the police and media afterward.

He moved on to the systems integration and enhancements and gave a brief, high-level summary of progress, knowing Marcel Dubois was next on the agenda to provide more detailed insight.

Finally, he broached the subject of Amber Chan and her disappearance. Naturally, he left out all the personal stuff, made no mention of the suspicions surrounding her, and avoided any hint of animosity. Tragically, she'd disappeared, and the authorities were still trying to locate her. Of course, he added his thoughts and prayers for a quick return to her role at Multima as soon as possible.

He flipped to his next slide, introducing progress on rebranding Jeffersons Stores to Multima Supermarkets, and had just started to speak when Abduhl Mahinder waved a finger and interjected. "Before you move on, tell us more about this woman Amber Chan. I don't know much about her. The last I heard of her, she was leading the Asian supermarkets division and doing an acceptable job there. What's gone on with her over the past quarter?"

Shit! Abduhl was at the meeting when Nicole put forward her name. Was he now playing some sort of game? Would the next few minutes be akin to walking gingerly through a minefield?

"Sure. Good question." Gordon bought a couple seconds to organize his thoughts. "We realized we needed a Multima person to lead the Jeffersons Stores integration. As you mentioned, Amber was our high-performing Asia leader for the past five years and was on my radar for possible advancement throughout that time. But it was actually Nicole Gagnon, our new HR leader, who brought her name forward. She pointed out that Amber not only spoke Mandarin, Cantonese, and English but was also proficient in Japanese. With many Japanese Americans both working and shopping at Jeffersons Stores, we saw that as an asset."

He paused to give the directors time to absorb the value of those skills. "As a bonus, we learned she was not only a strong business operator but also has superior technology skills. In addition to her honors MBA, she has a minor degree in computer sciences, where she ranked second in her class of more than four hundred international students at the University of Tokyo."

He took a breath again, giving everyone enough time to understand why she had been an excellent candidate for the role. "We moved her over to Atlanta to oversee everything related to the Jeffersons Stores integration, but she became so deeply immersed in the technology side of the equation that operations suffered somewhat. She realized that, and offered to move away from the technology and let the very capable headquarters team assume control, while she focused on shoring up operational performance in the stores. Eventually, it made more sense for her to live and work from San Francisco where Jeffersons Stores is headquartered. She was making good progress with the store performance metrics when she disappeared."

Abduhl Mahinder listened intently while Gordon answered his question. When he finished, all eyes in the room shifted to Mahinder. He nodded slowly but said nothing for a moment or so. Dramatically, he tilted his head to the side and looked up at Gordon.

"The woman surely has good academic credentials, and it's easy to see why everyone considered her a good candidate for the role." He turned in Suzanne's direction but addressed his question to Serge Boisvert, seated beside her. "May I ask what background checks your security team used to clear this Chinese national to work at a senior level in our new acquisition?"

Holy Shit! The powerful director representing the Bank of The Americas seemed to be casting blame on Suzanne's live-in partner.

"The security team didn't perform any additional background checks. I presumed the decision to promote her was made based on those checks performed by HR when she was hired and her multi-year experience in a management role." Serge's tone was factual with no hint of mistake or apology.

Mahinder nodded but wasn't satisfied. He shifted to look directly at Serge and his interrogation continued. "In retrospect, do you think background checks for senior executives should become Multima policy and a standard operating procedure?"

"I think that might be a good idea going forward."

Mahinder nodded and shifted his eyes back to Suzanne. His tone was polite but cool. "Can the board of directors expect to see that policy implemented without delay?"

Suzanne nodded. Her eyes burned with the dressing down, but she wasn't prepared to fight the logic, even if his manner appeared to annoy her.

But Mahinder wasn't finished. "I have another question for anyone on the management team. I've heard a rumor that Ms. Amber Chan was sexually promiscuous. Some say she slept with several of her colleagues. Is there any truth to that rumor?"

Gordon felt the blood drain from his face. His legs weakened, and he felt like he might lose his balance. He fought to maintain his composure and find the words to reply, but none came. Worse, he found himself stammering incoherently when he tried.

Suzanne jumped in. "I'll take this one. There have been rumors, but we investigated each one when it surfaced and were not able to conclusively substantiate any such incidents. We did learn two Chinese technicians in Atlanta were rumored to be involved in inappropriate sexual activity, and their employment with Multima was terminated. Not because of sexual dalliances, but due to concerns about their technological competence."

This seemed to satisfy Mahinder. He nodded. "I'm glad to hear management is taking her behavior seriously, investigating rumors of inappropriate behavior, and taking action when necessary. I apologize for the interruption. Please carry on, Gordon."

Somehow, he found the strength and courage to continue and finished his thirty-minute presentation without further interruption or questions. It was hard to read the crowd, though, because almost all the directors appeared to be studying papers on the table as he spoke. When he finished, every director around the table studiously avoided making eye contact with him as Gordon returned to his seat. No one could miss the stark contrast with the raucous applause awarded earlier to Pierre Cabot.

The rest of the meeting was a blur. Gordon sat there, forcing himself to appear interested and engaged. He prayed silently for the strength to persevere, but he sensed that every person in the room suspected he'd played a part in those malicious rumors.

During the lunch break, he felt nauseous and picked at a few fresh vegetables and a glass of water. He had only brief conversations with his colleagues rather than the all-important directors, fearing follow-up questions to the allegations planted by Mahinder and lacking a strategy to avoid wading further into the sexual cesspool.

When Alberto Ferer declared the directors meeting officially closed at the end of the day, Gordon gathered up his phone and files and stashed them quickly in his briefcase. He leaned over Suzanne while she was still seated and murmured that he wasn't feeling well and would return immediately to Atlanta. He'd take a commercial flight.

She glanced up at him for a moment, her brow furrowed in sympathy, and said that she understood and would call him tomorrow. He had difficulty continuing to look into her probing eyes, dropping his in shame as he backed away from the table.

Forty-Eight
San Francisco, California, Saturday October 28, 2023

Suzanne loved shopping on Hayes Street in the Hayes Valley area. Serge tolerated it. That morning, she scurried in and out of the quirky shops and boutiques on a mission. It was time to freshen up her wardrobe, and what better time than the day before departing for Asia? She'd planned it that way.

Leaving Montreal for the board of directors meeting in Florida, she brought only enough clothes for two days, but she packed them in the large suitcase she used for overseas trips. So she had lots of space, and Serge's cheerful assistance, for choosing a few new outfits before heading out to China later that evening.

She'd prepared for that flight with some trepidation. There were several dangling issues she'd need to monitor from afar, but Serge persuaded her he'd feel more comfortable knowing she was out of the country for a while. He was convinced Tak Takahashi and his gang would attempt a cyberattack sometime before the end of the year. A disruption before the crucial US Thanksgiving and Christmas selling periods would give them more negotiating leverage than at any other time.

When Suzanne's jet left for Shanghai around midnight, Serge would use a borrowed Financial Services jet and fly to Atlanta. There, he'd set up shop with her chief of technology, Marcel Dubois. Together, they'd try to complete work on the Multima computer systems upgrades before Thanksgiving. She'd given the pair *carte blanche* to divert whatever resources they needed and spend whatever amount was necessary for overtime or other costs.

They planned to meet for a weekend in Hawaii once during her three-week voyage. Otherwise, she expected their interaction would be limited to brief daily phone calls and occasional text updates. She'd focus on Asia, and Serge would try to outsmart the cyber bandits.

As they walked back to their suite at the Four Seasons

Hotel, she took his free hand and squeezed it playfully. Still moving, she tilted her head and flashed her best smile. "Let's order lunch to the suite. If we only have a few hours together this month, I want to make the most of them. Let's order from here, have it ready when we arrive at our room, wolf it down, and then let me make love to you until we have to leave for the airport."

Serge agreed, stopped for a second to retrieve the hotel's number, then resumed their pace once the phone started to ring. Suzanne used that opportunity to reach for her phone and pressed the number for Gordon Goodfellow. She owed him a call, and it was already late afternoon on the East Coast.

"Are you feeling better today?" She tried for an upbeat, but not overly cheerful, tone.

"Marginally. I still didn't sleep well after my lame performance at yesterday's meeting. Are the directors pushing you to toss me out?" His tone suggested genuine remorse about his performance, but what about the deed?

"You know I'm not easily pushed about by directors or others. If you were in my position, what would you do?" She kept her tone light. By asking the question, she was intentionally taking the issue to another level, so she waited for him to make his mental calculations and formulate a response.

"You never ask easy questions, do you?" He laughed uneasily, buying time.

Suzanne made no reply.

"If you want me to resign, I will. I made a couple big mistakes, there's no doubt about it. I know you once fired James Fitzgerald for a single indiscretion far less serious. He told me all about it. But you hired him back again when you truly needed his expertise. That tells me that, while you have rules and standards, you can adjust them when circumstances warrant. It gives me hope you might consider my long years of dedicated service to you and Multima, accept that I have realized the error of my ways, and feel confident you'll never see a repeat of my poor behavior."

Some contrition in there, that's good. Now let's see if there's enough.

"Which specific error of your ways are you referring to?"

For at least a minute, Suzanne heard only the sounds of cars and trucks on the busy street, voices of people laughing and chatting as they strode behind her or passed on the crowded sidewalk, and the sound of her own breathing as she continued to walk beside Serge at a brisk pace.

Gordon cleared his throat when he was ready. "Clearly, the list of my mistakes is long. I was wrong to flaunt the company policies with my use of the jet and my inappropriate personal interactions with Amber, which led directly to my current divorce case. But my biggest shortcoming was probably my poor judgment about Amber and her role in all this. I messed up badly there, and whether you ask for my resignation or not, I plan to get together with Serge and Marcel Dubois. While I've been sitting here thinking the past few hours, I've recalled a few inconsistencies in conversations I had with Amber. They might be useful as the team works to fix the computer systems' vulnerabilities."

Bingo! The right answer. But how useful might that information be? "What kind of inconsistencies?"

"I'm not sure how important they are. I'm no technology expert, but I'm interested in learning more about it, so I asked Amber lots of questions when we were together, away from the office. Serge and Marcel will have to decide. But I remember comments she made in conversations with me about things in the computer systems she discovered and fixed, but when I read the assessment reports now, I see they weren't fixed; or someone modified them differently from what she described to me."

The hotel entrance was only a few yards away, and she needed to cut the call short.

"I want you to spend a few minutes with Serge today." She made eye contact with Serge as she said it, and shrugged her shoulders with a grimace of apology. "We're just arriving at the hotel and have lunch waiting in the suite. Make a list of the things you want to discuss with him, and Serge will call you in an hour."

It turned out they consumed the succulent salmon dish faster than originally planned. Serge was intrigued by the new development and anxious to ferret out any information with a sense of urgency. He called Gordon before the agreed-upon hour, and they both listened on speaker while he explained the inconsistencies that had caught his attention after he thought more about his past conversations with Amber. Serge made extensive notes, his enthusiasm visibly growing.

It was past six o'clock in San Francisco, nine on the East Coast, when Serge said that was enough for the day. He begged Gordon to keep thinking about his conversations with Amber and make notes of any issue that didn't seem entirely right. They'd meet with Marcel when Serge arrived in Atlanta on Sunday morning.

A quick call to Marcel Dubois followed. Excited, Serge asked him to get a team together immediately and recounted his major takeaways from the conversation with Gordon. "Get your best guys working on the internal firewalls. Have them compare every line of code with the diagrams in the assessment reports. I think we're going to find the source of the new vulnerabilities you discovered."

When his call ended, Serge unbuttoned his shirt and belt buckle.

"Hurry up. I'm ready for that lovemaking you promised. We've only got three hours before we leave for the airport." He giggled before tugging Suzanne down onto the bed, smothering her with kisses.

Forty-Nine

Seville, Spain, Saturday October 28, 2023

Those Russian *sonsofbitches* didn't respond to Fidelia's demand. By today, they were to reach Klaudia with their proposal on where and when they would meet to discuss ways they could cooperate to avoid a gang war. She'd be completely justified in ordering an execution or two that morning to get the bastards' attention, but she decided not to issue any murder orders just yet.

Instead, she stood behind Amber and Klaudia, who sat beside each other, in front of a huge monitor parked on one side of the dining room table in the luxury apartment in Seville where they were all staying. Hours earlier, two technicians working for her Spanish country boss, Juan Suarez, had lugged in the big screen and a powerful new laptop computer they promised had every single one of the latest chips and technology features known to man.

The young technophiles giggled in anticipation as they unboxed the computer, connected all the wires, and started up both devices. Their faces glowed when they saw how rapidly the device processed data, downloaded software, and responded to commands. After the two women took control, both guys gawked at the huge screen with mouths agape while another universe of technology opened before their eyes.

At that point, Amber whispered into Fidelia's ear that the guys should probably leave. Amber's status had morphed positively away from "that Chinese woman" the moment she claimed she still had the ability to hack Multima's system—despite the millions of dollars the company was spending to block intruders.

That day, Fidelia had brought Klaudia into the room where they held Amber captive, naked and hungry. The women chatted for about ten minutes. Fidelia listened intently but only understood about twenty-five percent of their conversation. Instead, she relied on Klaudia to both filter and translate what the woman said.

Klaudia had smiled when she turned to face Fidelia. "She's very good, maybe the smartest technician I've met. What she says is plausible. We need to test it to be sure, but it looks like she engineered enough new vulnerabilities, in the most unlikely places, to still bring Multima's computer system down—even if they found and blocked all the vulnerabilities Tak's people planted from Japan."

Without delay, Fidelia had ordered food and clothing for Amber and had her moved from the bodyguards' quarters one floor below to Juan Suarez's luxurious third-floor apartment. They gave her the room Fidelia had used, allowed her to shower, arranged some food, and rescinded the invitation for the guards to play with the woman whenever they pleased.

Klaudia told her that she and Amber had talked well into that night, long after Fidelia left with two bodyguards for a suite reserved at the nearby luxury hotel King Alfonso XIII. When Fidelia returned to the apartment the next morning, they had their technology shopping list ready for Juan Suarez's men.

The two female computer geeks giggled like their male counterparts as they moved onto the dark web and along a path Amber navigated to peek into Multima's computer systems. Not two minutes later, she pointed to a vulnerability and demonstrated to Klaudia how she could open and close the software gate at will. She did it only once. More than one try might attract attention and corrective action by the Multima technicians.

Klaudia's high five with Amber, combined with their squeals of delight, told Fidelia all she needed to know. She sent Amber to her room to relax while she discussed the plan with Klaudia and Juan Suarez. Then they brought the country managers for Italy, France and Portugal into the conversation via burner phones with encrypted security. Everyone agreed it was time to set the wheels in motion.

Fidelia gave the order, and Pierre Boivin left their call to carry out that command. When he returned several minutes later, he confirmed an execution would take place later that day.

Fidelia and Klaudia then met to draft a message to Yuri Federov. They did their work on another laptop connected to an IP address in Rabat, Morocco. They typed, revised, typed again, and revised further. When they were satisfied, Klaudia saved it and waited.

It was after dinner before Pierre Boivin called from France. "It's done. As planned."

Fidelia nodded to Klaudia, who picked up the laptop they'd later destroy, and found the message they'd crafted. It was addressed to Federov using his private email address in St. Petersburg. She read it one last time and took one further long glance at Fidelia before she pressed the "send" button. Their message used words sparsely but left few doubts.

It is Saturday. FSB agent Dima Andropov had an unfortunate accident today while walking in the Forêt Sidi Amira near Rabat airport. As a result of his fall, he broke both legs in multiple places and succumbed to his injuries.

Fifty

Atlanta, Georgia, Sunday October 29, 2023

They met in his office rather than the normal project meeting room two floors down. Gordon had offered up his expansive suite, and Serge accepted immediately, saying it was another way to keep the group small and limit the number of ears listening to their conversation.

Serge brought in a couple of his people, and they wandered around Gordon's office with wands and another apparatus, checking for listening devices. It could have all been for show, but Gordon supposed their caution was advisable—although the guys could be planting new devices while they worked.

Marcel Dubois arrived with his two most senior programmers. They all laughed and spoke French while wandering down the hallway but instantly switched to English as they stepped into Gordon's office and said their hellos. Despite their strong accents, all understood English well.

Marcel looked like a typical computer geek that Sunday morning. He hadn't shaved since at least Friday, and his hair was ruffled as though he hadn't touched it since he got out of bed the previous day. Large dark eyeglass frames drew attention to his brown eyes, which danced with the cadence of the conversation. He and his colleagues all seemed alert, although each of them had worked through the night with a couple short naps.

Serge took control of the meeting. He asked Marcel what they had found. The chief technology officer provided a quick summary. They'd found twenty-four variations from the expected code and hadn't finished yet. So far, they were bewildered. At least a half-dozen of the variations occurred in software created by the two guys in the room.

They'd spotted the deviations right away, without a need to verify against written records. Somehow, the code they wrote had changed. Yet security records showed no access from outside the system by anyone. It was almost as though something in the internal code changed automatically, without human intervention.

"We've created a team of five AI specialists. This morning, they're scanning all the known software programs running in the system. We'll see if they can detect an app that's not supposed to be there or an app that's been modified with artificial intelligence," Marcel explained.

"When should we know?" Serge smiled, apparently to soften his demand.

Marcel shook his head, then answered. "It's too early to know. When we came up here, they'd finished scanning less than ten percent of the apps in the system. They scan some of those apps in a minute, but some take more than an hour."

"Are we using artificial intelligence in the system already?" Serge asked.

Marcel grinned at his colleagues, then took a moment to formulate his response so a layperson might understand. "If you're asking if we have apps like ChatGPT, the answer is yes. Many individual servers have it installed. We also have to remember that even basic word-processing apps like Microsoft Word use AI to spellcheck documents. So lots of servers have lots of AI—to varying degrees—accessing our systems."

Marcel paused to be sure Serge got it so far. Once he saw Serge's nod, he carried on.

"On the other hand, if you're asking if we use artificial intelligence to perform specific activities we direct, the answer is 'sort of.' Part of the expense we're incurring with this systems upgrade is for smart apps that will let us improve security by issuing instructions to those apps to change coding on the fly, scrambling previous commands at random and creating new code automatically, with limited or no human intervention."

"When did you start installing the 'smart apps'?"

"About a week ago, but we didn't report it in the daily summaries. That guy you brought in from CSIS made some good suggestions. We're fine with this group knowing it's there, but it's better if no one else learns about this new feature." Marcel leaned in as he spoke.

Gordon processed both the information and its

implications. A thought occurred to him. "Any chance this new app in some way created the vulnerabilities you discovered?"

Marcel shook his head. "Not likely. We're checking that, of course. But our sense is that our smart app isn't yet smart enough to perform that level of code modification."

Everyone took a moment to think and process. Serge took another tack. "Let's talk about the team composition and information-sharing protocols."

Marcel pointed to his technology expert on his left. A younger guy, probably just out of school, pulled out a few pieces of paper and distributed them around the table. It was a chart with the names of all the people who received the daily report and their role in the company. There were more than fifty names.

Serge asked the young fellow to explain why each of the names received a daily update on progress. Painstakingly, the fellow went through every name and title describing why that person needed the information. It was laborious, and by name forty-three, everyone's attention had waned. Suddenly, at name forty-four, he lurched in his chair and almost shouted it out.

"I don't recall seeing this name before. I don't know what they do or why they're on the list."

Serge pounced. "Do you have a record of when names are added and by whom they're added?"

The young fellow nodded and started tapping his computer keyboard furiously. Everyone waited in silence, thinking about the name, trying to recall if they knew the person and what role they played. After three or four minutes of working his keyboard, the young fellow looked around the room, gauging the mood before he spoke.

"I think we have a problem. The person who added this name was one of the Chinese technicians we fired last month. He added the new name the morning we terminated his employment. Name number forty-four is Susan Wilson. There is no one in the company's HR records by that name. Worse, when I followed the email address listed for the reports, I ended up at an anonymous site on the dark web."

Marcel leaned over to see for himself, swore, and banged his fist on the desk. "That sonofabitch never had access to this distribution list. He used someone else's access to get in, then altered the access list to include his ID. We're just seeing this name now because he overrode the tracking device."

"A vindictive last gesture?" Gordon asked.

"Not likely. Seems too calculated," Marcel replied. "Someone on the dark web knows every change we made to our systems over the past month. Who knows who that person might be? And who else they've shared it with?"

"I'm taking Susan Wilson, number forty-four, off the list right now," the young fellow said.

"The smart apps are trained to distort actual changes in reports, right? Are we sure only the five of us in the room know about them?" Serge looked each person in the eye with a short, penetrating glare. He held his piercing look for an instant longer on Gordon.

"Like you, I just learned about them now. I haven't talked to anyone about any of this stuff, but take me off the list if you have any concerns. I don't need to receive the daily updates. Periodic chats like this are fine with me."

The young fellow removed Gordon from the list seconds after Serge's nod of instruction. They carried on for another few minutes, reviewing the list and querying each name. It looked like only that one name gave cause for concern.

Serge looked around the table and proposed next steps. "Marcel, let's move downstairs to your office. I want to know more about those smart apps, and we'll let your guys get back to their jobs. Gordon, I don't think we need to eat up any more of your weekend, so feel free to leave whenever you choose."

Alone in his office, Gordon plunked himself in his executive chair, shook his head and rubbed his shoulders. Leaning back, he looked skyward again.

"She's smarter than I ever imagined, Lord. You've got to help me get out of this one!" he whispered.

Fifty-One

Beijing, China, Thursday November 2, 2023

It was Suzanne's third day in China. Yesterday, she'd been in Shanghai, visiting Multima Supermarkets' China office and store locations. This morning it was the capital, Beijing.

Although her Asian president for Supermarkets had begun working to get an appointment with China's minister of commerce, Wang Fùyù, three weeks earlier, she only received confirmation about nine o'clock last evening of a meeting scheduled for 10:15 this morning. The minister's assistant had emphasized the hour precisely and warned their session would end after exactly thirty minutes.

Suzanne recognized the power play and took it in stride. She was grateful to get even thirty minutes with him, given current tensions between the leaders of China and both the US and Canada. She doubted their conversation would be productive, but Jennie Xìngyùn, the woman who'd succeeded Amber Chan, insisted they should appeal for the government minister's intervention.

They flew to Beijing right after the call to avoid any complications or delays the morning of the meeting. After the two-and-a-half-hour flight and car ride to the Four Seasons in Beijing, they'd checked in about two thirty in the morning, so she'd had about four hours of sleep.

Despite the twelve-hour difference from her normal body time, and the intervening time in San Francisco, her jet lag had waned, and she felt energetic that morning. Suzanne ordered a large American breakfast to her suite and ate it quickly as she dressed and prepared herself in formal business attire. She'd need every ounce of energy possible because she was scheduled to meet with one of the titans in China. Wang Fùyù carried clout not only with the party apparatus; he was considered highly influential with China's president.

As a hired chauffeur drove Suzanne, Jennie, and their two bodyguards toward the minister's office, she checked in with Serge. After her meeting in China finished, it would already be late in Atlanta, and she preferred to avoid disturbing his rest if possible. After all, he was still pressing every possible button to hasten the completion of the cyber security upgrade project.

"We made good progress today," he said. "Marcel brought in another six programmers, and they think they've secured the inner wall. They'll test it again tonight. The outer wall still has some vulnerabilities, but he thinks he can finish it on the weekend." Serge's tone was more positive than during any other conversation they'd had over the past two weeks.

"Now, to be sure I'm clear on the timing, this completion you're talking about is only securing the Jeffersons and Multima systems, and they're still separate from one another. Is that correct?" she asked.

"Yeah. Marcel wants to achieve one hundred percent security on both systems before they start migrating all the Jeffersons' data to the Multima servers. Once he gets started, he thinks the migration will take about a month."

That meant confusion in the marketplace for a while. Jeffersons Stores signage was already coming down from their buildings, replaced by the distinctive new Multima signs.

In a few more days, customers in the Southwest would shop inside stores identified as Multima Supermarkets. They'd see lots of materials promoting the Multima name around the locations, but their purchase receipts would still say Jeffersons Stores. She made a mental note to contact Edward Hadley after the meeting to see if he was on it.

Their ride from the Four Seasons Hotel to No. 2 Dong Chang'an Avenue, in the heart of Beijing, took less than a half hour. As she said goodbye to Serge, the driver pulled up to the curb in front of the government offices.

A tall, well-dressed Chinese woman, cradling a clipboard in one arm, smiled and waved to Suzanne after they entered the lobby of the large building. She immediately stepped forward to meet the group halfway and bowed respectfully before offering her hand first to Suzanne, then Jennie. She said something to Jennie in Chinese. Her smile had disappeared.

Jennie replied in Chinese, then turned to Suzanne to explain. "She was concerned about your bodyguards. I forgot to let her know you travel with security, and she asked if they could wait outside the room while you meet with Wang Fùyù. I told her I'd ask you."

Suzanne nodded to the greeter and turned to confirm the bodyguards heard and understood the request. The Chinese host's smile returned with the interactions. She motioned for the group to follow her toward an elevator held open by a uniformed attendant.

While the elevator traveled to the eleventh floor, no one spoke. When it glided to a stop, Suzanne's group followed their host to a meeting room at the end of a long, well-finished corridor, the walls laden with photos and paintings. Before opening the doorway to the meeting room, their host pointed toward two green chairs upholstered with detailed needlepoint artwork and motioned for the bodyguards to stay there as she spoke with Jennie in Chinese. Two uniformed and armed guards stood on either side of the doorway, staring forward, making no sound or gesture of welcome as Suzanne and Jennie followed their guide inside.

The meeting room appeared luxuriously finished with dark wood paneling, subdued lighting, a round mahogany table, eight dark-brown leather chairs, and a plush tan carpet.

Their host pointed toward two chairs facing a flag of China and spoke again to Jennie.

"She wants to know if she can serve us tea while we wait for Wang Fùyù."

"*Shì de, qǐng,*" Suzanne said to their host, adding a cheerful smile and the hint of a bowing gesture she'd observed usually accompanied a Chinese acceptance of an offer of hospitality. She glanced at her watch after she accepted the offered teacup. 10:10.

Jennie had already warned all conversations in the room would be recorded, so they sat silently, sipping their tea. By the scheduled meeting time, there was no sign of Wang Fùyù or anyone from his team.

Suzanne started to simmer. She wasn't accustomed to waiting and took some offense to the minister's tardiness—especially after the earlier warning about punctuality from his office. But she waited in silence, checking her phone for messages.

At 10:27, the meeting room burst open, and Wang Fùyù

entered the room at a brisk pace, bowed formally, and moved directly to greet Suzanne with an outstretched arm and a smile that was difficult to read, neither friendly nor apologetic. Rather, it appeared pasted onto his face as a last-minute requirement.

"I apologize for the delay." To Suzanne's surprise, he spoke English perfectly and motioned for her to sit down again after their handshake. She noted the tailored cut of his designer-label suit and guessed his tie might have cost as much as her entire outfit. The guy liked to flaunt it.

However, the three assistants who trailed him didn't merit either an introduction or formal greeting. One younger member of the team gave her a tentative wave and smiled shyly as he took a seat farthest from Fùyù. Once everyone was in position, the government minister began without any small talk or pleasantries, again entirely in English.

"I understand you're here to complain about delays in winning approvals for twenty-five new store locations in Guangdong Province. Is that correct?"

She hadn't anticipated such an abrupt start to the discussion, so she took a moment to smile and chose her opening words carefully: "Over the past twelve months, I understand our Chinese management team has submitted several requests for permits to build supermarkets on land we've purchased in Guangdong."

Suzanne spoke slowly, calmly, and respectfully. "Our team here realizes the offices of the commerce ministry are extremely busy and burdened with many requests, but these seem to be taking far longer than the usual few months expected. We thought it might be helpful to understand if there were any problems with the submissions that we might explain or clarify."

Wang Fùyù listened, then responded the second she finished her explanation. "Are you an American or a Canadian?"

"I have dual citizenship." She smiled politely despite his confrontational tone. "I used my Canadian passport at immigration this visit. Has there been some problem reported with it?"

"The main problem is your lame prime minister and his

unjust accusations about the Chinese people and their government. He's surely not made of the same stuff as his father. But, if you had used your US passport, I would have complained about your president and his senseless tariffs. They make everything we ship to your country more expensive for your people to buy, and line the pockets of both your country's lobbyists and your government."

"Are you suggesting the delays we are encountering with permits and approvals in Guangdong are in some way related to Canadian and US government behavior toward China?"

"Not at all. But I'm sure you understand people in my department are human. They think. They have feelings. And I can imagine that should some of the people working on your files feel disrespected by your leaders or governments, they might not proceed with haste. Especially—as you noted—since they are already burdened with requests from Chinese companies and corporations in other countries that aren't showing China hostility."

Suzanne didn't reply immediately. Instead, she maintained eye contact with the minister and fought to retain a neutral expression.

It worked. He got to his hidden agenda for this meeting. "I'm not inclined to ask my team to move Multima Supermarkets' requests for permits to the top of the pile. We already have lots of food stores in China. Our people already can choose from many competitors who call China their home or are owned by companies located in countries that are friendlier toward us. But, more urgently, I cannot support requests from a company that doesn't take care of Chinese citizens it employs."

That comment shocked Suzanne. "I'm sorry. I don't understand your meaning. We treat our Chinese team members like all our employees, with care and respect."

"Then explain why Amber Chan, one of our citizens, has been reported missing and can't be located after an explosion in one of your stores."

"It's true Amber is missing. The police in Houston are looking for her, and they've requested the help of Interpol. Police authorities around the world are looking for her. Of course, I trust she is well, and we all hope they find her soon."

Wang Fùyù stood up from the table abruptly and glared down at her. "She's alive. She sent us a message. She's being held in a secret location somewhere in Europe. Amber Chan blames you personally for her kidnapping in Houston. If you have any hope for approval of your permits, Amber Chan must first be returned to us."

His assistants stood in unison and followed him from the room without the courtesy of a bow, a handshake, or a goodbye. Seconds later the woman who ushered them to the meeting room reappeared, motioning for Suzanne and her group to follow her. No smile was evident, nor any of the earlier hospitality the woman had shown.

No one spoke as the elevator descended. In the lobby, the woman continued to lead her guests toward the exit as though they might not remember their way out. Jennie called for their car as they marched and said something in Mandarin to their host when they reached the door.

Guards opened the massive front doors, and Suzanne heard their host say something else to Jennie before she stopped abruptly, bowed in one quick, formal motion, and backed away without looking directly toward her guests. In the car, Suzanne wanted to know what was going on.

"She sort of apologized for his behavior. Her message to me in Chinese was that he wasn't usually so rude. But he got a call this morning from the West Building, where the president of China works and resides. That's why he was so late for our meeting."

"Are you suggesting that the president of China is aware of Amber Chan?" Suzanne couldn't hide the surprise, maybe even disbelief, in her tone.

"Amber comes from a very influential family. Her father works for the party and is high in the political apparatus. He probably knows—and has access—to the president."

"Wow. This gets more complicated by the minute." Suzanne reached for her phone and dialed Serge's number. The device showed it was after eleven on the US East Coast, but he likely wasn't asleep yet.

He answered on the third ring, and she recounted both the details and tone of her meeting with the minister of commerce and the ultimatum he'd delivered. Serge sighed audibly. He took a moment to process it all and replied with another question.

"You don't want to let them know where Amber is. Am I right?"

"I'm not sure. I can't talk privately now, but approval for twenty-five new store locations in China isn't a matter I can ignore. How do you see it?"

Serge didn't take even a moment to think about his answer. He started the instant she finished asking her question. "Candidly, I think you're in a no-win situation. Even if you divulge the location where they can find Amber, I don't think there's any chance they'll grant you any approvals until this matter comes to an end, whenever and however that occurs."

"Agreed."

"I also think you are in grave personal danger. When I recommended you spend a few weeks in Asia to get away from the mess here, it never once occurred to me the Chinese might be involved in this debacle. Now that we know they are, I recommend you leave the country immediately. I think you should call your pilots, get them to the jet right away, and have your driver take you directly to the airport."

"I hear your concern, but do you really think the government here would be so bold as to detain me?"

"I do. Remember the Huawei affair? When they held two Canadians in prison for more than a year because a Huawei executive was arrested in Vancouver? I think you should leave immediately."

"Okay, we're almost at the hotel. That's where the pilots are, anyway. I'll gather up my clothes, and we'll all get on the jet as soon as possible. Sorry to disturb your sleep, and don't worry. I'll call in the morning. Love you!"

Suzanne turned to Jennie and asked, "Do you have your passport with you?"

Jennie nodded once, so Suzanne shifted her attention to the bodyguards. "Call the pilots and tell them to meet us in the lobby in thirty minutes. Tell them to file a flight plan with a destination of Shanghai, leaving as soon as we get there. We'll all need to pack our things and get back down to the lobby, ready for departure."

Jennie nodded tentatively but looked perplexed. "I won't need a passport for a flight to Shanghai ..."

"That's right," Suzanne interjected. "That's right. You don't need a passport for Shanghai."

Fifty-Two

Tenerife, Canary Islands, Sunday November 5, 2023

Fidelia checked into the five-star hotel Barceló Tenerife with Klaudia, Mia Vasquez, and six bodyguards in tow. They left Amber in Seville, still under guard but with a degree of movement within the deluxe apartment complex provided by Juan Suarez.

Unfortunately, her security detail had become thin with contingents in both spots. Fidelia had ordered Ricardo Schirillio—who had been babysitting the place in Dubrovnik and making the young Cuban, Agueda, a satisfied young woman—to fly to Spain and keep Amber occupied in Seville. They could play as much as they wanted, but she must not leave the apartment or contact anyone outside in any way.

Fidelia kept Amber as a bargaining chip with Boris Ivanov, who'd finally come to the table after a week of bloody losses on both sides. The bastard had retaliated for the loss of his guy in Rabat with the murder of Pierre Boivin's closest protector in France. Of course, she had to take out another Russian, so she picked one of their drug runners in Portugal, and so it went for several days.

Ivanov still hadn't contacted Fidelia directly. Instead, he communicated through Yuri Federov and Klaudia. At first, he insisted any meeting would need to take place in Russia. Over the ensuing days, he softened with suggestions of countries close to Moscow, places she knew would bend to any request from the FSB. Only yesterday, he finally conceded to a one-hour meeting in the Canary Islands and only in the private jet lounge of the Tenerife airport.

Klaudia subsequently persuaded Federov, who then convinced Ivanov, that they needed the privacy of a hotel room to demonstrate how their plan could work. He still limited their meeting to one hour, but agreed to meet her in suite 306 on the Royal Level at the Barceló Tenerife at 2:00 p.m. Klaudia reminded Fidelia that Ivanov could still return to Moscow that night and be ready for work in his office there the next morning.

Juan Suarez took a suite next to Fidelia's, and his guys had installed all the necessary listening devices to assure her safety. Although his men would be sure Ivanov—and whoever else joined him for the meeting in Fidelia's suite—was unarmed, she insisted on an extra level of monitoring. Suarez would personally direct the bodyguards in the event of an emergency.

The hotel suite was a modest but comfortable place with earthy tones. Bright, the walls were painted a color almost white, with matching furniture and window drapes. The floor tiles were also the lightest beige, and the floor-to-ceiling windows looked out over a magnificent cliff. She couldn't imagine Ivanov spending time to admire the view of the ocean and volcanic landscape that drew visitors to the islands, but she snapped a few pictures with her phone and breathed in some salty air from the balcony.

Inside, two people could sit comfortably on the sofa. If the seating in the living room proved inadequate, they could bring three chairs from the balcony inside. With her checklist complete, Fidelia and Klaudia sipped coffee and munched on fresh vegetables from room service while they waited.

At 1:30 p.m., they received a call from Suarez. His people had called from the airport. A private jet matching the description of Ivanov's had landed and was taxiing to the terminal. Ten minutes later, he reported that Ivanov had left the airport with two burly bodyguards. Ten minutes after that, he reported their guest was in the elevator en route to Fidelia's suite.

Moments later, they heard voices in the corridor, then a single firm knock on the door. Klaudia swung it open tentatively.

"There are only two of us here. She prefers you enter alone, leaving your men outside."

Ivanov looked around Klaudia until he met Fidelia's eyes, then dismissed his bodyguards with a brush of his hand and a few words in Russian. He breezed past Klaudia wordlessly and took a few steps to stand in front of Fidelia, removing a dark leather bag strapped over his shoulder.

Ivanov stood taller than she'd imagined, about the height

of an American football player with an equally fit physique. His skin was pale from the Russian fall season, making his black eyes appear even darker. There was little doubt he would be proficient in the martial arts and able to eliminate both women with his bare hands in a matter of minutes.

Without a greeting, smile, or gesture of warmth, he spoke. "You asked to meet." He spoke in clear English, with an accent, and waited for Fidelia's reply.

She remained seated on the sofa and motioned for him to take a chair facing her.

He set his leather bag on the floor between his feet.

She mirrored his grim expression and spoke curtly. "We offered you a steady income and a bonus payday if you'd stay out of our territory. Instead, we've each lost at least six people. Why not cooperate?"

Klaudia moved toward the sofa and took a place beside Fidelia. Both waited for the FSB chief to reply. It took a moment.

"No one tells us where we do business. Not leaders. Not governments. And certainly not you. So far, we've been patient and measured. We've only eliminated one of your people for every one of ours. Just wait. If you continue to attack, we'll return with ten times the force. And Klaudia knows we have the resources to outlast you and the methods to turn your stomach while we accomplish our goals."

"We know that. But what's more important to you here? Power or money? You may have greater power, but today we have much more money and access to hundreds of millions more. We're willing to share it if you agree to play nicely and stay out of our playground. And the amount we're willing to share will replace the half-billion you lost on Monday, March 16, 2020. We know where it is, and we know how to get it back. Would I be right to assume your all-powerful leader isn't aware of that loss yet?"

He didn't answer her question, and his poker expression revealed little. But one involuntary blink of his eyes suggested he'd heard her question and clearly understood its implications.

She continued. "We offered to become a good, steady customer of women you recruit, taking on all the risks of human trafficking and eliminating all your expenses from paying off European government officials. We think we're being generous and good neighbors. Why do you see it differently?"

"We already have good customers and enough government officials in our pockets, probably paying them a fraction of what you pay because we have better methods of winning their cooperation. If we did consider selling women to you, we'd need more money per woman and a much higher number per month."

He started with the women. As Klaudia had expected, that meant he first wanted something for the FSB to justify the trip. If they eventually talked about the lost half-billion, that would be a private matter.

Fidelia went fishing. "We offered to buy a hundred women per month from you at twenty thousand each. That two million dollars would pay a lot of FSB overhead with very little expense. Klaudia here knows you pay less than five hundred US dollars to harvest the girls in your poor neighboring countries. I'm willing to take another ten women per month at twenty thousand each."

He refused her offer, and they volleyed back and forth for a few minutes, his manner softening slightly as Fidelia showed some flexibility in both the price and the quantity per month. It took a few minutes, but Fidelia eventually increased her price to twenty-five thousand each, with one hundred and fifteen girls a month until the end of 2024. They clarified how the funds would be transferred and when. They agreed on the contact people and communications channels. When he offered his hand across the small table between them, she shook it firmly before moving to the more important subject.

"You limited our meeting today to one hour. We have less than thirty minutes left to discuss the half-billion. We need more time for Klaudia to show you what we can do, where we'll get the money, and how we plan to do it—with or without you—the week before American Thanksgiving. Want to extend your time by a few minutes today to discuss it? Or do you prefer to just leave with the nice order for women and your undertaking to leave Europe to us?"

Fidelia allowed a smile to form. She knew he'd tell her to

carry on. After all, the truly appealing part of their discussion was the massive amount she might divert to his personal offshore accounts somewhere in the world. If he agreed, and they pulled it off, he could retire from the FSB whenever he chose, disappear anywhere in the world, and live a life of almost unimaginable luxury.

"Tell me about it. I'll decide later if I'm interested in staying longer."

Fidelia nodded to Klaudia that she should begin.

She opened the lid of the laptop she'd placed on the table between them and invited Ivanov to slide his chair around beside her so he could see the screen. He shifted where she pointed, leaving his leather bag sitting on the floor within his view.

"I'm using the dark web, as you see, and with a few more keystrokes, I'll be at the entrance to Multima Corporation's main servers. If you don't know the company, I can tell you they are the fourth largest supermarket business in the world with operations in North America, Europe, and Asia. This company, particularly its CEO, benefited directly from that money the FSB lost three years ago."

Ivanov raised an eyebrow slightly, but no other reaction was visible.

Klaudia typed while talking and began navigating the software from the point of entry. She went to the first screening software Amber had shown her and keyed in codes she had learned. Nothing happened. She remained quiet but tried again.

A large lump formed in Fidelia's throat but she managed to remain calm.

Klaudia backtracked and tried another pathway in. More carefully this time, she keyed numbers while she consulted some notes at her side. This time it worked. They watched the software trigger another flow of data and waited for it to stop. Then she keyed in another series of codes. The flow of codes and characters slowed, then suddenly faded, then disappeared, leaving a large dark blob in its place. Klaudia pointed to the screen and Ivanov realized instantly what she had done. He smiled while she quickly snatched away the blob from the screen, and data resumed its rhythmic flow inside the Multima server.

"So, can you insert more of those, enough to bring down the entire system?" he asked.

Klaudia nodded. "We think it will take less than ten minutes to bring down the entire North American computer system for the stores and headquarters. The European and Asian servers would continue to function for some time at the store level, but none of their info would go beyond the country where regional data accumulates for consolidation and upload to headquarters."

"So business activities in North America would come to a standstill but not other regions. However, sales and revenue earned in those other regions couldn't be reported until the system was repaired. Brilliant," Ivanov said. "And you're planning to demand one billion in ransom?"

Fidelia nodded but said nothing.

"And you're willing to share it. Why?" His tone indicated both interest and suspicion.

"I want an understanding you'll leave us alone in Europe far beyond 2024. Your guy will probably be around for another decade. Beyond that, I realize it's impossible to give assurances, but I want your agreement to leave Europe to us until 2035."

"I can't give you those kinds of assurances. Even the one-year deal I agreed to for the women might cost me my job." His manner became more aggressive, not yet angry but approaching that threshold.

Fidelia looked at him, allowing a small smile to reappear. "I know that. You'll need to decide how much of that five hundred million you're willing to share with your guy at the top. I want those assurances from him, personally. Not you."

Ivanov shook his head in disbelief, his face reddening as realization set in. To share in the wealth, he not only had to be satisfied with a fraction of the total heist, but he also had to find a way to convince the most powerful man in his country to forego millions of dollars of future income from Europe for a few hundred million added to his personal bank accounts in the coming few days.

"Good luck with your cyberattack. I hope it works. But you can count me out." Ivanov's tone was resigned now, no longer angry. It almost sounded meek.

"Whether you consider yourself in or out is immaterial." Fidelia adopted a stern expression so there could be no misunderstanding. Then she repeated her statement for emphasis.

"Whether you consider yourself in or out is immaterial. If you decide not to play, before your flight touches down in Moscow tonight, your guy will learn about that half-billion loss you've hidden from him all this time. We thought you might appreciate a chance to introduce a new opportunity to him instead."

"When do you expect the cyberattack to go?"

"About two weeks from today. We'll make our demands the Tuesday morning before American Thanksgiving when chaos will reign in a few thousand American Multima stores as people realize they can't buy groceries for their most important holiday of the year. We expect to have the ransom within twenty-four hours and distribute the proceeds one day later." She crossed her arms confidently and waited for his response.

"I'll talk to him," Ivanov said, almost in a whisper, as he stood up from the chair beside Klaudia.

Fidelia reached out to grasp his leather bag, now sitting at her feet, and offered it to him immediately, still maintaining direct eye contact with the large Russian.

"I'll need to know if he's prepared to give me those assurances before the end of this week." Her tone was firm, her expression hard, held just short of anger. "One more thing. Fedorov has left you. His treatment of my friend Klaudia was despicable—in past years and recently in Morocco. Tomorrow, you'll read in the newspapers about his accidental fall, moments ago, from the balcony of a friend's apartment."

There was no handshake, and he met her eyes only for an instant before he stepped out the door. Fidelia closed it behind him, then turned to face Klaudia. She moved a step or two closer to whisper her question.

"What the fuck happened with that demonstration?"

"I was blocked at the first batch of software code I encountered. They've fixed it. Either Amber failed to update those records she's been downloading every day, or she's been removed from their list. Either way, we could have a massive problem. If they've discovered those vulnerabilities and are fixing them, we might not have two weeks left to launch the attack."

Fidelia nodded. They might have to move sooner. But she knew that was not her friend's immediate concern.

"Don't worry. I got the AirTag into his bag while you held him entranced with the screen. You should be able to track his movements immediately."

Fifty-Three

Atlanta, Georgia, Wednesday November 8, 2023

The ten days since Gordon had been shut out of the computer upgrade and conversion project had been a whirlwind regardless. His business unit was ramping up for the best Thanksgiving sales in the history of the company. Even the annoyance of James Fitzgerald shadowing his every move became less important as the good news compounded.

Although Serge had effectively cut him off from specific activities with the computer conversion, the security guy courteously called at the end of each day to provide a verbal update, avoiding any precise details. Essentially, the company's chief of security provided measured reassurance. The team was on track, making progress, and an end was in sight.

Each time they talked, Serge also took pains to update him on the lack of progress law enforcement had made in locating Amber Chan. Usually, he had little to report about his conversations with Houston police, but his latest conversation suggested they might have a lead on her somewhere in Europe.

James Fitzgerald also turned out to be a surprisingly helpful companion. It was easy to see why Suzanne relied so heavily on his observations and advice. In the past week alone, after meetings with executives who previously reported to Amber, Fitzgerald had pointed out individual strengths and weaknesses that Gordon hadn't detected among those team members. When asked, he offered ideas to hone deficient skills or suggest more appropriate roles for some individuals. Gordon lapped it up.

The makeover of Jeffersons Stores to Multima Supermarkets was right on track. Each day, the project manager reported on the number of signs changed on buildings, and it looked like the job could be done before Christmas. After Suzanne asked Edward Hadley to spend an extra twenty-five million on advertising in the run-up to

Thanksgiving, he created new TV commercials making light of the name change and leaving customers giggling about buying Multima-branded products in a store named either Jeffersons or Multima depending on the day.

The ads had run for less than a week, yet stores already reported favorable customer feedback, and sales of the house brand products had already skyrocketed.

With all the good news surrounding him, it might have been easy for Gordon to forget that his job was probably still in peril. Suzanne had called him only once in the three weeks since she'd assigned James Fitzgerald as his constant traveling companion, although Gordon knew she spoke with her watchdog almost every day.

As he prepared to meet James for breakfast that morning, concern about his future slowly crept into his thoughts. Was it too early to start updating his resume? Should he talk with a lawyer? Was it time to start putting out feelers to his excellent network of contacts across the food industry?

As he took a sip from the cup of coffee that he'd brewed in his room that morning, Gordon felt the situation grate on him more than usual. Like a good Christian, he'd admitted his indiscretions and lapses in judgment and apologized for them. He'd asked the Lord for forgiveness, too, and assumed that had been granted.

Why was Suzanne Simpson holding a sword over his head? It was more than ironic that she, too, had violated the Multima policy against inappropriate relationships with colleagues and direct reports. Although she and Serge had made a big deal of announcing their relationship to the world last year, did anybody out there think they hadn't been sleeping together for much, or maybe even all, of the year before that dramatic announcement?

It was a double standard, and it was unfair. Still, it was his job at risk, and it was unclear how the messy disaster would end.

Over breakfast with James, he broached the issue. "I'm feeling a little insecure in my role right now. I know you went through this before with Suzanne, and she ended up firing you at the time. Do you think I have the same fate waiting?"

James looked over his eyeglasses and smiled, setting

down the coffee cup previously headed toward his lips. "You're feeling uncomfortable. It's completely understandable, but I don't think I'm equipped to predict the outcome."

He changed his mind, picked up the cup again, and took a long sip, looking directly at Gordon before he continued. "I'm not sure I understand the way her mind works better than you. But I see a significant difference in our respective circumstances. Yes, when she forced my retirement that first time, I had an inappropriate relationship with a subordinate. No question. And it's her company. If she decides to enforce a rule to make an example or to punish, it's her call."

He paused again, then shrugged his shoulders before he got to the heart of his response. "In your case, if I read the tea leaves correctly, she's not so much concerned about possible indiscretions that led to a violation of company policy. It's there. But I see her more concerned about your judgment. Getting involved with someone under suspicion, rightly or wrongly. Then, perhaps not hiding, but camouflaging your involvement for some time. I think if it was only a case of involvement with a subordinate, she might have been more understanding. It's more related to who the subordinate was. Candidly, I can't predict how it might turn out."

Gordon left it there. The guy had been forthright, direct, and probably honest.

The rest of the morning unfolded in a blur. With one scheduled appointment after another, Amber Chan's former subordinates paraded through the conference room attached to her former office in half-hour increments carrying news. First, the previous day's sales results, then Thanksgiving purchasing challenges, negotiations with the labor union on a new agreement to replace the one expiring at the end of December, then the conversion project and customer satisfaction. There was little time to think about job security.

Reaching for his phone, Gordon checked messages and emails from the morning. There were more than fifty in total. One caught his eye.

Heard you might consider a new job. I've got one you might like. Call me. US Senator for Georgia, Milly-Jean Mailor

Gordon instinctively reached for his phone, then stopped suddenly. If they were monitoring him as part of his corporate humiliation, they were probably also tapping his cell phone and office line. He'd need to try her later.

Just before leaving the office with James Fitzgerald, Gordon had quickly Googled where he could buy a burner phone. Shockingly, he learned the devices were now no more than prepaid phones because the police had a right to ping the phones to track location.

His elevated heart rate returned to normal. It was unlikely the police were already tracking him. If there were wiretaps, Serge Boisvert and his team probably planted them, and they wouldn't have information on a new cell phone until they squeezed information about it from the selling store or somehow got their hands on it.

He begged off dinner with James and slipped out of the hotel. He grabbed a cab, showed the driver a T-Mobile outlet address he had written down, and buckled up for the ride. After what seemed like only a moment or two after the buckle clicked, the taxi stopped, and its driver announced they'd arrived. The fare was fourteen dollars and ninety-five cents, and tips were much appreciated.

Minutes later Gordon left that shop with his new prepaid number and grinned at his new toy—a tool used by real criminals. Before he set out walking, he performed a full circle of surveillance to see if any untoward characters or familiar faces lurked about. Satisfied, he set out for the hotel and keyed in the number left by the US Senator for Georgia as he walked.

He'd met her once or twice at church fundraising events for her election campaigns. She claimed to be a Christian, but her foul language and erratic behavior had always raised doubts about her fidelity to the faith. However, her greeting that day was effusive when he identified himself, and she thanked him again for his previous contributions to her PAC account.

He tolerated the chit-chat and political rambling, waiting for her to get to the purpose of her email and his call, but found his interest waning quickly. After more than a few minutes, she thanked him for calling and said she was relaying a message from someone important who wished to remain anonymous for the moment.

"This person is extraordinarily well-connected to the American business community, and one of the richest people in the country. They learned from an impeccable source that the board of directors of Multima Corporation is secretly looking for a new CEO. Your name has been mentioned as a prime candidate. Because this person is a major shareholder in Multima—through a private equity fund—he'd like you to meet one of his trusted advisors for an interview. Could you be available for a secret meeting in San Francisco on Friday afternoon?"

"Look, Milly-Jean, I barely know you. You won't share the name of the person who made the request. You want me to make myself available for a meeting in less than forty-eight hours, and you haven't revealed who I will be meeting with. Would you consider it impolite of me to say this all sounds a little weird?"

"I take no offense. You're an astute executive. Being cautious. Just as he told me I should expect. He said I could tell you the name of his trusted advisor if you're interested. It's Abduhl Mahinder, CEO of the Bank of The Americas. He would like you to join him Friday at 2:00 p.m. in his private dining room at Estiatorio Ornos San Francisco. Shall I tell my friend you'll be there?"

Fifty-Four

Honolulu, Hawaii, Wednesday November 8, 2023

The ten days since Suzanne first left San Francisco for Asia flew past like a nasty spring storm, not quite a hurricane, but lots of turbulence in the air. The visit with the Chinese minister of commerce was most unsettling, and the reason she was now in Hawaii rather than Bangkok. For once, she'd agreed with Serge's recommendation not only to leave China quickly but also his suggestion that she head toward American soil immediately.

It was hard to argue with his reasoning. If one of them had been a target for a shooter in Singapore by an unknown assailant, who knew what might await her in another Asian country in the current unsettled environment. There was no doubt the Chinese government's reach extended throughout the continent. If its apparent anger about Amber Chan continued, even an American safe harbor like Hawaii might become suspect. But Serge eventually rationalized his misgivings about the island and thought she'd be alright there for a few days.

Staying off the mainland also made sense. After a bombing attempt outside her home in the Laurentians and a successful bombing in a Jeffersons store in Texas, someone clearly wanted her attention.

She made the time in Hawaii productive. Eileen had traveled with her and organized the multitude of requests for time and attention with her usual precision. She knew Suzanne's priorities well, and organized days for optimum efficiency despite the five-hour time difference with the US East Coast where most communication focused.

It was approaching nine o'clock that sunny morning in Honolulu, and she'd already finished one-hour meetings with Serge and Marcel Dubois in Atlanta on Zoom, Pierre Cabot at headquarters in Montreal by phone, and James Fitzgerald with Gordon Goodfellow in San Francisco, again on Zoom.

None of the meetings produced dramatic news, but each

provided positive progress on the company she ran. From the computer systems upgrade to changing store signs in California and the impressive increases in retail sales as business ramped up for Thanksgiving, Suzanne took satisfaction that her company performed well despite the challenges.

She paused for a short break to stand, stretch and gaze out over the harbor from the balcony of her suite. In a clear sky, the sun shone brilliantly, and its reflection shimmering off the turquoise-blue water was captivating, almost mesmerizing. She gave her head a shake to break its spell and breathed in deeply, relishing the scent of salty air and its soothing sensation deep in her lungs.

Dressed oddly in a beige button-down blouse to appear professional during the Zoom calls, yet wearing gray, casual sweatpants for work-from-a-hotel-suite comfort on the bottom, she giggled, stretching her arms, back and legs before returning to Eileen's carefully plotted agenda.

Next on her list was Abduhl Mahinder, CEO of the Bank of The Americas and a member of her board of directors. Eileen pointed to her phone on the suite's polished hardwood desk. Abduhl was already on the line, waiting.

After their usual brief but cheerful greetings that never took longer than a minute, he got right to the point of his request to chat with her—politics. "A friend of mine in the Republican party called to ask me about Multima's political donations for the year. He said he checked with Pierre Cabot in Montreal and learned that Multima had no plans to chip in this year. He asked me if I could twist your arm a bit for the party."

"Well, you can twist away if you like, but it's true. I asked Pierre to withhold support for the party this year. I know John George always donated equally to both parties and I've continued that tradition for the past few years. But, from what I read and hear, the Republican Party has become a dysfunctional tool for their resident idiot. I don't agree with their choice of leader and don't want to encourage either him or the party in any way."

Abduhl heard her out with no interruption or comment, as she'd expected, then tried to change her mind, also as expected.

"I fought an internal battle with the question of support myself for several months. I think their leader's a jerk too. In the end, though, I swallowed hard and sent them the same amount as I contributed to the other party. As a director of Multima, I'm suggesting you might want to reconsider and do the same."

"Why?" She kept her tone positive but telegraphed impatience with her curt reply.

"Some strange things are going on in our country today. I won't say I like all of them. However, as CEO of the bank, it's my responsibility to put the interests of my publicly traded bank before my own. I'm sure you feel the same way about Multima, maybe even more so, since you own such a large chunk of the shares. It might be a dangerous time in American history to put too much weight on our personal values and ideals rather than pragmatically assessing the alternatives."

Suzanne processed his message. He chose his words diplomatically and maintained an almost fatherly tone as he shared his advice, but she roiled at the implied threat cushioned inside his message.

"So you're saying we need to give the party a couple million dollars so they won't punish us if they win the election?"

"Polls we've sponsored, and well-informed people I talk to, suggest the Republican candidate has a very strong chance of winning. Its leader is the most corrupt person to play the political game, and he demands absolute loyalty. If he perceives personal disloyalty, he seeks revenge almost like a Mafioso. This guy thinks of the party as an extension of himself, and every indicator suggests he will try to punish every person, company, or political figure he considers disloyal. Candidly, if he's elected, I fear the price Multima might pay could be far greater than a couple million dollars."

She continued to process the message, even as she shifted uneasily in the comfortable swivel chair in front of her phone, relieved he couldn't discern her features or assess her internal struggle. "I'll think about it some more, Abduhl. You know I respect your views even when I disagree with them."

"One last thought. Remember, I'm the messenger here.

The guy I'm relaying it for is a bit dodgy and not a favorite character of mine. But he insisted I mention during our conversation the recent Jeffersons Store bombing in Houston and the bombing attempt at your home. He asked me to remind you the party includes some real crazies no one can control. He implied there could be more violence against you or Multima should some in the party see you as an enemy."

Suzanne almost fainted. Blood drained from her face. Her shoulders slumped forward, and her throat became dry with a large lump threatening to block her breathing. Eileen, sitting on the other side of the suite, punching info into her laptop, noticed her change in demeanor and jumped up from her chair, approaching to see if she was okay.

Suzanne waved her off and eventually assured Abduhl she'd give his warning serious consideration before she said goodbye. With merely a moment's hesitation, she hit Serge's name on her phone. He needed to know.

"Now we're fighting a battle on another front, and a director of your company is involved?" His tone blended anger with incredulity as he spat out the words. Just as quickly, his tone shifted almost to a plea. "I don't trust any of these bastards. Please come to Atlanta. I'll find you a safe and comfortable place to stay where we can be close to each other, and I can protect you better."

The moving parts had increased both in number and intensity. She caved, opting for some increased personal security until things calmed down around her.

"Agreed. Find that nice secure spot. I'll fly overnight and should arrive there early tomorrow morning."

"Thanks, Suzanne. I'll feel much better about your safety, and I'll make it worth your while when you get in." His tone offered relief but also a hint of suggestion. "A little gossip for you to think about. My contact at CSIS let me know that a known Russian operative was killed a couple days ago. His contact at Interpol learned the FSB discovered that someone used an Apple AirTag to track his whereabouts. Apparently, they traced the sale of that AirTag to an Apple store near the address in Seville where they're also holding Amber Chan."

Fifty-Five

Seville, Spain, Friday November 10, 2023

When Fidelia and Klaudia returned to Seville after their meeting with Boris Ivanov in the Canary Islands, four bodyguards, with heads hanging and shoulders stooped, stood in a cluster outside the apartment door awaiting their punishment. Fidelia pointedly ignored them, swept past without a word, and furiously slammed the door to the luxury apartment once inside.

Both Amber Chan and Ricardo Schirillio were gone, just as the team leader had reported by phone hours earlier. Obviously, they couldn't file a police report, but Juan Suarez had put out the word to all his people across Spain with instructions to get the immediate attention of every person on The Organization's payroll within law enforcement, immigration, and secret services throughout Spain.

Estavo Sereno in Portugal and Pierre Boivin in France had issued similar orders, including to the handful of pawns they controlled at Interpol. Hours had elapsed. Despite thoroughly searching the surrounding streets of Seville within minutes of the reported discovery, so far there were no tips or evidence about where the pair may have headed.

"Did she take the computer?" Fidelia snarled at Klaudia, who was desperately searching through the apartment for precisely that reason.

Rummaging through drawers and inspecting closet crevices as though her life depended on it, the German woman finally gave an exasperated reply. "It looks as if they took the new computer and the backup drive. The bitch left nothing. She even stole some of my clothes for their escape. We're screwed."

Multima technicians in the US were fixing security gaps in their systems at breakneck speed. The daily download of enhancements that Amber had used to track remaining open vulnerabilities was gone. The next time Klaudia hacked her way into Multima—if a hack was even possible—she'd fly blind, unaware of which vulnerabilities might still be there and which were now too secure to penetrate.

Fidelia stormed around the apartment, checking once again those places Klaudia had already searched and left behind disheveled heaps of discarded clothing.

"How the fuck do two people just walk out of here with a few pieces of clothing and a large laptop computer under their arms without anyone even noticing?" She screamed into the faces of the four bodyguards now standing in front of her with hands behind their backs in fearful subjugation.

No one volunteered an answer. Juan Suarez jabbed one in the back with his fist and bellowed in Spanish, "Answer her, for Christ's sake."

"It was my four-hour shift to guard the doors while the others slept. I fell asleep, and when I woke up, I saw the door ajar. I ran inside the apartment and checked everywhere, but they were already gone."

"How long did you sleep?"

"I'm not sure. Maybe a couple hours."

"So they could have got as far as Portugal or Malaga before you were even aware they'd escaped." Suarez growled at his man, jabbing him in the lower back again.

Klaudia opened her computer amid the finger-pointing and confessions and pounded on the keyboard for a few moments. When there was a pause in the accusations and recriminations, she called out to Fidelia.

"I'm in again. It was tougher this time, and the code has been modified in more places. But if we act quickly, I think we can still bring down Multima's systems. There's no way we can wait for November 20 like you planned. At the pace they're fixing the vulnerabilities, we'll be locked out entirely by then."

Fidelia stepped away from the four bungling bodyguards and approached Klaudia at the dining area table, where she continued to poke and prod digitally.

"Send a note to Ivanov. Remind him we need an answer from him and his guy by tomorrow or they're out of the deal. Say nothing more. We'll switch the cyberattack date once we know whether we're sharing the take or keeping it all."

Klaudia followed Fidelia's instructions and then immersed herself again in her laptop. A few minutes later, she called out,

"Two things. First, the AirTag in Ivanov's bag is still working. Second, here's an interesting news item you'll want to see."

Fidelia looked over her friend's shoulder at a Russian media website in the direction Klaudia pointed. "Russian citizen Yuri Federov died yesterday after an accidental fall from the twentieth floor of an apartment building in St. Petersburg."

It was old news in one sense, but seeing the media's confirmation counted as something extra. They looked into each other's eyes. Fidelia read satisfaction in Klaudia's, although her face displayed no other emotion.

Six hours later, after midnight in Moscow, Klaudia received a message on the dark web.

> *He agrees but only if the ransom is 5 billion USD. All for him.*

Fidelia studied the email for several moments and said nothing. She stepped away from the table and paced the room for several more. Finally, she glared at Juan Suarez and said, "Do what you want with these bungling fools of yours, but I don't want them around me or to have anything to do with me."

It was effectively a death order, but this lapse was so severe they deserved it. The entire scheme was now at risk. The greedy Russian wanted more, and now they had no idea how to find the woman with the knowledge and skills to bring down Multima.

To Juan Suarez, she gave one more succinct order. "Pull out every stop to find that Chinese woman immediately."

To Klaudia, "Keep monitoring the situation at Multima. It's safer if we have Amber and her knowledge. We'll give it till Monday. If we don't find her by then, you'll have to bring down the computer system by yourself."

With a wave of her arms, she chased Juan Suarez and his men from the room and picked up her phone. She had to search for the number because two years had passed since she'd last called it. When a voice responded to the ringing, she used only a few words to get the attention of a guy working at the summit of Interpol.

"I still have the video. You have forty-eight hours for your outstanding organization to track down someone, or I release the video to TV5 Monde."

She ignored his howls of protest until they finally stopped. "The people I want are Amber Chan, a Chinese citizen, and Ricardo Schirillio, a Uruguayan. I need them both. Alive. By Sunday, midnight. I assume you'll use a Code Red. You can reach me at this number when you have them."

"Amber Chan!" He screamed into the phone. "Amber Chan the Chinese woman? There's been a Code Red out for her for several days already with no success. Your deadline is impossible."

"You'll just have to turn up the heat, or your red-hot video goes viral."

Fifty-Six

San Francisco, California, Friday November 10, 2023

As James Fitzgerald left the office at noon for the airport and a flight home to spend some time with the still-new love of his life, Gordon wished him a good weekend. He added that he'd stay and relax in San Francisco and looked forward to seeing James again sometime on Monday. Most of that was bona fide.

Most importantly, though, it hadn't been necessary to create a lie to spring himself from the office for a lunch meeting at 2:00 p.m. at Estiatorio Ornos San Francisco. He Googled the restaurant and noticed it didn't open until 5:00 p.m. Of course, Abduhl Mahinder had enough clout for any restaurant owner to bring in a chef or two for a private dining room. He decided to walk there from the office and grinned when he saw his path took him past the same T-Mobile store where he'd bought his first-ever burner phone.

Indeed, he found the restaurant entrance locked and scouted around the exterior. He quickly spotted a button near the top of a doorway and rang it twice. After a few minutes, a stooped, gray-haired, middle-aged character, probably a server, answered and peeked around an unlocked—but only partially opened—solid-glass door. The expression on his face invited an explanation for the disruption.

The fellow nodded after Gordon introduced himself. He opened the door wider. There was still no hello or other greeting, just a "follow me" and wave to do that. He led the way along a corridor on the perimeter of the restaurant's main seating area to the back, then up a flight of stairs.

Piped-in music played more loudly than usual in the restaurant, and dishes clattered noisily from a kitchen they passed on the way upstairs. Gordon heard a few voices laughing, joking, and carrying on, probably also from the kitchen area. There were few lights, and those illuminated were recessed, so the entire complex had an eerie, unwelcoming atmosphere, more like a dingy warehouse than a fine dining destination.

They arrived at a door where the middle-aged man knocked loudly. He opened the door and announced, "Your guest is here."

The small private room was more brightly lit and free of the noise from downstairs. Gordon noticed a round table in the center was set for six guests, glasses and cutlery arranged neatly on a red and white checkered tablecloth. He looked around the room as his guide left and saw five strangers. Abduhl Mahinder was nowhere in sight, and none of the faces were familiar.

"I'm sorry," Gordon said with a forced smile. "He must have brought me to the wrong dining room."

"Are you Gordon Goodfellow?" a man in a tailored, dark blue suit and pale blue dress shirt asked. When Gordon silently nodded in the affirmative, the man spoke again. "Abduhl won't join us today. You will have most of the planned discussion with me, and my colleagues will participate as necessary."

Gordon tensed. His heart rate suddenly spiked upward, and he felt queasy. Something was wrong. Instinctively, he started to back away from the group, looking for the doorway again. The well-dressed one spoke English well, but with a Latino accent, and none of his colleagues looked at all like bankers.

"Don't be alarmed. My name is Mauro Alvarez. Abduhl is a good friend of mine. I also own a lot of Multima shares through my private equity firm. He couldn't make it today as planned and asked me to share our ideas with you and chat about your future with the company."

"Thanks, but I don't have conversations about my employer or my employment with people I don't know." Gordon moved toward the door again, and over his right shoulder, he noticed one of Alvarez's colleagues step toward the same door.

Alvarez called out again. "Hear us out. It's not only Abduhl who wants us to meet. A friend of yours also wants us to have a chat. Her name is Amber Chan."

Gordon froze. Had he heard the fellow correctly? Amber Chan?

He turned to look at the group again. Alvarez had a broad grin on his face, almost a smirk, but he said nothing, watching Gordon and waiting.

"What does Amber have to do with this?"

"She's part of our team. Unable to join us live, but we can bring her up for a chat online if you like. It'll only take a minute."

Gordon took another few steps toward the door. "This whole affair is completely bizarre. I want to know where Abduhl Mahinder is, what he has to do with this nonsense, and no, I have no interest in the whereabouts of Amber Chan."

The large man who shadowed Gordon toward the door nimbly stepped around in front of him, blocking his path. Then, with one hand, he twisted him around to face Alvarez. Gordon started to mentally recite the Lord's Prayer.

"Sit down and listen to us for a minute. No one's going to force you to do anything, but you do realize your current job is fried with Suzanne Simpson at the helm of Multima, right?"

Gordon sucked in a deep breath, calmed himself, and took the chair another "colleague" offered. He immediately regretted the next word that came out of his mouth. "Shoot."

Alvarez pulled up a chair and waved for the others to give them some space. He started to speak, but a knock on the door interrupted him. The same middle-aged guy who had let Gordon in was at the door again, this time wearing a tie and apron. He carried two bottles of wine: one red, one white.

"May I pour your wine at the table before the food arrives?"

Alvarez stood up and slid his chair to the table, motioning for the others to follow. The room remained mostly quiet while the server poured generous quantities of wine into the glasses according to each diner's simple "red" or "white" instructions. Finished, he shuffled off to the doorway again and bowed slightly on his way out.

"Like I said, I'm a major shareholder, planning to become an even bigger shareholder in the coming days," Alvarez said. "So my colleagues and I have been watching Multima. You're toast with the current CEO. She and her lover-boy running security have been watching you. They listen to your phone. They tail you around the clock. They've done so for months.

She's only waiting for the right moment to fire your ass. Then what will you do?"

He let Gordon stew about that for a while. Of course, he realized all that, but how did this gang know about it? And Amber?

"I'm a successful executive. If it doesn't work out with Multima, I'll find another company."

"Maybe. That all depends on how badly she tarnishes your reputation. There's bad shit about to happen at that company. Far worse than the little bomb that damaged the store in Houston and killed or injured a few people. She's setting you up as the fall guy, not a hero. If they blame you like we expect, you could spend the rest of your career behind bars, not at another company."

That possibility had never occurred to Gordon. The guy now had his attention.

"What kind of stuff is going to happen?"

"Thanksgiving week at Multima is never going to be the same again. We know an outfit that will take down the whole company's operating system. All the time and money you guys have spent is worthless. These folks we know have technology you've never heard of and artificial intelligence tools. Multima's team can't even spell the software, let alone defend against it. Your company will have to pay billions in ransom."

Gordon listened. It didn't entirely make sense. If the guy truly was a shareholder, why would he want to see Multima suffer such devastating harm? He asked and the guy had his reply ready and rehearsed.

"Suzanne Simpson will be dethroned within hours of the hack. Her shares will be worth far less than today, but she'll no longer want to own the company if she can't run it. Some folks will be ready and willing to buy as many of her devalued shares as she chooses to sell. It'll take a while, but the company will one day return to its former glory, and buyers of her distressed shares will be far richer people than they are today."

His eyes drilled into Gordon's, showing fire and passion, almost like the eyes of a drunk about to wage a personal war of revenge.

Gordon blinked but said nothing.

"We're offering you a chance to become the company's CEO. We'll double your salary and bonuses to start. We'll give you fifty thousand of the diminished value shares the day you start the job and give you all the support you need to rebuild the company."

"What are you asking me to do?"

"On Monday, November 20, we need you to enter Supermarkets headquarters in Atlanta at 4:00 a.m. and leave one door just slightly ajar on your path to the executive suite, open just enough to trigger an alarm and draw security to that specific area. That's all. We'll handle the rest."

As he finished speaking, there was another knock at the door. The middle-aged server wheeled in a tray loaded with food and set bowl after bowl on the table, almost covering every available space on the red and white checkered tablecloth. It took him more than a few minutes. Then he slowly wheeled the cart into a vacant corner, left it there, and stepped out of the room.

To say Gordon felt awkward was a monumental understatement. Clearly, the gang around him not only knew who the cyberattack perpetrators were, but every indication led him to believe they were the people planning the attack. How could he spend the next hour or so breaking bread with criminals, even if they offered him a job he coveted and a ton of money? Silently, he prayed for guidance.

Alvarez helped himself to the nearest bowl and scooped food onto his plate, motioning for everyone else to do the same. After enough scoops, he passed on the bowl to Gordon and accepted another one from the guy on his right. They all passed around bowls and loaded their plates for a few minutes before Alvarez broke the cycle, grabbed a fork, and started eating.

Gordon probed a bit more. "Where does Amber Chan fit into this scheme?"

After thoroughly chewing a mouthful of fish, Alvaraz answered. "She'll shut the system down while security is preoccupied with your door distraction. She only needs about a minute to get in and do the damage."

"Why does she need to get into the building at all? Don't hackers usually crack security codes and enter from the outside, often from the other side of the world?"

"I don't know the technical details. That's her job. Apparently, one of the fixes Multima used in their systems conversion requires someone in a high-security compound in Atlanta to flip a special switch to disengage some monitoring tools. She'll get it done. So, can we count you in?"

"I presume somebody gives me a written confirmation of our discussion today?" Gordon framed it as a question rather than a demand.

"Fuck no," Alvarez laughed. "You think you're dealing with idiots here? You want a piece of paper you can take to the police or your company security chief? No, you'll tell me you're prepared to do the job in return for my word you'll be rewarded as I described it."

"And if I decide I don't want to play?"

"It's your call. But your walk back to the hotel might include some unexpected excitement."

Gordon had lost his appetite much earlier, but he continued picking away at the dish, lifting a morsel to his lips from time to time. Finally, he spoke again. "Okay, but I want to talk to Amber first."

Alvarez raised his eyebrows in response, tilting his head slightly, but he didn't reply immediately. Instead, he took a napkin, tapped his lips a couple times, and stood up from the table, reaching into his pocket for his phone as he walked away. He stepped out into the corridor and was gone for several minutes. No one around the table spoke.

Alvarez's colleagues continued wolfing down the food as though this might be their only meal of the day. None made eye contact with Gordon, yet they watched him suspiciously from the corners of their eyes.

When he returned to the room, Alvarez didn't immediately approach the table. Instead, he waved for Gordon to join him in a corner over by the door. He held up the phone. In the middle of the screen, Amber sat on a floor, her legs beneath her, leaning her back against an unpainted dirty cement wall. Zip ties circled her hands, and her face looked dirty, bruised and swollen. A laptop computer sat on the floor at her feet.

Beside her, a young man tried but couldn't lift his battered head to the camera. Blood oozed from the corners of his mouth, and his eyes were glazed.

The room was poorly lit, but there was no question the woman sitting on the floor was Amber.

Gordon repeated his request. "I want to talk to her."

Alvarez shook his head. "Not going to happen. Tell me you'll work with us. Perform your duty, and you can talk with her all you want after she's done the job."

He clicked the red button on the screen to end the Messenger video call.

Gordon's stomach felt like he carried a load of lead. His throat was dry. His shoulders were tight. There was no way he could return to the table. Instead, he stood across from Alvarez and stretched out his hand. "Okay, I'm in."

Gordon set out for the hotel once he'd stepped from the restaurant into the street. But first, he looked around in a slow full arc to see if indeed someone stood hidden in the shadows somewhere, spying on him as Alvarez had claimed. If they were hiding out there, they were damned good.

The late afternoon sun was warm, and the air off the bay was fresh. Still, to Gordon, it seemed as if he carried the weight of the world on his shoulders. His brain struggled to think logically. Emotions ranging from intense fear to abject disgust took turns toying with his brain, swamping his ability to process it all. How did a seasoned business executive find himself mixed up with criminals plotting to destroy the company he'd worked tirelessly to build over more than two decades?

At the hotel, Gordon rode the elevator up to his suite and headed directly to a closet where he stored his clothes. Within minutes, he'd packed and presented himself to the front desk, paid the bill they printed, and headed to the hotel's taxi stand.

Minutes later, the car stopped at a site named Lands End Lookout.

Gordon dragged his carry-on bag with rollers to the doors of the popular tourist attraction, paid his fee, then looked for the quietest space in the crowded viewing area. There, he prayed. He closed his eyes and silently asked the Lord to give him the wisdom to make the right decisions and guide his life back on course. It felt better after a few minutes there; his faith was renewed. He took a few photos of the sunset with his phone, then headed toward the exit with newfound confidence.

At the airport, they accepted his American Express credit card without question as payment for a first-class ticket to Atlanta on the red-eye flight leaving just after midnight and arriving around breakfast time.

He still didn't know which choice he would make on arrival but trusted the Lord to help him make the right one. With that consoling thought, he stretched out in his assigned leather, reclining seat the moment he boarded and fell asleep before the jet left the ground.

Fifty-Seven

Atlanta, Georgia, Saturday November 11, 2023

Since the day she'd received an implied threat during her phone conversation with Abduhl Mahinder, Suzanne and Eileen had taken refuge in the Stonehurst Place Bed & Breakfast, a lovely, quaint spot in mid-town Atlanta.

Before she left Hawaii, Serge had booked the entire hideaway for a week. He assigned additional bodyguards who were waiting for her at the airport and again at the small hotel. The Atlanta sheriff's office also parked two cars outside the place and sprinkled a half-dozen armed deputies around the hotel's perimeter. She felt secure. Serge claimed it would probably take a small army to penetrate the security wall they had built around her.

In theory, he would share the comfortable room and bed with her. But she hadn't yet seen him over the past two days. Instead, they had frequent chats by phone or text. It was some comfort that he'd virtually taken over the massive project of fixing the computer systems and upgrading them to better security levels. While Marcel Dubois remained technically in charge of the project, he willingly shared information with Serge, listened well to his advice, and worked with her chief of security to get the most out of every employee.

Their working environment seemed to be more trepidation than panic. All week, key programmers and technicians worked twenty-four seven. One of the large meeting rooms became a communal bedroom. Serge had ordered cots for the staff to use whenever they tired, and the employee cafeteria operated around the clock with staff added from local caterers. Serge had also taken over Gordon Goodfellow's office and slept on the sofa there for a few hours each day.

The Atlanta sheriff's office had reacted with alarm when they learned of new threats against Multima. After all, Supermarkets' headquarters had called Atlanta its home for almost half a century and was one of the city's highest profile and most prestigious employers. They knew Suzanne almost as well as they'd known John George Mortimer. She'd lived in Atlanta for more than a dozen years until a bomb destroyed her home there, and they knew she still waited for contractors to complete its reconstruction. Serge had recounted to her, in glowing terms, several ways the sheriff's team had assisted him and the technology experts to ward off the cyber attackers.

That morning, he called her just after five to alert her that Gordon Goodfellow was on a flight to Atlanta. Two members of the security team planned to meet him at the airport at about eight thirty and escort him to the office. Serge also sent a car to Stonehurst Place Bed & Breakfast with two extra bodyguards to oversee her short trip to the office to meet with Goodfellow.

The bodyguards followed her all the way to the president's office, where Serge spent more than an hour reviewing all he'd learned over the past few hours. She trembled at times and felt sickened at others, but agreed she needed to be there.

After a bodyguard called from the airport to say they'd found Gordon and were on the way to the office, Serge sent out his text for everyone to join them there. When Suzanne stepped back into the meeting room from a brief break, she was surprised at how the crowd had grown and shot a glance of concern toward Serge. He nodded in reassurance.

Four deputies in uniform stood outside the doors to the meeting room. Inside, two detectives sat at one end of the table, dressed in their usual business attire. Serge and two members of his team took the side of the table closest to the outside windows. Suzanne noticed three new faces on the other side of the table. She introduced herself as she worked toward her seat at the head of the table. They identified themselves as FBI agents from the Atlanta office.

As the team escorting Gordon approached the room, Serge signaled to the sheriff, and they left the room together. From her seat at one end of the table, Suzanne heard the law enforcement officer outside calmly explain to Gordon that they had some questions for him. He wasn't under arrest, but they wanted to read him his Miranda rights so he would understand he had no legal obligation to speak with them.

Gordon confidently acknowledged those rights and assured, "I've done nothing wrong. I'm happy to answer your questions, and I think I have valuable information to share with you."

Gordon stepped into the room first, and his jaw dropped. Probably anticipating a *tête-à-tête* with the sheriff and Serge, he hesitated in the doorway, uncertain if he should enter.

"Who are all these people?"

Suzanne suddenly realized he'd directed his astonished question to her, and she prepared to answer when Serge interjected. "They're all either with my team, the sheriff's office, or the FBI. Don't worry."

Hesitantly, Gordon made his way to a vacant chair in the middle of the table, right next to the FBI team. Before he'd settled into his chair, he asked to say a few words before they asked him their questions.

Suzanne nodded.

"I wasn't expecting an escorted welcome when I got to the airport and surely didn't expect such a crowd in my office, but I flew back last night because I have crucial information to share with you. I know you've had some suspicions about my loyalty to the company, but I think what I want to share with you can save the corporation if we act quickly."

For the following fifteen minutes, he recounted the call from a US senator, the request for him to meet Abduhl Mahinder, his surprising meeting with Alvarez, and a summary of the conversations about the planned cyberattack on Multima. As he spoke, the sheriff recorded, and law enforcement officers took copious notes, flipping pages continuously to make space for more details.

No one interrupted his monologue. No one challenged the accuracy or veracity of any claim he made. Everyone listened.

When he paused for breath after those several minutes, he poured a glass of water from a pitcher on the table and took a long sip. When he appeared comfortable, Serge asked him softly if there was any other information he was prepared to share.

Gordon thought about it for a moment. He looked confidently around the room like a schoolboy who'd just scored one hundred percent on a history test. He shook his head at Serge. "No, I've given you everything I have."

Once again, Serge asked his question. "Are you *sure* you've left nothing out? No small detail?"

Gordon drew a breath, thought about the question, then shook his head again emphatically. "I've told you everything I know."

As though on cue, someone knocked on a door, and the meeting room stayed silent as one of Serge's people stepped over and opened it.

He ushered in a short, middle-aged man with graying hair who walked with a shuffle. Suzanne watched Gordon Goodfellow as a stark realization set in. His face reflected abject panic as his mouth froze open, his eyes enlarged to about twice their usual size, and his face flushed a brilliant red.

Everyone watched the middle-aged fellow shuffle to the table, handing a phone to Serge, who pressed a few keys, then adjusted the volume before he set it on the table. The conversation was between Gordon and a Latino with accented English. They talked about the cyberattack and the role Gordon would play—crucial details he hadn't mentioned when he'd outlined the risks of an attack to the group moments before. Eyes around the table gradually shifted toward Gordon.

When the recording broadcasted his fateful words, "Okay, I'm in," Serge stood and reached out to click off the phone.

Gordon blanched, and his head drooped before he muttered, "I think I'd like to speak to an attorney before I answer any more of your questions."

Again, the room remained silent. Serge nodded to the sheriff, who whispered into Gordon's ear and led him away from the table out into the corridor with a hand on his shoulder. As Serge closed the door behind them, she could hear the law enforcement officer reciting the Miranda rights again as he took Gordon into custody.

Passing behind her chair at the head of the table, Serge paused and squeezed her shoulder gently. Barely audible, he mumbled, "It's better this way."

After Serge returned to his seat, a woman with the FBI was the first to speak. She formally introduced herself as

Agent Riley Andrews and first addressed Serge.

"The contact you gave us with the RCMP proved very helpful. When we shared the profile of the person we strongly suspect had some involvement in the bombing of Suzanne's house here in Atlanta three years ago, she confirmed with Canadian Immigration that the fellow was, indeed, in Canada in the weeks before the drone bombing attempt at your place in the Laurentian Mountains. The guy in question is a transplanted New Yorker now living in South Florida who drank the Kool-Aid of Make America Great Again. He doesn't seem to be part of any formal gang but hangs out with a loosely connected bunch that leans toward extreme right-wing politics and has some connection to a guy in Florida who likes to call himself the Shadow."

'Who is this Shadow?" Suzanne interrupted.

"We can't be sure. We strongly suspect it's someone close to the former president, but we have no proof. We have innuendo and a couple distorted voice recordings but no concrete evidence. During the past president's term of office, we detected several calls linked directly to misadventure or misfortune originating either in the White House or very nearby. While we don't have unequivocal proof of the former president's direct involvement, be sure you understand this, for his entire adult life, the people in his circle of influence have been characters of interest to law enforcement around the globe."

Suzanne nodded, understanding the agent's delicate position. She drove right to her concern: "Okay, if it is this character you call the Shadow, does he have the expertise to pull off a cyberattack on Multima?"

"If you're asking if he or the people around him have the technical know-how to pull it off, the answer is probably no. Does he have enough money to pay off an expert? That answer is probably yes. More concerning is the Shadow's pattern of apparent willingness to use violence to force some people to do his will. Currently, our greatest concern is your former employee Amber Chan."

She paused and looked intently at Suzanne for emphasis. "Although Gordon Goodfellow didn't mention it in his statement earlier, he saw her held captive somewhere. We know that from the full recording of the conversations in the San Francisco restaurant. Serge has also made us aware the woman has expert technology skills. It's possible the Shadow could force her, or someone else like her who might have the necessary technical expertise, to pull off an attack."

If the dates Gordon Goodfellow remembered were correct, they had less than a week left to bolster the computer systems of the entire company and avoid a catastrophe too ugly to imagine fully.

Suzanne turned toward Serge, who waved for her attention.

"There's another bit about Amber Chan we should all be aware of. Interpol now knows where she's hidden and it's outside Spain. They had an apartment under surveillance in Seville, and saw her and a male suspect carried away from that apartment to a vehicle. They followed it to the location in Gibraltar where a guy locked them in a basement. They continue to monitor the apartment in Seville as well because Interpol believes the head of the outfit known as The Organization is using that apartment and expects a new Interpol Red Code alert will return Amber Chan to her."

"So Interpol is using Amber as bait to catch the big fish?" Suzanne asked.

It was the FBI agent Riley who answered. "We know there's at least one big catch in play, but there may be more, several more. So, we urge Multima to make full use of every day to get the security of your computer systems in order. We think an attack is imminent."

Fifty-Eight

Seville, Spain, Saturday November 11, 2023

Her phone rang late in the evening. Fidelia expected the caller to be the highly placed official at Interpol, letting her know they'd found Amber Chan before the midnight deadline. It wasn't him. Pleasingly, though, it was Juan Suarez, and he'd successfully tracked down the Chinese woman. The mark at Interpol had dodged another career-ending bullet and probably didn't know it.

"It was Eduardo, the big one. The one who told us he fell asleep. I was tempted to finish him off immediately after we found her missing. Instead, I decided to have a guy I trust tail him. Sure enough, this afternoon, he followed Eduardo down to Gibraltar. The bastard delivered a plastic bag of food, trying to keep alive both Amber Chan and your guy from Uruguay."

Juan paused, probably to be sure she understood everything so far. She told him she got it.

"The guy tailing him asked me what he should do. I told him to put Eduardo to sleep and give the prisoners food and water until I could get him some help. Right away, I sent over two enforcers I had in Marbella. They got there about an hour ago. Eduardo was still unconscious from the tap on the head my guy delivered, and the prisoners were better after some food and water. My guys thought they hadn't eaten since the day they were kidnapped and the room where he held them was stifling hot."

"Where are they now?"

"About halfway to Seville. My guy's driving them as fast as he can. You should have them in about an hour."

"Do they need medical attention?" This would all be in vain if the Chinese woman couldn't perform.

"Probably. I'll get a doctor over to the apartment. She should be there before they arrive."

"Where's Eduardo?"

"He's in the trunk of my guy's car. I was tempted to off the bastard immediately but thought you might like to have the honor."

Fidelia nodded her satisfaction with his judgment but didn't tell him that. "Tell your guy to keep him tied up in the trunk of his car. I want some time with the victims when they get here. We'll deal with Eduardo later."

Juan's guy called her as he parked the vehicle in the street near the apartment. She ordered four of the bodyguards downstairs to help get the victims up the three flights to the apartment she and Klaudia shared on the third floor.

Neither victim could walk without help. One hefty guy finally decided to carry Amber up the final two floors to speed up the laborious process. Juan Suarez arrived with a doctor, who skipped up the steps with her medical bag and moved directly to Amber.

The hefty one had dropped her on the sofa, and the doctor kneeled beside it to begin her assessment. Wordlessly, she pulled out equipment from her medical bag, starting with a stethoscope to check her lungs and a blood pressure monitor to measure BP and pulse. She held a thermometer to Amber's forehead. Then she ordered a glass of water, helping her patient drink the entire glass slowly.

"Give him some, too," the doctor ordered Fidelia, pointing to Ricardo Schirillio, slumped on the floor beside the sofa. "They're severely dehydrated, but I think both will be all right if you give them small amounts of water every few minutes for the next couple hours."

Fidelia nodded to Juan, tilting her head toward the doctor. "We'd like you to stay with them for the next two hours as you suggest. I'll add two hundred euros for your trouble."

The doctor grimaced but appeared satisfied with the extra compensation on a Sunday evening she'd surely hoped to spend elsewhere. Fidelia told Klaudia to take care of things for a while and pulled on a sweater for the chilly evening air outside. She motioned for Juan, his guy who had brought the victims, and two other bodyguards to all follow her down the stairs.

"Where's the car?"

The driver pointed to a black Lexus SUV parked a few yards down the street, and Fidelia signaled for everyone to follow.

"Direct your driver to a quiet spot out of town where we can work undisturbed for a while." Fidelia kept her tone civil, but there could be no doubt about her intentions.

The driver took Highway E-803 out of Seville toward the north. Within a few minutes, they were in rolling terrain and, minutes after that, into the start of the Sierra Morena. On one dark side road, the driver left the pavement, followed a gravel path for more than a kilometer, and pulled to a stop. Everyone left the car and walked to its rear.

Fidelia nodded to the driver, who unlocked and raised the hatch. Eduardo was a mess. Zip ties secured his hands and feet. A small towel held in place with tape wound around his head several times covered his mouth. Just to remove it all would be a form of torture. His jeans were soggy and brown, and the odor from them was repulsive from even a few feet away.

She motioned to yank him out, and Juan added instructions to the bodyguards to cut the covering over his mouth but not the zip-ties. As they hoisted him to his feet, the big brute blubbered like a baby, pleading for mercy and understanding as soon as he could speak.

Bodyguards stood on each side of the bound man, a few feet away from the stench. Without a word of warning, Fidelia stepped forward, slapped the side of his face hard, and told him to shut up. The blubbering reduced to whimpers, then subsided completely as Fidelia threatened to smack him again.

"Why? Why did you do it?" Her tone was controlled, but her eyes surely conveyed anger.

"They stole my daughter." His voice broke, about to cry again. "She's only fifteen. They threatened to sell her!"

Fidelia was unmoved. It was his problem, but the jerk had made it hers. "Who were you dealing with?"

"I don't know the guy's name. Tony, the bodyguard who brought Amber Chan here on your jet, put me in touch with him. An American, from Miami I think."

Fidelia momentarily calculated the odds, then swirled around to the largest of her Uruguayan enforcers. When she spoke, she almost spat out her disdain with an order.

"Break his left foot."

The enforcer calmly walked back to the SUV, opened the

rear door, then rumbled about for a minute or two. When he closed the hatch and resurfaced from behind the SUV, he held a tire wrench in front of him so it would be easily visible to any onlooker. He casually approached Eduardo, who started to whimper again as the guy approached.

Fidelia was tempted to give the cowardly bastard another chance, but she resisted it with a nod toward her enforcer. With a reflex as quick as lightning, he lashed out with the tire rod and smashed it against Eduardo's left ankle with such force that the ankle sprang more than a foot off the ground. His victim collapsed in a crumpled heap, trying to reach out to clutch his foot, screaming in agony.

They all stood and watched. The two enforcers lit cigarettes and inhaled deeply, knowing their work might not be done.

It was a still night. Other than Eduardo's cries of agony on the ground, there were no signs of nightlife among the birds or animals hiding in the bushes. A cool breeze rustled the few leaves remaining on the trees, and a bright moon provided enough natural light when clouds moved on.

"Stand him up again," she said after a while. The pain he'd feel putting weight on the ankle would refocus his attention. Sure enough, as soon as the pair yanked him vertical again, he let out a yelp of new agony. It lasted only a moment.

"They'll kill her. They'll kill my daughter if I give you a name. I can't do it!"

A noble outburst. Completely understandable. But stupid. She nodded again to the tall enforcer. As he stepped forward, with tire wrench in hand, Eduardo recoiled and tried to shift away. With the added weight to his left ankle, he lost his balance and collapsed again in a heap on the ground. The enforcer swung at his flailing right foot anyway, and a crunch of crushing bones momentarily drowned out Eduardo's screams of suffering.

She waited for his cries to subside. It took a few minutes, and she noticed the bodyguards shuffling their feet uncomfortably. They'd do what she told them, but it didn't mean they enjoyed it. They knew the guy. Maybe even had a couple beers and played some cards with him in their downtime. It would be best to wrap it up soon.

Fidelia walked over and stood above his face, glaring directly down. It was time to change tactics. "Look Eduardo, I don't want to hurt you more. Think about it. How will whoever you're protecting ever know you squealed? Do you think that Juan over there and the boys will call the character up and tell him? You can't control your daughter's fate. The guy you're protecting is going to do what he wants to do. But if you tell me, I can get some revenge."

She let him think about that for a moment or two before she pressed. "Tell me all about it, and I can work on getting your daughter back from him or extract some justice if he's harmed her."

Whether he bought her questionable logic, or his weakened state guided his mental calculations, he caved. "Tony said the guy was a billionaire or something. Gave me his number. I called him on a burner phone just like Tony instructed, and he offered me fifty thousand dollars to steal Amber and hold her for a few weeks. I told him I wasn't interested. A day later, the same guy called me and told me he had my daughter. Said he'd sell her for prostitution if I didn't cooperate. But if I stole Amber, and hid her away someplace safe until he had a friend pick her up, he'd let my daughter go free and still give me fifty grand."

"You're telling me a story. I want a name."

"He never told me his name. Said he was the Shadow. Said that was all I needed to know."

Fidelia spun on her heel the second he divulged the name and faced Juan Suarez. "He's yours. Handle it as you wish."

She strode to the SUV a few yards away and didn't flinch when she heard the loud pop of a single shot fired from a silenced handgun.

Fifty-Nine

Atlanta, Georgia, Saturday November 11, 2023

It was entirely different from what they portrayed in the movies or on TV. No one slapped handcuffs on Gordon's wrists. There was no perp walk before flashing cameras or shouting reporters. In fact, the sheriff politely asked Gordon to ride over to the office with him and opened the front passenger door as an invitation to sit up front for the ride.

There were no flashing lights or sirens, and the sheriff chatted about the fine weather they were having for November. He asked no questions, appeared relaxed and, dare Gordon use the term, almost friendly. When they parked the sheriff's large SUV in a reserved spot in the underground parking, no one else was around, nor was there any activity he could spot.

Walking toward the elevator, the sheriff told him they'd need to do a few formalities upstairs, photos and that sort of stuff. Then they'd get a phone for Gordon to call his attorney. *Attorney*? True, he'd said he wanted one, but he'd never used a criminal attorney. For God's sake, the only attorney he knew was the one handling his divorce.

As they took his photos and fingerprints, technicians repeatedly used the phrase, "It's just a formality," and seemed almost as embarrassed about the process as Gordon. They each made small talk about meaningless things like the weather, the Atlanta Falcons, or their upcoming Thanksgiving plans.

Handing him a phone, the sheriff explained the law required them to give Gordon one free call, but he might need to make more than one. However, he should restrict calls only to those from whom he sought legal advice. Any call to a media personality or reporter would change the rules entirely.

He first dialed the number for his divorce attorney, who had slept late that Sunday morning and hadn't yet sipped from his first cup of coffee. Gordon had to repeat his name twice before the guy realized who was disturbing his free time. The divorce lawyer bailed out once Gordon gave the guy a brief overview of his circumstances.

"Wow. I'm so sorry to learn of this complication, but I'll be candid with you. I handle divorces only. We have attorneys in the firm who handle criminal matters. If you like, I can try to track one of them down."

The sheriff guided Gordon to a room toward the back of the office complex and asked him to stay there while everyone waited for an attorney to call back. It was a comfortable room, something like one might see in a motel, except there was no bed. He saw a full bathroom in one corner, including a shower and clean towels on chrome racks.

On the back rim of a clean, white washbasin, toothpaste, a toothbrush in a plastic wrapper, a small bar of soap, a tiny bottle of shampoo, and a comb wrapped in plastic all formed a neat line next to the wall.

There was a TV in one corner. A bookcase on an opposite wall displayed a few dozen hardcover books, with a stack of newspapers on the shelf below. Cheap tile covered the floor, but it was clean. All four walls were off-white, so no one could call the decorating anything but functional. But there were no bars on the windows, and Gordon wasn't even sure the door was locked.

Since he hadn't cleaned up for more than thirty hours, and all the amenities were available, Gordon quickly stripped off his clothes and showered. Afterward, he felt like a new man and even allowed himself a smile as he picked up a copy of that morning's *The Atlanta Journal-Constitution*. He scanned the pages first and was relieved to find no mention of him or Multima in the headlines.

He sat in a comfortable armchair, reading, until a knock on the door broke his concentration. It squeaked open immediately, and a short black woman poked her head around the door.

She smiled broadly. "I have some lunch for you. It's nothing special, but there's a sandwich, a cupcake, and an apple. Would you like me to leave it on the table?"

Gordon returned her smile and told her the table was fine.

She entered, carrying a tray toward a low, rectangular bureau about the size and height of a TV tray. "I can also come back with a bottle of Coke, Sprite, or water. Which do you prefer?"

Of course, in Atlanta, home of Coca-Cola's headquarters, the water would undoubtedly be Dasani. He stood up, told her his choice, then unwrapped the plastic from the sandwich. His last meal had been a muffin of some sort with orange juice on the flight from San Francisco.

It was early afternoon before Gordon heard his assigned phone ring. A new voice identified herself as Emma Jones, attorney.

"I'm sorry to learn you have some legal challenges, and I apologize for the delay in getting back to you. I was on a flight from New York this morning and just spoke with my colleague about your circumstances. Are you still looking for legal counsel?"

"Yes. I surely am. They're holding me in a room here at the sheriff's office. I'm comfortable, but I'd like to get out of here as soon as possible."

"Did I hear you say a room, not a cell?"

"Yeah. It's a small room near the back of the facility. I've been here since about ten this morning. Are you able to come right away?"

"I'm in a taxi from the airport, almost at my home. I can visit you after I drop off my bags and get my car. Have they interviewed you? Have they formally charged you with anything?"

Gordon explained the meeting at Multima Supermarkets' headquarters earlier that morning and the chain of events until then, confirming no charges had been laid yet.

It was another two hours before his attorney knocked on the door and stepped in with her right arm outstretched in greeting. She was tall, a good few inches taller than Gordon, with jet black hair that fell comfortably below her shoulders. Her eyes were a shade of blue but without a sparkle. He thought maybe blizzard blue, like the color of water just below arctic ice, might be appropriate.

Her handshake was firm. Her smile was brief and formal. He sensed she'd be a tough questioner and a formidable foe or ally. Immediately, she reached for a nearby chair behind Gordon, pulled it closer facing an armchair, and motioned for him to take a seat.

"The law requires the sheriff to provide a room like this where we can openly and freely discuss your case. They aren't allowed to record or listen to conversations, so you can be comfortable that everything you tell me will be entirely between us. To provide you with the best defense, I need you to tell me the full truth about everything that's happened leading up to today."

She paused for emphasis and arched her brows slightly. He nodded in understanding.

"Take as long as you like," she said. "There are no time limitations on this conversation. First, I will need you to confirm you're engaging me as your attorney and understand that I bill for my time at nine hundred ninety-five dollars per hour, with an initial retainer of ten thousand dollars due tomorrow and payment for services rendered due upon receipt of a monthly account."

Gordon nodded in acceptance, then began talking. He started at the beginning and walked her through the acquisition of Jeffersons Stores, the background fears of a cyberattack, and the decisions to fortify the computer systems and integrate Jeffersons Stores. He candidly explained his relationship with Amber Chan and the complications that it caused.

From time to time, Emma Jones asked a question or two for clarification, but for most of the two hours, she listened and recorded. When he finished, he took another sip from the Dasani water bottle and waited for her to explain where they went from there.

"Your explanation of the circumstances and events as you remember them was very helpful. It also helps me better understand my curious conversation with the sheriff earlier. It took me longer to arrive than you probably expected. He was waiting for me when I came in and asked for a chat before we met."

Gordon tensed. Why hadn't she divulged all that before he spilled his guts? He opened his mouth to protest, but she cut him off with a wave of her hand.

"Before you say anything else, let me explain their proposal. When I asked him how quickly we could arrange bail today, he asked me to discuss the wisdom of not requesting bail. Instead, he's proposing to hold you—for the next few days at least—at FPC Pensacola, a minimum-security prison in Florida."

Gordon's mouth dropped. Blood rushed to his head in a classical fight-or-flight response to unexpected danger. He'd expected to be home long before now. Yet this woman was proposing he voluntarily succumb to imprisonment without a trial, and even before criminal charges were filed!

He exploded. Jumping up from his armchair, he screamed, "There is no fucking way I'll agree to go to some prison. Not now. Not ever! If that's the best you can do, I'll get another attorney, somebody who actually knows how to do their job. Let me talk to the sheriff right now!"

She didn't cower or make any move to leave the room. Instead, Emma sat quietly and let him vent, almost as though she'd expected this reaction. She glanced at her watch and then turned off the recording on her phone. When Gordon stopped shouting and slumped back down into the comfortable armchair, she stood up and looked down at him with an expression resembling pity.

"I understand your surprise and your anger. The sheriff's proposal is extremely unusual. I've never encountered a suggestion like it before. But understand this. FPC Pensacola is a federal facility. An invitation to accommodate you there must have involved the FBI and someone near the top of the Federal Justice Department. If you stay there a few days, you'll be in America's cushiest prison. It's more like a country club than a jail."

She paused again to let him process her words. Her eyes softened, and her manner relaxed. Still, she drew a deep breath before she continued.

"It's your call. If you want another attorney, I'll leave and won't charge for my time today. I'll let the sheriff know you want someone else. That will buy you a few more hours in this lounge before he eventually transfers you to a cell. But I still strongly recommend you consider his offer. To be candid, it seems to me they're offering you something like protective custody." She turned on her heel and headed toward the door.

Gordon remained dumbfounded, in shock.

At the door, she turned and faced him again, her forehead creased with worry lines and her mouth forming a tight grimace. "Think about it, Gordon. I'm still willing to help, but I've accomplished all I can today."

She closed the door behind her, and a multitude of thoughts raced through Gordon's muddled mind. He panicked and ran over to the door, grabbing the door handle and twisting it urgently. It was locked. In exasperation, he cried out for help and collapsed on his knees, his shaking hands helplessly gripping the doorknob.

Sixty

Atlanta, Georgia, Saturday November 11, 2023

Neither could recall a day so emotionally charged and demanding. Suzanne pulled Serge aside late in the afternoon for a quiet corridor conversation, took him by the hand, and led him to the end of the corridor where no staff worked that day. They were both exhausted, and it showed on their faces.

She'd checked hers in the bathroom mirror minutes before requesting this *tête-à-tête*.

Red and swollen eyes were just the beginning. Her face was so pale she added a dash of makeup to make her skin color passably lifelike. Her lips were dry, and the lipstick added color but hadn't helped much. Worst of all, worry lines creased into her forehead and cheeks. She looked as if she'd aged years in just the past few weeks, and the prevailing aches, tightness, and fatigue she felt inside compounded her concern.

As she looked into his face and eyes, she saw the same physical characteristics in Serge. They'd seen each other so little over the past weeks that his new appearance almost shocked her. During the earlier meeting with Gordon, twice she'd caught him trying to hide hands that trembled involuntarily from fatigue, tension, or maybe both.

"Any news?"

"Which front are you asking about?" His attempt at humor failed, and he grimaced as soon as he said it. Then he added a bit. "Interpol reports there's been movement in Spain. The FBI thinks a cyberattack is imminent. With Gordon out of the loop, the Shadow—or some other outfit—will be looking for another way in. And the private jet registered to Tak Takahashi is parked in Seville, but there's no sign of him. None of those factors bodes well for us."

"You didn't mention China. Other than Amber Chan, and maybe this guy they call the Shadow, has anyone found a link that might help us understand what the Chinese are so upset about?"

"Strangely, no one has found a connection. But here's

another odd development I should mention. My contact at Interpol reported that someone there leaked news about our surveillance in Seville to the Russians. Authorities at Interpol arrested that guy—somebody high up in its ranks—but not before he let the FSB in on all the details about Amber Chan that Interpol had learned. My contact fears that might draw the Russians into the game, too."

"Why?"

"Remember, I told you the FSB lost one of their people last week. There's little doubt someone outside Russia, maybe even The Organization, killed him. They'll surely seek revenge. One never knows if that will trigger a gang war or some other competition. Who knows? Maybe the Russians might try a cyberattack to beat a rival to the punch."

With that sobering thought, Gordon popped back into her thoughts. He was still in limbo at the sheriff's office. Serge had called over twice that afternoon and learned that although he'd conferred with legal counsel, there was little progress on either bail or outright release.

They were still considering charges. Suzanne had called Alberto Ferer, Multima's chief legal counsel for his opinion and advice. He was sympathetic but demurred about getting involved. "My area of expertise is corporate law, not criminal. I would probably just muddy the waters. You're better to leave it with a local professional," he said.

A few hours later, she could no longer continue. Fatigue was surely a factor, but the emotional burden was no longer bearable. "We need to leave it to the professionals. Let's take a night off. Come to the cute little hotel with me and have a meal, a good sleep, and maybe even cuddle a bit." She dug deep for a smile that hinted at possible mischief.

"Yeah. You're right," Serge said. "Marcel has the technology stuff under control, and he's pushing his people as hard as possible. They're close enough to the end now that they can taste it, and I'm sure they'll do everything they can to be ready."

They agreed to have a car come around for them at five, with two bodyguards to ride with them until the contingent around the hotel took over.

At precisely the agreed hour, Suzanne stopped outside the

door where Marcel and Serge were sharing last thoughts, waved her hand for him to come, and bid goodnight to Marcel.

"We can't thank you enough for all you're doing here. When it's over, pick your destination. We'll fly you and the missus there for a couple weeks, pick up the tab, and make sure a special bonus check fattens your bank account." She managed a half-smile and carried on.

After the short drive to the inn, Eileen greeted them at the door and introduced the caterers who'd prepared their special meal and were ready to serve. She wished them a wonderful evening and then scooted out the door for her own evening out with one of Serge's security guys.

Entering the small dining room, Suzanne became speechless. Slow, romantic music oozed from overhead speakers. Lights were dim, and several candles on the table flickered with an inviting ambiance. One square table sat in the middle of the room, covered with a brilliant white tablecloth laden with fine bone china and gleaming silverware. Only two chairs sat on the floor beside the table, arranged at a ninety-degree angle for cozy seating and intimate conversation.

The catering team offered chairs and pulled them out for Suzanne and Serge, their smiles broadening as they noted the warm reaction from both guests. Before they stepped away, they offered to open the bottle of vintage red wine sitting in the center of the table and poured it after Serge's go-ahead.

While they savored their ceremonial toast and an initial sip of the wine, Serge slid his hand across the table and put it over one of hers gently and with a squeeze of affection. It was amazing how comforting such a small touch could be.

It was their first meal together in weeks, and it felt much longer. FaceTime, texts, and phone calls never could substitute for proximity. Simply being close added a dimension of relaxation that helped release built-up tension, frustrations, and the constant prevailing fear of the potential damage from the threatened cyberattack.

Their meal lasted for almost two hours as the caterers slowly worked their way through four courses, each more delicious than the one before. The fresh smoked salmon was flavored with a spicy sauce they both raved about. A salad followed using a dozen different lettuces and vegetable ingredients that were flavorful and satisfying. Their main course was beef, roasted to perfection with thin medium-rare slices, a baked potato, and more vegetables. To finish their meal, the caterers served bowls of colorful and delicious fresh fruits. Suzanne counted six different varieties.

After their first few sips of wine, she asked the caterers to take away their glasses and the remainder of the bottle. They loved it, she told them, but tonight they couldn't risk being anything less than one hundred percent alert. There was too much going on around them.

Two hours of dining flew past. It was surprisingly enjoyable catching up on all the little things they didn't take time to chat about during calls or business meetings, and their laughter grew louder and longer as the meal progressed.

After they dabbed their napkins to their mouths and thanked the caterers profusely, Serge and Suzanne wended their way up the steps to their room, arms around each other's waists, and engaging in lingering and more passionate kisses every few steps.

Neither had any doubts about what came next. Before the door to their room clicked locked, his arms had already wound around her shoulders. He pulled her tightly to him, he was already partially erect. She could feel him harden further as they kissed, mouths and tongues locked in passion, equally hungry to explore each other more.

They loved to undress each other, and she let Serge lead the way. Within only a few minutes, her top, skirt, and undergarments dropped casually to the floor while he kissed, touched, and probed her body. She was damp before her panties fell at her feet, and she kicked them away. Unexpectedly, he swept her off her feet with one strong grip around her bottom and shoulders, then gently placed her on the bed.

When she reached out to his shirt, he swept her away with one hand and reached down between her thighs with his other, touching her both urgently and passionately. Slowly, he started kissing her bare breasts, alternating light touches of his lips to her aroused nipples with gentle sucking to enlarge them even more. She felt her legs gradually spread wider and wider with his gentle nudges and a more forceful penetration of his forefinger.

She pulled him toward her, desperate to undress him. Still, he resisted. Instead, moving farther from her reach and kissing her tummy, then her curly pubic hair, and finally tasting her clitoris with his tongue. Repeatedly. Deeply. Lustfully. Her legs opened wider, and his passion grew more intense as she heaved her hips and embraced his head and shoulders with welcoming thighs. She groaned in satisfaction. This was new, exciting, and stimulating. But she wanted his penis, and she wanted it immediately.

Suzanne twisted out from under him, forcing his mouth to withdraw. From there, she raised herself to a seated position, then lunged for his penis, grabbing hold of his pants with one hand, yanking down his zipper with the other. With her hands inside his pants, she groped behind his underwear and finally connected. He was harder than she could remember ever feeling him. Stroking him gently with her left hand, she unbuttoned his shirt with the other, then loosened his belt before yanking off his underwear and trousers in one motion. Before he could adjust or protest, she climbed on top, took his penis in her hand, and guided him fully inside.

Her desperation was so great and his penetration so satisfying, she finished surprisingly soon and before him. Without missing a beat, Serge slipped out from under her and reversed positions, entering her again with ease and passion. Unexpectedly, she came again and in perfect sync with him this time. They collapsed in an exhausted heap, holding each other tightly like it was their first time, and maybe their last.

At some point, they separated and took showers. Serge went first and when Suzanne returned cleaned up, he was already asleep, breathing deeply but with a tone and rhythm of satisfaction. She kissed him gently on one cheek and glanced at her phone. It was approaching midnight. That was her last thought before she fell into a deep sleep as well.

Serge's phone rang the next morning at 9:38, waking them both. He hit the speaker button as he answered in the still-darkened room. "Something's going on you probably want to know about. Somebody's trying to get in. We can't call it an attack yet, and their first attempts have been unsuccessful, but you might want to come over and watch the show."

Both scrambled from bed and threw on the closest clothes they could find. Serge was first to the bathroom, then rushed down the stairs to round up the bodyguards and car. Suzanne followed as soon as her teeth were clean and a capful of mouthwash did its job.

There was no rush hour that weekend morning. Still, their trip to the Multima offices seemed to take far longer than the night before. One of Serge's security people greeted them at the main entrance and sprang open the door as they mounted the cement steps at the entrance. Another held open an elevator across the main lobby before it quickly climbed to the technology team's floor in the building.

Suzanne noted that everyone was on the job as they hurried past the area where employees usually snatched a few hours of sleep on the rented leather cots. Most cubicles had technicians hunched over keyboards or fixated on large monitors with flashing lights and rolling columns of data.

In the meeting room, the situation was too tense for anyone to sit. Instead, a cluster of Marcel's closest advisors and direct reports stood around its outside wall, pointing at indicators on the screen, occasionally sharing whispered comments with each other.

When he noticed they'd arrived, Marcel hurried over and gave a quick explanation. "They've made only two attempts with no success. Both were from the same IP address in Kraków, Poland. After the first attempt, it was a good hour before we saw the second. But there, do you see that blue flash on the screen? That's another attempt blocked by our firewall."

Suzanne had to ask. "Will you be able to keep them out?"

"That's the billion-dollar question, isn't it?" He allowed a tiny smile to form before dampening any tempting enthusiasm. "Unfortunately, it's still too early to tell."

Sixty-One

Seville, Spain, Sunday November 12, 2023

Because the Spanish thug, Tony, had found a way to kidnap Amber and Ricardo once, Fidelia knew she had to get out of the country. To connect with that jerk, someone had discovered where they were in Spain, and if the Shadow was behind the kidnapping, he'd likely have someone else try again.

The Shadow remained an enigma to her. She'd never met the guy in person. Her mentor Giancarlo Mareno had known him, and they'd worked together on a handful of crooked schemes. But he'd detested the Shadow and refused to reveal or use the scoundrel's name. Fidelia was confident she knew his true identity but still couldn't be entirely sure.

Fidelia, Mia and Klaudia had already done the research while Juan Suarez's men tracked down Amber and Ricardo, and had agreed Poland made sense as a base for the cyberattack. Once they had Amber and saw she would soon be healthy enough to carry out the job, they set the wheels in motion.

In the hours after Tony got his just punishment that Sunday morning, she'd wasted no time. Returning to the loaned apartment in Seville, she scrambled up the three flights of stairs, nodding at new bodyguards on each level.

Inside the apartment, Amber looked better. She sat on a sofa and sipped water from a glass while the doctor cleaned up some scratches and cuts on her face and the side of her head.

Amber managed a half-hearted smile to acknowledge Fidelia's arrival but said nothing. Fidelia took a few seconds to assess the situation, then motioned to Klaudia to follow her to one bedroom.

Standing a few steps away from the door, she whispered, "Any information from the doctor?"

"Not much. She's not very conversational. Seems more than a little piqued to be here." Klaudia shrugged.

"Amber done much talking?"

"She woke up just before you came in. She's been sleeping continuously except for the minute or two each time the doctor woke her to take on water."

Fidelia nodded, and they returned to the living room. "How are you feeling, Amber?"

The doctor stopped her work to listen to the reply.

Amber shifted uncomfortably on the sofa, and took a deep breath, then cleared her throat before she spoke. "I feel a little light-headed, not dizzy or anything, just a bit of a fog like I had when I had COVID."

"Would you like to try walking around?" the doctor asked.

Amber, pressing down with her hands, pushed off from the sofa and stood erect. She then took a few slow steps toward the door before turning around somewhat unsteadily and bracing against a nearby wall.

The doctor observed. Fidelia wanted to see more.

"Why don't you try running on the spot for a bit?" the doctor said. After a few seconds, she suggested jumping jacks and then touching her toes a few times.

Amber followed her instructions with no apparent difficulty.

The doctor asked again how she was.

"Okay. I feel more normal. I think everything's okay."

Fidelia looked at the doctor, who appeared relaxed but again anxious to leave as she packed up her medical kit.

"Is she okay for a flight?" Fidelia asked.

The doctor stopped her packing momentarily and faced Fidelia. "Are you suggesting a flight within the next few days?"

"Yes," Fidelia said. "Tomorrow."

The doctor protested but to no avail. Juan Suarez promised her another thousand euros and told her to stay. When she refused, he ordered one of his men to strike her. After the third violent punch to her stomach, the doctor collapsed in a heap on the floor, weeping and begging him to stop. With her continued cooperation assured, Fidelia carried on.

First, she sent Mia Vasquez and Klaudia ahead to Kraków on her private jet to settle into a suitable Airbnb they'd booked for a week. Klaudia's orders were to detach all the apartment owner's existing Wi-Fi technology and replace it with new equipment from a nearby Exatel outlet in Kraków, paying with cash and a false name. Meanwhile, Mia would buy and stock the apartment's refrigerator with enough food for a dozen people for a couple days.

By late morning, her private jet would be back for the rest of the crew. Provided Amber was well enough, the jet would make yet another flight and have everyone in Poland ready to attack sometime on Monday.

She'd picked Kraków because the Polish city was physically closer to the Russians than the Americans. Fidelia had also instructed Klaudia to create new IP addresses, sure that Multima would call in the FBI once a cyberattack occurred. Everyone knew they had sophisticated software that could track and locate where the hack actually originated.

It was important to lead the FBI down a false path, and it was better in a country still partially under the influence of the Russians than in any Western European market she controlled. She may have made a deal with the Russians, but she still had no love for them. The idea of the Americans harassing the Russkis for a while held some appeal.

After a few hours of sleep and confirmation the pilots were back in Seville, Fidelia rousted the sleeping doctor and demanded she wake Amber and check her status. The doctor still held a hand on her battered stomach and limped slightly as she moved around the bed, checking her patient.

Amber didn't speak except to answer the doctor's questions. She appeared fine, but Fidelia knew the effects of beatings sometimes weren't obvious and might take days to appear or regress. She needed the Chinese woman in top form if they were to pull off the cyberattack.

Several minutes after she started, the doctor nodded toward Fidelia. "She'll probably be alright. It would be better to give her a couple days to fully recover from the dehydration and trauma, but she'll probably be okay."

Fidelia looked at her sternly but spoke very calmly. "Call home. Tell them you'll be away until Tuesday evening. You're coming with us. Negotiate your fee for two more days with Juan while I pack."

Her jet left Seville for a second time a few minutes before noon, carrying three women and Fidelia's eight male

Uruguayan bodyguards—nine, including Ricardo, who needed help even to get up the steps of the plane.

Juan Suarez and his people left them at the aircraft without knowing its destination. Under potential intense questioning, her country leader and his people would better withstand the pressures if they truly didn't know.

Unfortunately, regardless of the amount of compensation the doctor negotiated with Juan for the extra days, it was unlikely the woman would make the return trip. But Fidelia needed Amber awake, alert and in top mental form in mere hours, so she might have to sacrifice the doctor.

Overflowing with anticipation of the coming day's events, Fidelia couldn't sleep, but she encouraged all the others to try. During the flight, most of her companions dozed off, while she continued to anticipate outcomes and plot alternative steps should they become necessary. The low growl from the pilots cutting power to the engines broke her concentration, and minutes later, they parked at one end of the Kraków airport terminal just after 5:00 p.m.

Four cars were parked at the front door of the terminal, waiting for their arrival, and their drivers stood outside with all doors open, ready for passengers. Their drive was less than ten minutes, and everyone piled out when they arrived at the four-bedroom apartment on the top floor of a modern, functional building.

First, she gave instructions as the gang stood in a semi-circle in the large living area. Mia had stocked the refrigerator and cupboards with enough food for everyone to eat as much as they wanted, whenever they wanted it. Next, she ordered the bodyguards to divide into two teams, half sleeping for the next six hours and the remainder guarding the perimeter of the building.

Then she ordered the doctor to perform another assessment of Amber. She found her in better health with normal fitness indicators, so Fidelia instructed Amber to take one bedroom and sleep there until she called. Then she ordered the doctor to switch her focus to Ricardo. She needed him to fully recover before their next flight.

Klaudia had already assembled the large, thirty-inch monitor on the back ledge of the huge desk the apartment provided. That desk had caught her eye when she'd searched the Airbnb site. From that photo, she could see the old, polished wood desk measured more than six feet across and about four feet deep. It made a perfect surface for a monitor and two people working side-by-side with laptops.

Already, Klaudia sat at the computer, testing and retesting the Wi-Fi and dark web connections. Fidelia watched her German friend for a moment. As the sun began to set, the late afternoon light created a colorful halo above her head, making her recently colored dark-brown hair look younger and more vibrant.

She liked the new hairstyle. While shorter than before, it still covered the back of her neck and fell almost sensuously around the tops of her shoulders. More importantly, seated like she was now, her previous long, flowing hair no longer blocked a clear view of her breasts. When Fidelia saw them outlined beneath her top, her thoughts always wandered in hope. If everything went well today, there might still be an opportunity before she dropped her off again in Germany. Successes sometimes left them both aroused and wanting.

Fidelia abruptly shut down the daydream and started with the necessary phone calls as Mia prompted her. It was early morning in Australia, so they started with Aretta Musa, who reported that she'd found another dozen women in Mexico. If Fidelia wanted to pick them up, she'd be happy to share. If not, she'd bring them to Australia, where business was picking up with Chinese tourists. Fidelia told her to keep this batch for her rich Asian customers.

The next scheduled call didn't happen. "I've tried Tak Takahashi at all the numbers I have on file. There's no answer at any of them. I also tried a couple of his people whose names I have on file. Both claim they haven't seen him for a few days and don't know where he is."

It was not only odd, but the timing of this unavailability was suspicious. She hadn't told him about the issues with Amber or any of the details of their earlier-than-originally-planned cyberattack on Multima. She asked Mia to keep trying.

Working across time zones, Mia reached Zefar Karimov, the deputy finance minister in Uzbekistan. The only condition he had ever attached to arranging her passport for that country was that she let him know in advance when she intended to visit the compound in Muynak.

"I'm not sure when I'll arrive," Fidelia said, "but it will probably be late tomorrow evening."

"Wonderful! Call me again when you know. I'll pop up there to ease your entry." That meant he'd probably spend the night again, but she promised either she or Mia would phone.

Mia had all the European calls organized, with each leader waiting as Fidelia took the line. The calls were quick, last-minute checks that nothing had changed with their grand scheme and no new twists or hurdles had been discovered. In France, Pierre Boivin confirmed the Russians had notified him their first shipment of girls from Belarus was ready for delivery.

Juan Suarez confirmed the apartment in Seville had been cleaned and swept again for electronic devices and guards remained in the area. They had observed no unusual activity or visitors.

Estavao Sereno confirmed all the new bank accounts were open and ready to accept deposits in Gibraltar, Cyprus, the Caymans, and Thailand. As soon as Multima caved, it would be a formality to receive their ransom payments, then almost instantly transfer those funds into other countries and accounts before anyone could begin to track them down.

Fidelia was satisfied that everyone appeared ready for success. Moments later, she regretted her premature sense of satisfaction. Mia had Louise Dependente from the US on the secure Zoom line, and Mia's body language signaled distress.

"Two things," Louise said. "I just got a call from Tak Takahashi. The FBI hijacked him in Macao and spirited him off the island. They're holding him in a jail somewhere in Oregon."

"Macao? What the fuck was he doing in Macao? And now Oregon? Why would they detain him there?"

"He didn't say. What he did say was that he was using his one phone call so I could get him some legal help urgently. What they've charged him with might explain why he was in Macao. I don't know. He says they've charged him with trying to sell an atomic bomb!"

"Are you kidding me? That's ludicrous. What's the head of the Japanese Yakuza got to do with atomic weapons?" Fidelia didn't expect an answer. She just needed time to think. This was most unwelcome news at a most unwelcome time.

"Get an attorney for him out in Oregon. Try to post bond, but they'll probably refuse because he's a flight risk. Be sure you use a lawyer that'll share everything they know with us." She waited for Louise to acknowledge the orders, then added another thought. "I don't know why, but I have a feeling that asshole the Shadow might have something to do with this. It sounds like the kind of ridiculous frame-up he might try, and he probably has the clout to get the FBI to make such a ludicrous charge."

"Okay, I'll get our people in Florida to poke around and see what they can learn, but there's one more odd issue you probably want to hear about. My folks in Atlanta reported earlier that Suzanne Simpson and Serge Boisvert just dashed out of the little hotel they were staying at. A guy followed them to the Multima Supermarkets' headquarters. They've been there since."

"Keep me posted on both." She needed coffee after news like that.

The moment she returned from the bedroom—where she'd made her calls—into the living area where Klaudia was setting up for the attack, her German friend looked up with an expression of bewilderment and despair.

It took her a moment to force out the words. "We've got some problems. In Russia, it looks as if Ivanov found the AirTags. They've stopped transmitting." She wouldn't realize her dream of revenge any time soon. "In Atlanta, the news is no better. I've tried three different entry points to the Multima computer systems that I used during the tests with Amber last week. I got blocked at all of them."

"Get the bitch out of bed. We can't lose any time now." Fidelia started to work on contingency plans.

Sixty-Two

Atlanta, Georgia, Monday November 13, 2023

After that first blue flash indicating an attempt to hack their computer system, nothing happened for many hours. Suzanne finally left Serge with Marcel waiting and watching, slept on the sofa in Gordon's office overnight, then called for Eileen to come over from the hotel the next morning. She had two cups of coffee waiting and motioned for her executive assistant to sit beside her on the sofa.

"It looks as if someone's trying to hack our system this morning. I may get called away at any time, but I've still got a business to run. Try to get my regular Monday morning calls arranged, starting with Alberto Ferer this time." Eileen nodded and made a note. "I also want you to see what you can find out about this odd story I noticed on X this morning."

She held up her phone to display a CBS news headline on the site formerly known as Twitter that read "Head of Japanese Yakuza Held for Trying to Sell an Atomic Bomb".

"Serge thinks the guy they're talking about is the one trying to launch a cyberattack against us. But if the FBI's got him, I'm wondering if someone else might also be involved. Call Beverly Vonderhausen, that attorney we've used in Washington. She knows people at the FBI. Ask her if she can find out any background about Takahashi's arrest, anything at all. Let her know I need to hear back from her with some urgency."

Eileen got the message, picked up her mug of coffee, and headed to a desk outside the office. Within moments, she buzzed that Alberto was on the line.

"We haven't heard anything from the attorney here about Gordon Goodfellow's status over at the sheriff's office," said Suzanne. "I'm worried and feel a little uncomfortable about his position in all of this. I know you told me you didn't want to get involved, but I'm going to give you her name and number. As chief legal officer for Multima, can you please call and just inquire about his current status?"

He hemmed and hawed for a moment or two then agreed to do it.

She signaled to Eileen that she was ready to continue her phone meetings. Suzanne had completed useful and productive calls with both Pierre Cabot, her CFO, and Natalia Tenaz over at Multima Financial Services before Eileen passed her a note that Alberto Ferer was on the line again.

"I spoke with Gordon's criminal attorney in Atlanta. He's gone. Disappeared. Sometime between two and four this morning, he just walked out of the sheriff's office. Only two deputies were on duty overnight. While one slept, the other apparently showed Gordon the way out, and she's missing as well."

Before she could say goodbye to Alberto, Eileen burst into the room, waving her arms. "Serge called. The attacks have started again!"

Sixty-Three

Kraków, Poland, Monday November 13, 2023

Although it was now afternoon, and Amber had slept for more than a few hours, the doctor gave her an injection of something she said would help her stay alert and offset some lingering grogginess. Fidelia also insisted she drink a cup of strong black coffee as Klaudia explained what happened when she tried to hack Multima's computer systems.

Her friend used the Chinese woman's charts and diagrams—the ones she received digitally from Multima without their knowledge—to show what happened as she tried to crack the Multima security codes. Then, both women moved to the upright wooden chairs in front of the huge monitor and a pair of laptops.

Amber started first. She pounded on the keyboard of her computer for several minutes with her eyes fixed on the monitor. After a few minutes of activity, she shook her head twice, then hunched forward again, trying different codes and combinations of digits. Every time she tried, she failed. The software of Multima's computer systems sat there, unmoving. No combination seemed to work.

After about a half-hour, she sighed deeply and shook her head in frustration. "They've changed everything since I was in the last time. They also must have found and deactivated the AI software we embedded in Japan before the deal closed. I'll need to call Tak for help."

"Tak is in jail in the US." Fidelia broke the news as directly as possible to gauge the Chinese woman's reaction. "He's impossible to reach. What are you going to do now?"

Amber's eyes widened as the news registered. Her eyes reflected sadness, fighting back tears. Might there be more of a spark between the two than the young woman had first claimed? The Chinese woman stood up from her chair and started pacing in circles.

Klaudia looked at Fidelia with a shrug but said nothing. Fidelia watched in silence, anger surging from deep inside.

After several minutes of pacing, Amber mumbled that she had an idea. "Tak worked with a Chinese programmer to create the AI software. I can contact him to see if he can find a way to reactivate it, but it's the middle of the night in Shenzhen."

"Wake him up," Fidelia demanded, as she handed her secure burner phone to the woman.

It took a while. First, Amber had to locate his number. Her own phone had disappeared during the kidnapping nonsense by Juan Suarez's guy. She had to access some directory she'd cached in a personal email app somewhere in China and had trouble remembering the password. It took several attempts before she found one that worked and keyed a number into Fidelia's phone.

The phone rang several times before the guy responded. They spoke in Mandarin for a couple minutes before she pulled the phone away from her ear and announced they might have a solution.

"We'll need to connect via Zoom, move into 'share screen' mode, and grant him access to one of our laptops. He'll find a way to hack into the Multima system. He's among the best in the world. He has a tracking device to locate the AI software inside the system. If he can find it, he thinks he can reactivate it and thwart any defensive measures the Multima team installed."

Another partner. Fidelia sensed danger. She knew nothing about the guy. She already had recurring concerns about Takahashi and the Chinese woman. Plus, Multima might now be aware of their attempts. They already knew the company's CEO and her chief of security were summoned to the headquarters. With the top Russian guy involved, failure would be lethal. Given the bastard's reputation, if Fidelia came up short on their deal, she should probably avoid tall buildings for the rest of her life.

She nodded her okay to Amber.

Another hour or two elapsed. They completed all the Zoom steps and watched the guy from Shenzhen take control of the probes. All three women in Poland watched. He tried a multitude of codes and combinations of codes before Klaudia suddenly squealed, "He's in."

Next, they waited. Thousands of characters flooded across the monitor for several minutes. They watched rows of characters evolve into different columns, with continuous motion vertically and horizontally. After an hour, he spoke to Amber again in Chinese. Her pale face telegraphed the story before she relayed his message.

"Multima's technicians found our AI software. They not only disabled it; they destroyed it. It's gone. He says he can probably bring down one or two feeders into the system, but Multima also installed advanced AI software. It instantly detects any intruder and blocks the software path quickly. He sees no way to infiltrate that system immediately. He'd need a team of engineers for at least a month to disable enough of the system to demand a ransom."

Klaudia nodded a silent agreement. As the two women shut down all the equipment, Fidelia calculated in silence. What first seemed to be a brilliant scheme that would kill multiple birds with one stone now appeared to be the worst tactical disaster of her life.

The top Russian guy would be livid and kill the agreement to provide women. His undertaking to stay out of Europe in return for a share of the take would become worthless. Her guys in Europe—already unhappy about Russian interference—would almost certainly start questioning her leadership, maybe worse.

Now, her German friend and the Chinese woman were probably already calculating.

"Who does he work for?" Fidelia demanded.

Amber looked away. "I don't know."

Fidelia recoiled in anger, reached for her bag, and pulled out the handgun she always carried. She pointed it directly at Amber's face. "I asked you a question and I won't ask again. Tell me now, or I'll pull the trigger. You know I've done it before."

Amber visibly shrank away, knowing the answer might be her last in any case. "He works for the Chinese government in their cyber intelligence."

Fidelia nodded. "I thought so. So Tak was also working with the Chinese throughout this entire fiasco."

The Chinese woman cowered in growing fear before she

mumbled a whispered answer. "Yes."

"And, if Multima hadn't found a way to block us out, the ransom money from Multima would never have found its way into my bank accounts either, would it?"

"Yes!" Amber screamed. "You would have got everything, just like we discussed." She collapsed to her knees in tears.

Fidelia took one step forward, checked to confirm the silencer was engaged, and pulled the trigger of her gun gently once.

Klaudia gasped and covered her face in horror. She'd been around The Organization but probably had never seen revenge up close before. Fidelia waved for her to collect her things just as the Spanish doctor came out of the room with Ricardo. She probably heard the first pop but didn't have time to hear a second one before she too crumpled to the floor.

Fidelia called the pilots at a nearby hotel to get to the airport, to start the engines and be ready to leave in minutes. Then, she called out for Mia in another bedroom before dashing to the door to rustle up the bodyguards. Within mere minutes, three women and nine bodyguards climbed into three SUVs parked outside the building.

Their ride to the airport was uneventful. Traffic was light, and weather conditions were favorable. The two bodies wouldn't be discovered until cleaners came to tidy up at the end of their scheduled booking.

Still, Fidelia carried the burden of defeat. She longed for the peace and tranquility of her remote compound in the desert in Uzbekistan.

At the airport, the pilots warmed up the jet's engines as the SUVs arrived, and one stepped down from the aircraft to help load everyone's baggage into the compartment below the seating area.

No one spoke, but furtive glances suggested no one was comfortable. Amber Chan had deserved her brutal end. But the doctor had no reason to die. Life wasn't always fair, and Fidelia had her own burdens to bear. So she blocked out the blood, gore, and tragic loss of life as she had every previous time. It's what a leader had to do.

Within minutes, the luxury jet slowly crawled away from the terminal, then worked its way toward the runway, preparing for take-off. The pilots revved the engines for departure and soon dashed down the assigned runway at increasingly roaring speeds before soaring gracefully into the air.

Takeoffs always exhilarated Fidelia. On that somber day, the powerful upward thrust seemed to stimulate her senses even more than usual. She closed her eyes and leaned back in her comfortable swivel seat. As the jet soared, a small smile gradually formed as elation took hold.

At that precise instant, her plane shook violently as her ears ruptured and a massive ball of fire exploded into her face.

It was the last thing she saw.

Sixty-Four

Atlanta, Georgia, Monday November 13, 2023

Early in the afternoon, Serge dropped by Gordon Goodfellow's office, which Suzanne had confiscated temporarily. He proposed a sandwich and a quick chat. They had Eileen fetch a few things from the employee cafeteria and bring them to the office, where they caught up on each other's mornings, chatting together on the comfortable leather sofa.

"It seems the attacks are done for the day. We haven't had a peep for a few hours now. Marcel's work held up well considering the awful barrage we took for a while there. Still, we can't be sure we're done with it yet. That might have been a test run. Remember, all the chatter on the dark web called for next Monday to be the big day. Today might have just been an elaborate practice session."

Serge's life in law enforcement had prepared him to expect the worst, but she didn't contradict him this time. No one could say the attacks were finished for sure, but strong signs of optimism were evident—enough that she'd set in motion the generous bonus payouts she'd promised her staff.

"Marcel and his team did a fantastic job," she said. "We'll reward them after we get through next week. But he told me that much of the credit goes to you. He said that techie you borrowed from CSIS for a few weeks made all the difference."

"We were lucky to get him. He recommended that we embed Artificial Intelligence in every aspect of the security wall. Every day, from the first installation, Marcel and his team trained, coached, and improved that AI software to better recognize threats and thwart them before they got any traction. It was amazing to watch."

She asked if the police had made any progress in finding the people who bombed the store in Houston.

He shook his head with an exaggerated grimace before he answered. "Both the Mounties and FBI think it was probably some two-bit repeat offender looking for a quick buck when somebody approached him with an offer he couldn't refuse.

They figure he's either somewhere out of the country, waiting for things to cool down, or perhaps he might have had an unfortunate accident if the guy who was supposed to pay him wasn't entirely happy with the outcome."

"I heard back from Beverly Vonderhausen. Do you remember her? The attorney in Washington we work with sometimes? I asked her to check with some of her FBI sources about Takahashi's arrest." Suzanne couldn't suppress a spreading and mischievous smile as she recounted the gossip.

"According to her FBI contact, they acted on an anonymous tip from a caller in Florida who called himself a very fine American with some unbelievably important news they needed to act on immediately. He said it involved national security and heads would roll if the FBI didn't act urgently on his warning."

Serge raised his head and looked at Suzanne with his brow furrowed and shook his head twice. "Doesn't that sound exactly the way a certain former US president might speak?"

She nodded. "Beverly thought the FBI might have similar suspicions. Her contact said if the allegations against Takahashi don't stand up, they'll have to investigate the anonymous caller more fully. But if the courts think he's immune to prosecution it might not matter."

Finishing up their brief lunch and chat, they agreed to meet again and leave the office together at five. Suzanne coyly added that she'd ask Eileen to organize another catered meal so they might carry on from where they left off the night before. Maybe celebrate their victory.

They shared a long, tender kiss. Just as they broke away, Eileen knocked on the office door and stepped forward, then stopped suddenly. Her open mouth and flustered face portrayed shock and horror.

"I just received a call from the attorney working with Gordon Goodfellow. State police in Alabama just discovered his body in a ditch near Interstate 20."

Eileen barely managed to get the words from her mouth before she burst into tears and lunged toward Suzanne for comfort. Tears flowed from Suzanne's eyes as well, and she hugged her long-time assistant tightly, but with more than a little discomfort.

Serge suggested they all sit down for a moment. It was shocking news. A jolt for everyone. His voice sounded hoarse, and he took longer to form his words than usual. He brought three bottles of water from a small refrigerator while both women strained to regain their composure and wipe away tears.

"I'll speak with the sheriff's office and get all the details," Serge said. "Once we know exactly what happened, someone will have to break the news to his wife and family."

He left the office to make his call, and Eileen regained enough composure to eventually wander back to her workstation. Suzanne sat alone with her thoughts. She rose from the sofa again, closed the door to her office, and replayed in her mind everything she could remember. And silently questioned her role in her longtime colleague's death.

Were they wrong to bring in law enforcement after Serge heard the recordings from California? Was a killer out there targeting someone else at Multima? Would this cycle of violence toward her business ever end?

When Serge returned to Gordon Goodfellow's former office, his eyes were downcast, his emotional load heavy. He seemed to need a moment to choose his words.

"So far, law enforcement has no suspects, no clues, no information. Both Gordon and the deputy sheriff were murdered. Single bullets to their heads, laying in a ditch. So far there are no witnesses, no video from other cars. We did our best to keep him safe, but it seems someone out there was determined to send us a message. Unfortunately, I have no idea what that message is."

Suzanne nodded. "I feel the same way. My public comments probably didn't help. Edward Hadley gave the media a recording of my criticism of organized crime at the meeting with the Canadian cabinet ministers ... it was then circulated far more widely than he expected. My speech in Hawaii also drew a lot of media coverage ... I guess maybe I need to revisit the wisdom of taking on the whole gang single-handedly. It might create an unacceptable risk for us all."

Serge put his arm around her and gave a gentle squeeze of support. "We have lots of time to think through the best business strategies going forward. Let's first go and offer comfort to Gordon's wife and family."

She nodded.

It was only a short drive from the Multima office to the suburban home of Gordon's wife and children. Both took a few deep breaths before approaching the front door, and Serge rang the doorbell once they arrived. Priscilla Goodfellow opened the door. She recognized Suzanne and started to smile in greeting before she sensed tragedy and screamed without restraint before Serge could get out, "I'm sorry we have some bad news to share with you."

Suzanne first tried to find words to comfort the woman but gave up and just held Priscilla tightly while she sobbed uncontrollably. When the teens came to see what had happened, Serge put his hands on their shoulders and guided them toward a sofa. There, he explained their father's fate, embracing them gently as both broke into tears at the news.

Once full realization of the tragedy set in, Suzanne remembered Gordon's strong religious beliefs. She asked Priscilla if she might call their pastor, let him know what happened, and see if he might come to help them cope with their loss. Through tears, deep breaths, and painful gasps, she called out the ten digits and Serge keyed them into his phone, then made the call.

The pastor arrived within minutes, and Suzanne realized their role was finished. They offered their sympathies, condolences and farewell only minutes later, with Suzanne emphasizing that Multima was there to provide any support, counseling, or financial assistance they might need in the coming months.

Approaching the SUV, bodyguards jumped to open their doors and await instructions. Serge confirmed they'd head back to the small hotel again.

Neither mentioned that there would be no catered dinner that night nor any continuation of where they'd left off the night before. Each accepted that reality intuitively. Instead, they held each other's hands.

After several long, silent moments, Suzanne reached toward the large red button that closed the glass shield between their compartment in the rear of the SUV and the bodyguards up front. When it finished its slide upward to the roof, she shifted in her seat to face Serge as directly as possible.

"Is it me? Do I have some sort of blind spot that prevents me from better detecting and deflecting all the greed and betrayal we seem to constantly encounter?"

Serge looked back at her, his eyes softening when they met hers. He sensed her unease and reached out to touch her hand before he asked her, with a wry smile, "Are we talking about Gordon Goodfellow or Amber Chan?"

"Today, we're talking about both, but there have been others before."

"I can't speak about cases that came before me, but I have no doubt there was little any of us could have done to detect Amber's avarice earlier. She was trained, groomed and polished to be the perfect Chinese government infiltrator. And I think it was more than coincidental that they chose to launch their cyberattack on Multima through the Japanese Yakuza. If the government in China continues to behave badly, I expect businesses of all sizes will be subjected to this kind of sinister international subterfuge. Going forward, you might want to tighten HR background investigations, but that's about all you can do."

"And with Gordon, someone I worked with and trusted for more than a decade?"

"That's a different and tougher one. I, too, liked Gordon, and his behavior surprised me to the end. I see him more as a guy who simply morphed into someone else. Amber Chan was probably the trigger. It's easy to understand why he was lured to her. She's a beautiful, charming, smart woman who apparently enjoys sex. She also knew her strengths and used them."

While Suzanne processed that mouthful, he shrugged and took another breath before he continued. "By definition, as a fundamentalist Christian, Gordon lacked critical-thinking skills. I think it's impossible to think critically and put your faith in religion at the same time. Critical-thinking tests might be another senior management qualifier to consider and emphasize."

It was too deep for her to deal with that day. Suzanne shifted her body forward again and decided to just park certain pressures. She'd revisit possible lessons learned another day.

Instead, she took temporary solace in her phone and checked her X feed in silence for a while. It took her mind off the other Multima worries in the world. Just before they reached their hotel, a post caught her eye.

"Serge, do you believe in omens? I think I'm seeing one that suggests there can never be a satisfactory ending to the Multima story. Probably for as long as I serve as CEO. Look at this new twist."

She held up her phone for him to read the news copy.

> *A private jet exploded and crashed today in Krakow, Poland, killing all 14 passengers and crew. It was registered to Tak Takahashi, head of the Japanese Yakuza, currently in the custody of the FBI in Oregon awaiting formal charges.*

He looked at her phone, then reached out to take it from her hand and study it more carefully. His lips twitched perceptibly before he looked her directly in the eye and said, "I don't think you're seeing an omen at all. I think our guy from CSIS astutely shared information that helped with much more than our computer security walls."

The End

Acknowledgements

With my eighth novel since *Three Weeks Less a Day* launched in 2016, I thank readers around the globe for reading my stories. I write to entertain, and your positive feedback confirms I succeed on that level.

I always start off with an outline of a story I think readers will enjoy, and tell it as effectively as I can. Once a manuscript draft is complete, two excellent writing professionals tell me all the mistakes I've made. I listen to them.

Paula Hurwitz and Val Tobin have worked separately, but together, to help me deliver the novel you're about to read. They did much more than detect mistakes. Both provided valuable suggestions that improved my story meaningfully, and I think you're going to enjoy reading it. I thank both for their dedication and patience.

To catch those nasty little typos and errors that try to work their way into every book, Deborah Armstrong of Terrahill Publishing and Paula Hurwitz carefully proofread the final drafts and pointed out their discoveries. If you find any remaining errors or shortcomings, they are entirely mine.

Early in the review process, I asked Cathy & Dalton McGugan and Heather & Dan Lightfoot, for their thoughts about the characters and plot. Each provided excellent suggestions that added significant value to the story.

Sharon Brownlie of Aspire Book Covers designed the impactful cover and pleasing book layout. I enjoyed working with her across continents, and hope we can do it again in the future.

To each of these excellent collaborators, I express heartfelt thanks and appreciation.

About the Author

Gary D. McGugan loves to tell stories and is the author of Three Weeks Less a Day, The Multima Scheme, Unrelenting Peril, Pernicious Pursuit, A Web of Deceit, A Slippery Shadow, and CONTENTION.

After a forty-year career at senior levels of global corporations, Gary started writing with a goal of using artful suspense to entertain and inform. His launch of a new writing career—at an age most people retire—reveals an ongoing zest for new challenges and a life-long pursuit of knowledge.

Home is near Toronto, but Gary thinks of himself as a true citizen of the world. His love of travel and extensive experiences around the globe are evident in every chapter.

Follow Gary D. McGugan

Author Gary D. McGugan Website:
www.garydmcguganbooks.com
Subscribe to Gary's VIP Readers Newsletter:
https://www.subscribepage.com/garydmcgugan
Facebook: www.facebook.com/gary.d.mcgugan.books
Twitter: @GaryDMcGugan
Instagram: Authorgarydmcgugan
Threads: Authorgarydmcgugan
LinkedIn: https://tinyurl.com/rmbhfzer